Betrayal

MORE BY THIS AUTHOR

The Anniversary
The Travellers
A Running Tide
The Testament of Mariam
Flood
This Rough Ocean
The Secret World of Christoval Alvarez
The Enterprise of England
The Portuguese Affair
Bartholomew Fair
Suffer the Little Children

Praise for Ann Swinfen's Novels

'an absorbing and intricate tapestry of family history and private memories ... warm, generous, healing and hopeful'
VICTORIA GLENDINNING

'I very much admired the pace of the story. The changes of place and time and the echoes and repetitions – things lost and found, and meetings and partings'
PENELOPE FITZGERALD

'I enjoyed this serious, scrupulous novel ... a novel of character ... [and] a suspense story in which present and past mysteries are gradually explained'
JESSICA MANN, *Sunday Telegraph*

'The author ... has written a powerful new tale of passion and heartbreak ... What a marvellous storyteller Ann Swinfen is – she has a wonderful ear for dialogue and she brings her characters vividly to life.'
Publishing News

'Her writing ...[paints] an amazingly detailed and vibrant picture of flesh and blood human beings, not only the symbols many of them have become...but real and believable and understandable.'
HELEN BROWN, *Courier and Advertiser*

'She writes with passion and the book, her fourth, is shot through with brilliant description and scholarship...[it] is a timely reminder of the harsh realities, and the daily humiliations, of the Roman occupation of First Century Israel. You can almost smell the dust and blood.'
PETER RHODES, *Express and Star*

Betrayal

Ann Swinfen

Shakenoak Press

Cover design by JD Smith www.jdsmith-design.co.uk

For

Nikki & Pascal

Chapter One
Mercy

The flood was receding at last. We had been nearly a week in the village church, after that terrible day of flood and blizzard, all of us huddled together hugger-mugger: villagers, soldiers, and foreign settlers. The rising ground where the church stood, together with the rectory, its glebe lands and farm buildings, had been our Mount Ararat, the church itself our Ark, but just as the voyagers on that first Ark must have suffered, we were all feeling the strain of our confinement, although every soul in that church was thankful to be alive.

Two braziers, at either end of the nave, provided us with some warmth, but only if you were close by. Besides, they were dangerous for the small children, so we had constructed a sort of pen out of pews to confine them in safety. Fortunately the kitchen of the rectory was but a short distance away, where several of the village women, including my friend Alice Cox and her mother, Mistress Morton, were now preparing meals for everyone, gathering together whatever food had been rescued in time before the waters flooded the village houses.

I confess I was of little use those first few days. The long journey from the sluice which the soldiers and I had demolished, fighting the blizzard and wading through icy water sometimes up to our waists, had brought on a fever and chest congestion which laid me so low that I took little notice of my surroundings until nearly a week had passed, but at last I was well enough to make my way to the church door. I wanted to see how bad was the world outside.

The door was flung open just as I reached it, and Jack Sawyer, my brother Tom's friend, came in, stamping the snow off his boots. Over his shoulder I saw a landscape of glassy plains and hills of snow. The flood waters had frozen. The snow which had begun on the night of the flood had lasted several days and now blanketed the half-submerged houses and barns of the village. It lay along the bare branches of the trees, and crusted thinly those shallower parts of the flood water which had frozen first. Where the waters lay deeper, the snow had ceased before they froze.

'The flood is going down,' Jack announced to the faces which turned towards him. He brandished a stout stick. 'I smashed the ice in some of the hollows and the water has seeped away somewhat, leaving a space under the frozen layer.'

'God be praised!' someone cried out.

Jack made a face. 'Do not be in too much of a hurry with your praise,' he said. 'I could not reach the village. At the bottom of this hill there is a great frozen lake between us and the houses. I'd not risk trying to cross it yet.'

To anyone familiar with other parts of England, our Mount Ararat would hardly have counted as a hill, but here in the Fens any ground more than a few yards above sea level is regarded as a hill.

'No need to take risks,' Gideon Clarke said. 'We have food enough for ourselves and feed enough for the livestock to survive another two weeks, if we are careful.'

'Do you think the men of Crowthorne have halted the pumping mill on their land?' Tom asked.

'Must have done,' Jack said, flinging himself down on the nearest pew and pulling off his boots. 'With the one built in our medland out of action, and theirs too, it's to be hoped that the excess water pumped out of the moss will drain back, instead of forcing the river and Baker's Lode to burst their banks again and drown us.'

There was silence. One man had been drowned in the flood, George Lowe, who had leapt into the raging waters of the Lode to save Tom, when – crippled by the loss of his amputated leg – he had slipped off the sodden bank. George was an outsider, one of the soldiers billeted at our farm, but everyone had been both shocked and humbled by his heroic action and we grieved for him. Our days together, sitting out the flood here in the village church, had created a curious comradeship between natural enemies. The soldiers had been brought here in order to put a stop to our resistance against the drainers trying to steal our common lands, but we had come to recognise that they were just young men like our own, many of them impressed into the Model Army and anxious to go home. As for the Dutch tenant farmers, illegally installed in settlements on our land, they had been misused by the adventurers as much as we had been. Their houses had been erected on land which normally flooded in winter, as anyone local could have warned them. In this latest terrible flood, more widespread than even the oldest villagers could remember, they had lost their homes, their livestock and most of their possessions, except for what they had been able to catch up as they fled before the rising waters. Few of them spoke much English, but we made ourselves understood to each other and they had shared the tasks of our common home, the women cooking, washing and minding the children, the men trudging through the snow to feed the livestock and milk the cows. That milk, thin and wintery as it was, had been a godsend in feeding the children.

Jack stood his sodden boots near one of the braziers to dry. 'If the water continues to go down,' he said, 'I am minded to try for the village in a day or two. There are cheeses stored in our attic, and turnips, and oats. Hay in the loft of our barn. The flood seems only to have reached halfway up the ground floor.'

'If you go,' Gideon said, 'you shall not go alone. We will make up a party. No need to run risks.' He reached out and took my hand. He knew I could not forget the sight of George being swept away, when he had been but inches from our reaching arms.

The next moment Alice's mother touched my shoulder. 'Mercy, your mother is wanting you.' She gave me a sympathetic look. It was rare these days for my mother even to know who I was, so if she was indeed asking for me, I must go. I left the men discussing a foray into the village. Tom watched and listened, his face tight with frustration. With but a single leg and one of his crutches lost in the flood, he knew he could take no part in it.

If my mother had indeed asked for me, she had forgotten it now.

'See, Abigail,' Mistress Morton said gently, 'here is Mercy come to you.'

My mother's vacant look must have been nearly as distressing for Mistress Morton as it was for me, for they had been close friends since childhood, just as Alice and I had been. Now my mother sometimes knew the companion of her youth, for her

3

memory was better for things long past than for an hour ago, but me she sometimes took for her long-dead sister Elizabeth, sometimes for someone quite unknown. She looked at me now as at a stranger, and shook her head.

'I do not know this girl,' she said defiantly. Then her face crumpled.

It was impossible to predict her moods. Sometimes she would grow angry and violent, sometimes she was piteously lost in some dark world that no one could penetrate. Now she began to sob, rocking back and forth on the narrow pew, clutching her arms around her body, as if that way she could hold her world and her mind together. I tried to put my arms about her to comfort her, but she pushed me away.

'I don't know you. I don't know who you are.'

Mistress Morton shook her head.

'Leave her to me,' she said.

I turned blindly away, unable to hold back the tears spilling down my cheeks. Gideon was there beside me. He had left the other men and followed me, knowing what I was likely to find. He handed me a handkerchief and I tried to blot away the tears.

'She is so unhappy, Gideon, and I cannot help her.'

'I know, my love. All you can do is to be ready at those moments when she does recognise you.'

'They are so few.'

He put his arms around me and I leaned my cheek against the rough homespun of his jacket. When he had returned secretly to the village, he had discarded his clerical dress so that no outsider should recognise him as our exiled rector, driven out by the Puritan regime now in control of England. But there was no privacy here in our Ark. Not only our own friends knew who he was, so now did all the soldiers and the Dutchmen. And since we had declared our love openly here in the church, our intended betrothal was common knowledge also. How we were to live in future, he an exile, and I now the owner of a farm marooned in the floods, we could hardly bear to think.

In the end, it was another four days before the men considered it safe to make the attempt to reach the houses of the village. Further smashing of the icy surface in the smaller depressions in the glebe land showed that in these areas the standing water had seeped away, although the ground below was near as boggy as the Fen. Venturing through deep snow as far as the margin of the frozen lake which lay between the church lands and the village, Jack Sawyer and Toby Ashford had taken axes to the ice and found that here too the water was beginning to diminish, although it would be some while yet before the flood waters retreated altogether.

They made quite a large party setting out for the village: Gideon, Jack, and Toby, Will Keane, the village blacksmith, Rafe Cox, Alice's husband, two of the soldiers who had been billeted with us, Seth and Aaron, and the Dutchman who had the most English and acted as their spokesman. His name, I had learned, was Hans Leiden. Gideon was determined that they should run no unnecessary risks. Will had found a length of strong rope in the rectory barn and with this the eight of them roped themselves together. Although the level of the water was not much above a man's height, and the frozen lake might appear motionless, yet if one of them should fall through the ice, he could be sucked away under that fatal frozen roof before the others could reach him. Joined together, they could not lose one of their number. Had we but had a rope when Tom fell into the Lode, George might have survived.

Soon after sun-up they set off, carrying heavy sticks and with knapsacks on their backs to fetch what goods they might find that were worth saving. The flood waters had risen almost to the top of the ground floor of most of the houses. The Coxes' house and Jack's and the smithy stood on slightly higher ground on the other side of the village green, so the water had reached just to halfway up the windows, but everything on the ground floor, unless it was exceptionally sturdy, would be ruined. At the far end of the village, out of sight from the church, there was a cluster of poorer cottages where the road to Crowthorne dipped down toward a delph which flowed into the Lode and was crossed by a simple plank bridge. This bridge had been swept away in the early hours of the flood and the one-roomed cottages had been swamped entirely, consisting as they did of a single rough-built storey topped with a low gable roof which allowed no more than a small space for limited storage. Although something might be salvaged at the upper end of the village, the poorest of our neighbours would, like the settlers, have lost everything. The cottages themselves were probably gone.

I stood at the church door, watching the exploring party set off. If you did not know of the terrible damage that had been done, the sight would have seemed quite beautiful. There had been a hoar frost in the night, so that every twig coruscated like a diamond necklace in the low fingers of the early sun. The sky was a cloudless dome of chilly blue, reflected in the ice of the lake which lay where the village green and street should have been. Even the snow looked almost blue, lying in a smooth blanket over the glebe land, except where the men's feet had trodden a path around the church to the farm buildings and now down the hill to the lake.

'What will they find, do you think, mistress?'

I turned round, startled. It was a woman who had spoken in accented but perfectly clear English. I recognised her as the wife of Hans Leiden, a woman a few years older than myself. Months ago I had seen her in the Dutch settlement, spreading out washing to dry, while her little boy, not much bigger than Alice's son Huw, had played at her feet. I found myself blushing. Mevrouw Leiden had worked amongst the other women while I was lying ill, but I had never spoken to her. What I remembered all too clearly was that hers had been one of the houses Tom and I and the other young people of the village had half torn down in our rage at the building of the settlement on our barley field. I knew now that she also had a daughter of about five. It was this child who had screamed when I ripped the thatch off their roof.

If Mevrouw Leiden knew I had been of that company, she gave no sign of it now as she smiled at me shyly.

'They will find little that has not been destroyed by the flood, I fear,' I said, 'except perhaps in the upper rooms of the houses on this side of the village. The cottages over there–' I waved with my right hand towards the far end of the street, 'they will probably be destroyed altogether.'

I turned back to watch the men. They were gingerly testing whether the ice would take their weight.

'We are used to floods at home,' the woman said, 'but usually they come from the sea.'

'We are used to our own normal floods,' I said bitterly, 'for they bring fertile soil down from the wolds to feed our fields, but

6

this is a man-made disaster, caused by men who understand nothing of how the Fens themselves absorb our flood waters. For generations we have managed and understood the fenlands, but now your people have destroyed us.'

It was unkind of me to blame her for the misdeeds of Piet van Slyke and his party of drainers, but the sight of what lay in front of me in the village, and the fear of what we might find when we returned to the farm at Turbary Holm, made me unforgiving.

Then, ashamed of my words, I held my hand out to her. 'I am Mercy Bennington.'

She nodded, taking my hand briefly and dropping a curtsey. 'Aye, I know. I have heard you spoken of. I am Griet Leiden.'

The men had tested the ice first with their sticks, then with tentative steps. Now Seth, who was the lightest weight, took a few hesitant paces out over the frozen lake.

'Shut that door,' someone shouted from within the church. 'We shall all freeze to death.'

I heaved the heavy door closed. Ever since the attack of the soldiers, egged on by Edmund Dillingworth the previous summer, the door had dragged on the stone threshold. As Griet Leiden and I turned back into the nave, I said, 'You speak very good English. Better even than your husband.'

She made a little deprecating gesture. 'My father was a merchant in Amsterdam and I was sent to a good school there. We were taught English. Then my father lost two ships and died soon after.'

She stopped, as though she thought her story would be of no interest to me.

'But now you are farmers?' I prompted. I could not keep a note of incredulity from my voice.

She smiled sadly. 'Hans worked for my father as a clerk, and had invested in the business. We were married not long before my father died and we lost everything. Hans found some work in the city, and we struggled to live there for a few years, but we were very poor. Then there came this offer of land and a farm here in England. As a boy, Hans had sometimes helped on his uncle's farm and he thought we should take our chance, so we borrowed some money from his uncle for the passage to England, and for the rent of the farm. He also gave us a cow and six sheep. It would be a start, we thought.'

I wondered that anyone could suppose that it would be so easy to set up as farmers, with no experience and little livestock, in a foreign country where you knew nothing of the land and no more of how to farm. Yet there were tales of settlers travelling from England to the New World just as ill prepared. Were all these settlers as naïve as children?

'I suppose you lost the cow and the sheep in the flood,' I said.

Her eyes filled with tears and she nodded.

'My little girl loved the cow. It has broken her heart.'

Even I was not immune from a feeling for animals. I would have wept myself if Blackthorn, my favourite amongst our cows, had been drowned in the flood. But we had seen it coming and had known we must move the livestock to the higher ground of the glebe lands.

'What will you do now?' I said. 'When the flood goes down and we are able to leave the church?'

She shook her head. The tears were falling freely now. 'I do not know,' she whispered. 'We have no money left. The animals are gone, and our seeds for next year. We had very few possessions, but most of those are lost, even our cookpots.'

We sat down together on one of the pews near the font.

'You know that you should never have been allowed to build where you did,' I said, but I said it quietly. It seemed to me that these people had been treated even worse than we had. 'That is common land. What that means is that it belongs to all of us commoners, the people of the village. We have a right to it in perpetuity.'

She frowned. The word must be unfamiliar to her.

'We own it forever,' I explained. 'Our ancestors owned it. Our descendents will own it. There is a charter, made centuries ago and granted to us by the king. The men who have made these drainage schemes and flooded the land, they have been breaking the law and stealing our land.'

'But,' she said, 'how can that be? If it is the law, you must go to court.'

I shook my head. 'My father went to the court and it killed him.'

Her eyes widened in horror.

'Later,' I said. 'Some day I will tell you what happened when my father went to court. We need the charter to prove our rights. There was a lawyer in London who was supposed to find it and take it to court for us, but nothing has been heard from him.'

I shrugged. At the moment the question of charters and claims in court seemed remote when we were confronted with the need simply to survive the winter with our homes destroyed and most of our supplies of food as well.

It was past midday when the men returned from the village, and we saw at once from their bulging knapsacks that they had managed to salvage some food for us. Rafe was also carrying with pride his son's beautiful carved cradle. Alice rushed to him, holding out her hands for it.

'It is unharmed,' he said cheerfully. 'All the upper floor of our house has escaped the flood, though there is no denying that it has a dank, musty smell.'

The cradle still held little Huw's bedding and the delicate shawl I had knitted for my godson as a christening gift. Mistress Cox stood looking down at it, wringing her hands.

'Everything upstairs is safe?' she said. 'You are sure?'

'Aye, Mother.' Rafe patted her shoulder uncertainly. Mistress Cox could be difficult at times. 'All the blankets and linen will need drying out from the damp, but there is no damage done.'

'And downstairs?'

He shook his head. 'Flooded to the height of my chest, I fear. The ice in the houses is thinner than outside. It broke up as we waded through it, but most of the furniture is still under water. I could see the top of the dresser, and the dishes on the high shelves are still there.'

'Rafe,' Alice said suddenly, 'you must take off those clothes.'

Like the other men, Rafe was sodden nearly up to his neck. Although he was standing near one of the braziers, he was shivering. He nodded and followed the others into the vestry – our only private place – to change into a dry tunic and breeches.

9

Altogether, the exploring party had managed to salvage a fair amount of food from the winter stores squirreled away in the attics of the houses at the upper end of the village. We were the richer by strings of onions, two pots of salted beans, a sack of late apples, another of turnips and one of dried peas, a whole cheese and one excellent ham found in Will's house, hanging from the roof beam in his kitchen, just inches above the level of the flood. Will's wife Liz handed it over to the common stock with a touch of pride.

'Meat for all,' she said.

'The waters are clearly going down,' Gideon said, when the men had spread out their spoils to be admired. 'We could see the clear marks on the interior walls where the highest level reached. Outside, the flood is seeping away beneath the ice, so that it forms a precarious surface with a foot or so of air beneath it. The ice is beginning to collapse in places. Will fell through it.'

'Aye,' Will said ruefully. 'I was glad of the rope then, you may believe me. Mind, I was so wet already from wading through the houses that I could not get any wetter.'

In truth, although they were now in dry clothes, all the party looked grey with cold and our company of cooks hastened to finish the hot vegetable pottage they were preparing for our midday dinner. We lined up with our assorted bowls of pottery or wood or pewter, like orphans lining up for a charity meal, but the helpings were generous and we ate with gusto, knowing that our supplies had been augmented. The goodness of the meal was somewhat marred for me by a bout of the hacking cough which still seized me from time to time, leaving me weak and angry at my weakness. I knew that as soon as conditions permitted, I must ride back to the farm and assess just how bad the damage was. Although we had herded all the four-footed beasts to the glebe lands, our little maid Kitty Parish and I had carried all my hens to the attic, where they should be safe from the flood. We had left piles of grain for them, but I was fearful that the supply would be exhausted and I would return to find nothing but emaciated bodies.

However, I was determined not to give way to my lingering illness and a few days later I persuaded Gideon, Tom, Will, and Jack, together with Hans and Griet Leiden, to sit down with me to discuss what we should do as soon as the retreating waters allowed us to assess how serious was the damage to the whole village.

'I checked the level of the flood this morning,' Jack said. 'It has gone down again and the surface of ice in the centre of the lake is sagging and cracking up. Once it is possible to make one's way along the Crowthorne road, I want to go and see how they fare, whether their lane is clear through to the old Roman road. That is raised up on its ramper, so if we can but reach it, we can go north to Lincoln or south to London.'

Tom shook his head. 'It would not be clear yet after one of our usual winter floods. Surely not after this.'

'Besides,' I said, 'it is more urgent to think what we must do here, so that people may return to their homes. And how we may provide for those who have lost their homes.' I nodded toward Griet and her husband. 'The settlers have nowhere to go, and there are many young children amongst them. And it is likely that the three furthest cottages along the Crowthorne road will have been washed away.'

'We must take our neighbours into our homes,' Gideon said. 'I have no rights to the rectory any longer, but until the outside world reaches us, it will hold two or three families, if they do not mind crowding together.'

I laughed. 'After we have lived all of us together in the church, I cannot think they would have any objection.'

'The houses at this end of the village will be clear first,' Will said. 'We should set to, all of the village together, and work our way along the street, house by house, rather than each man trying to repair his own house.'

'Well thought of, Will,' I said. 'That way we can move the oldest and youngest into the houses as they are made fit, never mind whose home it is.'

Tom grinned. 'Some may not like the idea. Mistress Cox may not wish to yield her fine home to the likes of Joseph Waters.'

We all laughed, those of us who knew Joseph, a jobbing labourer who carried about with him the strong aroma of a farm midden. It had ripened mightily since we were crowded together. Griet and Hans smiled politely. So far they had said nothing, but now Hans spoke.

'We know you do not like us. We take your land. We did not know. Men told us–' He turned to his wife and said something rapidly in Dutch to her.

'We were told that the land belonged to these men,' Griet said, 'and that we could each rent a portion for a house and a . . . I do not know what you call it . . . a small farm. Enough for a few animals and grain crops, and what we do best, growing good vegetables to sell in the towns. Now we understand that we were tricked, as you were tricked.'

She wiped her eyes on her apron. 'We do not know what to do. We cannot go home. We have no money, no houses and no food, but Hans says we will help you all we can. The men are all good workmen. They built our houses in the field and they can help you repair the houses here.'

Her voice took on a desperate note. 'If you will just allow us to feed our children and keep them safe, until we know what to do.'

I reached out and took her hand. 'Of course we will not turn you away, Griet.' I looked around at the others, somewhat defiantly. 'We will contrive something, will we not?'

'Certainly,' Gideon said, and the others nodded.

'But first,' he added, 'and before work can begin on the houses, let us not forget what occasion it is next week.'

I clapped my hand to my mouth. 'Christmas!'

'Aye. Christmas. Our services here have been makeshift, but I intend that we shall celebrate Christ's birth in joy and thankfulness, especially for the children.'

I smiled at Griet. 'Aye. Especially for the children.'

It was the strangest Christmas I had ever passed, yet a joyous one for all that. Our little maid Kitty and some of the other youngsters, even a few of the Dutch children, had gone foraging for Yule greenery about the glebe lands. They had found one holly tree with berries on it, as well as plenty of ivy clothing the wall which separated the churchyard from the lane leading to our farm. Returning bright-eyed from the cold, they wreathed the pews and windowsills with their spoils and wove a garland to lay across the chancel steps where the altar rails had been ripped away and smashed by the soldiers in the summer. Those other soldiers, not our soldiers, as I had begun to think of them.

It was agreed that Will and Liz's ham should form the centrepiece of the feast, cooked in the rectory kitchen and served with roasted turnips and some of the beans. There was some discussion about killing one of the hens, but we all felt they were too precious for the sake of their eggs. Mistress Morley and Alice, together with Mistress Sawyer, Jack's mother, found enough ingredients to contrive a vast plum pudding. Tied up in a cloth, it was put to simmer away over one of the braziers in the church. All through Gideon's Christmas service I was aware of the soft bubbling and the occasional rattle of the pot lid as the pudding cooked to perfection.

Until now we had eaten anywhere, standing, or sitting in the pews or on the floor, but this would not do for Christmas. Toby and Will, with some of the Dutchmen, carried in planks and trestles from the barn, where they had last been used at the harvest supper the previous year, and set up a table large enough for all of us. With pews drawn up on either side for seats, and some of the rectory sheets laid over it for a cloth, it was as fine a communal Christmas table as you could wish. Kitty laid sprigs of holly down the centre and persuaded Gideon to add some stump ends of church candles. At the last minute Jack rolled out a small barrel of ale.

'I went back to my house yesterday,' he explained, 'while everyone was occupied. I knew I had this barrel in our kitchen and I managed to free it from the flood water and mud. It is not much above knee height in my house now.'

'Will it be spoiled?' Tom said.

'If it is proof enough to hold the ale in,' Jack said, 'then it will have held the flood waters out. In any case, I have tasted it.'

So we sat down to our first formal meal since we had taken refuge in our Ark. By the time we had poured fresh cream from our cows over the sturdy helpings of plum pudding, few of us could have moved but slowly and carefully from our seats. A few games had been organised for the children, who seemed none the worse for full stomachs, and after that we sang carols. Our English carols were followed by Dutch ones, sometimes sung to familiar tunes, so that in the end our voices blended, two languages, two peoples, but one faith.

At last the flood seeped away from the village green, leaving behind a filthy deposit of mud mixed with great slabs of dirty ice,

13

still unmelted, for it remained very cold. There was another fall of snow on the day we had appointed to make our first general foray into the village, so that it had to be postponed for a day, but at last all of us who were able-bodied set off down the hill, leaving behind the children, the old people, and a few of the women to mind the young ones. It was difficult to pick our way over the broken ice, which was sharp-edged and treacherously slippery. The Coxes' house was to be the first to be cleared, for it stood the highest and was spacious enough to hold a number of the weaker members of our community. The outside walls were stained from the flood almost as high as my shoulder. What would we find inside? I glanced at Alice, who gave me a nervous smile. She and Rafe had lived here with his parents since their marriage, and Mistress Cox was a fearsome housekeeper.

'Now we shall see.' Rafe Cox dragged open the door, which was somewhat warped with the wet, and we stepped inside.

I caught my breath. My first thought was relief that Mistress Cox was not strong enough to be of our party. The floor was a foot deep in wet mud, from which, here and there, household objects poked up – dented copper pans, broken dishes of delftware, linens, strings of rotting onions. There was a strong and unmistakeable stench. It was clear that the flood had washed filth from the midden through the house. Alice looked about her, appalled.

'Oh, what shall we tell your mother, Rafe?'

'We will not tell her,' he said grimly. 'Come, there should be shovels hanging in the barn, if they have not washed away. Toby, Hans, will you help me to fetch them? We will shovel all this muck on to the midden.'

'But be careful,' Alice said. 'There may be some things unbroken mixed amongst it.' With some distaste, she pulled a saucepan out of the mud. 'This has but a small dent, it can still be used.'

'We will put everything to one side,' Rafe said, 'and you can decide what is to be saved.'

With that, he went off in search of tools.

'Alice,' I said, 'let us leave this to the men.' She was standing helplessly holding the saucepan, a look of despair on her face. 'When they have shovelled away the mud we can wash down the floor and walls, and the furniture. Look, the good oak chairs and table have withstood the flood. Meanwhile, let us go upstairs and see to airing the beds and the clothes.

She nodded mutely. Together with the other women, she followed me upstairs. Mindful of the filthy state of our boots, we set them aside halfway up. Fortunately, the scene here was not nearly so bad. The upper floor and attics had been untouched by the flood, but Rafe had been right about the musty smell he had described before Christmas. Fortunately, the Coxes' house was well-built and modern, with a fireplace in every room. Fortunately, too, there was a basket of logs beside each fireplace. Although the flood water had not reached the logs, they were still somewhat dampish and took a while to catch light, but eventually we had a fire going in each room, so that soon a much more pleasant scent of burning wood filled the air.

We shook out all the bed clothes and feather beds, and draped them over the bed rails to air. The clothing, which was stored in deep oak coffers, with lavender and rosemary to keep it sweet and free of moths, was in a better state than the bedding. Nevertheless, we shook this out too, laying gowns and tunics and breeches and hose over chairs and chest lids to benefit from the warmth of the fires. I thought that Mistress Cox would not have been pleased to see strangers handling her chemises, but she need never know of it,

When we had done, we ventured downstairs again. The thick layer of mud had gone, though everything was covered in slime. It also felt very cold after our fires upstairs. There was no dry wood here.

'Is there any firewood in the barn which was out of the flood?' Alice asked Rafe. She turned to me. 'We should have saved some of it for downstairs.'

I nodded. It was one of many lessons we were to learn as we cleared the village. Rafe went in search of dry wood and managed to find two small bundles, which he lit in the large kitchen hearth. Then he and the other men moved on to the house Jack shared with his widowed mother. Next after that would be the house and workshop of Ned Broadley, the village carpenter. When they were gone Griet, without being asked, found a couple of buckets.

'Where is your well?' she asked.

Alice led her out into the yard, where they filled the buckets and brought them back to heat the water for our cleaning.

'The well is polluted,' Alice said drearily. 'It will serve for rough cleaning now, but how long before it is clear enough for cooking and washing?'

I shook my head helplessly. Our normal managed floods did not pollute our wells. I had no idea how long it would take for a well to draw clear again.

There were twelve of us women working together to scrub down the house, and it must have taken us four hours at the least. Some things we were forced to throw away. The cushions from the chairs and benches were past saving, although they had been exquisitely embroidered by Mistress Cox. Griet filled the stone sink with hot water and carefully washed all the kitchen pots and dishes, the broken ones as well as those which had escaped undamaged.

'Many of these you can glue together,' she said to Alice. 'See, this plate is broken in two clean halves. I am sure it can be fixed.'

Alice nodded. She knew, as I did, that Mistress Cox would never eat off a mended plate, but perhaps Alice could make use of the broken dishes when once she had a home of her own.

As we scrubbed down the walls and furniture, I was relieved to see that they had withstood the flood waters well, although the lime-wash on the walls was stained. I hoped that the same would be true of our farm. By mid afternoon the winter dusk was setting in, but we were satisfied with our work. The house was as clean as we could make it and the warmth of the fires was beginning to rid it of that unpleasant mouldy smell. Rafe had found a store of peat forgotten in the loft of the barn. Because of the invasion of the drainers during the last year, there had been little of our usual peat-cutting for fuel. We dampened peats and laid them in a layer over the embers of the fires to provide some continuing warmth during the night, then trudged wearily back over the ice field to the church.

This was to be the pattern of our days for the next week, as we worked our way along the village street, house by house. Not all the houses had survived intact, so that the building skills of the Dutchmen were called upon to make good the weakened structures. After we had folded away the clothes and made the beds in the Coxes' house, Rafe's parents, who were both somewhat frail, moved back in and found room for several old people, including the widow Peterson. To do her credit, Mistress Cox also gave sanctuary to one of the pauper families from the far end of the village, who had lost everything. Alice and Rafe chose to stay, with baby Huw, in the church with the rest of us, declaring that the more feeble should be housed first.

By the end of that week, we had made six houses habitable, though the losses in household possessions and stores of food were considerable. Fortunately most families in the village used their attics to over-winter their supplies, but the flood had come so fast, and everyone had been so taken up with saving people and livestock, that regular kitchen supplies had been left where they were, and were spoiled. We were especially short of salt. The damage grew worse as we worked our way down the hill to the brook, for the houses on the lower ground had been drowned deeper.

On the last day of that week, Jack declared that he would make his way over to Crowthorne, to see how that village had fared. We were not on very good terms with the people of Crowthorne, but in the face of such a disaster as this flood, even our old enmities might be set aside for a time.

Jack must cross the delph at the bottom of the street, and possibly others on his way, but like all fenlanders he was accustomed to vaulting over waterways, and carried his leaping pole with him. When he returned late in the afternoon, he brought us their news.

'Like us they managed to stop the drainers' pump on their land,' he said. 'Truly, I think if we had not both disabled the pumps, the flood would have risen over the church and drowned us all. They think they may be able to get through to the Roman road in a week or so. After that, we may be able to reach Peterborough for supplies of food, but it also means others can reach us.'

'Do you mean the drainers?' Tom asked. 'There will be the devil to pay when they find we have interfered with their pumping mills.'

Jack shrugged. 'They will be back, you may be sure of it.'

17

'Somehow we must make them understand that by drawing the water out of the Fen, instead of letting it soak up the winter rains, they have caused this flood,' Gideon said reasonably.

Hans was looking uncomfortable during this conversation, which was taking place, as before, amongst a small group of us in the vestry.

'The drainers,' he said apologetically, 'they do what they are told. Piet van Slyke is well known at home. He has drained polders from the sea. But it is different with us.'

Once again, his English failed him, and he turned to Griet.

'We build dykes,' she explained. 'Like a wall between the sea and the marshland to be drained. Then the pumping mills take the water from the marsh and put it in the sea. When the land is drained, we can farm it.'

'But you can see how different that is from the Fens,' Tom said, with an edge of anger to his voice. Had it not been for the drainage works, he would not have lost his leg. Our farmhand Nehemiah Socket had made him a replacement for the lost crutch, so that he was now able to swing himself about in the church. Grimly every day he worked his way up and down the nave, trying to strengthen the muscles of his shoulders and arms, so that he could move more easily.

'We are only flooded from the sea occasionally, when there are bad storms and very high tides,' he said. 'Even so, that does not affect us much here, but along the coast. Sometimes the river may back up and spread out near the estuary, but we're not troubled by it. Our floods come from the winter rains which are a benefit to us, enriching our fields with soil from the higher ground inland. During those winter months we expect certain of our fields – like the one you built on – to be covered with a shallow flood for a few weeks. Afterwards the marshland of the Fen slowly absorbs the extra water. By watching the natural floods over the years, our ancestors dug ditches and channels like Baker's Lode to carry away excess water to the river.'

'But you can only dig these ditches where you know they will do good,' Jack interrupted. 'What you do not do is try to take water out of the bog. It works like, like . . .' He shrugged.

'Like a sponge,' I said. 'And that also keeps the peat from drying out. Further south, where they brought in drainage in our grandfather's time, the peat has turned to dust, no use to anyone.'

'And where the wetlands have vanished there,' Jack said, 'the fish and the eels have gone, the waterfowl vanished. Reeds and osiers no longer grow, which we use for thatching and baskets and hurdles and eel traps – when we have any eels.'

Their voices had grown strident, so that Hans and Griet looked more and more unhappy. Gideon laid a restraining hand on Jack's arm.

'You can understand now why the work of the drainers is such a disaster for us,' he said. 'Our traditional ways of farming and fishing and wild fowling will be destroyed for ever if these schemes go ahead. And at the same time they would take possession of our common lands where we graze our beasts and grow our crops. Our people will be made destitute.'

Griet nodded. 'But Mercy told me that you have a charter which proves in law that the land belongs to you.'

'If we had it,' Tom said grimly, 'there would be no problem. Or rather,' he corrected himself, 'we would be one step nearer to proving possession of our common lands. We would still need to fight the company of speculators in the courts. They are rich and we are poor. However, we do not know where the charter is. It is nearly a year since the local squire, Sir John Dillingworth, set his London lawyer to secure the charter and prove our claim in court, but nothing has been heard from him.'

'If indeed Sir John ever instructed him.' Jack's voice was scornful. 'Which is doubtful.'

'It shall be my first task,' Tom said, 'when I get to London. To search out Sir John's lawyer and discover whether he has been able to trace the charter.'

'You are still determined to go back to Gray's Inn?' Gideon asked.

'I am. I can do no good here. I will take up my studies in the law, so that I may have a profession even a one-legged man can practise.' His tone was bitter, but who could blame him? 'Sir John's man is at Lincoln's Inn, but it should not be difficult to track him down. As soon as a carrier is able to get through to the

London road, I shall be on my way. You may be sure I will not let a moment go past but I will search out the charter.'

To tell the truth, I was reluctant for Tom to go. I feared that the difficulties he must confront in London, with no one to help him get about, might prove too much even for his indomitable spirit. And for selfish reasons of my own, I would have been glad of him here on the farm. He could no longer carry out the physical tasks of farming, but he had undertaken much of the management ever since he had abandoned his studies and returned home to help our father. I had done a good deal of late, but Tom had always been there with his advice and knowledge. In future I would have to cope without that.

Sooner than expected, a carrier did manage to reach us, the very day after the men of the village had rebuilt the wooden bridge over the delph, on the road leading to Crowthorne. He brought with him a passenger from Lincoln – Will's cousin, Abel Forrester, the gaoler who had helped me when I was tried for witchcraft. Having left his position at Lincoln castle in disgust, he was returning to his original trade as blacksmith, coming to work as partner to Will.

Abel brought with him news from the outside world, though it held little as dramatic as our own affairs. The king was a prisoner, his army scattered. It seemed the war was at an end, yet the soldiers billeted in the village had not received any order to disperse. As they had not been paid for months, most of them were not minded to leave until that happy day arrived.

The carrier stayed overnight at the yel-hus, and when he left in the morning, Tom would go with him.

'He goes as far as Peterborough.' Tom was sitting with Gideon and me at the back of the church. 'I shall easily find a carrier in Peterborough to convey me to London.'

'Have a care,' I said. I did not want to cluck over him like an old wife, but it was a fearful journey for a one-legged man, with little prospect at the end of it. 'Promise that you will write as soon as you find lodgings and have enrolled again in Gray's Inn.'

'I shall see if any of the fellows I knew are still there. I might be able to share lodgings with them.'

'A good plan,' Gideon said. 'You will be close at hand for – what do they call them? – moots and readings?'

'Aye, if the teaching carries on as before. In the early days of the war, everything fell apart.'

I brought out of my pocket a small purse, which clinked as I laid it on the seat of the pew next to Tom.

'You remember when Gideon went to Lynn, to take ship for the Low Countries, he left all the money he possessed with me. Most is still unused. We want you to have it.'

He shook his head.

'I cannot take it and leave you penniless.'

Gideon laid his hand on Tom's arm. 'Mercy and I have agreed this. We have kept back a little, in case we need to buy food in the lean months of spring. This should be enough for you to have a wooden leg made, and to keep you until you can find work.'

It was Tom's plan to try for work as a clerk or a tutor while he took up his studies once more. With his university degree and a year's training in the law, we hoped it would not be too difficult. As for the artificial limb, he had been assured by Jack (who had been to sea, where such injuries were not unknown) that a wooden leg would improve his balance and enable him to get about with just one crutch.

At last he agreed to take the money, but swore he would pay it back as soon as he was earning. The next morning, before he heaved himself into the carrier's cart, he hugged me and kissed my cheek.

'I am only sorry that I shall not be here to see you wed, Mercy, but I shall think of you. Send me word, once you are Mistress Clarke.'

I nodded, finding it difficult to speak. A year ago we had been a family. Now my father was dead, my mother lost in confusion, and my brother setting off on a long and difficult journey.

As the cart trundled away down toward the bridge, I stood watching until it vanished from sight.

Tom was gone, but I must not give way to grieving. I had other work to do. The lane to our farm was passable now. Within the next few days, I was determined that I would ride to Turbary Holm and confront the damage to the farm that was now mine.

Chapter Two
Tom

The carter Edy was travelling as far as Peterborough, which we reached before nightfall that first day. Although I had coin enough for a bed in the purse Mercy had given me, I was mindful of how much I might need it once I reached London, so I asked Edy whether I might sleep in his cart. He himself had taken a shared bed for the night, but he was willing enough for me to use the cart, as I might also keep a watch on his horse, for not every ostler is an honest man. We took a pot of ale and a mutton chop together in the low-ceilinged common room of the inn, then I went off to the stable for the night.

I was glad no one was there to see my struggles in getting myself back up into the cart. Gideon had given me a heave up when we left the village, and it had not been difficult to lower myself to the ground when we reached the inn, but lifting myself back up into the cart was almost more than I could manage. At last I lay on the floor of the cart, sweating with effort and pain despite the icy wind whistling through the gaps in the stable walls.

For a long while I lay there, reflecting on my rashness in setting off for London alone and maimed as I was. More alone, indeed, than ever in my life and sobered by my struggle, I felt for the first time that I might fail in my attempt to take up my studies and to find the charter. Or worse. Who knew what London would hold, after these years of war? Mercy had often chided me for acting without thinking. I believed I had reflected carefully before undertaking this journey, but I was forced to confess that I was more disabled than I had allowed myself to admit until now. At home on the farm, and during our weeks in the church, there had always been someone at hand to ease my difficulties. From now on I must depend on no one but myself.

The cart contained a load of Jack's fleeces which had escaped the flood waters. They were bound for a dealer in Northampton, so the carter and I would part company in the morning. Tonight, however, they would provide me with a reasonable bed. When I had regained my breath, I rearranged them into a kind of nest and unrolled one to serve as a blanket. The familiar smell of untreated wool was comforting in the cold darkness of the stable, but my newly confronted anxiety about what lay ahead kept me awake and unsettled far into the night.

In the morning, I shook Edy's hand and offered to pay him for carrying me as far as Peterborough, but he refused my money.

'Nay,' he said. 'You have had troubles enough. I wish you well in London, Master Bennington.'

He gave me a look of half-ashamed pity, which I endured with a forced smile, and we said our farewells.

'There is a regular carrier service to London,' he said as we parted. 'Go to the market place and ask for Joseph Thompson. Say that I sent you.' Then he climbed into his cart with ease, clicked his tongue to the horse and was gone.

I found Joseph Thompson without much difficulty and learned that I was in luck.

'I leave in half an hour by the church clock,' he said, pointing, 'if you can be ready by then.' He was looking at my crutches and the empty leg of my breeches.

'I am ready now,' I said, 'but I'd be glad of your help in getting up on to your cart.'

After my trouble the previous night I had realised that I must humble myself to ask for help. Joseph, like others before him, was fearful of hurting me, but I reassured him, and with his assistance I was soon sitting next to him on the driver's bench. The previous day I had ridden in the body of the cart, but this was a much larger vehicle, with a solid bench for the driver, partially protected from the weather by a projection forward from the roof of the cart and a plank for shelter on each side. The smaller cart had been roofed with nothing more than a hooped canvas, while this one was like a solid wooden shed on wheels, drawn by two horses.

The journey to London took us three days, for Joseph made deliveries on the way and collected other goods for transport onwards. Each night I slept in the cart to save my money, and although it was more weatherproof I was less comfortable than on the first night. There were no fleeces to make a bed. Mostly Joseph carried barrels and crates, though I also shared the accommodation with a flitch of bacon, three hens in a wicker cage, and – on the last night – a strong smelling billy goat.

By dusk on the third day we were within sight of London, on the high ground of the heath land that lies to the north of the city, but Joseph would not travel the last few miles in the gathering dark.

'Too chancy,' he said. 'This has ever been a haunt of rogues who prey on travellers, and since the fighting began, with so many masterless men and deserters from the army, no one but a fool would cross the heath at night. We'll stop at an inn I know and reach London by daylight tomorrow. You must know your inns as well, for some of the innkeepers are in league with the bands of robbers. This man is honest.'

So I spent that last night in the goat's company, aware that when I arrived in London I would probably carry his pungent aroma with me, no very welcome scent when I was trying to persuade Gray's Inn to readmit me as a student. In the morning I was dirty and crumpled, and very stiff from the last three uncomfortable nights. I wished I had some friend in whose lodgings I could make myself more presentable, but I knew of no one. If any of my former fellow students were still in London, they might not be easy to find. For all that I knew, some might have joined the army on one side or the other. Some might even have died in battle.

We reached the city wall at Aldersgate, where I asked Joseph to set me down, for it was the nearest he would come to the Inns of Court. I could think of nowhere to go, save directly to Gray's Inn, though it would be hard walking so far on crutches. He offered to drive me there, but I could see he was reluctant, being urgent to dispose of his goods. Like Edy, he refused payment.

'Nay, Master Bennington,' he said. 'I have been glad of your company on the road. And if you should want carrying back to Peterborough at any time, you may find me at the Three Dolphins in Billingsgate. I make the journey at least once a week, except in foul weather.'

I thanked him, though I saw his kindness arose mostly from pity for a poor maimed fellow. It is a hard thing, to accept pity, when you have once been as strong as any other man, but beggars, as they say, cannot choose otherwise. I was not yet a beggar, but who knew? It might yet come to that. Once I had slipped down from the cart and balanced myself upon my crutches, he passed down to me my knapsack, saluted with his whip, and drove into the city through the gate. I slung my knapsack over my shoulder and turned away, first along Little Britain and the south side of Smithfield Market, which echoed with the noise of the beasts, then along Holborn.

Never before I had ventured more than a dozen yards or so on my crutches with my knapsack on my shoulder, and I now discovered how difficult it was, for every few strides the knapsack would slide down my arm and entangle itself in one of my crutches. I tried shifting it from shoulder to shoulder. Nothing solved the problem. It was worst on my left side, the side of my amputated leg, for it was more likely to unbalance me, but I also needed my right side to be dependable, and the sliding knapsack unsteadied me there. I was constantly stopping to heave the wretched thing back on to my shoulder, while passers-by either hurried past, averting their eyes in embarrassment, or – like a gaggle of half grown apprentices – jeered openly, shouting abuse.

'Hey, Master Hop-a-Leg! Let's see you dance a jig!'

One of them picked up a clod of earth and heaved it at me, but his aim was poor and it fell to one side. In the past, I would have laid into the fellow with my fists, but what could I do now, teetering on my crutches, against six youths? They were poor, pale-faced, pimply fellows, not like our strong country lads, but all I could do was set my jaw and hobble on. They followed me for a while, but soon grew bored and ran off.

After two more tangles with my knapsack, I pulled it off my shoulder in disgust and hung it round my neck, where it bumped against my chest. I felt a fool, but at least I was able to get along more easily.

When at last I found time to look about me, I thought London seemed dirty and shabby. I had not thought it so when I had first come here, fresh from my studies at Cambridge. I had been full of hope then, confident that I would qualify as a lawyer and begin the life of a gentleman, perhaps with a post in the service of government. There had been talk in Cambridge of the growing tension between Parliament and the King, but I had paid little attention to it, for it seemed unreal amongst our bookish days and our evenings in the town's taverns. Coming to London, I had thought it a city of promise, where I would break out of my chrysalis as a country yeoman's son and rise to great heights.

It had not taken more than a week or two for me to realise that something dangerous was brewing in the land. And my fellow law students were hotly debating the merits of some strange new ideas that had begun to circulate. That was when I first heard the name of Freeborn John, John Lilburne. His pamphlets circulated amongst us, with their revolutionary ideas of equality amongst men, of a fair society in which poor men would not be oppressed by the rich, where even a king must be subject to the law. We young men were mostly excited by these ideas, though some declared that opposition to the King was tantamount to blasphemy, for was he not God's anointed?

I do not think we suspected, then, that it would lead to bloody war, but as my first year of studies in the law came to an end, war did indeed break out and all teaching at the Inns of Court was suspended for the immediate future. At the time, I suppose that most thought life would return to normal after a few months. The King and Parliament would reach some compromise. As all studies were at an end for the moment and my father that summer was not very well, I went home to the farm, expecting to return to London at the start of the next law term.

Now, here I was, nearly seven years later, come back to a London where the people were ill dressed, their faces pinched, their eyes furtive. The streets were surely more clogged with rubbish than before, where skeletal stray dogs scavenged. On nearly every street corner beggars in their rags stretched out bony hands, too weak even to cry out for alms. I hardened my heart, for my early time in the city had taught me not to trust the claims of beggars. There had always been a foul smell in the streets, where the kennels meant to carry away rain water were more often choked with the contents of piss pots tipped from the neighbouring houses, but the stench seemed worse than ever. I need not have worried about the smell of goat that I carried.

By the time I had hobbled up Gray's Inn Lane and reached the gatehouse of the Inn, I was exhausted. Despite the winter cold and the bite of an east wind, I was sweating with the effort of swinging myself along. The pain in my armpits from leaning on my crutches had spread to my shoulders, my back, and my neck. My whole body was screaming for rest. Had the distance been much greater, I think I should simply have slid to the ground and stayed there.

The gatekeeper was a new man who did not know me and eyed me with suspicion, barring my entry. I cannot have been a pretty sight, stained and dirty with travel, my face running with sweat and my ridiculous knapsack flapping about on my chest. It seemed that, after all my efforts, I might not even be able to gain admittance to the Inn. I lifted the strap of my knapsack from my neck and let it slide to the ground. Fortunately I had brought writing materials with me, intended for taking notes during moots and readings. I could send in a letter to the Treasurer, the master of the Inn, asking for a meeting.

Just as I was unbuckling my knapsack, a young man came up behind me and was about to enter the gatehouse when he stopped and looked at me, frowning.

'Tom? Is it Tom Bennington?' he said. 'God's bones, Tom, what has happened to you? Have you been in the fighting?'

He was looking frankly at my injury. It was a natural assumption.

'Anthony Thirkettle! The Lord be praised! I thought this fellow was going to kick me into the gutter.' I glared as the unfriendly gatekeeper.

Anthony turned to the man. 'This is Master Bennington, Potter, a former student of Gray's Inn. He will be coming with me.'

Without another word, Anthony led me through the gate and into Chapel Court. Halfway across, he paused.

'So, have you been at the war?'

'Nay.' I shook my head. 'Stand me a mug of beer and I'll tell you the whole story.'

'We'll go to my chambers.'

He started off again, but I laid my hand on his arm.

'I am not able for stairs.'

'My chambers are on the ground floor. Two shallow steps.'

'That I can probably manage.'

Seeing how awkward I was, with my knapsack now thudding against my chest again, he simply lifted it from around my neck and carried it himself. It was one of the things I remembered about him: how he would quietly set about doing whatever might be needful, while other fellows argued and wasted time.

'Here,' he said, unlocking a stout wooden door and holding it open for me.

I managed the two steps without falling flat on my face, though my arms had begun to shake with the long labour of my walk from Aldersgate. Anthony waved me to a cushioned chair beside a cheerful fire and I sank into it gratefully, propping my crutches against the side, where they promptly clattered to the ground.

At first I closed my eyes, for I was overcome with a wave of nausea and dizziness, then I felt Anthony pressing a mug into my hand.

'Drink that. It will soon set you up. Despite the times, we still have a good strong brew here at Gray's. When did you last eat?'

I took a long draught, then wiped my mouth on my sleeve, which still definitely carried the stink of goat.

'I had some thin pottage at an inn last night, on the far edge of the heath land.'

'I haven't much food here, but there's a fresh loaf and some hard cheese. You may help yourself.'

He fetched the food from an inner room and set it out on a table next to my chair. While I ate, he asked no questions.

'Are you not eating?' I said. The cheese was somewhat bland, compared with Mercy's cheeses, but I was too hungry to mind. And the beer was strong and strengthening.

'Nay, I had a good breakfast not long since in Hall.'

When he saw that I had finished eating, he poured me more beer and some for himself, then sat back in a chair on the other side of the hearth

'Well? And how do you come to be in this state? And what are you doing in London?'

Anthony was perhaps three or four years older than I and had progressed further in his studies than I had, before I left for home. Like me he came from the Fens, though he was a townsman. His father was a modestly prosperous merchant in Ely, trading mostly in raw wool and woollen cloth with the Low Countries and France. I do not think he owned any ships, but the family had done well, at least until the war.

'As for my leg,' I said, 'I injured it twice last year in battles with the adventurers who are attempting to drain our Fens and steal our commons. Then my leg turned gangrenous. It was necessary to amputate, else I'd have been dead by this. So, yes, I lost it in battle, though not the kind of battle you meant.'

He shook his head. 'It is a bad business, this draining. They are wreaking havoc.'

'They are indeed.' I told him of the terrible flood caused by the blind mismanagement of the waters, and how we had struggled to survive, despite the damage.

'I am of no use now on the farm. I cannot do even half a day's work. My father is dead and I have made over the farm to my sister.'

He raised his eyebrows. 'Can a woman run a farm?'

I smiled. 'Someday you must meet my sister. But aye, she was near enough running it already before the flood. I have left them restoring and rebuilding while I came to London.'

I looked about me. This was no student's room.

'Have you been called to the bar?'

'I am an utter barrister, not fully qualified yet, but all is in such confusion in these times, even in the courts, that I sometimes act as assistant to one of the Readers or Benchers. Though we can hardly speak of Readers any more, for there have been no readings this long while. Indeed, sometimes I am even left to do most of the court work myself. No one has been called to the bar since the start of the war. You just completed one year, did you not?'

'Aye.' I hesitated. 'As I am useless now as a farmer, I thought to resume my studies in the law, if they will take me back. I had paid my fees.'

I would not yet mention my other reason for coming to London.

'I do not see why they should not. You must see the Treasurer, and he will put it to the next meeting of Pension. Though I must warn you, there is little formal teaching now. Last year Pension gave an order that every student must attend a moot once every day, but it is an order more broken than observed. We are in a sorry state.'

'Here in Gray's Inn only?'

'Nay. It is the same at all the Inns. We must get by now, it seems, merely by studying the law books. At any rate, we have a good library, better than it was when you were here, thanks to several bequests from former members.'

'I cannot see the Treasurer in my present state.' I waved a hand at my muddy breeches and my stained and crumpled shirt. 'May I wash and change here?'

'Of course.' He paused, eying me thoughtfully. 'You have just arrived in London this morning?'

'Aye.'

'Have you lodgings?'

'I thought I would wait until I spoke to the Treasurer, then decide what to do.'

'Would you like to share these chambers with me? My fellow – Jonathon Dawes, do you remember him? – he shared with me, but grew so disgusted with the present state of affairs that he left after Christmas and went home to Yorkshire. He had qualified as an utter barrister too, and it seems that is enough for him to practice there. His share of the rent is paid up to Lady Day, so you may live rent free until then. I mostly eat in Hall, but sometimes I send out to a pie shop, or cook over the fire when I want to save the chinks. What do you say?'

What could I say? I flushed, partly with relief, partly with shame that he should think me a charity case. 'I can pay my way,' I said, somewhat stiffly.

He laughed. 'Of course, but the room is empty and going a-begging. Why not use it? We can see how we fare. If by Lady Day we find we are heartily tired of each other's company, then you may look about for other lodgings.'

'Then I say hearty thanks.' I grinned at him. 'A ground floor room in chambers will suit me very well. And I am told that here in London I may have a false leg made of wood, which will help me to get about more easily.'

'Aye,' he said soberly. 'You are not the only man in London who has need of such help. There's many a soldier to be seen about the streets who has lost one or both legs.'

'Then I need not feel so much a freak,' I said, trying to make a jest of it.

'Nay, it is an honourable wound earned in defending your land against those scoundrels. You should be proud.'

I shook my head, but said nothing. It is easy enough to say such things when you are not the one who feels himself but half a man, maimed and disfigured. I let it pass. At home no one had spoken to me so frankly, but Anthony had always been as open and honest as clear glass. My luck had surely taken a turn for the better in meeting him.

He showed me round the rest of the chambers. The room where we had been sitting was the largest, with comfortable chairs and also a table with joint stools to serve when he took his meals here. On the other side of the outer door there was an office or study, with two desks and a shelf of law books. At the back there were two small bedchambers, a privy chamber and a very small room, not much more than a large cupboard, which was a sort of kitchen, with a pallet bed against one wall.

'The fellow who lived here before us was a full barrister and had a servant who cooked and valeted for him. He slept in here. I don't aspire to such grandeur,' Anthony said. 'But it is useful if we want to cook, or even brew up some spiced ale.'

Everything was immaculately clean and tidy, and I remarked on it.

'There's a woman comes in once a week to clean all the chambers on this stair. Fortunately her services are included in the rent. She keeps us all in order. Quite a tyrant, Goodwife Gorley. Even the Benchers dare not say her nay.'

I laughed. 'I shall mind my manners with her, then.'

'This is the chamber you can have,' Anthony said, leading me back to one of the bedchambers. 'It isn't much, but I find it is adequate. And one advantage of living on the ground floor is that we have piped water, so you may wash in the kitchen. I'll warm some water for you on the parlour fire. The kitchen fire is not lit.'

'I don't want to trouble you.'

'No trouble.'

Half an hour later, I had washed thoroughly in hot water, with Castile soap, a luxury Anthony allowed himself in the dirt of London.

'You would not believe how much dirtier London is than the country,' he said as he handed me the expensive soap. 'The sea coal leaves a filthy film over everything, and so many people crowded together seems to multiply the dirt.'

'At least here we are outside the City proper.'

'Aye,' he said. 'Henry III did us a good turn, banning the teaching of law within the confines of the City. Here we benefit from being on the edge of the country.'

'Are the Walks still maintained?'

'Aye. Somewhat untidy, for several of the gardeners joined the army, but they are as beautiful as ever.'

After I had washed and combed the tangles from my hair, I donned a clean shirt and hose, and my best doublet and breeches, which I had carried with me in my knapsack. Mercy had cut away the foot of some of my hose, so I could roll the left leg up to my stump. I must find out whether the Inn still employed washerwomen, for the clothes I had worn for travelling were not fit to be seen in company.

'I feel a new man,' I said, as I hobbled back into the parlour. 'I cannot tell you how grateful I am, Anthony.'

He brushed my words aside. 'What do you want to do about seeing the Treasurer?'

'No time like the present.'

'He is not here today, he was sent for to go to Westminster. Why do you not write a message to his senior clerk, asking for a meeting tomorrow? He is not unreasonable. I am sure he will see you.'

Taking Anthony's advice, I wrote a brief note to the clerk, which was carried to the Treasurer's chambers by one of the Inn's servants. I had a reply within the hour, naming ten o'clock the next day for the meeting.

In the meantime Anthony had settled to his papers in the office, where I took him the news of the appointed meeting.

'Excellent. Then today you may rest after your travels.'

'I would rather make myself useful. Is there anything I can do to help you?'

'Well, if you mean it, you could help by copying out the precedents from these casebooks. They are marked with slips of paper. I am assisting one of the Benchers in a case of land inheritance. It is complicated through the deaths of several direct heirs in the war and now there are three claimants, all with more or less equal rights.'

'It cannot be divided three ways?'

'Nay, it is a case for Solomon's wisdom. Which is somewhat lacking in these modern times.'

I sat down at the second desk and we worked together contentedly for the rest of the morning. Although copying out precedents was a clerk's task, I enjoyed it, though I found it far more interesting to root about in the casebooks, searching for ancient precedents like a pig hunting for truffles. Anthony had already made the necessary searches, but I did find one more judgement which might prove useful. At midday we stopped for more bread, cheese and beer, followed by a slice of apple pie purchased from the redoubtable Goodwife Gorley.

'This is excellent,' I said.

'She augments her small income by selling her baking to members of the Inn. I believe her father was a baker.'

Anthony stretched out his long legs to the fire. It had been chilly in the office, where he had not lit a fire, although we had kept the intervening doors open to benefit from the parlour fire. He explained that both coal and firewood had become very expensive since the war.

'Fewer miners and woodsmen, I suppose,' he said. 'And we cannot go out and dig up a load of free peat, as you fenlanders may.'

'Not in the future,' I said grimly, 'if the drainers have their way.'

'By the by, I appreciate your help,' he said. 'It is clerk's work, I know, but I cannot afford to employ one, so mostly do it myself. A few of us share a clerk. I have his services one day a week.'

'In order to keep myself in London, I thought I would seek some clerking work myself,' I said, 'a few days a week. Perhaps with one of the merchants in Cheapside.'

'You might even get one of the Benchers here to take you on. Some of the clerks, like the gardeners, have joined the army. And you will understand the work. You should ask the Treasurer when you see him.'

'I will so.'

We carried on working at Anthony's papers for the rest of the day. Just as it was growing dusk and we needed candles, he stretched his arms above his head, until his shoulders creaked.

'That is surely enough evidence to take to court. You have saved me a whole day. I shall send out for a pie and a bottle of wine to celebrate.'

'Do you not dine in Hall?'

'Sometimes. Not tonight.'

He went off to send a servant out for our meal and would not take a contribution from me.

'Nay, you have more than earned it with all the work you have done today.'

I suspected that he would have dined in Hall – and dined far better – had I not been there, but I said nothing, not wishing to embarrass him. Only if I were readmitted to the Inn would I be able to dine in Hall. In any case, I would not be able to afford the bills unless I could find some paid work. Otherwise I must needs live on bread, cheese and beer, which might grow somewhat tedious after a time.

Anthony insisted that we should lay the table as if we were at home.

'My mother would chide me if she saw me still living like a student, sitting cross-legged on the floor and tearing my meat with my fingers. The wine glasses are in that hanging cupboard to the right of the hearth, and the napkins are there as well.'

'Your mother would be shocked, then, to see how we have had to live at home these past weeks, all huddled together in the church. These glasses?'

'Aye. Can you manage?'

'One at a time.'

By the time the servant returned we had the table laid well enough to satisfy Anthony's mother's standards, and sat down to a very acceptable dinner: a dish of sprats fried in batter, a pigeon pie with crisp pastry and a gravy rich with onions and red wine, roasted parsnips, and a custard tart to finish. The French wine, too was excellent.

'The pie shops hereabouts must have improved mightily since I was last in London,' I said, wiping my mouth and sitting back with my last glass of wine.

He laughed. 'Nay, I sent him to the Peacock in Holborn. You remember. Best of the nearby inns. They will send over food to Gray's if they know you. One may eat very well.'

I was glad to retire soon after we had eaten, for the fatigues of the journey and my uncomfortable nights had begun to overtake me. I laid my decent clothes on the coffer and pulled my wool night shift over my head before lowering myself carefully on to the bed. It was not very wide, but it was comfortable, with tightly strung ropes and both a flock and a feather mattress. It had grown colder as the evening drew in, so I was glad of the good blankets and the feather bed for covering. Anthony had said he let the fire go out at night, because of the cost of fuel, so I pulled the bedclothes close round my ears.

My first day in London had been remarkably fortunate, after that agonising walk from Aldersgate. I shuddered at the thought of what I could have done, had Anthony not come along as I was turned away at the gate. Since the Treasurer was away, a note sent in to him would have done me no good. I would have had nowhere to go, and in my weakened state I am not sure if I could have made my way even as far as the nearest tavern.

After that morning's experience, I realised that my plan of applying for work with a merchant in Cheapside was folly. I could never make my way over so great a distance every day. Anthony's suggestion that I might find clerking work here in the Inn was far more practical. As for the lucky chance that he had a spare room in his chambers, I could hardly believe my good fortune. I hoped that he was telling the truth, that the rent was indeed paid up until Lady Day. Still, I had never known him prevaricate. Whether or not Pension agreed to readmit me as a student, I could stay here for the coming weeks, provided I could earn enough to pay my share of the food and fuel. Perhaps by then I would have located Sir John Dillingworth's lawyer and through him discovered the whereabouts of our charter. I would take Anthony into my confidence about the charter. After I had seen the Treasurer. Tomorrow. I slept.

Although the Treasurer's chambers were also on the ground floor, Anthony said they were reached by five steps. He offered to come with me, but I was determined to manage without help. I allowed myself plenty of time and negotiated the steps slowly, pausing after each one to steady myself and catch my breath. The door was heavy, solid oak, and gave me almost more trouble than the steps, but I struggled through, finding myself in an outer chamber, an office with three clerks. A junior barrister was also there, in consultation with the senior clerk. As I entered, everyone stopped speaking and their eyes went immediately to my amputated leg. I bit my lip. At home everyone was accustomed to it now, but here in London I would have to endure such looks every time I encountered someone new.

'Master Bennington? It is good to see you again, sir, after so long.' At least Theodore Somers, the senior clerk, had recognised me. He stood up, with a murmured apology to the barrister, and came forward to shake me by the hand.

I saw him hesitate and knew what was passing through his mind. Should he or should he not make a reference to my injury? He would not. He gestured me towards an inner door.

'The Treasurer is expecting you, sir, if you will just step this way.'

He opened the door for me.

'Master Bennington to see you, Treasurer.' He bowed me in.

My first thought was that the Treasurer had aged far more than I had expected. During my time as a student, he had been one of the Readers, but now filled the most senior position at the Inn. Why it was designated 'Treasurer', I did not know. It had puzzled me, coming from a Cambridge college. I would have expected 'Master'. It looked to me now as though the position had taken its toll on him during the recent difficult years.

'Good morrow to you, Master Bennington,' he said, half rising from his chair and bowing across the large desk which stood between us. 'Please take a seat.'

I sat down on one of the hard straight chairs which faced him across the desk.

'I had not expected to see you again, I must confess.' He took off his spectacles and polished them on a silk handkerchief. Putting them on again, he peered at me keenly. His eyes had flicked swiftly to my leg and away again. 'How many years is it?'

'Nearly seven, sir.'

'Seven years! A great deal has happened since then, has it not?'

'It has indeed.'

'And what can I do for you?'

I drew a deep breath. 'You may remember, sir, that I returned home at the end of my first year, expecting to come back in the autumn. My father was ill. I was needed on the farm during the summer, but I did not plan to abandon my studies. Then when war broke out, and teaching at Gray's was suspended–'

'Indeed, indeed. Very troubling times. But we are hoping to restore teaching. We have made a start.'

'That is why I am here. As you can see, I am not fit to manage the family farm any longer.'

'You have been in the army?'

He nodded toward my leg.

I gave him a brief account of my injuries and the gangrene. I had decided not to mention how I had received the injuries. For all I knew, he might be acting in a legal capacity for one of the companies of adventurers. Let him assume that the injuries had been sustained on the farm. Many such injuries occur.

'So,' I concluded, 'I hoped I might be able to resume my studies here. My fees were all paid and I believe I completed my first year satisfactorily.'

He steepled his fingers and rested his chin on them.

'I remember that you were a good student, though sometimes a little wild.'

'I have not much capacity for wildness now, sir, and I am seven years older.'

37

He nodded and smiled briefly. 'It is not a decision I can make myself, you understand. I must put it to Pension. We have a meeting in two days' time. We will be able to give you a decision then. Where are you lodging?'

'Anthony Thirkettle has a spare room in his chambers. I am lodging there at present.'

'Good. Good. Well, I hope we may be able to welcome you back, Master Bennington.'

He began to rise, to dismiss me. I struggled to my feet, leaning on my crutches.

'There is one other matter, Treasurer.'

'Aye?'

'I shall need to earn enough to keep myself in London. There has been a disastrous flood at home, and I cannot expect money from my family. I thought, perhaps, if any of the Benchers need some clerical work done?'

He cocked his head. It was a strange suggestion from a student, for law students were normally too grand for such work.

'I will enquire. However, I think you might find work in our library. We have received a large number of books in bequests from former members of Gray's, who are now, alas, deceased. I know that our librarian, Master Hansen, is having some difficulty in cataloguing and arranging them all. You might ask there.'

'Thank, you, Treasurer. I will do so.'

I bowed and made my way out of the room. The Treasurer's response had been the best I might expect, but what the will of Pension would be, I could not tell. Some of the ancients, the most senior members, might vote against me, deploring my long absence. I must simply wait the next few days to learn my fate.

In the outer office the lawyer was gone and Theodore Somers opened the outer door for me.

'Will you be rejoining us, Master Bennington?'

'I hope so.' I smiled at him. 'That is a decision Pension must make.'

'It will be good to have you back. These have been difficult times, and we have lost several members. It is to be hoped that life may return to what it was, before too long.'

'Indeed,' I said. 'Can you tell me where the library is now? Is it still housed in one of the Bencher's chambers?'

'Oh, no, sir. We have a new library building, in Coney Court, and our own official librarian, appointed two years ago, Master Hansen. It is the new half-timbered building on your right as you enter Coney Court.'

I thanked him and manoeuvred my way down the five steps. There had been a frost in the night, but fortunately someone – probably one of the Inn servants – had scattered sand over the steps, so there was less risk of my slipping.

As for my meeting with the Treasurer, it seemed that there was no point in wasting time. I would go at once to the library and ask if there might be work for me there. Crossing Chapel Court and entering Coney, I passed several members hurrying to and fro, their gowns flapping in the icy wind which had arisen again that morning. I was glad of my thick cloak, but as always the stump of my left leg was cold, and I shivered. I recognised some of the faces, mostly senior members, although there was one younger man, about Anthony's age. His face was familiar, but I could not put a name to it. It seemed to be the same with him, for he hesitated, looking slightly puzzled, then bowed and walked on. I must ask Anthony who he might be. Altogether the whole place seemed much emptier than I remembered, but perhaps the cold weather was keeping people withindoors.

I found the new library building at once, its oak timber frame still the pale colour of freshly cut wood, where the beams of the older buildings had weathered to the beautiful silver grey of established oak. I was relieved to see that there were but three steps up to the door. It seemed that for the future I would be forever counting steps.

Inside, the building consisted of one large room, like a smaller version of the Inn's Hall. It was well lit by tall windows, while there was a pleasant smell of leather bindings, fresh cut timber, and the lime wash on the walls. The room was divided into bays by tall bookcases, each bay containing a double row of reading desks, facing each other down the centre. Just to the right of the door a small area had been partitioned off with a low rail to provide a workplace for the librarian. And I saw at once what the Treasurer had meant. For the most part the bookshelves were empty. Instead every surface – reading desks, benches, even the floor – was covered with piles of books. Some mounted to four feet or more in precarious piles, some were still in half open crates. Everything was very dusty. It seemed that Goodwife Gorley or her like were not admitted to the library.

I thought at first that there was no one here, until a voice said, 'May I help you, sir?'

It came from behind the librarian's desk, which carried its own formidable wall of books. A head appeared, barely visible above the massive tomes filled with past case law. Master Hansen, it seemed, was a very small man.

He emerged around the side of his desk, indeed a very small man, not much above five feet, with a gnome-like countenance and very bright blue eyes behind his spectacles, which he removed in order to study me.

'Master Hansen?' I bowed as far as my crutches would permit. 'The Treasurer said that you might have need of an assistant.'

He gave a puzzled frown. 'There is indeed far too much work for one man, sir, far too much! But who are you? You do not appear to me to be a clerk.'

'I am a former student of Gray's, Tom Bennington, hoping to resume my studies, if Pension agrees. However, I must earn my keep while I live in London and the Treasurer suggested the library. I am very familiar with law books, which would be an advantage.'

I strove to keep a note of pleading out of my voice.

'But my dear sir!' He felt about himself, it seemed for a handkerchief, then pulled out his shirt tail and polished his spectacles on that. 'I am paid a pittance, a mere pittance! I cannot afford to employ an assistant.'

I was somewhat taken aback. 'I do not think the Treasurer meant that you should pay me out of your own pocket, Master Hansen. Surely Gray's would cover any expense.'

'In that case it will be up to Pension to decide.'

It seemed that every aspect of my future lay in the hands of the members of Pension.

'But you would be glad of assistance? You could request that I should be employed?' Remembering the Treasurer's words, I added cunningly, 'There is a meeting in two days' time. You could send in a request to be considered then.'

'I do indeed need assistance. Do you think you would like the work? Are you able for it?'

'Why do I not help you now? I am at liberty.'

Anthony was spending most of the day discussing the land inheritance case with the Bencher who was employing him. I would be as well getting an idea of the work here as idling away in his chambers.

Hansen gave me a sharp look. 'But I say again, are you able?'

I clenched my teeth. I would need to be honest.

'I cannot climb a ladder to the high bookshelves, no. And I cannot carry heavy boxes of books, no. But I can manage single books, even large ones.'

I hoped this was true.

'However, I understand from the Treasurer that the chief task is first to catalogue the books.' I nodded toward the untidy piles and full crates. 'I write a fair secretary hand, and I am quick. If you show me your system for sorting and arranging the different categories of books, I am sure I can save you a great deal of time. Let us see how we fare. I am glad to offer you my services today.'

He could hardly refuse such an offer of help. I looked about, feeling some sympathy for the fellow. The task was truly daunting for one man, even for two. He beckoned me round to the far side of his desk, where he had a row of ledgers laid out and explained which books were to be listed in each: case histories, general law books, Latin and Greek classics, and a great variety of general books which had been bequeathed to the Inn, including philosophy, poetry, history, memoirs, books on navigation and exploration. The list was unending.

'These books have nothing to do with the Law,' he said, waving his hand dismissively at some collections of poetry from the last century and a seafarer's account of a voyage down the coast of Africa. 'However, as they have been given to us, we must find a place for them.'

For myself, I thought there was much of interest here. How Gideon would have rubbed his hands in glee, and Mercy would have snatched up the poetry to read at once, but all I said was, 'It is good for students to broaden their minds by reading widely. So we were taught at Cambridge.'

He gave a snort at this, but I did not pursue it. My task here was the simple recording of books, not a discussion of their use.

'We have columns here,' he said, pointing with the clean end of his quill, 'for the author, the title, a brief description (you may usually find this on the title page), the date it was received by the Inn if that is known, and the benefactor, if it was a gift. The final column holds the key to where it will be shelved.'

'How do I know what to enter there?'

He drew a sheet of foolscap from the far side of his desk.

'I have set out here a table showing all the major categories of books, with a description of each category and the key letters and numbers to the shelves.'

I looked about at the empty shelves.

'But I do not see any key on the shelves.'

'I have not progressed that far yet.' He was impatient. 'Once I have an understanding of how many books fall into each category, then I shall know how many shelves should be set aside for them.'

I nodded. 'I understand.'

'You may work at this other table.' He swept the pile of books off a smaller table next to his desk. 'It will be necessary for us to have the table of categories available for us both to use. There are quills and ink here. Take care you do not make any blots.' He gave me a fierce look. 'If you do the work well, I will consider making a request for your services to Pension. See to it that you make no mistakes.'

I felt this was somewhat ungracious of him, since I was generously giving up my day to help him, but I held my tongue. I would need his good will if I were to find employment here. I took off my cloak and laid it on top of one of the crates, but he clicked his tongue and carried it off to be hung on a hook by the door. I rolled my sleeves up to my elbows, for I had no wish to stain my good shirt and doublet with ink, which is impossible to remove. With some difficulty I managed to shift a stool next to the table he had allotted me, and leaned my crutches against the table's edge. I helped myself to inkwell, quills, sand sifter.

Hansen carried over a pile of books and placed them before me.

'These are from the bequest of the late Reader, Sir Thomas Bordman. They are all casebooks, so they are to be entered into this ledger with the blue binding. We cannot be for ever passing ledgers back and forth between us. You must catalogue one group at a time.'

I nodded. I sharpened a quill to my satisfaction with the small knife I carried in my pocket and set to. When Pension met in two days' time I should know whether this would be where I would be spending many hours in the coming weeks. It would hardly prove exciting, but if it enabled me to live in London, I was grateful.

Chapter Three
Mercy

Our horse Blaze was as eager as I was to escape the confines of the church and the glebe lands, and set off at a brisk pace up the lane to Turbary Holm. Unlike me, he had no apprehensions as to what would confront us there. The road home meant his own welcome stall in a peaceful barn, away from the crowding he had endured for more than a month. For my part, I rode with a sense of dread. Our home had already been flooded several feet deep when the soldiers and I had trudged past it through the blizzard, carrying a half-conscious Tom, and ourselves numb with despair. We had watched helplessly as George was swept away on the flood and there had been nothing left for us to do but to reach the sanctuary of the church.

I did not undertake the ride back to the farm alone. Gideon had borrowed a horse from Will, while Nehemiah half walked, half trotted alongside us. I had tucked up my skirts and rode astride, as I always did, for we did not possess a side saddle, and I doubt whether I could have managed to stay mounted on that barbarous invention. The lane was pock marked in some places with new holes, hollowed out by the flood, and ridged with frozen mud in others, so we had need to go carefully. Despite Blaze's eagerness to reach home, I was forced to hold him on a tight rein and pick our way with caution.

At last the farmhouse came into sight. I must confess I had almost dreaded that it might have been washed away, but it stood there sturdily on its slight rise, with the barn and dairy and hen-hus and well-hus beyond, though I could see that the roof of the hen-hus was damaged. One wall of the barn was sagging, which we had been hastily propping up before we had abandoned the farm.

'You will need to ask the help of the Dutchmen,' Gideon said, his eyes on the barn as we rode through the gateway into the yard. The gate itself had been partially torn from its hinges and lay askew against the supporting post. 'That wall needs urgent repair, before the whole side of the barn collapses.'

I nodded. The repair to the barn was urgent and looked difficult. However, the roof of the hen-hus would be easy enough to replace, once we had gathered reeds for thatching, but I could not return the hens there until it was done, for fear of foxes. I wondered whether the local foxes had been drowned in the floods. Probably not. Wild animals have an instinct at such times. They would have fled for the higher ground further inland, though one or two had been seen about the glebe land.

Dismounted, I tethered Blaze to the ring in the house wall and shook down my skirts.

'The house first,' I said.

Best to confront the worst before all else. Then I jumped in alarm as something pushed against the back of my legs.

'Jasper!' Our dog must have followed us up the lane from the church. Like Blaze, he was anxious to return home.

Gideon laughed and rubbed Jasper behind his ears. 'You'll not find your usual warm place beside the fire, lad.'

'I hope we can make a fire.' I frowned. 'The whole of our wood store beside the barn will have been saturated. Nehemiah, have we any peat left?'

'We had some in the barn loft, Mistress Mercy. I'll climb up and see.'

Nehemiah crossed the yard to the barn, while Gideon and I struggled to open the house door, which, like others in the village, had warped in the wet. We stepped over the threshold.

I had steeled myself to expect the worst, after what I had seen in the village houses. My own home was no worse than some, and a good deal better than many. Like the Coxes' house, Turbary Holm stood a little higher than the surrounding ground. That was why it had been built here and why it was so named, for 'holm' is an old word for 'island', so I had once been told – a word brought to these parts by the Danes – while 'turbary' referred to the rich peat bogs nearby. It had not been island enough in the flood, but was raised sufficiently that the flood had reached not much above waist height, judging by the dirty marks on the walls.

As elsewhere there was a layer of mud on the floor about a foot deep, but the stench was not as bad as it had been in the Coxes' house. Somehow the movement of the flood waters had spared us the midden. But there was the same destruction of small household goods, although the heavy furniture had survived. In the corner my mother's loom was a pile of shattered sticks, tangled up in a half finished blanket Kitty had been weaving. The door to the small chamber which had once been Kitty's stood open. Since his amputation, it had been Tom's, for he had not yet found a way to manage stairs. The bedclothes had been torn off the bed and lay in the mud.

'There is a ham left,' Gideon said, pointing to where it hung above the fireplace.

'And there will be cheeses and other stores in the hayloft over the barn,' I said. 'We hid them there when the court officers seized our goods as security for Father's fine. We never moved them.'

'Some good has come of that bad time, then.'

Nehemiah came in, carrying two shovels. 'Aye, there's a small store of peat left in the barn, but let it stay until we have cleared this mud, eh, Reverend?'

'You'd best not call me that, Nehemiah. Not until I may return to my church, if ever I may.'

He nodded. 'Aye. Master Clarke it shall be, then. Shall us set to and clear this clag?'

He had brought a wheelbarrow to the door, and as they began to shovel the filth from the floor into it, I picked my way to the barn. Jasper kept close at my heels. It seemed he was worried by the state in which he had found his familiar home. The beaten earth of the yard had been softened and churned by the flood, then frozen into uneven hillocks, so there was every likelihood of turning an ankle. It would be better not to bring the cows back until there was safer footing for them.

The large lidded crock which held the hens' food still stood safely on a shelf in the barn, away from rats. The rest of the barn was in much the same state as the house, though there was little here that could be damaged. Everything of value was stored in the hay loft or hung from pegs high on the walls. Normally I took a single scoop to feed the hens, but I feared they might be starving, so I made a bag of my apron and filled it with as much of the feed as it would hold.

Back in the house I could hear Gideon and Nehemiah working away in the back parlour, seldom used by the family. They had not begun yet on the kitchen, where we mostly lived. Holding my apron tightly with one hand, I felt my way cautiously up the stairs to the first floor. The first few steps were slippery, but after that they seemed sound enough. As in the Coxes' house, I decided to shed my muddy boots. The attics were reached by a ladder, which was still in place. This was even more difficult to climb with my burden of hen food. Unable to follow me, Jasper watched anxiously from the foot of the ladder, whining softly. As I pushed up the trap with my free hand I was engulfed in a stink of hen droppings and something worse, so that I closed my eyes and prayed that I should not find them all dead.

Two had perished. Their emaciated bodies showed clearly enough that they had starved to death. Hens have a fierce pecking order and the strongest will always prevail over the weakest, pushing and clawing them away from the food. These were two of the young pullets, and I was glad that I had not brought Kitty with me, for she had reared the brood herself and was mighty proud of them. The remaining hens crouched here and there, with lacklustre eyes and ragged feathers. Clearly they had been pecking each other in their distress. All the food, naturally, was gone.

I scattered several handfuls of grain in a wide sweep over the floor, so that all the hens could reach it without being bullied. They staggered or scrambled to their feet, some certainly in a worse case than the others, but animated by the prospect of food. I was relieved that Hannah's pet hen, Polly, was still alive, although she looked very weak. She had been taken in by us, along with her mistress and the cat Tobit, when the drainers burned down Hannah's cottage. After Hannah's death at the hands of the witchfinders, I had felt a particular care for her two pets.

Once the hens were all feeding, I searched the attics to see how much damage they had done. Kitty now slept up here, in the room she had once shared with Hannah. Fortunately she had closed

47

the door before we left the farm, but the rest of the attics, those used for storage and the one where the billeted soldiers had slept, were now covered in hen droppings. Every inch would need to be scoured. That would have to wait until the hens could be returned to the repaired hen-hus. It must be one of the first tasks, for the smell permeated all the floor below, where our bed chambers were.

I scattered the rest of the grain, then carried the dead hens down the ladder and out to the midden. They were not fit for eating, having been dead some time and already crawling with maggots. As I came back round the corner of the barn away from the midden, I stopped suddenly at the sight of the two bee skeps, overturned and lying broken in the mud. The bees! Hannah's bees. I had quite forgotten them when we were herding the stock to the glebe lands. If I had remembered, we could have moved the skeps to a safer place, the hay loft, or a high shelf in the dairy where the big cheeses were sometimes kept. The bees would have been deep in their winter sleep when the floods came. No chance of escape. They must have drowned, every one.

Somehow the loss of the bees seemed to hit me like a blow in the stomach. Until then I had thought that everything about the farm could be cleaned and repaired, soon all would be well again, but those were Hannah's bees, which had followed her here from her cottage, and everyone knows the importance of bees to any household, especially a farm. They are part of the luck of the family. Suddenly I found myself weeping, unable to stop.

At the sound of the trundling wheelbarrow, I rubbed my face with the edge of my apron. It smelled of the hens' grain. Why should I weep for the bees? There had been so much lost, so many families bereft. What were two skeps of bees, compared to that? Yet I could have saved them, had I not forgotten them, hidden round here in the shelter at the side of the barn, where the bees had a clear flight path to our small orchard.

'Why, what ails thee, Mercy lass?'

Nehemiah had dropped the handles of the barrow, and at the same time lapsed into the way he had always spoken to me as a child. I pointed to the tattered skeps, which Kitty had helped Hannah make, back in the spring.

'We have lost the bees,' I said. 'I should have remembered.'

'Nay, lass,' he said gently, 'what you did was grand. You got all the stock to the glebe land, and all the folk too, even those foreigners. And if you hadn't seen to breaking down the old sluice gate to run off some of the water from the Lode, the flood would have been deeper still. We'll make new skeps, and happen we'll find us a new swarm, come the spring.' He patted my shoulder clumsily. 'How have the hens fared?'

'Two of Kitty's pullets are dead, and the rest thin and in a bad state, but I think they will live. I wish we could move them back into the hen-hus. There's a fair stink in the attic.'

'I'll thatch it again tomorrow, but there's a bit canvas in the barn we could tie down over the roof tonight, if you like.'

'Aye, let us do that,' I said. 'When you and Gideon have finished shovelling the clag from the house.'

'Nearly done,' he said, and set off again with his barrow for the midden.

'Bring the peat back with you,' I called. 'I will light a fire upstairs to air the bed chambers.' I walked slowly back to the house, with Jasper still clinging to my heels. I felt suddenly tired and defeated, but I was determined that I would keep such weakness hidden.

For the next few hours we all worked hard. I lit a fire in my chamber, leaving all the doors open so that the heat would reach the other chambers – my mother's, the one which used to be Tom's, and the little room at the back where Nehemiah slept. As we had found in the village houses, the bed clothes were damp, and even the clothing stored in the coffers. By the time I had spread everything out to air, I came down to find Gideon on his hands and knees scrubbing the kitchen floor. He had lit a small fire on the kitchen hearth and brought in stacks of the damp logs to dry out in the warmth.

Something twisted in my chest as I looked down at Gideon crouched like a poor scullion, his hands red and sore.

'That is no task for an Oxford trained clergyman,' I said, trying to make a jest of it, though my voice trembled a little.

He looked up at me sideways, a lock of his hair fallen across his face, and grinned.

'We must forget the Oxford trained clergyman until better times return, my love. I am a farm labourer now, like Nehemiah.'

49

'You do not sound like Nehemiah,' I said. 'And where is he, leaving you to scrub the floor?'

'Fixing a canvas on the hen-hus roof, so you may move your poultry back where they belong.'

'You found some dry logs?'

'Aye, the top of the stack was above the level of the flood, so there is a dry layer. The ones just below are only a little damp. They should dry out soon.'

I started to sort out the crockery, separating the broken from the undamaged, and I put the muddy bedding from the small chamber off the kitchen to soak. Soon after, Nehemiah came in, rubbing his hands together against the cold.

'More snow coming, I'm afeared,' he said. 'But the hen-hus is snug enough. I've put a layer of peat over the canvas for warmth. Shall us move them?'

'Aye,' I said, 'then I think we have done enough for today. Tomorrow I will scrub out the attics.'

It took the three of us two trips to restore the hens to their home and settle them with a good supply of water and feed, then we laid damp peats over the fires in the house to make them safe, before setting off to ride back to the village, Nehemiah and Jasper trotting behind the horses, perhaps not quite as briskly as earlier in the day.

Dusk was drawing over us as we came to the village. It was heartening to see candlelight in the windows of the houses that had been restored, and smoke rising from their chimneys. I began to think that some sort of normal life was returning. I wondered how Tom was faring, far away in London.

The following day Alice, Kitty, and Griet walked with me to the farm, and with the four of us working together, the unpleasant task of scouring the attics was quickly done. I had carried a load of small logs on my back, to make up better fires and hasten the drying out of the house, while Alice brought a basket of small loaves and cheese and ale, so that we were able to sit down to a midday meal around the kitchen table, almost as if the farm had been restored.

'My attic is quite as good as ever,' Kitty said cheerfully, biting into a large slab of bread and cheese. 'I could sleep here tonight.'

'You shall not sleep here alone,' I said sternly. 'Not until we all move home.'

'And when will that be?'

I looked around. We had tidied the kitchen before we sat down to eat and apart from a few broken dishes and the loss of the loom, it did not seem too severely damaged. The walls throughout the ground floor would need to be lime-washed, but Gideon and Jack had promised to do that the next day. They had followed us to the farm with Nehemiah and four of the Dutchmen and were busy repairing the wall of the barn, where the flood waters had undermined the foundations. Back from taking them food, Kitty had reported that they had nearly finished and would then set about levelling the yard, so that it would be safe for the cows, while Nehemiah thatched the hen-hus.

'Perhaps in two or three days we can come home,' I said. 'I want it to be as comfortable as possible for my mother.'

'Her chamber is quite warm and dry now,' Alice said. 'Griet and I have made up the bed and folded her clothes away. Once the painting is done, I think you should come back. It will be less confusing for her.'

I nodded. 'Aye. But she will be sad at the loss of the loom.'

'Nehemiah thinks he can repair it,' Kitty said. 'I asked him just now. He must carve some new pieces, but he says it is not past mending.'

'And the spinning wheel is fine,' Alice said, 'now that we have cleaned it, and thrown away the spoiled wool.'

'Aye,' I said. 'Once she has the spinning wheel under her hand, she will be more content. We will keep the broken loom out of sight until Nehemiah can see to it. You can move the pieces into the dairy, Kitty, when we have eaten. I am sorry that your blanket is destroyed.'

'I can weave another,' she said stoutly. 'I am only sad that the wool is lost.'

Despite our best efforts, the half-woven blanket could not be saved, but scraps of it would serve as bedding for sick lambs in the spring, or to rub down Blaze after a hard day's work.

Alice and I cleared away the food while Kitty and Griet cleaned the parlour. When we had finished and I was reaching for my cloak to see how the work on the yard was faring, Alice laid her hand on my arm to stay me.

'Mercy, have you thought what is to become of Gideon when we have all moved out of the church? He cannot stay at the rectory, once there is the risk of a new rector being sent to us, or the Reverend Edgemont riding over from Crowthorne.'

I looked at her in surprise. 'He will come here, of course. He will help me run the farm.'

'He knows very little of farming, Mercy. He always hired Joseph Waters and his nephews to manage the little farming he did on the glebe lands. Besides–'

'What is worrying you, Alice?'

'It cannot be right for him to be living here before you are married, now that Tom is gone.'

I laughed. 'I shall not be alone with him. My mother and Kitty and Nehemiah all live here.'

Still she shook her head. 'I fear there may be talk.'

I was astonished. In truth, I had hardly thought ahead as far as this, we had been so preoccupied with trying to survive and repair the damage of the flood. Yet now that Alice had put the idea into my head, I supposed there might be talk. Gideon had lived here before, when he was recovering from the terrible injuries inflicted on him during the attack on the church, but Alice was right. Tom had still been in sound health and living here, as had Hannah. My mother had not grown feeble in her wits. Indeed, there might now be talk. I could defy it for myself, but a clergyman must take care that no whisper of scandal comes near him. Some day Gideon might be able to take up his vocation again and I must not allow anything to endanger that.

'We would take him into the Coxes' house,' Alice said, 'but already it is so full of the homeless that Rafe and I and Huw are going to board with Jack and his mother, living in their attic. Will has two settler families at the smithy.' She gave me a shy smile. 'It would be best if you could be married at once.'

Married at once! I hardly dared think of it. Who would marry us? We could not ask the rector of Crowthorne, a rigid Puritan, who knew that Gideon had been expelled from his parish. We must keep his return here hidden from the Reverend Edgemont. Gideon could hardly perform the service himself. I thought of Alice's marriage last year, all our joyous preparations, the whole village joining in the celebrations. It had been during the dancing on the green afterwards that I had the first inkling that Gideon might love me.

'How can it be?' I said. 'Who is to marry us?'

'Perhaps that little fat parson will come back. What was he called?'

'Apsley. He ran away for fear of floods, long before there was sign of any.'

'Aye, he did. I do not suppose he will return. Gideon must know other parsons.'

'If they keep to Queen Elizabeth's church, they will have lost their places, like Gideon. And I will not be married by a ranting Puritan, who will tell me that I am already damned. Besides–' It was my turn to hesitate. I fastened my cloak about my shoulders.

'Aye?'

I realised the colour had mounted to my cheeks. 'I cannot say to him straight out, that I want to be married at once.'

'Indeed you may.' Alice was her usual brisk, practical self. 'And if you do not, I shall.'

'Alice!'

'Fear not. I shall be very discreet. I shall drop a little word in his ear about impropriety.'

'You must not!'

'I shall keep a watch on you, Mercy. If I find you have said nothing to the point, I shall feel I must preserve your good name.'

I was unsure just how serious she was, but Alice could be very determined, once an idea had taken hold. I realised I might need to say some word to Gideon, for fear of what she might do. Now, though, I stepped out into the cold, pulled my hood over my head, and went to see how the men were faring in the yard.

It was another three days before we judged it practical to move my mother back to Turbary Holm. The lane had dried, although snow still spread over much of the land. The ground which normally lay above the winter floods was now free of standing water, though very boggy in places, while the fields which normally flooded were still under water, like the barley field where the settlers had built and the medland through which the drainers had cut the ditch leading to their pumping mill. There was some hope that the flood would have broken down the banks of that misjudged new ditch and filled it in, at least partially.

The day before we moved, Nehemiah, Jack and the young soldier Ben drove our cattle back to the farm, with the aid of our dog Jasper. Ben, who was a boy of just fifteen, was beginning to show a liking for farming. The soldier who had drowned, George Lowe, had been a farmer before he was pressed into the army and Ben had clearly admired him. He could not stay permanently on the farm, however. Once orders came through for the soldiers, no doubt he would be snatched away. When the cows were settled, Nehemiah and Ben would stay to milk them. Nehemiah would sleep in the house and have good fires going to warm it throughout before my mother arrived. Ben offered to sleep in the hay loft.

'Nonsense!' I said. 'It will be much too cold. You may sleep in the room off the kitchen tonight.' I had washed and dried the dirty bedding. The room was clean and fresh again.

At that moment I realised that our five remaining soldiers would expect to move back to the farm with us, for they had been billeted there. So much for Alice's fear that I should be unchaperoned.

Over the past weeks a small group of us had somehow become the leaders of the community, deciding which houses should be repaired first, which of the elderly and the children should be found homes away from the discomfort of the church. That evening we gathered again in the vestry, sitting around the table – Gideon and I, Alice and Rafe, Jack, Will, and Toby, and Hans and Griet Leiden. Gideon also asked Seth, one of the most senior of the soldiers, to join us as well.

'Many will be moving out of the church tomorrow,' Gideon said. 'Mercy's family is returning to Turbary Holm, and Alice and Rafe are to move in with Jack. The families from the three lost cottages down by the stream have found shelter for the moment in other houses, and so have two of the Dutch families, but the rest of your countrymen,' he bowed his head toward Hans, 'have still nowhere to go. Then there are all the soldiers billeted among us.

Any spare rooms they occupied before the flood are now taken up by the needy. So we must think what to do.'

'Our five soldiers may return with us to the farm,' I said. 'Their attic is now free of chickens.' I smiled at Seth, who grinned back. He had heard the tale of the hens' droppings.

'As for the rest of our men,' Seth said, 'they can stay here in the church for now. It is better than a tent in camp, or a rough bivouac under a bush in a field.'

'Aye, I think they might do that,' Gideon agreed. 'Sometime soon I expect a new rector will be sent to us, but until that happens, they should stay here. The greater problem is the settler families.'

Hans and Griet exchanged a look, but seemed at a loss what to say. Before they could speak, I cut in.

'Clearly they have nowhere to go at present,' I said, 'other than here in the church, and I think few have the coin to pay their fare home to the Low Countries. It is the middle of winter and there are many children amongst them. How can we call ourselves good Christians if we do not find a home for them amongst us? For one, I am happy for Hans and Griet and their children to stay at Turbary Holm with us. They may sleep in Kitty's attic, while she shares with me.'

Hans opened his mouth as if to speak, but I forestalled him.

'The incomers have all worked hard to repair our houses and barns, to clear them of filth and make them habitable. The men are good builders, even though the settlement they built has been washed away.'

At this Hans looked uncomfortable, no doubt at the thought that they had built illegally on our land, but we too had reasons for guilt, having done our best to destroy their homes.

'I think we should allow them to build here in the village,' I said. 'All this is common land, whatever the speculators may say. It must be a decision of the whole village, of course, whether we will allow them to build here. Here, but not on our farmland.'

Gideon smiled at me across the table. 'You are running ahead of me, Mercy. This is what I planned to suggest myself.'

'Where the road runs on past the Coxes' house and Will's smithy,' Toby said, 'on the way to the hay meadow and the medland. There is a stretch there which is high enough not to flood in the normal way of things.'

'Aye,' Jack said. 'It's a patch of poor soil and gravel, no good for cultivation. Widow Peterson and the two other cottagers from by the delph – they hope to build there. There would be room for houses on both sides of the road.' He turned to Hans. 'You are eight families. You could build five houses on one side of the road, three on the other, next to the three cottagers.'

The Dutch couple were gaping at us, amazed. It seemed they could not believe we would let them build in our village, after their trespass on our land and the ruin of much of our barley crop.

'We are so grateful,' Griet said, and there were tears in her eyes, 'that you should allow us to stay. But we must work. We must earn our bread.'

Hans cleared his throat. 'In our country we make a new way to grow vegetables. We grow them very close, very big.' He made extravagant gestures with his hands. 'We can sell to market. To Peterborough, not so?' He broke off and spoke to Griet in Dutch.

'My husband says, it will be several months before we can sell our vegetables and earn money, but if you will let us have a piece of land, where we can grow for market . . . I do not know how we shall live until then.'

'I am sure we can find a way,' Gideon said. 'But we must have the agreement of all the village that you may stay.'

'Call a meeting tomorrow morning,' said Will. 'The sooner started, the sooner done. And I know there is a blacksmith amongst you. There will be a need for tools and nails and cooking pots. He can earn his bread with me, for one, and with my cousin Abel.'

The following morning, all the adults of the village gathered once again in the church, where Gideon put to them the proposition we had discussed. Before our shared misery during the flood, I am sure the village would have rejected it out of hand, but matters were different now. There were a few grumbles, but when Hans said that he and his fellows would build the three cottages for the villagers first, those grumbles were soon forgotten. The whole village agreed that the Dutchmen should be allowed to settle amongst us. They would be given a patch of land on which to grow their vegetables. A small patch, to start with, but if they proved successful, they might be allowed more.

When the others had left us, I turned to Gideon.

'I need to speak to you,' I said, and felt the blood rushing to my cheeks. 'Let us go into the vestry.'

He closed the vestry door and we sat down, facing each other across the table. He reached out and took both my hands in his.

'What is it, my love? What is worrying you?'

I fixed my eyes on our joined hands, so that I need not meet his eyes.

'Alice has been speaking nonsense to me,' I said.

'Alice? Alice is one of the most sensible women I know. What is this nonsense?'

'Tomorrow we all move back to the farm.'

'Aye. And high time too, to pick up the threads of our life.'

'Alice says – she says – she thinks there will be talk if we are living in the same house before we are married.' I spoke in a rush, to get the words off my tongue and out in the open. 'I said it was foolishness. She said I would be unchaperoned, but beside my mother and Kitty and Nehemiah there will be the five soldiers living with us. I would not have repeated her nonsense, but that she threatened to speak to you herself.'

He began to laugh softly, and ran his thumb over the back of my hand.

'Do you want me to stay in the village? I am sure I could sleep in a corner of Will's smithy, or Jack could find me space in his hay loft.'

'Nay!' I looked up to see whether he was teasing me. He was smiling, but I was not sure whether or not he was serious. 'Nay, I need your help on the farm. And besides–'

'Aye?'

'I want you near me.' I pressed his hands with mine and he leaned forward over the table and kissed me.

'There is a very simple answer to the problem,' he said.

'Is there?'

'Let us be married at once.'

I felt my colour rising again.

'How can that be? Who is to marry us?'

'You do not care for our friend from Crowthorne, the Reverend Edgemont?'

'Gideon! That prattling Puritan!'

He laughed. 'Perhaps not. But I have other friends in the church, though they may not be easy to find. Many have gone into hiding. Others have left the country. Nevertheless, I am sure I can find someone, even if it means riding to Oxford.'

'That might not be safe, if the fighting breaks out again between here and Oxford. Is it in Royalist hands now?'

He shook his head. 'I cannot tell. It used to be the King's centre of power, but we have been so cut off here that I have not heard if that is still true. It may be that it is in Parliamentary hands now. But I should travel as a simple civilian, no threat to anyone.'

I tightened my grip on his hands. 'I fear it would be dangerous.'

'Well, there is no need to decide yet. Let us move your mother back to Turbary Holm and set all in order there. Then we will discuss this again.' He grinned. 'For my own part, the sooner we are married, the happier I shall be.' He kissed me again.

'We must go,' I said, feeling confused. 'Everyone will be wondering–'

'Do you want me to come and live at the farm tomorrow?'

'Of course,' I said firmly.

The next morning Gideon mounted upon Blaze and Jack lifted up my mother to ride pillion behind him. Because we feared that she might not grip him firmly enough about the waist, risking a fall, we passed a long strap around both their waists to keep her safe. Kitty, Nehemiah and I walked behind them, carrying our few possessions tied up in bundles, and Alice's mother came with us, for she felt her familiar face might help to keep my mother calm. The soldiers and Hans were to spend the day helping to dig foundations for two of the new cottages and would follow in the evening, though two of the Dutchmen were to help with the final repairs to our barn. Griet would bring her children some time in the afternoon, once my mother had time to grow accustomed to being back at the farm.

It was all planned carefully. However, because of my mother's unpredictable moods, I was unsure whether she would settle so easily. As we made our way along the lane, I saw how frightened she seemed, staring about wildly and calling out, 'Isaac? Isaac, where are you?'

It near broke my heart that she still believed that my father was alive. They were cousins and had known each other all their lives.

Once we reached the house, Gideon and Nehemiah between them lifted her down from the horse and Mistress Morton put her arm around my mother's shoulders.

'Come, Abigail, let us go inside away from the cold. Nehemiah had a good fire going before he came to the village. Let us make some spiced ale to warm us all in this bitter weather.'

Kitty ran ahead of them into the house. She was anxious to prepare her room for the Leiden family and move her few small possessions into my room. Nehemiah had already gone to the barn to knock together two simple truckle beds, one for Kitty, which would slide under my bed during the day, the other for the Leiden children, while their parents would sleep in the large bed Kitty and Hannah had once shared.

Gideon had led Blaze into the barn and returned now with his own small bundle.

'You shall have the room which used to be Tom's,' I said, 'before he lost his leg and could not climb the stairs. I have made it as comfortable for you as I can. I have put your books on the little table.'

'I gave those books to you, Mercy.'

'Aye, well, we will share them. But do you keep them in your room for now. And Gideon–'

'Aye?'

'When we are not too occupied about the farm, I wonder whether you would teach Kitty to read? I made a small start last summer, but there has been no chance in recent months. She is a clever little soul, and she wants to learn.'

'Of course. How old is she now?'

'Twelve. Thirteen soon.'

'She is not the first young girl I have taught to read.'

We both smiled, remembering my lessons in the rectory, all those years ago, when he was the schoolmaster and I the humble pupil.

'What would you like me to do now?'

'It is already past time to start the morning milking. Nehemiah has promised me that he will teach you to milk. It is not difficult. If you do not mind?'

He reached out and took my hand.

'Mercy, I want to learn everything I can about farming, so that I am not merely a useless encumbrance to you. Of course I must learn to milk.' He grinned suddenly. 'It will be good for me to be the pupil, and not always the master.'

'Give me your bundle, then. Take Nehemiah a bucket for the milking. I will put your bundle in your chamber.'

Gideon went out to Nehemiah in the barn, but before I went into the house, I wanted to check on the newly thatched roof of the hen-hus. I found that Nehemiah had done it well, for it was sturdier than it had been before the flood. I fetched feed for the hens, then let them out into the run. They were soon rushing to and fro, scratching about for the grain as I threw on to the frozen ground. Already they were beginning to look more healthy.

In the kitchen my mother and Mistress Morton were busy heating the spiced ale and putting away the meagre supplies of food we had brought with us from the village. Later I would bring in some of the stores from the hay loft, but now I carried Gideon's bundle up to his room. I laid it on the bed and looked around. It was certainly sparse, but in the rectory he had lived with very little, so I hoped it would not seem too unwelcoming. I could hear Kitty clattering about, climbing up and down the attic ladder. I hoped that Hans and Griet would not mind being lodged in the attic, but it was the largest chamber apart from my mother's, better for the four of them than any on this floor. The other attic chamber was much smaller. The soldiers slept there lined up on their straw palliasses on the floor, with hardly room to move about.

Back in her own home, my mother seemed more her true self than she had been for weeks. She even stopped asking for my father. Mistress Morton set up the spinning wheel in its usual corner and sent Kitty for a bundle of carded wool stored in the attic. Soon my mother was hard at work, and I could see that the gentle, familiar rhythm of the wheel somehow gave her comfort. Her hands instinctively moved to perform the familiar tasks almost as quickly as when she had been herself.

At midday all the men trooped in from the yard. I noticed that the Dutchmen removed their dirty boots at the door without needing to be reminded, unlike many an Englishman I have known, including my brother.

'Is the barn safe now?' I asked, as we all sat down to the pottage Mistress Morton and I had made. Nehemiah had been lucky enough to catch two eels the previous day, in a trap he had left overnight in the gap where the drainers' new ditch met Baker's Lode. And we still had onions and carrots stored in the attic.

'Aye,' Gideon said. 'That wall is quite sound now. And Nehemiah has nearly finished making the children's beds.'

I saw Kitty frown a little at this, for she did not like to be thought a child any more. Indeed, she worked as hard as any woman grown.

'Good,' I said. 'And how much milk did we get today?'

'A mite more than yesterday, Mistress Mercy,' Nehemiah said.

After so much disturbance, the cows were not yielding much, but it was to be hoped that they would soon be back to normal. There was always less milk in winter in any case.

The two Dutchmen said little as they ate their meal. I was not sure how much English they understood, but after our weeks cooped up together, most of the settlers were able to speak a little. They smiled and nodded their thanks as they were served, but made no attempt to join in the conversation. After the meal, they set off back to the village, where they would help with the house building. It was clear all the settlers were anxious to complete the cottages for the villagers who had lost their homes, in order to demonstrate their good will.

When they were gone, I persuaded my mother to lie down in her room during the afternoon, for she tired very easily these days. As I returned to the kitchen, Mistress Morton looked round from washing the dishes with Kitty, and gave me a nod.

'Good. If Abigail rests in her own room, she will soon forget that she was ever away. Did you see how much wool she managed to spin?'

'Almost as much as in the past.'

She dried her hands on her apron.

'All you can do, Mercy, is to try to make her life as much like the old days as possible. That way she will be less confused.'

'I shall try, but it will not be easy, with my father and Tom both gone, and Gideon and the soldiers living here. The Leiden family as well. She might remember the soldiers being billeted here, and she has known Gideon for years, though not living with us. The Dutch family, however, are strangers to her.'

'You can only do your best.' She patted my shoulder. 'That Griet, she's a good woman. You'll be glad of her.'

'Aye,' I said. 'Aye. So I shall.'

Mistress Morton set off back to the village soon afterwards and must have met Griet and the children in the lane, for they arrived not long after she left. Kitty had gone out to the barn, to help Nehemiah at his carpentry work. She was eager for him to finish the beds so that he could make a start on rebuilding the loom. Gideon was helping as well, so I sat down at the kitchen table for a few moments and rested my head on my arms. I must have fallen asleep, for I woke only when I heard a tentative tapping on the door.

'Griet, come in! And the children too. You must not knock on the door. This is your home now, until you build your own house.'

She looked confused but pleased, and whispered something to her little girl, Margit.

The child curtseyed. 'I thank you, Mistress Mercy, for–'

She stopped and looked at her mother in a panic.

'For giving us a home.'

'For giving us a home.'

I smiled at her, returning the curtsey, then bent down to kiss her on her forehead.

'You are very welcome to Turbary Holm, Margit.'

I had learned that the Dutch word for 'welcome' sounded much like the English, so I was sure she understood me.

Before there could be any awkwardness, Nehemiah and Gideon appeared, carrying one of the truckle beds between them.

'This is for the Leiden children,' Gideon said. 'I will string the ropes once we have it in place. Good day to you, Mistress Leiden.'

Griet and Margit both curtseyed, while little Maarten looked on, his thumb in his mouth.

'Can you carry it up to the attic?' I said. 'It will be difficult up the ladder. Then when you have strung the ropes, we will come and make it up with a mattress and bedclothes.'

'We could build a staircase to that top floor, you know, Mistress Mercy.'

'Some day, perhaps, Nehemiah. When there is less to do. Not now.'

He grinned and nodded. Since he had come to live on the farm, Nehemiah was for ever full of schemes. He had always been clever with his hands, weaving baskets and eel traps and hurdles, but his own small cottage had been very simple, before the drainers attacked him and burned it down.

There was a good deal of banging from upstairs as they struggled to carry the bed up the ladder. I tried to ignore it, hoping they would not wake my mother. Instead I showed Griet what I had done in the house since she had last been here to help me.

'It is so fresh and good,' she said with a smile, 'with the new lime wash.'

I nodded. It was surprising what a difference it had made. There was now no lingering smell of chickens or mud or mould, only the clean scent of the lime wash. Alice and I had even laundered the curtains, which I would not usually have done in winter, for they must be dried inside before the fire, but I wanted to be rid of every trace of the musty smell.

Fortunately, the noise did not wake my mother, not even when the second truckle bed was carried into my chamber. There was a spare palliasse in the soldiers' room, which had been George's, and we put this on Kitty's bed, then filled a new one for Griet's children. Margit enjoyed stuffing the straw into the sacking, while little Maarten enjoyed strewing it about the floor, until Griet put a firm stop to it.

By the time we had finished making up the beds, Hans had arrived from the village and Gideon had helped Nehemiah with the evening milking.

'Mistress Cox, she sends you this,' Hans said, holding out a basket containing two large loaves of bread and a lump of butter wrapped in a cloth. 'She says, you do not have time to make bread today.'

'Thank you for bringing it, Hans. Was that young Mistress Cox?'

'Ja. Young one. Not the old vrouw.'

It was thoughtful of Alice. I had had no time to make bread, though I would set some to rise overnight.

'There is enough of the pottage to make us supper, I think, now we have the bread.' I had realised just how many mouths I now had to feed, for Hans was followed by the five soldiers. The army had promised us chits, so that we might reclaim the cost of the soldiers' rations, but naturally nothing had come of it.

'I will put a supper on a tray for my mother, Kitty, if you will take it up to her?'

The food did not look very much when thirteen of us sat down around the kitchen table. They say that thirteen at table is unlucky, but Maarten sat on Griet's lap, so perhaps he did not count. Gideon spoke a brief grace and we began our meal, all of us holding back, for there was barely enough to stay the pangs of hunger.

After we had eaten and the soldiers, Kitty, and the Leidens had gone to their beds, I was sitting by the kitchen fire while Gideon shut the hens away. Nehemiah came in and stood before the fire. He had taken off his woollen cap and ran his fingers through his hair, which I noticed had gone greyer in recent months.

'Mistress Mercy, food – it will be a problem, won't 'un?'

'It will, Nehemiah. It was difficult before the flood, after the soldiers were billeted here, but now–'

'I think I'd best set more eel traps. And go out a-fowling. There's only that one ham, and the hens don't lay much in winter.'

'Not at all, in their present state, I expect. Aye, you are right. And fish. There must be plenty of fish, with all this water!'

'Are you going fishing, Nehemiah?' Gideon had come in as we were speaking. 'I may know little about farm work, but I can fish.'

'Can you net wild fowl, Master Clarke?'

'Nay, but I can learn.'

I left them discussing how they might augment our food supplies, and went to bed.

We soon fell into pattern of work at Turbary Holm. Nehemiah spent much of his time fishing and fowling. Gideon helped me with the milking. He was slow, but he was gradually improving. I nursed the hens back to health and we began to have a small supply of eggs. Kitty and Griet undertook much of the household work, cleaning and washing. Griet made bread every day, sometimes with Kitty helping her, and the three of us cooked the large meals that were required for so many. Most of the time my mother was content to sit at her spinning wheel, and later at her weaving when Nehemiah had rebuilt the loom. She still seemed lost in her own world, but to my relief she had not been violent since we had returned to the farm.

Gideon had not forgotten his plan to seek out one of his parson friends and still thought the likeliest place to discover their whereabouts was Oxford. Once the road through to Crowthorne was clear, the Reverend Edgemont rode over some Sundays to conduct one service in our church. When we first heard he was coming, the few people still accommodated there hastily found cramped quarters in the village, so with a quick clean, the church presented an innocent appearance. I fear the Puritan minister would have considered it a just punishment for us sinners if we had all perished in the flood, instead of finding sanctuary in the church. However, we attended his grim services dutifully, all of us except Gideon, who must keep out of the way.

'I will hold my own private service,' he said. 'I shall not neglect my duty to God.'

As the weather improved and the last of the snow disappeared, the fenlands began to come back to life. The first of the little wild flowers showed their faces amongst the grass in the hay field, and the first of the migrating birds began to appear.

One evening, as Griet and I sat knitting by the fire and Kitty was trying out her letters on a piece of slate with fragment of chalk, Gideon looked up from the book he was reading.

'It is time I made the journey to Oxford, Mercy. If I delay much longer, we shall be into the fighting season. It will be safer if I travel now.'

I looked up in alarm. 'How soon?'

'Edy the carter arrived in the village last night. He returns to Peterborough tomorrow. I can travel with him and hire a horse there for the rest of the journey. I will not linger. Three days from here to Oxford? The same home again. A day in Oxford. I need not be gone for much above a week.'

My heart was pounding. Perhaps it was unreasonable, but I felt this journey was dangerous. Yet I could not prevent it. How were we to marry, unless Gideon could find a fellow clergyman of our own persuasion?

'You will be careful?' It was all I would allow myself to say.

'I promise,' Gideon said.

Hans and Nehemiah were both dozing after a hard day's work, but Nehemiah opened his eyes at this.

'I had a word with Edy at the yel-hus. He said that Piet van Slyke and his men are back. They are surveying over beyond Crowthorne. It cannot be long before they discover that we broke into their water pumps and put a stop to them.'

I shivered. Was it all to start again?

'I think,' Gideon said slowly, 'that you also must promise to be careful.'

Chapter Four
Tom

The following days at Gray's Inn passed in impatience and frustration. I offered to contribute to the cost of our food, but Anthony refused to accept any money from me until I knew whether I should be given employment in the library. I filled the long hours by spending half the day in the library with Master Hansen, hoping that by demonstrating that I could work swiftly and accurately I would persuade him to ask for my services permanently. He gave no hint as to whether he had applied to Pension. I believe he took some enjoyment from keeping me in suspense. The mornings were thus given up to the somewhat tedious but undemanding task of cataloguing books. It was clear to me that, with my assistance, Master Hansen no longer seemed quite so overwhelmed by the tasks as we began to made inroads at last into two of the great stacks of volumes.

In the afternoons and early evenings, I assisted Anthony. Some of this work was clerical, the mere copying out of precedents, as I had done on the first day, but we soon began to discuss the finer points of the cases in which he was involved. I found my interest in the law awakening again. To tell the truth, I had chosen to come back to Gray's because I could see no future for myself on the farm, and not because I wanted to become a lawyer. That ambition had perished long before. But as we talked and argued and ferreted about in Anthony's law books, my old excitement returned.

'We are holding our own moots!' Anthony said on the evening of the second of those days, pouring us both large cups of beer. He had sent out again for food from the Peacock and the table

67

was scattered with crumbs of pastry. 'I must invite Henry Grantham to join us. We may establish our own inn within the Inn, to argue out our cases.'

'That is who it is!' I said.

'Who what is?'

'I have twice seen someone I thought I recognised, coming or going about Coney Court. Henry Grantham, of course. I remember him now.'

'He is an utter barrister as I am, and has chambers in Coney Court. Top floor, with a fine view over the Walks. Expensive rooms, but he does not have piped water.'

Anthony was justly proud of our water supply, though it sometimes failed. As we were nearer to the source of the New River scheme out in Hertfordshire, it came to us quite fresh, unlike the water further along the pipes into the City, which was sometimes tainted. It was nowhere near as fresh as the water from the well-hus at home, but for London it was remarkable. You could even drink it.

'So, tomorrow you will know what Pension has decided,' Anthony said.

'Aye'

'And you still do not know whether the librarian has solicited them for your services?'

I shook my head. 'I believe he likes to exercise his power over me by keeping silence on the subject.'

'Small men are often eager to exercise power. It gives them an advantage over bigger men that they cannot enjoy physically.'

'I am hardly a physical threat,' I said bitterly.

'Oh, I am not so sure. I think you could land quite a blow by swinging one of those crutches of yours.'

'I have been tempted, a few times, but I fear it would not win me a place in the library.'

We both laughed. I knew he was trying to ease my worries, but they would not go away. I slept badly that night. What should I do if Pension refused to readmit me? Should I make my way home, humiliated? Or try to find some other employment? I pondered my original idea of clerking for a Cheapside merchant. I would be forced to find lodgings near my place of work, instead of living rent free here until Lady Day, for I could not walk that distance between Gray's Inn and the City twice a day.

I abandoned my pretence at sleep soon after the first softening of the dark of night to the grey shimmer of the winter dawn. I rose and dressed, with my usual clumsiness, then crept to the parlour as quietly as I could, so as not to wake Anthony. It was very cold, so I set about lighting a fire, which was remarkably difficult on crutches. In the end, I lowered myself on to a small joint stool close to the hearth, which made it easier to lay the fire and to tend it as it took hold, but it was awkward to raise myself on to my crutches again.

Once the logs had begun to burn through, the room grew a little less chilly, though the inside of the window facing on the court was thickly coated with swirls and flowers of frost. I found myself ale and bread, but left the cheese, for I felt guilty about the food I was eating, despite Anthony's assurance that I had earned it, clerking for him. The clerk he shared with two other lawyers – one of whom I had learned was Henry Grantham – would be coming tomorrow to work for Anthony. I hoped I had not deprived him of his income. Still, I supposed he was paid by the day and not by the number of sheets he managed to cover in good lawyer's script.

'Up already?' Anthony came yawning through from his chamber, barefoot, with a long house gown of faded velvet over his night shift.

'I could not sleep.'

'Pension will meet at ten o' the clock, and they usually finish by midday. You can probably expect a summons from the Treasurer this afternoon.' He yawned again. 'Shall you go to the library today?'

'I think not. I want to be here if he sends for me. It would not do to keep him waiting.'

'Nay, it would not. Though the decision will have been made by then.'

'No need to tempt the Fates.'

'Indeed. Why have you taken no cheese with your bread? I know it is not the breakfast of princes, but you will be hungry again in an hour.'

'I do not want to consume all your stores.'

'Nonsense. And besides, Mistress Gorley comes tomorrow. We have finished that apple pie, so I shall buy another, and some of her preserves. She makes some excellent pickles, a good accompaniment to sausages from the butcher who supplies the Inn. Sometimes she has fresh pasties. I always stock my cupboard on the day she comes. It does her some good, and me too.'

'I wish we had had such a paragon when we were students,' I said. 'Either we ate expensively in Hall or we supped at one of the local taverns, where you needed plenty of beer to wash down the gristle stew and the stale bread. I think I only went once to the Peacock, when it was someone's birthday. Probably yours.'

He laughed. 'Perhaps. I cannot remember. There have been a good number of birthdays since then.'

Anthony had a meeting about the land inheritance case that morning, where all three claimants were to be present. The Bencher handling the case for one of the claimants was trying to persuade them to arrive at some sort of compromise, so that one would inherit the land and the other two would settle for a financial compensation, but they were proving stubborn. Each of them wanted the land together with all the money. Anthony went off gloomily, certain that the entire morning would be wasted in recriminations.

I took out paper and ink, thinking that I might write at last to Mercy. I had sent her no word during these days I had been in London and I knew she would be worried, but I wanted to be able to report my acceptance at Gray's. I found I could not start my letter until I knew for sure which way Pension had leaned. Was I back at Gray's, or was I not?

To occupy myself and keep my mind from dwelling on the possibility that I might be refused, I tried to read one of Anthony's law books, but I found I was reading the same paragraph over and over, but I could not have repeated what it had said. I heard the chapel clock strike midday, but Anthony had not returned. It seemed the three possible heirs were still bickering.

A certain nausea in my stomach put all thought of a meal out of my head, so I merely sat, chewing my nails and throwing the occasional log on the fire, until I heard the clock strike one. How much longer would I be kept waiting?

Then at last, around half past the hour, Anthony arrived at the same time as one of the Inn servants, bearing a note from Theodore Somers instructing me to report at once to the Treasurer's chambers.

As I slung on my cloak and fastened the clasp, Anthony clapped me on the shoulder.

'The best of luck to you, Tom. Come straight back when you know.'

'I will that.'

I made my way cautiously across the Court. The severe frost in the night had left the ground hard frozen and the thin winter sun had done nothing to thaw it. Suddenly I was convinced I would fall flat and be left sprawling on the icy ground like a fool, unable to get up again. I went slower and slower, partly for fear of a fall, partly to postpone what might be bad news.

The steps up to the Treasurer's chambers had been sanded again, to my relief, and Theodore Somers greeted me cheerfully.

'This way, Master Bennington. The Treasurer is awaiting you.'

Would he be so cheerful if I had been turned down?

'Ah, Master Bennington, come in.' The Treasurer waved me to the same chair as before. 'I am pleased to tell you that Pension has decided that you may be readmitted to the Inn, to take up your studies where you left off at the end of your first year.'

I felt relief flood through me like a burst of heat. My hands were shaking, so I clasped them together.

'We must ensure, naturally, that you have not forgotten everything you learned. I am assigning you as a pupil to Bencher Whittaker. He will examine you on your knowledge and direct your studies. As you will probably have learned from Master Thirkettle, most of our teaching is now done by making use of our excellent law books, although we do encourage our students to take part in regular moots.'

He shook his head. 'I have to say that they are often reluctant to participate, yet there is no better preparation for a barrister's appearance in court. One must have case law at one's finger tips and be able to argue cogently and persuasively, without the use of printed sources. I never thought we should come to this.'

71

'I am most grateful to you, Treasurer,' I said, 'and to the rest of Pension, for the opportunity to begin again. I shall do my best to earn your approval.'

'Excellent, excellent. You will start with Bencher Whittaker next week. He will see you first thing on Monday morning.'

I was wondering whether I could raise the matter of the library, or whether I should wait to hear from the librarian, when the Treasurer stood up to dismiss me. I gathered my crutches and heaved myself up.

'Ah,' he said. 'There is also the matter of the library. I understand you have given Master Hansen a good deal of your time during the last few days. He has found you of great assistance in the work of cataloguing, though it is understood that you will be unable to undertake much of the shelving. One of the servants may do that, under your supervision. Pension has agreed to pay you the equivalent of a senior clerk's full salary, and you will work either two full days a week or four half days, to be arranged between Master Hansen and Bencher Whittaker. I hope you will find that satisfactory.'

'You are very kind, sir,' I said, bowing.

Somehow I managed to make my way out of the room. I was a Member once again! And a full clerk's salary for less than half a week's work. I could hardly believe what I had heard. Theodore Somers was beaming at me.

'Good news, then, sir?'

'Aye, Somers,' I said. 'Very good news.'

Anthony knew at once from my face that I had not been refused.

'Thomas Whittaker, eh? He's somewhat of a stern fellow, but very able. You should do well under him, if you work hard. And what of the library?'

When I told him the terms of my employment, he whistled softly.

'That is good news! We must celebrate.'

'Indeed we shall. And this time I shall pay.'

'Very well. But do not run mad. Did the Treasurer say when you would be paid, and how often?'

'Nay.'

'Well, let us hope it is not quarterly. In arrears. You must make sure you are paid regularly and soon. Have a word with Somers. He will handle it.'

I was a little dismayed at this suggestion, that I might have to wait for my money, but I was still determined to stand Anthony an excellent meal. Had I been able to get about more easily, I should have liked to go to the Peacock, but it would have been folly on crutches in such icy weather.

'Before we send out for our dinner,' I said, 'tell me how you fared with the disputing heirs.'

Anthony pulled a long face.

'I had rather deal with a parcel of rogues and pickpockets than with that trio of preening, self-important fools. In truth, their claims are all equally valid. The last owner bequeathed both land and money divided between his two sons, but both were killed in the war and predeceased their father. He had no time to make a fresh will, he was already in his last illness himself. All he could do was to add a codicil – the one you have seen – that the property should go to his nearest male relative.'

'And he did not specify which one, or whether the property could be divided, I remember.'

'Aye. The three claimants are each the grandsons of the last owner's three aunts. All related to him in the same degree.'

'But we found that precedent – that in a case of equal claims, the property could be divided, though you say that the house and manor lands could not easily be broken up.'

'Nay. Which is why we suggest that the land goes to one and the money is divided between the other two, but they will not accept this as a solution. Each thinks he has the best claim to everything.'

'One, you said, is descended from the eldest sister.'

'Aye. So he believes he has the best claim. Another is the eldest man of the three, which he believes gives him the better right, while the third holds the adjacent manor and was always close to the old man and his sons. Claims he was brought up in their household like another son, so he should take precedence.'

'A nest of vipers.'

Anthony shrugged.

'They will not settle out of court. Our client is the third one and to my mind he has the better claim on moral grounds, but I am thankful I need not make the decision. It will go before a judge in Chancery now, and could take months before there is a decision. The Court of Chancery is overburdened with work and cases move at the speed of a tortoise. They would have done better to accept our solution.'

'Well, put it out of mind for the rest of the day. I shall write a letter to my sister now, to tell her my good news, then let us send out for our dinner.'

We ate well that night and I felt all the pleasure of the benefactor on this occasion. Afterwards we made up a good fire, for it had begun to snow, and we mulled a pot of spiced ale to drink while we sat close to it, eating the pears preserved in red wine sent over by the Peacock.

'I have another reason in coming to London,' I said, 'besides this return to Gray's.'

Anthony stretched out his legs and scooped up the last fragment of his pears.

'I know. You are in search of a wife. A wealthy widow, perhaps, who owns her own house and will make you a gentleman of leisure for the rest of your days.'

I laughed. 'I cannot imagine any wealthy widow finding me desirable, with my country ways, crouched over and hobbling about on crutches.'

'You do yourself an injustice. With a scrub and a London doublet, and perhaps a fine new hat with a feather, you would pass muster on a dark night.'

'A very dark night, perhaps. Nay, I have no plans for matrimony at present.'

'Wise man. You never know where it may lead. A house full of squalling brats, all expecting to be clothed and fed. I shall not wed until I am at least forty and have a good store of coin put by. Enough to afford a household of servants, to make life more easy.'

'I am not sure I shall wait that long. Nay, my purpose in coming to London is quite different. You know what we have suffered in the Fens. We had thought we were done with it. The drainage works in the south near Cambridge, in our grandfather's time – those were undertaken by companies of adventurers made

74

up of courtiers and nobles, great landowners. Most of them are now fled abroad. But the thievery has not come to an end. Instead, a new breed of speculators has sprung up, men of the middling sort, city merchants, country squires, Model Army generals. Even Cromwell himself, it seems.'

'So I have heard. They are unscrupulous.'

'Aye. They claim our commons are a wilderness, fit for nothing, and therefore ripe for plundering, yet they have been farmed for generations. Centuries.'

'Even we townsmen know this. If they wreak havoc in the lands around Ely, we too shall suffer. We are barely more than an island ourselves.'

'Not only do they plan to take possession of our land,' I said, 'but if they drain the Fens we shall lose the other half of our livelihood, the fish and waterfowl. Then there is the peat we use for fuel. With the drainers trespassing on our lands last year, they attacked our men who tried to dig peat. We have been short of fuel, for you know there is little firewood to be had in our fenlands.'

'And the reed beds?' he said. 'Material for baskets and eel traps.'

'Aye. And thatching and hurdles. Then, even more disastrous, they do not understand how we manage the winter floods, which bring such fertility to our arable and grass lands.'

'You would think,' he said, 'that both these sets of men would have read the ancients like Herodotus. For surely the Nile floods in Egypt were the same, restoring the land.'

I shrugged. 'They think of nothing but drying out the moss to create more arable. Yet the areas where they have drained before, south of us, have produced wastelands of peat turned to dust, and unmanageable floods.'

'All of this is unfortunately true, but what has that to do with your coming to London?'

'There was an ancient charter,' I said, 'given to our surrounding parishes, five in all. I believe it was in the time of King Henry II. It granted possession of our common lands in perpetuity to the inhabitants of the parishes. They may not be alienated.'

'Then you can fight them in court.'

75

'Aye. We could fight them in court, if we had the charter in our hands. We have not.'

'Do you know where it is?'

I shook my head. 'Last spring, when the surveyors appeared on our land, under a Dutchman called Piet van Slyke, employed by the adventurers, my father and other men of the village sought the help of our local squire, Sir John Dillingworth. He himself holds a small portion of common land, but most of his land lies within the boundaries of his own manor. He promised his help.'

'And did he fulfil his promise?'

'I was doubtful of such tame measures from the start. Sir John said he would write to his London lawyer. He was to locate the charter and take our case to court. We waited months, and in the end some of us attacked the workings, which had gone ahead willy-nilly. We set fire to a pumping mill they were building, and a sluice gate, and filled in some of the ditches. That was when I received my first injury, a bullet in my leg. My sister managed to get me home, two to a horse.'

He raised his eyebrows. 'So you abandoned the case at law?'

'My father went to Lincoln, to put our case before a local judge. Some fellow was sent up from London to argue against him. My father was not even allowed to speak in court. Instead he was thrown into prison until he could pay a fine which was far beyond our means. He caught gaol fever and died then.'

Anthony looked down at his hands. 'I have heard of other such cases. Many of the local magistrates and judges are in league with the adventurers. By imposing these fines, they hope to frighten people so much that they will not dare to resist. I did not realise your father had died thus.'

'My sister even went afterwards to Sir John, who swore that he was acting for us, but nothing has been done. I thought that if I came to London, I might be able to trace the charter. Or at least find Sir John's lawyer and discover whether he has done anything on our behalf.'

'Do you know who he is?'

'I know that he is a Member of Lincoln's Inn, but not his name.'

Anthony sat in silence, clearly turning over my account in his mind.

'Ordinarily, I suppose, a copy of the charter would be deposited in Rolls House, the old Domus Conversorum, in Chancery Lane. I spend a fair amount of time there, searching out documents relating to the land disputes I have worked on. Another copy of the charter would be held locally, usually by the greatest landowner. That would be your Sir John Dillingworth, I suppose.'

'If the Dillingworths held it in the past, they no longer do so. Or if they do, Sir John is not admitting it.'

'You sound as if you suspect him of dishonesty.'

I shrugged. 'I have never much liked the man. He claims to be some distant cousin of Cromwell's, but has a foot in each camp, shifting as the wind blows. Indeed, we are related, for my mother's grandmother was a Dillingworth, but they do not admit the connection. Yeoman stock is beneath them, though I believe our ancestors have held the land as long as theirs.'

'You say he is some connection of Cromwell's, and Cromwell is involved in the drainage schemes?'

'Aye.'

'Does Sir John support the Parliamentary cause, now that the struggle has lately gone their way? You say he shifts.'

'Sir John keeps his head down. However, his son Edmund fought on the King's side, a fact he is striving to make people forget.'

'You do not like him.'

'I do not. He tried to defile my sister.'

He gave a low whistle.

'Never fear,' I said with a grim smile. 'She fought him off, and he was humiliated in front of their servants. He has not forgotten it. He brought a troop of soldiers to attack our church and they near killed our rector. Then he was behind an allegation of witchcraft against my sister and an elderly neighbour. Hannah was hanged by that devil Hopkins, but Mercy was acquitted after trial by water.'

'God's bones, Tom! I had no idea that your family had suffered all this. What was the second injury to your leg? Were you shot again?'

'Nay, it was due to my own folly. I fell over a scythe as we ran off from pulling down the foreign settlers' houses. It laid open the same place in my leg and I did not allow time enough for it to heal. Then the gangrene set in.'

Anthony ran his fingers through his hair. 'After hearing this, all I can do is offer you my help in searching for the charter.'

He glanced at the window, where we could see snow piling up on the sill.

'As soon as the weather permits, we will start our hunt, and not rest until your charter is in our hands.'

On Monday morning I presented myself at the chambers of Bencher Thomas Whittaker in Coney Court. Like most of the senior Members of Gray's, he now preferred the title of Bencher, though when I had been here before he was a Reader. With all the upheaval of the war, the practice of giving readings – similar to the lectures I had attended at Cambridge – had lapsed. In the past, only Readers were members of Pension, then the practice of appointing Benchers had crept in, sometime in the last century, I thought. They could be members of Pension, but were no longer required to give readings. Anthony said that the full barristers much preferred the current arrangement.

'It means they have more time to take on paid work,' he said.

'You are very cynical.'

He shrugged. 'They might not admit to it, but it is true. Although some cling to the title, there are no true Readers now, for there are no readings, just as there are no moots, or very few. We must get by with the written word.'

Bencher Whittaker's chambers, fortunately, were also on the ground floor. I wondered whether that had dictated the Treasurer's choice of mentor for me, but perhaps he had not even considered it.

'Come in, Master Bennington.'

Whittaker showed me into his outer office himself, although he had a clerk sitting in a corner, writing busily. He did not even glance at the space where my left leg should have been, but he had probably been made acquainted with my physical state at the meeting of Pension. He was a tall, lean man of middle years, peering at me over the thick spectacles he wore for reading. He had always reminded me of a heron, for he had the same capacity for stillness and the same forward-leaning, acute attentiveness.

We sat down on either side of his desk and he moved a pile of papers to one side. He drew out a single sheet and studied it for a moment.

'We need to establish how much you remember of your former studies in the law before we decide how to direct your reading from now on. I have made a list of subjects here. I want you to write me two or three pages on each, whatever you can remember, and hand it in to me on Friday.'

He passed the sheet across the desk to me.

'I have arranged with Master Hansen that you will work in the library on Wednesdays and Thursdays, while the rest of the week will be devoted to your studies in the law. I also want you to start reading the following books. Have you pen and paper?'

'Aye, sir.'

I took some folded sheets of paper from my pocket and flattened them on the desk. From a pouch at my belt I drew out two sharpened quills and a portable ink well I had borrowed from Anthony. I unscrewed the lid, dipped my quill and waited.

Whittaker rapidly dictated the titles of twenty law books. I had to write fast to keep up with him, and I saw him watching me, assessing how accurate I was, even though he was reading my writing upside down. My heart sank a little. How long would he allow me to read all of these? I did not like to ask, but I foresaw I should be reading far into the night. Candles would be another expense to add to my budget.

'That will do for now. Hand in your answers to those topics on Friday and I will see you again next Monday. We will then have a better idea of how you should proceed.'

I realised I was being dismissed, so I screwed the top on the ink well and gathered up quills and paper, fanning the list of books in the air to dry the ink.

Whittaker stood up and watched me struggle on to my crutches.

'How serious a problem is that?' He nodded toward my missing leg.

Few people spoke so frankly, and oddly I liked him for it.

'As you see, sir, I can only get about with difficulty, using two crutches. Walking any distance is painful and tiring. I cannot manage more than a few stairs.'

'There is a fellow I know of,' he said. 'Trained in Paris, where they have been improving false limbs for sixty or seventy years. Far more skilled than any English craftsman. My cousin's son lost a hand at Marston Moor and this fellow built him a new one. He's very skilled, so my cousin says. I will enquire his name and his place of work here in London.'

I found myself flushing. 'I thank you, sir. I was hoping to have a wooden peg fitted. It might help my balance.'

'These French designs are more than pegs, Bennington. They have joints. Something like a marionette, I believe.'

'That seems remarkable.'

'Aye, well, I will see what I can learn. Off you go now.' His stern face broke briefly into a smile.

Once outside, I paused, drawing a deep breath. A jointed leg? It seemed impossible. How could it possibly work? And in any case, it would surely cost a king's ransom. Now I thought about it, I remembered hearing about some German nobleman who wore a silver hand after he had lost a hand in battle, but how could a poor law student pay for a silver leg? It was a wild dream. I would be lucky if I could afford a wooden peg strapped to my stump, which would take some of the weight on my left side and ease the pressure of my crutches on my shoulders and back.

For the remainder of that day and all the next, I applied myself to Bencher Whittaker's topics, and they were not easy. I felt it would be deceitful to ask Anthony for help – although he volunteered. I did check a few points in the law books he kept in chambers. And I was relieved to find that he also owned most of the twenty books on the list Whittaker had given me. The other two I hoped to be able to find amongst the chaos of the library.

'It is a little hard,' Anthony said, 'if he requires you to hand in your answers on Friday, when you must work in the library all day on Wednesday and Thursday.'

'It will remind me of my time at Cambridge,' I said, 'when much preparation was a mad scramble at the last minute.'

'You were younger then.'

'Aye. So I was. But now I am older and I hope I may work harder, with fewer distractions and more sense.'

Nevertheless, I found it difficult to complete the task in time, even though I continued to work on the topics during the evenings of the days I spent in the library. I suspected that the short time allowed me was part of the test of my abilities. In the end, I did my best, wrote out a fair copy of my answers, without all the blots and crossings out, and handed it in to Whittaker's chambers on Friday morning.

When I had stumped my way back through the snow to Anthony's chambers I found Goodwife Gorley on her hands and knees scrubbing the stairs which led past Anthony's door and on to the upper floors of the building. I had forgotten that it was her day to clean. It was best to keep out of her way. I knew that Anthony was in court today.

'Good morrow, Goodwife Gorley,' I said politely.

'Don't you be tracking mud across my clean floor.'

'The ground is still too frozen for mud.'

She sniffed, turning her back on me and scrubbing all the more vigorously.

When Anthony had told me of the widow who was such a tartar, I had expected a fierce grey-headed old woman, thin and hard. Meeting Goodwife Gorley for the first time the previous week, I had been taken aback. She could not be more than her middle thirties, a blooming buxom woman with plump cheeks and light brown curls escaping from the edges of her cap. However, she had the muscled arms of a farm labourer and she was indeed a tartar. She kept us all in order.

I sidled past her now, hoping that my single foot and the tips of my crutches would not drop lumps of snow on her shining floor. Safe within the sanctuary of the parlour, I sank down on to one of the cushioned chairs and took up the first book on my list to read. Later she would be cleaning our chambers, but as she started on the top floor and worked her way downwards, I was safe until midday at least. Anthony had taken his clerk with him to court and it occurred to me that it could not always be convenient to have Goodwife Gorley and the shared clerk both arriving on the same day. I wondered whether she scrubbed round their feet while they worked in the office, or whether she drove them away with her broom.

I settled to my book and began to take brief notes. Paper was expensive, so I would need to keep them short. The Treasurer had been right, in what he said about participation in moots being an excellent training for a lawyer. The more one wrote down in notes, the less one committed to memory and the less one would have ready for argument in court.

The time passed quickly as I became absorbed in the book, which was one Anthony and I had consulted for his case on land inheritance, so that I was taken by surprise when Goodwife Gorley gave a brief tap on the outer door before marching into the chambers with her bucket, brushes and broom.

'I will be out of your way, goodwife,' I said hastily, as I laid aside my book and rose from my chair. 'Master Thirkettle has left money on the table for some pasties, a pot of raspberry preserve, and another of your excellent pies.'

I waved my hand toward the money, aware that I was flattering her. She merely nodded briskly. Hopping to the door, I took down my cloak from its peg and let myself out into the court. The air was so cold it made me gasp. I had decided that this would be a good time to approach Theodore Somers about my salary for working in the library. I had seen the Treasurer go out of the gatehouse a little while before, and I preferred to speak to Somers when there was no danger of running into the Treasurer.

'Your salary for the library work, Master Bennington?' Somers said, reaching into a drawer of his desk. 'I was about to send you a note about it.'

He laid a cloth purse on the desk. 'The Treasurer has given me this for you. It is your first month's fee.'

I picked up the purse gratefully. I had hardly needed to ask, and the purse was a comfortable weight in my hand. I tucked it into a pocket in my doublet.

'Should I come to you again, in a month's time, Somers?'

'Aye. That will be best. I will be sure to have it ready for you. And how are you faring with Bencher Whittaker?'

I grinned. 'I shall know better on Monday, when he has read the answers to his topics which I handed in today. I feel like a schoolboy again, or a student back at Cambridge.'

He returned my smile. 'Ah, sir, but you will soon be back into the way of it. In no time you will be an utter barrister, like Master Thirkettle.'

'I hope you may be right. Good day to you, Somers.'

I made my way slowly back across Chapel Court, the weight of the purse comforting against my hip. I hoped Goodwife Gorley had finished her work and left, for I wanted to count my coins. I would have been shamed to do it before Somers.

I met Anthony and his clerk, Edwin Latimer, at the door. Edwin was carrying a basket, from which arose an appetising aroma. A hot beef and kidney pie, I suspected.

'We bought our lunch as we came past Pie Corner,' Anthony said. 'Let us set to while it is still hot.'

We trod warily into chambers, but Goodwife Gorley was gone, every surface gleaming, my book and papers lined up severely into a neat stack, and the new stores put away on a shelf in the small kitchen.

When we had made quick work of the pie, Anthony drank deeply from his cup of beer. 'Latimer and I have been discussing the likely whereabouts of the charter you seek. It is most likely that a copy will be held in the Rolls House in Chancery Lane, as I said. If it was indeed granted by Henry II, it will be shelved with the other state documents of that reign.'

'I cannot be certain,' I said, 'but I remember my father saying that he believed it was King Henry who made the grant.'

'I shall need to go to Rolls House next week,' Anthony said. 'My senior has a case involving the purchase of monastic lands in Sussex in Henry VIII's time. That was a fine time for men grabbing land that was not theirs, like your speculators in the Fens. Although there was at least I kind of sham legitimacy about it, the king having decreed all the monastic lands belonged to him, so that he could sell them to whomsoever he wished.'

Latimer shook his head. 'It may have been legitimate but it was a ruthless land grab nonetheless. And so much of it done in haste, with ill-conceived bills of transfer, that we are still trying to sort the confusion, more than a hundred years later.'

'Aye, you are right.' Anthony nodded. 'Two or three cases a year, where a poorly written bill of purchase is called into question.'

I laughed. 'Profitable work for lawyers, then?'

They both grinned at me. 'Where would our profession be, without the folly and greed of our fellow men?' Anthony asked.

83

On Monday morning, as I set off nervously for Bencher Whittaker's chambers and the judgement on my answers to his points of law, Anthony followed me out into Chapel Court, where a few more wisps of snow were falling, like feathers from a leaking pillow.

'I am off to the Rolls House to hunt out the documents relating to those monastic lands in Sussex,' he said. 'I am not sure how long it will take me. I may stay there all day. If time permits I will start the search of state papers from the reign of Henry II, but he was a prolific legislator and it was a long reign, so it is likely to take me more than today. You are quite sure you do not know the date?'

I shook my head. 'I am afraid I do not. I only remember what my father said, and he may have been wrong. He said Henry II, but he may have meant Henry III. He may even have been told the wrong king by my grandfather. I know my grandfather had hoped to take a case to court, but they arrested him and he died in Cambridge castle, without ever having the chance to be heard in court.'

'Like your father.'

'Aye. Like my father. Let us hope history does not repeat itself even in the third generation.'

'At least you will pursue the case as a trained lawyer, with lawyer friends to support you.'

'If you mean yourself, then I thank you, Anthony. But we must find the charter first. It will be the strongest weapon in our defence.'

He pulled his cloak tightly about him and drew the hood up over his head. 'At least it is not far to the Rolls House to walk in this weather. Will spring never come? Just down Chancery Lane, opposite Lincoln's Inn.'

'Aye. It would have been easy for Sir John's lawyer at Lincoln's Inn to search there for the charter.'

'Indeed. I hope you meet with Bencher Whittaker's approval. He will be a hard task master, I expect, but an excellent mentor.'

Unsure whether this should cheer or depress me, I raised my hand in farewell and began my laborious way through the snow to Coney Court.

It seemed that my discussions of Whittaker's topics had been satisfactory. He did not praise my efforts and pointed out one or two omissions, but it seemed I had answered well enough that we could move on. He outlined a course of reading I was to pursue for the next week.

'You will come again next Monday and we will see how much you have understood and remembered,' he said. 'It is unfortunate that moots are no longer held daily. There are, of course, far fewer students than before the war. Have you become acquainted with any?'

'Only in passing. I cannot get about easily.'

Also, with working two full days a week in the library and spending the rest of my time on the work he had prescribed for me, I had hardly had the opportunity to meet other students.

'You must dine in Hall. You will meet them there.'

I nodded. I knew that I must dine in Hall, which would give me the chance to get to know the other Members of Gray's, both senior members and students, but it would be more costly than our present practice of sending out to the Peacock. I fancied that Anthony was quite glad to save his coin too, for he could not be earning much as an utter barrister. Perhaps we might dine in Hall once a week. Anthony's friend, Henry Grantham, had twice eaten with us in chambers, but I knew that he usually dined in Hall. I also knew – but did not say – that I should probably find I had little in common with the other students, who were so much younger than I, fresh come from Oxford or Cambridge. Some would be country gentlemen's sons, here at one of the Inns of Court to pick up a smattering of the law to serve them when they went home to become Justices of the Peace in their own counties. The others would be those bent on a permanent career in the law, like Anthony They would take their studies more seriously, but it seemed there was no longer the same fellowship that had existed when I was first a student. In those days we all met daily to listen to readings or participate in moots. Now, most study was done privately or with a senior Member.

As Bencher Whittaker concluded his instructions for the following week's work, he handed me a slip of paper.

'This is the address of the craftsman of artificial limbs who made the hand for my cousin's son. His name is Gilbert Bolton, a good English name, although I believe his mother was French. That is why he studied his craft in Paris, at the Hôtel-Dieu, where the barber surgeons are trained.'

I glanced at the paper. At the sign of the Golden Ram, Bucklersbury.

'That is south of Cheapside, is it not?' I said.

'It is. Parallel to Cheapside. It meets Walbrook in the east. A good many of the apothecaries have their shops there, but also the barber surgeons. I understand that although Bolton trained as a surgeon, his trade is now mostly in artificial limbs.'

I wondered both how I could make my way there, and how I could afford an expensive artificial leg, but I thanked him politely and slid the paper, together with my other papers and writing materials, into an old leather satchel Anthony had loaned me.

Anthony returned from the Rolls House in the late afternoon, looking tired. He threw himself down on a chair and looked at his clothes in disgust.

'I am covered in dust. We should lend Goodwife Gorley to them in the Rolls House. She would soon sort them out. I do not know how the clerks can work there, day in and day out, without choking.'

'Goodwife Gorley would probably want to scrub all the ink off the ancient parchments, to make them fresh and clean again.'

'Aye. And she would not tolerate all those ancient cracked wax seals dangling off frayed ribbon or ragged strips of parchment. She would snip them off and throw them away, so that the bundles of scrolls would look all the tidier.'

We grinned at each other. We would never dare to speak to the goodwife so boldly, but in her absence we could take some revenge for her bullying.

'Did you find your Sussex documents?'

'Eventually. But the bills of sale for monastic properties at the time are stacked high, and you have to check at least the heading of each scroll until you find the right ones. They should be making a catalogue like yours for the library, but when you look at rack upon rack of documents, stretching back hundreds of years, you can see that it would be an almost impossible task, unless you set a hundred clerks to work, night and day, for several years.'

'Still, you found what you needed.'

'I did. And I had about an hour to look through documents from Henry II's time, but as I feared there are thousands of them. However, I have some free time this week, so I will go back again tomorrow and Wednesday, though I am in court again on Thursday.'

'I am grateful.'

'Nay, I have my nose on the scent for this charter. We will show these scoundrels that they shall not destroy our fenlands, shall we not?'

'Indeed. Between us, how can we fail?'

He sat up, brushing the dust off his breeches. 'What shall we order for dinner?'

'Bencher Whittaker thinks I should dine in Hall and meet the other Members of Gray's. I would prefer to carry on as we have done, but what do you say to dining in Hall once a week?'

'Very well. I suppose we should show our faces from time to time. Shall we dine there tonight?'

'Aye, let us do so.'

There were but five steps up to Hall, so I managed well enough, and we took our places at one of the tables set at right angles to the dais which held High Table. The lower tables were sparsely populated, compared with the full complement of students and junior lawyers which I remembered from the past, but there was a cheerful buzz of conversation as we stood waiting. Then silence fell as the Treasurer and the other members of Pension filed in and took their places at High Table. The Treasurer spoke the traditional Latin grace, then everyone sat down with a scraping of benches and a fresh outburst of conversation.

The meal was good, but not as fine as I remembered. Even here, it seemed, some effects of the war could be felt, though we had heard of no fighting recently. So many years of war had meant damage to crops and a shortage of men working the land. And there had been a severe famine two years before, which had cost many lives. All in all, I felt we dined as well in chambers. Anthony introduced me to several students sitting nearby, but to me they looked no more than boys. I had seen them stealing glances at my missing leg. I felt more as ease in the company of Anthony and Henry, for all that they were utter barristers and I was a mere student.

Anthony spent the next two days diligently searching through the state documents dating from the reign of Henry II, but could find no trace of a charter granting the common lands to our five parishes.

'Do not be down-hearted, Tom,' he said on Wednesday evening, when I returned from my labours in the library and he came in, dust-covered as usual, from the Rolls House. 'If you were to see the thousands of scrolls there, stacked shelf upon shelf, so high you must climb a ladder to reach the top, then you would understand that a single charter may be as hard to unearth as a grain of sand on a beach. As I have said, I am in court tomorrow, but if the case does not linger on to the next day, I will go back on Friday. If it is there, I shall find it.'

For three weeks, Anthony spent his every free hour searching the Rolls House. The longer he searched, the more grimly determined he became to find the charter. The last of the snow thawed and the days turned slightly warmer. Snowdrops and crocuses began to show their faces in Gray's Walks. Anthony continued to search.

But he found no sign of the charter.

Chapter Five
Mercy

My hands were covered in blood and the damp scrap of wool and bone lay lifeless in on the straw. Another lamb lost. That made four today alone. You must not weep when an animal dies, else how can you call yourself a farmer? Yet the tears were running down my face and I could not check them. I laid the dead lamb aside and scrubbed at my hands with a fistful of straw. My very skin seemed ingrained with the blood. The ewe had lost more than normal. There was nothing I could do for the lamb, but I must care for the ewe, who lay exhausted and motionless in front of me where I knelt on the barn floor. God grant we had not lost her as well.

Nehemiah gave me a sympathetic look from where he was bent over another labouring ewe, but there was nothing he could say. There seemed no reason for the stillbirths, yet we had already had seven. There had been no chance to go into the village to discover whether others were likewise blighted. All the sheep had been together in the glebe lands until they were driven back to their own farms in time for lambing, so I did not know whether some disease had afflicted all the sheep of the village or only mine.

The ewe stirred slightly, so she was not dead, but she was too weak to get to her feet. She had passed the afterbirth, so I swabbed her with warm water, then helped her rise. She drank a little water, then sank down again, glancing over her shoulder in a desultory way, as if she were looking for her lamb. She was three years old and had given birth before, but seemed to know instinctively that all was not well this time. She lay on her side, but was breathing normally, so I went over to see whether Nehemiah needed help.

This lamb slithered out easily, unlike the one I had just delivered. It was small, but its legs moved, and when Nehemiah wiped its muzzle free of blood and slime, it gave a faint cry. He laid it down beside its mother and the ewe began to lick it.

'Thank God,' I said. 'One survivor at least.'

Nehemiah sank back on his heels with a groan. 'I cannot make it out, Mistress Mercy. The ewes seem healthy enough, though something thin with the poor feeding this year, but I cannot guess why we are losing the lambs. I'm no stockman, you know that. I'm an eel man. You need to talk to Jack Sawyer. He's your man for the sheep.'

I nodded dumbly, and rubbed my sleeve across my face.

'I will see him when I can. Perhaps this evening. Is it evening yet?' I had lost all count of time. 'I don't think there are any more ewes due now, do you? I think you should take some rest. You were up all night.'

He stood up, stretching and yawning. 'I'll take a bite and sup, then I'll bed down in the straw here by the sheep fold. I'll soon wake if one of the ewes is in distress.'

I scrambled to my feet. I was stiff too, and my right leg was numb. I could see now, by the light filtering through the half open barn door, that it was late afternoon.

'Kitty was to come for the milking,' I said, realising that the cows were becoming restless. 'And she was to bring us some food. Do you start the milking and I will fetch us something to eat, then lend you a hand. Where can the girl have got to?'

Nehemiah fetched bucket and milking stool, while I hobbled across the yard to the house, as feeling came back to my leg and turned to cramp. I was worried that something I was doing wrong was causing the deaths of the lambs. I could not expect Nehemiah to know, for as he said, he was a waterman first and foremost. Until he had come to live on the farm last year he had had little to do with livestock. My father and brother had cared for his few beasts in return for the fish and wildfowl he supplied to us. Those few beasts of his had been stolen by the drainers last summer.

I had never been in charge of the lambing before. Last spring Father and Tom had seen to it, as they had every year for as far back as I could remember. I had helped only occasionally, when there was a sudden rush of lambs all at once. I knew what to do in simple cases, but if a lamb presented awkwardly, I would be in trouble. Yet I could not see how my inexperience could be blamed for this spring's losses. The lambs had been dead before birth. After the milking, I would ride to the village and speak to Jack. Perhaps he would know the answer.

The house was very quiet. The soldiers had been ordered over to Crowthorne this morning, for some kind of military training, and two days earlier Griet and Hans had moved back to the village. They now had a simple cottage there, with very little furniture, but Hans was eager to make a start on his vegetable growing. I was missing Griet. Somehow having her there about the house had made me feel less burdened. She did more than her share of the household tasks, leaving me free to manage the farm. And with Gideon still away, I was grateful for her companionship.

My mother was probably asleep upstairs. In the mornings she was wakeful and would spin or weave, or even sometimes make bread, but by the afternoon she was tired and would retire to her chamber, often sleeping for the rest of the day. But where was Kitty? It was not like her to have fallen behind with her tasks. Young as she was, she was sensible and reliable.

'Kitty!' I called as I entered the kitchen. 'Where are you, child?'

I did not see her at first, for the light was beginning to go. She was sitting at the kitchen table, slumped forward, with her head resting on her folded arms, and seemed to be asleep.

'Kitty!' I shook her by the shoulder. 'Wake up! What are you about, sleeping in the middle of the working day?'

She lifted her head slowly and gazed at me with eyes that did not quite focus. I saw then that her hair was damp, clinging to her forehead, and she was very flushed.

'I'm sorry, Mistress Mercy,' she said, 'only I had such a headache. I just sat down for a minute to rest it. Is it time for the milking?'

Her words were slightly slurred and she shivered suddenly. I laid my hand on her brow. She was on fire.

'Heavens, child, you are burning up! When did this start?'

'I did not feel quite right yesterday, mistress, but I did not want to worry you, what with the lambing and Master Gideon being away. I shall be all right, only my head aches so.'

'You are going to bed,' I said firmly. 'Here, you can use your old room off the kitchen. That way I can keep an eye on you. Come with me.'

She protested, but I steered her across the kitchen and into the little room which had once been hers, before it had been used for one invalid after another. She sat down heavily on the bed and her eyes took on that wandering look again. I left her there, while I ran up to our shared room to fetch her night shift.

She let me undress her and put her to bed, as unresisting and helpless as a cloth doll. Although she had been sweating profusely when I first found her, she was now shivering, her teeth chattering together.

'Tell me what else is amiss,' I said, taking hold of her hand and pressing it, as if that way I could gather her wits together.

'My arms and legs hurt.' She frowned. 'As though I had been working very hard, but I haven't, have I, mistress? And this morning–' she gave me a pleading look, 'this morning I brought my breakfast back up, but I managed to get to the midden in time.'

'Why did you not tell me? You foolish girl, you should not keep such a thing to yourself.' I patted her arm, so that she would know that I was not really angry.

'You were so worried with the lambing, and with Master Gideon being gone so long, I did not want to trouble you.'

She began to shake again. I tucked the bedclothes around her.

'Keep as warm as you can,' I said. 'I left Nehemiah doing the milking on his own. He will wonder what has become of me. I must take him some food and help him finish the milking, then I will come back and heat a stone for your feet. I have something which will ease your headache as well, with feverfew and poppy juice. You should have told me, not suffered like this without a word.'

I quickly made up a meal in a basket for Nehemiah, with bread and cold bacon, some dried apple rings and a flask of my ale. When I reached the barn, he had nearly finished the milking.

'I am sorry,' I said, setting down the basket on a shelf. 'I found Kitty ill and put her to bed.'

He looked up, though his hands went on milking.

'Kitty is never ill.'

'She is this time. Feverish and then cold. A terrible headache and pains in her arms and legs.'

He let out his breath in a soundless whistle, then picked up his bucket and stool and moved to the last cow.

'Marsh fever, do you think, Mistress Mercy?'

'I am afraid it may be. I will go back to her now, but I still want to ride over to Jack's. I wish Griet were still here, to sit with her.'

'Do you want me to?'

'Nay, you must get some sleep. You have been awake for two days and a night. I won't tarry with Jack.'

Back in the house I warmed a stone and wrapped it in an old towel to put by Kitty's feet. The last time I remembered doing that in this little room was when Gideon was so ill after being beaten by the rogue soldiers, set on by Edmund Dillingworth. Kitty was thrashing about in the bed, shaking uncontrollably, so I tucked her in firmly and went to fetch the feverfew tonic. The herb is excellent in the case of severe headaches. Pounded and mixed with poppy juice it should ease her pains and perhaps stop the sweats. If it was marsh fever, she would alternate every few hours between burning up and shaking with cold. Someone should really sit with her, but my mother was not able and I would be needed with the lambing and all the other farm work. Even the soldiers were likely to be away for a few days. I wondered whether I could ask Griet to come. I would not ask Alice, for the last time I had seen her she had confided that she was expecting another child. I could not risk her catching marsh fever and losing the baby.

Kitty seemed barely conscious when I brought her the tonic, and threw her head from side to side as I tried to persuade her to drink it, but in the end, as I held her up with my arm around her shoulders, most of it went down her throat and only a little splashed on to her shift and the bedclothes.

As soon as I had made her as comfortable as I could, I went back to the barn and saddled Blaze. Nehemiah had taken my advice and was curled up in the straw just outside the enclosure we make with hurdles for the ewes when they are dropping their lambs. He was snoring softly. I took a quick look at the sheep. The surviving lambs seemed well enough and none of the gravid ewes

93

were showing signs of giving birth yet. I led Blaze out into the lane, mounted, and set off for the village.

It seemed an ironic twist of fate that one minute I had a house so full of people that I was at my wits' end trying to feed them all, and then just when I needed help, there was no one. Nehemiah and I were doing our best, but we needed someone else. Even the lad Ben could have helped with the lambing while I cared for Kitty. I would have sent for Joseph Waters, who often did occasional work on the farm, but I knew he was fully occupied in helping to build the new cottages.

And where was Gideon? I had been pushing away the thought for days, but as I rode along the lane in the gathering dusk, I could not silence it any longer. He had said he would be gone a week or perhaps ten days, but it was more than three weeks now, with never a word from him. I could hardly bear to admit it, but he might have been arrested as a recusant priest – so the Puritans deemed those who retained the Anglican services of Queen Elizabeth. Or he might have fallen in with one army or the other and been pressed into service. In the early years of the war, he had served as a priest administering to the amateur soldiers of those days, an experience he had never forgotten, but if he concealed the nature of his calling, he might be forced to become a common fighting soldier. Between my anxiety for Kitty, the worry over the lambs, and the thoughts of Gideon that would not leave me, I was in a poor state when I reached the house where Jack lived with his widowed mother.

The first person I saw was Alice.

I threw my arms around her and began to weep. 'I had forgotten that you were still living here. Oh, Alice, I am so glad to see you.'

'What is the matter? Rafe, take the horse, will you? Come into the house, Mercy. Jack and his mother are there.'

They were all about to sit down to supper and were insistent that I join them.

'I cannot,' I said. 'There is the lambing. Nehemiah is taking his first rest for two days. I have my mother to see to. And now Kitty has fallen ill. I think it is marsh fever.'

'Sit,' Alice said, pressing down on my shoulders. 'You can eat while you explain to us why you have come. I can tell by the merest look at you. You have not eaten all day.'

'I broke my fast this morning,' I objected, but the smell of bacon and onions was irresistible.

Mistress Sawyer handed me a steaming plate. 'Eat, Mercy. You will do no good to anyone if you do not eat. Alice has made a dried apple cobbler to follow. I am grown quite idle with her living here.'

She smiled at Alice, who laughed and turned pink with pleasure. She received little enough praise from her mother-in-law when they were living at the Coxes' house. She gathered little Huw on to her lap and began to feed him small spoonfuls of chopped up bacon. He was not yet a year old, but he was well grown and almost walking.

As I ate, I realised that I had been nearly fainting with hunger. Jack's mother was right. It was folly to neglect meals when I had so much labour on the farm.

'I came really to see you, Jack,' I said. 'I am in trouble with the lambing. We have had seven lambs born dead already. I do not know what to do. I do not think it is my fault. The ewes seem healthy, though thin. I had just one bad delivery this afternoon. It lasted a long time and the ewe seems exhausted. It was another dead lamb.'

I felt the tears welling up again and bent forward over my meal. I did not want Jack to despise me or think I was incapable of running Turbary Holm. Tom had entrusted the farm to me and I must show that I was worthy of that trust. But I was very tired.

'Nay, Mercy,' Jack said, 'it is no fault of yours. I have had the same difficulty, and so have others. There are a large number of dead lambs this year. No one knows the reason. The ewes do not seem diseased, but there is certainly something amiss. Perhaps the water they drank was tainted by the flood. Perhaps some kind of parasite has got into the unborn lambs. Whatever the cause, we are all suffering.'

'So there is nothing I can do?'

'Nothing,' he said grimly, 'except endure and hope for a better time next year.'

'We have lost lambs too,' Rafe said. 'If it was caused by the flood waters, that is something else to set against the drainers' account.'

There was hardly much comfort in this, but at least it showed that I had not caused the death of the lambs.

'But young Kitty,' Mistress Sawyer said, 'do you truly think it is the marsh fever?'

'By all the signs, aye.'

She shook her head. 'That is serious. At least she is young and healthy.'

None of us said that after a hard winter on short rations, none of us was as healthy as we had been before. Two years ago there had been famine. Already this year the poor weather and the sodden ground had held up the spring planting. It might be another famine year. And if this was marsh fever . . . it could be fatal. Those who recovered were never quite rid of it, for it seemed to linger in the blood, to break out again, sometimes years later.

'I will come back with you,' Alice said, 'and help with Kitty and your mother. I may leave Huw with you, Mistress Sawyer, may I not?'

'Of course.'

'Nay.' I shook my head. 'I will not risk you taking the fever. Somehow I shall manage. I must get back to Kitty.'

I started to rise, but Mistress Sawyer placed a bowl of the apple cobbler in front of me. 'You shall finish your supper first,' she said firmly. 'I know Abigail would insist, if only the poor creature were her own true self still.'

I felt a choking in my throat, thinking of my mother lost in her dark world, but I spooned up the cobbler as I was bid, though as speedily as I might. I was grateful for their kindness, but the longer I was away from the farm, the more worried I grew for Kitty. At last I was free to go.

'We will put our heads together,' Alice said, 'and decide what we can do for you. It is a pity that you no longer have Griet with you.'

'Aye. She was a great help to me.'

'Is there still no word of Gideon?'

'None.'

Jack gave me a leg up on to Blaze.

'I hope you do not have too many losses amongst your lambs, Mercy. We cannot know what is causing the trouble, but I am keeping the ewes who have had stillborn lambs separate from the others, lest there is some unseen illness spreading amongst them.'

'Good advice, Jack. I shall do the same.'

Back at the farm, I led Blaze into the barn and found Nehemiah still asleep, though he must have woken while I was away, for he had lit a candle lantern and hung it on a peg by the door. I could not separate the ewes now without disturbing him, but I would follow Jack's suggestion and do so in the morning. I hurried to settle Blaze, then ran back to the kitchen.

The only light was from the embers of the fire, so I hastily made it up and lit some candles. Carrying one, I went softly into the small chamber. Kitty was moaning and throwing off the bedclothes. Her fever was so high I could feel the heat streaming off her body when I was still several paces away. I removed the heated stone from the bed, though it had mostly cooled by now. I would need to bathe her with cold cloths to try to bring the fever down, but I must also think about my mother. She had eaten a meal prepared by Kitty at midday, before she retired to her chamber, but she usually grew wakeful around this time, and would often start wandering about the house during the night. In the dark she was liable to hurt herself, and I had taken to wedging two chairs across the top of the stairs, to prevent her falling down them. I dared not leave a candle with her, for fear she might set the house on fire. I slept poorly these days, half listening for her stumbling steps, then worrying even more when I heard nothing. Sometimes I would creep to her chamber door and listen, to be sure she was still breathing. Alice had told me she had done the same with Huw for weeks after he was born. What an inversion of life that I should now listen for my mother's breathing.

Torn between Kitty and my mother, I went to the bottom of the stairs and listened. My mother was moving about in her room. I had best see to her first, then perhaps she would settle. I heated some of the thick soup Kitty had made earlier in the day and took a bowl of it, with some bread and a cup of warm milk sweetened with honey, up to my mother on a tray. She was fretting about the room, hunting for something.

'Come, Mama, I have brought your supper.'

I set a candle lantern on the mantelpiece and persuaded her to sit in her chair beside the small table which held her Bible. I put it aside and began spooning up the soup for her, until she took the spoon from me and began to feed herself. You could never be sure. Sometimes she needed to be fed like a baby, sometimes she would eat normally, and sometimes she would hurl the dish across the room.

In my anxiety to return to Kitty, I could hardly bear to wait while she ate, crumbling the bread into the last of her soup and scooping up soup and bread together. She seemed to enjoy the warm milk and honey, though she said never a word to me all the time she was eating. When at last she was done, I persuaded her back into bed and retreated downstairs, hoping she would sleep, at least for a little while. I made sure the chairs were in place at the top of the stairs before fetching a bowl of cold water and some clean cloths into the small chamber.

Kitty seemed almost on fire. She was such a slender little thing, I feared the fever would burn away what little flesh there was on her bones. I knew she must drink. Hannah had taught me that. Anyone in a high fever must drink as much as possible, to douse the fire burning within. Wiping over the sweating body with cold wet cloths would also help to fight off the fever.

I did my best to get Kitty to drink. The water from our well is very pure and sweet, and I could see that she was eager for it, but she seemed hardly in control of her body, which was seized by convulsive jerking. I was terrified that she might fall into a fit. Little by little I managed to pour the water down her throat and she gulped at it desperately, though a good deal poured over me and soaked the front of her shift. I had turned back the bedclothes and once she had drunk I peeled off her night shift, which was sodden with sweat, and began to bathe her all over with cold water. I could hardly believe that a body could be so hot and yet live. If it was the marsh fever, then she would soon be shivering uncontrollably again. I had no way of knowing how long each phase would last, and I feared trying to cool her when she had already turned cold again.

I dried her gently, then left her lying naked while I fetched another night shift. There was no sound from my mother's chamber, so I prayed that this night she would not wander. Back in Kitty's chamber, I dressed her in the clean, fresh shift. She seemed calmer now and even came to herself enough to speak.

'I am so sorry, Mistress Mercy. I am such a trouble to you.'

'Hush,' I said. 'You are no trouble. You must rest and get better soon.'

I hugged her gently and kissed her forehead, feeling a painful twist in my heart. Kitty meant more to me than a maidservant. She was as precious as a small sister and I loved her dearly. She had come to us as a parish foundling when she was seven and I was only thirteen. Our lives had been twined together ever since. I would fight this illness with every scrap of knowledge I had.

She slipped down into the bed again.

'I'm feeling cool now,' she whispered. 'Almost, I am feeling cold.' She shuddered.

'I will warm the stone for you again,' I said. I gathered up the basin and cloths, and the discarded shift, and carried them through to the kitchen.

'Mercy!' It was a thin cry. 'Don't leave me! It's dark and I'm afraid.'

'I am just here in the kitchen, Kitty. I will bring you a candle and the stone to warm you. Never fear. I'll not leave you.'

With the hot stone at her feet and two extra blankets, Kitty was not shivering constantly, but from time to time her whole body would begin to shudder convulsively. Her eyes were wide and frightened, so that I put my arms around her, blankets and all, and held her close, hoping that the warmth of my body and my closeness would reassure her. I sat with her all night, though I must have slipped into a shallow sleep from time to time, for like Nehemiah I had spent many wakeful hours with the labouring ewes.

After the shivering came the sweats again, sometime in the dead hours of the night. The pain in Kitty's limbs must have grown worse, for she began to sob with it, though she strove valiantly to endure. During those dark times, she mumbled incoherently, about the work she thought she should be doing, about Tom and his lost leg, and other things that made no sense. When she calmed a little, she lay slack in my arms.

'Mercy?' she whispered.

99

'Aye, my pet, I am here.'

'It is the marsh fever, is it not?'

There was no point in lying to her. 'I fear that it is.'

'Am I going to die?' Her voice was choked with a sob. 'I thought I was dead already and gone to Hell. The flames of Hell were burning me up and the devils were stabbing me with their pitchforks.'

Inwardly I damned the Reverend Edgemont and his like for terrifying children with their horrific visions of what awaited us hereafter, we who were not amongst the company of the Chosen, the Puritan Saints.

'That is all nonsense,' I said firmly. 'Our Lord has promised Heaven to all who believe in him, as you do. That burning Hell, peopled by devils, is an invention of cruel and evil minds, meant to frighten people into submission to those who set themselves up as our masters.'

'Rector Gideon does not believe in Hell?'

'He does not.'

I felt her body relax slightly, but she was still tense.

'So I will be safe from Hell, if I die?'

'Quite safe. But you are not going to die.'

'People do die of the marsh fever, Mercy,' she said, 'I know it.' And tears began to trickle down her cheeks.

I took a corner of a blanket and wiped them away.

'Only those who are old or sickly already. Not great strong girls of nearly thirteen.'

She did not feel like a great strong girl, there in my arms. Already the fever was wasting her away.

'Aye,' she said, with a valiant attempt at a smile. 'I am nearly thirteen. When shall I be old enough to wed?'

What had put that into her head? 'Not yet a while,' I said with a laugh. 'Wait until you are fully a woman grown. Once you are married there will be no time for play. Besides, you have not even made a start on your dower chest.'

She brightened a little at this. 'Can we make a start? I can weave now, and I can sew and knit and embroider.'

'Once you are well again, we will see. First, you must try hard to get better. I want you to try to sleep now. Sleep is the best healer.'

Obediently, she slid down under the bedclothes. She still had a high fever, but I had dosed her again and she said that her head did not hurt quite as much. Gradually her breathing slowed and she slept, but I kept up my vigil at her bedside until the morning dawned.

With the new day, Kitty seemed a little better. She was feverish, but it did not seem as high as it had during the night. She drank all the water I brought her as eagerly as if she were stranded in a desert, but she refused to eat.

'I know I should be sick,' she said, turning her head away and pulling a face. 'Please do not make me eat.'

I thought she probably knew what was best for her. She admitted that she had eaten nothing the day before, after vomiting her breakfast. I had been too preoccupied with the lambing to notice. I would not force her to eat today, but that would mean two whole days without food, it could not continue much longer. I would try to persuade her to take a hot beer toddy in the evening, for they say that beer feeds you as surely as bread. Wheat and barley are the great sustainers of life. Which naturally reminded me that we had been unable to plant either as yet this year.

When I had made Kitty as comfortable as I could, and set my mother to her spinning, after she had breakfasted, I fed the hens and let them out into the run before I took bread, ale and cheese out to Nehemiah, who had stayed all night in the barn. I found him carrying the last of the morning's milk through into the dairy.

'I must set about some butter and cheese making,' I said. 'The cows are giving generously and it must not be wasted.'

'You do that, Mistress Mercy,' he said. 'There is but one ewe restless this morning. I can deal with her on my own. Did you speak to Master Jack?'

'I did. It seems we are not alone in being afflicted. The whole village is losing stillborn lambs.'

I watched the look of relief wash over his face. Like me, he had been blaming himself.

'Jack is separating the ewes who have borne dead lambs from the others, in case the disease is spreading among them. I think we should do the same.'

'That's a canny idea,' he said. 'Shall us do it now, before you start in the dairy?'

101

'Aye. Best do it soon. We'll take Jasper and drive the ewes who have lost lambs up to the medland where the drainers were last year. That is where Jack has put his. We'll have the rest in the barn for now, where we can keep a watch on them. Perhaps we should separate the ewes with lambs from the gravid ewes, in case there are more affected ones amongst them. We can fence off two folds.'

It took some time to sort out the sheep, but the ewes driven out to the medland seemed glad to be out on the fresh grass. The abundance of flood waters meant that the grass was grown thick and juicy, so that they were soon tearing at it enthusiastically. Separating the flock in the barn was more trying, but we accomplished it at last, with a delay while one more lamb was born, this time a healthy one.

'It is time the cows were turned out as well,' I said, 'but I do not think between the two of us we can be fetching them in twice a day, not until the lambing is done. By then the calves will be due.'

'No need to fret about that,' he said. 'Calves usually come without much fuss outside.'

I nodded. 'We will turn them out as soon the lambing is done.'

Before I went to the dairy, I returned to the kitchen. I had left both my mother and Kitty too long. My mother was still spinning, a task which was so familiar to her that even in her present state she could produce a fine, even thread. Kitty was restless, but her fever was still lower than it had been the previous night. I knew that meant little, for the heat of a fever builds up during the day to break out in sweats during the evening and night, though no one has ever been able to tell me why. I gave Kitty another dose of feverfew and poppy syrup, for I could think of nothing that would serve her better. If she grew worse, I would need to send for an apothecary, though there was none nearer than Peterborough, and he might be unwilling to travel so far from home.

In the past, Hannah had ministered to the sick in the village. Her knowledge had been extensive and there were few cases where she could not provide some relief. Her friend Agnes Pettifer had done the same for the people of Crowthorne. Both had been accused of witchcraft by Matthew Hopkins, and both had hanged for it. We had a midwife, Meg Waters, a cousin of the labourer

Joseph Waters, a woman with hands like hams and a rough way with her. She was not known for any skill in treating sickness.

For the moment I must hope my homemade remedies would give Kitty some ease from her pain and the fever. She swore that her head did not hurt her so much, but I suspected that she was being brave and trying to spare me.

'I have drawn this jug of water fresh from the well,' I said to her. 'I will put it on the table here beside the bed, with a cup. Drink as much as you can. There is a piss pot under the bed.'

She flushed. 'You cannot be emptying piss pots for me, Mistress Mercy.'

We were back to 'Mistress Mercy' again, I noticed.

'Nonsense,' I said. 'I did worse when I worked as a maid at the manor house. Now you must sleep and drink, both as much as you can. I am going out to the dairy, but I will be back at midday.'

'What of the lambing?'

'There is a pause at the moment, and Nehemiah will deal, but if he needs me I am but a few steps away. Now, try to rest.'

Obediently she lay down and closed her eyes. I envied her the chance to sleep, though not the fever, for I could not remember when I had last had an unbroken night.

I had set the curds to drain for the cheese making and I was sitting on a stool at the door of the dairy, working the butter churn, when I saw two figures approaching along the lane from the village. The butter was just beginning to come, for I could hear the difference in the sound of the milk slapping against the sides of the churn, so I must not stop. It was Alice and Griet, both carrying large baskets.

'Griet,' I said, as they stopped in front of me, both smiling broadly, 'it is good to see you. Alice, I told you not to come near Kitty. You must not risk it.'

I gave her what I hoped was a meaningful look, for I was not sure how far she had shared the news that she was carrying another child.

Alice laughed. 'Never fear, Mercy. I shall pay heed. And Griet has been told my news.'

Griet touched her lightly on the arm. 'Alice comes with gifts, but she will not enter the house. Me, I am here to help you.'

'But you have children too.' I was distracted, for I could feel that the butter was nearly ready.

'We will go into the dairy,' Alice said, 'for we are hot from walking. Perhaps with this sun the fields will dry enough at last for the planting. Bring the butter when it is done.'

They stepped inside the dairy, which was on the north side of the farm and designed to stay as cool as possible. I soon followed with the churn.

'Let me.' Alice took the paddle from me and began scraping the butter off on to the butter trough, where she could work it and squeeze it until any remaining butter milk was pressed out. I would give Kitty some of the butter milk, for it is easily digested.

Griet had set their baskets on a shelf at the back of the dairy and was examining the draining curds.

'We have been busy making provisions for you,' Alice said, as she worked the butter. 'Some pies and a large pottage, which, I may say, was very heavy. Mistress Sawyer has sent you some of her preserves and sausages. We thought it would save you some cooking. Griet is going to stay here tonight, and as long as you need her.'

'But Margit and Maarten!' I protested.

'All the children are with Mistress Sawyer now. When I go back, I shall look after Griet's children as well as Huw until Hans has finished work in his vegetable garden. He will put them to bed and I will have them again tomorrow.'

'I shall stay as long as you need me,' Griet said.

'You are both of you so kind,' I said, sinking down on a stool and rubbing my hands over my face. My skin felt sore, as though I were the one scorched by fever.

'How is Kitty?' Alice asked.

'She was bad in the night, very bad. This morning the fever is down a little, but that means nothing. I know it will rise again in the evening. Last night she was burning up, then she was so cold she could not stop shaking.'

Alice looked worried. We all knew of people who had died of marsh fever, but we did not speak our fears out loud.

'Here is your butter finished,' she said. 'Shall I put it in this crock?'

'Aye. Then you must go back to the village. You had best not come into the house. Griet, I am not sure that you should come near Kitty. What if you should take the fever yourself? Or carry it to the children?'

She took both my hands in hers. 'You have helped us find a home here. What a small thing it is, to help you now. I will be careful. I too do not want to make my children ill.'

When Alice had set off back to the village, I looked into the barn, and explained to Nehemiah that Griet was come to share my work. 'I shall care for Kitty and help with the lambing, while Griet looks after the cooking and my mother.'

He nodded. 'They are not such bad folks, some of those foreigners.'

'Any more lambs?'

'Not yet, mistress, but there be two likely to drop tonight, I'm thinking.'

'I will come out again, when I have seen to Kitty.'

Griet had already gone into the house carrying one of the baskets. I followed with the other.

The next four days fell into a pattern. Griet managed the house and cared for my mother, who seemed to make no distinction between the two of us. Griet was no more a stranger to her in her confused state than I was. Nehemiah took charge of all the night-time lambing and slept during the day, while I milked and delivered any lambs who arrived by day, although he always came to help me towards evening.

During the day, Kitty lay quiet, still suffering from alternating bouts of fevers and chills, but I managed to persuade her to take a little broth and then some buttered eggs. At night I sat beside her bed and then the illness took a different turn, as though it had waiting mockingly during the daylight hours, holding itself in readiness to leapt out again in the darkness and seize the child in its claws as surely as any of those devils who had tormented her imagination.

On the third night, I came close to losing her. The fever mounted higher and higher. It seemed her body might burst spontaneously into flames. She could not bear anything to touch her, throwing off the blankets, ripping at her shift until I peeled it over her head. She even fought me when I tried to bathe her burning skin with cooling water, shrieking and babbling incoherently as though she was possessed. It woke Griet, who was sleeping in my chamber. She came creeping down to the kitchen, shielding her candle with her hand.

'Can I do aught to aid you, Mercy?'

Her eyes were wide with fear and horror. I think if those devils, the witchfinders Hopkins and Stearne, had still haunted our fenlands, they would have carried Kitty off at once to hang, for surely no Christian soul could rave like this.

I shook my head.

'I think it is coming to a crisis, Griet. If she outlives this night, then I believe she will recover.'

I stood up, stretching my cramped limbs. 'I will just fetch a bucket of fresh water from the well. It is coldest when drawn fresh. If only she will let me bathe her.'

We both looked at the emaciated girl, her hair soaking with sweat, her body shuddering as if with cold, yet her flesh was burning to the touch.

Griet reached out and took the bucket from me. 'I will fetch the water. Do you eat and drink something while you may. Take a slice of that cold ham pie Alice brought this morning. You cannot live like this. You have no sleep.'

'I doze a little when she is quiet. You cannot fetch the water, you are wearing nothing but your shift.'

She shook her head and laughed. 'Who is to see me? The hens? Nehemiah is busy with the ewes.'

She threw a shawl around her shoulders and was out of the door before I could stop her. I cut myself a slice of the pie, poured a cup of small ale, and went back to Kitty. When Griet returned with the water, Kitty had quietened and seemed to be sleeping, though her breathing was very fast and shallow.

'I think she is a little better, not so?' Griet set down the bucket just on the kitchen side of the doorway, for I would not allow her to risk coming near Kitty.

'She is no longer raving, certainly. I shall try bathing her again. Thank you for fetching the water. You must go to bed.'

She smiled and slipped away, her bare feet soundless on the floor.

That night we passed the point of danger. The following morning, when I laid my hand on Kitty's forehead, she felt cool, but not cold, and lay exhausted. I prayed that the fever had finally passed. It was still very early, barely past dawn, and she seemed to be sleeping normally. I made my way out of the house, across the yard and a little way along the lane, toward the arable fields. I had heard the men of the village passing along the lane yesterday with the ox-drawn plough. By climbing the shallow bank at the side of the lane, I could look out across the field which had been sown for wheat last year, but would be planted with beans this year. It was already ploughed and sown.

The yoke of oxen had belonged to Turbary Holm, but when we had needed money for my father's court fine, Tom had sold them to Jack, who promised to sell them back to us when we had raised the money again, though that time had not yet come. They were used by all the village in any case, and I had been promised that our share of the common lands would be ploughed and sown for us, while we were in such troubles.

The freshly turned earth had not dried yet but gleamed like brown satin in the low rays of the early sun. I remembered how Alice and I had clung to each other, laughing, as we sat on the harrow last year. It seemed a lifetime ago. I turned to where I could see part of the medland where our sheep were grazing. Alice had said yesterday that much of the drainers' ditch, which they had dug right across it, had collapsed in the flood. I could not see their pumping mill from here, there was a clump of sallows in the way, but it had been disabled by Will and others, to stop it pumping water out of the Fen to augment the flood. It had never functioned since.

Beyond the medland I could make out the rushes of the Fen, constantly rippling in gold-green waves. Even from where I stood I could hear their constant shushing, like a mother soothing her babe to sleep. The wind carries the voice of the Fens, and if you are a fenlander born and bred, you are never happy out of the sound of it. I thought how much Tom would be missing that sound amidst the violence and noise of London.

A blackbird had already begun his song before I came out to steal these few precious moments for myself. Now the other birds began to join in – a blue tit in the hedge not three feet away, a thrush somewhere over amongst our apple trees, a robin perched on the gate post. From the Fen I heard the booming call of a butter bump and with a rush of wings a flight of swans swept over, no more than a few feet above my head, with that strange whistling of the wind in their wings.

I must go back. My patient would need me. Perhaps she could be persuaded to eat a proper meal today. Then I must take over the day's lambing. We were nearly done. We had lost two more, stillborn, but the rest were healthy. Soon they could all be driven to the medland, and the cows too. The sowing of the crops would be late this year, but God willing, we would have a harvest. I turned back to the house.

The following day, Jack rode out to Turbary Holm. When he had asked after Kitty and looked over the last of our lambs, who were doing well, he came to sit in the kitchen. My mother had not yet risen, but Kitty was out of her bed for the first time, wrapped in blankets and tucked into the large chair where my father used to sit. She had taken up her knitting, but after a few rows her hands had dropped into her laps. I saw that she was still too exhausted even to ply her needles. She revived a little on seeing a new face.

'Well, Kitty lass,' Jack said, 'you have given us all a fright, have you not? And how are you now?'

'Much better, Master Jack,' she said, blushing at having so much attention paid to her. 'I shall be back about my work tomorrow.'

'You will not,' I said, poured Jack a cup of ale. 'You are weaker than those newborn lambs. You will be allowed to stay out of bed for a little longer each day until I think you are strong enough.'

As if to reinforce my words, Hannah's cat Tobit leapt on to Kitty's lap, turned round a few times and then settled comfortably in a nest of blankets and wool.

'You see. Even Tobit knows you must sit quietly.'

I took up my own knitting, for ever since last year all the women of the household had made finished woollen goods to send to market, instead of merely selling our fleeces as we used to do.

'This is more than a neighbourly visit,' Jack said, drinking deeply of his ale and setting the cup down on the table.

'You have come from Hans, to fetch Griet home?' I asked. 'She is out collecting the eggs now, but she is coming home this evening anyway.'

'I am sure Hans will be glad to see her, but he knows that she was needed here. Nay, I went over to Crowthorne yesterday, after we sowed the beans, and I thought I would bring you the news.'

Jack had a few friends in the other village, amongst those who were not such dedicated Puritans as the rest, in particular the two men, Joshua and Ephraim, who had worked with us to rescue our confiscated stock last autumn.

'And there is news?' For a moment my heart leapt. News of Gideon? But the people of Crowthorne knew nothing of his whereabouts, or so I hoped.

'Piet van Slyke has discovered how they disabled the pumping mill on their land at the time of the flood, and is threatening all kinds of vengeance against them. It will not be long before he discovers that we did the same.'

'But what right has he to take vengeance?' I said.

'His property, he claims, or at any rate the property of the company of adventurers which employs him.'

'Erected on our land. Without our consent. Nay, rather in defiance of our will. And neglected all through the winter.'

'Indeed. And I do not believe any serious damage was done, at least not to the one they built here where Hannah's cottage used to stand. Will knew what he was about. He disabled it, but did it no harm. If any harm has been done to it, it was the flood. I have not been inside it since, though I have seen that the sails of the windmill are badly damaged.'

'Aye, we saw that, Nehemiah and I, when we drove our ewes up to the medland. But was it not to be expected, when the whole mill was left unattended all these months? Surely van Slyke and his men are to blame?'

'I'll not argue with that,' Jack said. 'However, I thought I should warn you, in case van Slyke comes nosing about here again.'

'If he is looking for Tom, he will not find him.'

'Have you any word of him?'

'He has sent one letter. Gray's Inn has accepted him again as a student and happily he has met an old friend who has invited him to share his rooms – "chambers" they are called – at Gray's. He has even found some work in the library there, so all seems to be well.'

'Any word of the charter?'

I shook my head. 'Nay. But the letter was written soon after he arrived and the weather was still bitter, the roads icy.'

'He would find it difficult to get about.'

Privately, I did not know how Tom hoped to search for the charter, hampered as he was by the loss of his leg, but I had not wanted to discourage him. His spirits had been so low since the amputation that I was glad of his plan to take up his studies in the law again. It had lifted his heart, to have a possible future before him, instead of wasting away idly on the farm.

Jack rose to his feet just as Griet came in with her basket of eggs and they greeted one another.

'One other thing I learned in Crowthorne,' he said, fastening his cloak and pulling on his hat. 'It seems we are to have a new rector. Rumour in Crowthorne has it that some ranting friend of the Reverend Edgemont's has yielded to his persuasions to give up his position in one of the London parishes and take up the cure of the poor benighted souls of our village. Though why either he or Edgemont should care, since by their lights we are already damned, that I cannot know.'

Griet looked puzzled at this. We had never discussed religion and I knew nothing of her faith, save that she was Protestant. But this was bad news indeed. If Gideon and I were to be married in church, it must take place before this new man came.

'When does he come,' I asked, 'this new rector from London?'

'Some time in May, so my friends believe, but that is but hearsay.' He looked at me gravely. 'Let us hope that Gideon returns before then.'

Griet went home to her family. Kitty began to regain her strength, though slowly. And the last of the lambs were born. We had lost just two more. Finally, along with the rest of the village, we drove the remaining sheep and then the cows out to pasture. We had only two sows this year, each with a litter, so the care of the beasts became less demanding. Once the crops were planted, at least three weeks later than usual, the weeds began to grow as fast as the grain, so like everyone else I took my turn at hoeing out the weeds, backbreaking work. The new cottages in the village were completed, though barely furnished, and the settlers were hard at work creating their vegetable beds, which were fenced in with boards and raised above the ground, with a generous addition of manure dug in. They planted very close together, which seemed strange to us, but they cared for their young plants as carefully as if they were children.

I had walked one afternoon into the village to return Mistress Sawyer's baskets which had been left at Turbary Holm since Alice's first visit. I had had no opportunity to take them before, but Kitty was well enough now to look after my mother, Nehemiah was busy about the farmyard, and I had baked the day's bread before I set out. Outside Will's smithy a man was shoeing a horse, bent forward, with the horse's hoof gripped between his knees. As I came nearer I saw that the man turning over the points of the nails to hold the shoe in place was not Will, but his cousin Abel, the man who had helped me – who had, in truth, saved my life – in Lincoln. He had arrived in the village just as Tom left and I moved back to the farm, so that I had hardly exchanged two words with him since he had come to the village.

He set the horse's hoof gently on the ground and straightened up, laying aside the pincers he had used on the nails.

'That's done then, Ned,' he said. 'I've cleaned the hoof, too. She had some hard clay wedged between the old shoe and the frog.'

It was Ned Broadley, the carpenter, with his old mare. He handed Abel some coins, which chinked faintly, then they both caught sight of me.

After I had answered their questions about Kitty and the lambing and the state of the farm, Ned patted his mare and led her away.

'Abel,' I said, 'I am glad to see you well settled here with Will and at work in the smithy. I shall never forget what you did for me.'

He looked embarrassed and shifted from foot to foot. 'It was your own courage as much as anything I did, Mistress Mercy. You kept your head, when many would have drowned. And I hear you took very ill on your long walk home.'

'That is all over now,' I said. 'And forget the "Mistress". I am but "Mercy" to my friends. I hope I may count you among them.'

'I'd be honoured,' he said, with a sudden grin.

'And how are you liking the return to smithing?'

'Ah, well, I am somewhat out of practice, but it is coming back to me. Cousin Will trusts me with the simple jobs.'

I laughed. 'Will was boasting of your skills before ever you came.'

'Then he was too forward. I hope my hands will find those skills again.'

He removed his thick leather apron and laid it aside. 'Will you step into the house? I know that Will and Liz will be glad to see you.'

'Nay,' I said. 'I must return these baskets to Mistress Sawyer and then hurry home, or Kitty will be trying to do too much. She has not got all her strength back yet.'

I bade him farewell and was about to turn aside to the Sawyers' house when I saw the carter Edy trundling up the village street from the direction of the new bridge. Carters always bring news, so I waited. Then I saw that there was someone sitting up beside him. And I threw down the baskets and flew down the street, heedless of those who looked after me, gaping.

'Gideon!'

He jumped down before the cart had stopped and we fell against each other – and nearly down in the mud – clinging together, half laughing, half crying. It was most unseemly behaviour, and my mother would have been shocked. Or she would once have been.

For the next half hour I was forced to share him with the village, but at last we were able to set out for the farm, after I had rescued the baskets and thrust them at Jack to be given to his mother.

As soon as we were alone around the bend in the lane, he took me in his arms and kissed me.

'Oh, Gideon,' I said, when I could breathe again, 'you have been gone so long. What has happened?'

He tucked my arm under his and we began to walk on toward the farm.

'First, I had some difficulty hiring a horse in Peterborough, for the army had commandeered nearly everything on four legs. At last I secured an old nag who went so slowly it took me twice as long as it should to reach Oxford. Once I was there, I must tread carefully. Since the siege it has remained in the hands of the Parliamentary army, so one could not go about loudly seeking the whereabouts of an Anglican clergyman.'

'I feared you might be in danger.' I squeezed his arm. 'I have been imagining everything from prison to press ganging.'

'It did not come to that, though I had one or two bad moments.' He smiled down at me. 'Eventually I had word of an old college friend, Amyas Cooper. Like me he took orders after graduating and he had a parish in Kent, but he was driven out three years ago. I heard he was now in Burford.'

'You found him?'

He nodded. 'I rode my nag slowly over to Burford and made discreet enquiries. He was working as a clerk to one of the leading wool merchants there. All that area is very important in the wool trade, and this man is one of the great men in the wool business. And a Puritan. So I had to be careful.'

He shifted the knapsack he was carrying, and I realised he was very tired, but we had not much further to go.

'Eventually I was able to meet him and ask if he would perform the ceremony for us. He agreed, but he needed to get leave from his master, on the excuse of some family trouble.'

'He will come!' I cried.

'He will come.' He stopped and kissed me again. 'Do you remember last May Day, my village queen?'

I smiled, feeling again the weight of the ancient May queen's cloak on my shoulders. Our last celebration of May Day, and I the last queen. I remembered the touch of Gideon's hand as he led me to my flower-decked throne on the village green, and the shock it sent through me.

I could see that Gideon too was remembering. He smiled. 'Amyas will reach the village on the last day of April. This year you shall become mine. We shall be wed on the first day of May.'

Chapter Six
Tom

'There is nothing for it,' Anthony said, 'but to search the state records for the reign of Henry III. I have scoured to the bottom of the barrel with Henry II. Or rather, I have climbed up among the cobwebbed rafters of his reign's documents, and the charter is not there.'

'I feel guilty,' I said uncomfortably, 'that you should have all this trouble. It is not your case, nor your common lands.'

'Perhaps not, but like the proverbial runaway horse, I have seized the bit between my teeth, and I shall run with this.'

He lifted a large beaker of ale and drank most of it down in a single draught.

'Ah, that is good. I feel as though I have swallowed half the cobwebs and most of the dust in that place.'

We were sitting in a small tavern which stood not many yards along Gray's Inn Lane from the gatehouse. It was the first time I had ventured out of the Inn since I had arrived in London. With the last of the snow gone and the roads dry, I had decided I must make my way about more, now that I could move more safely. I was progressing well with my studies. Bencher Whittaker even gave me a few words of praise from time to time. In the library we had started to shelve the first of the books we had catalogued, so that it had begun to look more like a place of scholarship and less like a chaotic merchant's warehouse. Now that we had a better idea of how much space might be needed for each category of books, Master Hansen and I had put up temporary labels on the shelves, and under my direction a servant had carried books and shelved them according to our labels. Nevertheless, I was impatient that the Rolls House was too far away for me to accompany Anthony and help in the search.

'So,' I said, 'what is to be done now?'

'I shall make a start on the royal grandson. Mark you, it was the second Henry who was the legislator and administrator, in between conquering most of France and fighting with his wife, his sons and his friends. His grandson was more interested in endowing churches than legislating for the secular kingdom. There are certainly other land charters concerning the granting of common lands amongst the older Henry's documents. Your father's memory seems credible on that score.'

'You must not take too much time from your own work. I do not want to beggar you.'

Anthony drained the last of his ale and signalled to the tavern keeper's wife to bring him more.

'I have only the Sussex case at present, now that our three disputatious heirs have been taught a lesson and sent away to lick their wounds.'

The case of the three heirs had come to court earlier than expected, and the judgement had pleased none of them. The manor had gone to the one who lived close by, and the judge had divided the coin between the other two, the very solution which had been suggested to them before it went to court. However, they had now been forced to pay court costs and additional lawyers' fees, so that they were considerably more out of pocket. Anthony and his senior were glad to be rid of them, for the dispute had dragged on altogether for nearly two years.

'If, as you say, Henry III did little in the way of granting common land,' I said, 'is it worth your time to search the documents from that reign? He inherited young, did he not? How long was his reign?'

'Fifty-six years,' Anthony said, rolling his eyes, 'but there are fewer documents, at least as far as I can tell.'

'You know,' I said slowly, 'I am loathe to ask for help from Sir John's lawyer, but he was supposed to have searched for the charter a year ago. If we can find him, might it not save you a great deal of time, supposing he has already made the search?'

'But surely, if he had found the charter, you would have heard by now?'

115

'If he searched at all.'

'You are still suspicious.'

'Truly, Anthony, I do not know what to think. If he searched and failed to find any charter, would Sir John not have told us? If he has not bothered to search at all, of course Sir John might prevaricate.'

'There is a third possibility.'

'Aye. That he found the charter and has concealed the fact. But why would he do that?'

'Perhaps he is playing some double game, thinking to sell the charter to the speculators, so you have no evidence to support your claim.'

'That would be a crime, surely? Though I am not sure what kind.'

'Perhaps lèse-majesté, interfering with a royal decree? I am not sure myself.'

'I wonder whether he is an honest man. I wish I knew his name. I have written to my sister and asked her to try to discover.'

'I will make some enquiries amongst the clerks at the Rolls House. They may know whether a lawyer from Lincoln's Inn has been showing a particular interest in royal grants of common land, dating from the reign of the early Henrys.'

He tapped his thumbnail against his teeth.

'I hope there was indeed a charter. Some common lands are known as such by tradition, not charter.'

'What my father told me was that the lands had been held in common from earliest times, merely by tradition, but that one of the local abbeys tried to seize control of them. The commoners appealed to the king, the king supported their claim and granted the charter to confirm their rights. That is the story people remember.'

'If that is true, then surely it must have been Henry II, who was anxious to curb the growing power of the church.'

'And that was why he fell out with Becket.'

'Aye. It is unlikely to have been Henry III, who was such a friend of the church. He would have been more likely to take the part of the abbey.'

'In that case,' I said, 'you should not waste your time on the documents from the reign of the later Henry.'

'At least before I do, I shall enquire whether anyone from Lincoln's Inn has been ferreting in the same places as I have.'

The following morning, after Anthony had gone off to make enquiries of the clerks, I spoke to the gatekeeper Potter about some means of transportation to carry me from the Inn to Bucklersbury. After his initial hostility, Potter had been obsequious in his behaviour to me, hoping, I suppose, to atone for his ill manners. I did not care for his fawning any more than his rudeness, but he was the most likely person to ask.

'Why, Master Bennington, sir, I am sure one of the Inn carriages could convey you to the City.' He was bowing deeply and working his hands together as if he were washing.

'I do not require the use of a carriage,' I said – somewhat coolly, I fear. 'I merely wish to know whether there is a local carter hereabouts who might make trips into that part of the City.'

With much fussing and prattling, he finally conceded that a local man who supplied the nearby taverns with wine from a vintner's warehouse in Walbrook regularly drove into the City each morning and back in the afternoon with barrels destined for the taverns. I was too late to go with him today, and the next two days I would be working in the library, but I sent a message to the carter, asking whether I might travel with him on Friday. Before the end of the day, I received his reply, agreeing to take me to Bucklersbury.

When Anthony returned from the Rolls House later that day, he had something to report, though nothing very conclusive.

'At first none of the clerks could remember any particular search for charters granting common land from the time of the early Henrys. As you might expect, the lawyers from Lincoln's Inn are in and out of the Rolls House almost every day, as they have only to step across the road.'

'Of course. I should have thought of that.'

'Then one of the older fellows came in, who had been transferred to the Six Clerks Office a few months ago. It is in another part of the building. He thought there might have been such a search made some time last year, by one of the Benchers from Lincoln's Inn. However, he did not know the lawyer's name, nor whether the search was successful, so we are no further forward.'

'It does sound as though that might have been Sir John's lawyer,' I said slowly. 'I think you should cease your labours until I hear from Mercy, if she has been able to discover the man's name.'

'Aye,' he said, 'let us do that. Then I can go to Lincoln's Inn and tackle the man himself. See whether he managed to trace the charter.'

'We will both go,' I said firmly. 'I can manage much better now that the ground is no longer icy. Besides, on Friday I am going to see this barber surgeon, Gilbert Bolton. His elaborate jointed legs after the French fashion will be far too costly for me, but I am hopeful that he may be able to fit me with a simple wooden peg, such as sailors wear.'

'I wonder how costly they are, these jointed legs,' Anthony said thoughtfully. 'I could lend you some coin.'

'Nay, I have no wish to get into debt, though it is kind indeed of you to offer. Something simpler will do me very well. I cannot imagine how such a jointed leg would work in any case. With no nerves and muscles, how can they be made to move?'

'Bencher Whittaker said they were jointed like marionettes, did he not? Could they be worked by strings?'

I gave a dry laugh. 'I cannot imagine myself walking about, working my leg by strings! Nay, such fancy toys are not for me.'

When Friday came, I nearly called off my journey to Bucklersbury. I was suddenly afraid and ashamed, for I knew I should need to show my stump of a leg to this stranger and I had kept it hidden even from my family once it had healed. I hated the sight of it myself and always averted my eyes from it when I dressed. However, I made my way down to the gatehouse and the carter appeared a few minutes later. He heaved me up beside him and now there was no going back.

It was still very early in the morning, a warm spring day. Most of Gray's Inn Lane still runs through unspoiled country. Apart from the Inn and a few cottages and a tavern or two, it might be deep in the countryside, Gray's being the most rural of all the Inns of Court. We drove between hedgerows alive with courting birds, who flew past within inches of our noses, carrying nesting materials – robins and blue tits and blackbirds and thrushes and greenfinches – all the small familiar birds we see about Turbary Holm. Down by the river there would be gulls and swans and various ducks, but nothing like the rich life of waterfowl I was accustomed to seeing and hearing at home. And at home the treble songs of these small birds would be accompanied by that most mysterious of sounds, the boom of the butter bump, which sounds more like some deep throated musical instrument of brass than the call of a living bird. Hidden amongst the rushes of the Fen, it can send its strange cry reaching out for miles across our flat watery lands.

I found myself suddenly homesick for the call of the butter bump and the clean wide skies of the fenlands.

Instead, here we were, now skirting the lower end of Smithfield and passing through Newgate, past the prison on the right and the orphanage of Christ's Hospital on the left. The stench of the City under a warming sun caught at my throat. Out in the peace of Gray's Inn, with its elegant courts and the magnificent gardens, the Walks, you forget the stink and the noise of London proper. Crowds swarmed and jostled in the streets, the jettied houses leaned overhead, almost touching, so that only a narrow strip of blue sky could be seen. Flimsy market stalls narrowed the street still further, so that sometimes the carter was obliged to stop and shout at men with barrows and women with shopping baskets to get out of his way. We reached a stretch of Cheapside lined with butchers' stalls. Carcasses of pigs and sheep dangled like hanged men, crawling with flies, and the cobbles were sticky with blood.

Behind the makeshift stalls stood the elegant houses of the rich Cheapside merchants and I wondered how they could tolerate living here, cheek by jowl with the noise and dirt. Before the war, some of the richer merchants had begun to build themselves elegant houses out beyond the western wall of the City, in amongst the homes of the aristocrats along the Strand. Others had migrated up to the clean airs of Hackney Downs. But the war had sent many of them scuttling back inside the City walls, for I suppose they felt safer within a defensible city. Yet the old walls were crumbling away, like the City gatehouses. A determined army could take London without much trouble. I was no soldier, but even I could see that.

The carter set me down in Bucklersbury, outside a large double fronted shop. A freshly painted signboard proclaimed it as the Golden Ram. He would return, the carter said, in the early afternoon, when he had loaded the barrels of wine and beer, and taken a bite at an ordinary near the vintner.

I lowered myself to the ground and watched as he drove away before I turned to the door of the shop. I could not escape now, for I could hardly stand here in the street for the hours until he returned.

The shop front was freshly white-washed. On either side of the door, windows displayed a curious array of items. Like all barber surgeons, I supposed Gilbert Bolton practised a variety of crafts, pulling teeth, cutting hair, setting bones, stitching up wounds, as well as performing amputations like my own. At the side of one window there was the red and white pole which symbolised his trade – red for blood and white for bandages – but it was small and discreet, as though he considered this the lesser part of his business. I noticed he did not gleefully display a bone-cutting saw or a huge pair of forceps, as some of the coarser of his colleagues will do. Instead there were several artificial limbs, gruesome enough in themselves, so that they almost turned my stomach. Although it was for his very skill in such devices that I had sought him out, those stranded arms and legs and hands looked like the bloody litter of a battlefield.

Curiously, there was also a clock and two automata, such as the gentry like to have to amuse their guests. I remembered seeing one at the Dillingworths' house when I had gone there as a boy. It was a kind of doll, dressed like a gypsy, which performed a dance, twirling about and shaking a ring of wood decorated with bells, while a tune played on the musical box concealed in the base. Sir John had bought the toy in Paris when he had travelled in France as a young man.

I hitched myself forward and opened the door of the shop. It set a small bell jangling above my head as I stepped inside. The place was remarkably clean, a strong contrast to the filthy street outside, where rubbish lay in heaps, although not in front of this shop. It had a pleasant smell, of soap and fresh herbs. I was not as skilled as Mercy at picking these out, but I was sure I caught the scent of lavender and camomile. There was also something astringent, like vinegar.

There was no one to be seen, and very little in the shop, apart from a few items like those in the windows, laid out on a low table. There were some comfortable chairs, a bookcase, and a side table holding several wine flagons and glasses. It looked, in fact, more like a parlour or a gentleman's study than a shop. Except, of course, for those artificial limbs.

I heard footsteps clattering down stairs from the upper floor, where I supposed the proprietor lived, and a man stepped through a door at the far end of the shop. He was perhaps about forty years of age, wiry and quick, with bright, intelligent eyes and a shock of red hair which stood up on end, as though he was in the habit of running his fingers through it.

'I beg your pardon, sir,' he said, bounding toward me like an eager dog, 'I am sorry to keep you waiting.' He bowed and gave a charming smile. 'Gilbert Bolton at your service. Whom do I have the pleasure of addressing?'

'Tom Bennington,' I said, bowing in my turn. 'I am a student at Gray's Inn. I have been absent for seven years, but have returned to take up my studies again.'

'Ah,' he said, nodding briskly at the empty leg of my breeches. 'You have been at the war?'

It was the natural assumption that everyone made.

'Nay, a double injury, then gangrene.'

'And you would like me to see what I can do for you.'

'If you please.'

His eyes gleamed. It almost seemed that he wanted to rub his hands with pleasure.

'Please take a seat, Master Bennington,' he gestured towards one of the comfortable chairs. 'Let us discuss what has been done so far and how I can help you. I see that you have become quite accustomed to using crutches. When was the amputation carried out?'

I lowered myself into the chair, realising that it was higher off the ground than usual, making it easier for a crippled man to manage. I laid my crutches down beside it.

'I was injured in the spring of last year, then again in the same place on my leg, before it had fully healed. That would have been in the early summer.'

He sat down opposite me, watching me keenly. He nodded.

'And when did the gangrene set in? Was the wound not cleaned properly?'

'It was. I have no one to blame but myself.' I found I could speak easily to this man, who seemed to treat my maiming in such a matter of fact way.

'We had many family troubles at the time. My father had gone to court, then was fined and imprisoned in gaol until the fine was paid. There were . . . other troubles last summer as well. I rode to Lincoln to pay the fine and gain his release. The wound broke open again and what with the ride and the dirt of the journey . . . well, after I reached home, it became infected and then the gangrene set in.'

He nodded, as if this were the most ordinary thing in the world.

'I hope your father was recovered.'

'Nay,' I said bitterly. 'He was already dead of gaol fever.'

He clicked his tongue and shook his head.

'So, it became necessary to amputate. You made the wise decision.'

I smiled sadly. 'It was not my decision. I was delirious by then. My family sent for a surgeon from Peterborough. He amputated and cauterised the stump.'

To my surprise, he slammed his fist on the table. 'When will they learn! They should not cauterise! The wound may become infected or the patient may die of shock. Nowadays we can use much gentler methods, by applying a paste of egg, oil of roses and turpentine. The wound heals much more quickly and there is far less pain or risk of fever. Yet these fools cling to Galen and his followers as though his methods were handed down on tablets of stone.'

I was slightly shocked by this, for the reference sounded almost like blasphemy. And the man's passion was extraordinary.

'Forgive me, Master Bennington,' he said, running his fingers up through his hair and making it stand even more on end. 'I cannot control my temper when I hear of such practices, which should have been banned a hundred years ago. That was when the new method was first employed by the great Ambroise Paré. Yet I have seen with my own eyes men die in agony, not from the amputation but from cauterisation. Still, that is in the past for you. Fortunately you have survived.'

I gave him a twisted smile. 'I have survived. A maimed and despicable half man.'

'Now that is pure folly,' he said briskly, 'and no way to think of yourself. The real man lies here.' He struck himself in the chest. 'And here.' He tapped his head. 'If we employ our brains and our courage, then we are men. A leg is no more than an instrument allowing us to strut about on the surface of the world. And like any other instrument, if it is damaged, we must repair it. Allow me to show you what I mean.'

He got up and darted across to the book case. Laying a large book, somewhat battered and well thumbed, on a table next to my chair, he turned over the pages until he found what he was searching for.

'Look at this. Did you ever see anything more beautiful or more ingenious?'

It was a complex drawing of a leg. No ordinary leg, however, but one composed of gears and levers. Because it looked more like a piece of machinery than a severed limb, I did not find it offensive.

'This is, naturally, a cut away diagram,' he said, 'showing the interior machinery.'

'This is one of the mechanical legs I have heard about?' I said. 'Surely such a thing can only exist in the imagination, not in practice.'

He clicked his tongue in annoyance and turned over more pages. I saw drawings of whole legs, part legs from below the knee, arms of various types, hands which looked more like the interior of a clock.

'This is the work of Ambroise Paré,' he said, 'the greatest benefactor to the art of surgery that the world has ever known. Though,' he added thoughtfully, 'we nearly lost him during the St Bartholomew's Day Massacre, had the king of France himself not saved him, but that is another story.'

123

He closed the book and tapped it with his finger. 'I studied at the Hôtel-Dieu in Paris for six years, where Paré himself once trained, though in his student days they still followed the ancient practices of Galen, and later did not altogether welcome his new ideas in surgery and patient care. Artificial limbs of one kind and another have, of course, been known since earliest times. The Greeks and Romans made some attempt to provide assistance for soldiers who had lost limbs in battle.'

There was a gleam in his eye. I recognised the signs of a man launching upon a subject with which he was obsessed, so I attempted to divert him.

'I noticed the two automata in your windows,' I said. 'Do they not also have gears like clocks and like these pictures you have shown me?'

He jumped up again and carried one of the automata over to the table. It consisted of a man leading a donkey around a circular base. When Bolton wound up the key at the side, the man walked round the base, the donkey following after. There was no music this time, but the legs of both man and donkey, and the man's arms, were jointed and moved like real limbs, while the man's head moved from side to side. When they stopped moving, the donkey threw back its head and brayed, so unexpectedly that I jumped, then laughed.

'Very clever,' I said. 'I have seen but one automaton before. Was this one made in Paris?'

'Nay, it was made in my workshop here.' He grinned, clearly pleased with my reaction.

'You made it?'

'Aye. And the other one, the dancing girl. It's a common type, but normally the girl merely turns around, but mine kicks out her leg. Watch.'

He set the second automaton moving, and the female figure did indeed kick out her leg, which moved from hip, knee and ankle. The movement was remarkably smooth and realistic.

'These are not toys.' He returned the two automata to the window. 'They are a means of studying movement, so that I can reproduce it on a larger, a human scale.'

'And the clock?' I was truly curious now.

He waved his hand dismissively. 'I also trained as a clock maker. I must earn my living somehow. I make and mend clocks to put bread on the table, and to support me while I develop new techniques in the making of artificial limbs. Though to tell the truth, with the fighting we have seen in these last years, brother against brother and father against son, these latter skills of mine have been called upon more than ever before.'

'You are a man of great talents, Master Bolton.'

'I have dedicated myself to repairing those injuries which others besides yourself regard as making them less than whole men. Now, let us see what we can do for you. Come through into my workshop.' He gestured towards the door at the back, and I rose awkwardly.

'Before your expectations are raised, Master Bolton,' I said, 'I must explain that I am not a wealthy man. I am the son of a yeoman farmer, and my family has been comfortable enough in our rank in life, until a series of recent disasters. As I can no longer work as a farmer, I have returned to my studies in the law, but I must pay my way by doing clerical work. I have little coin to spare. These mechanical limbs appear to be quite marvellous, but I fear I can afford nothing better than a simple wooden post to strap to my stump and give me some support on my left side. I hope that I may then manage with just one crutch.'

'Oh, that is simple enough, and you will be able to discard one crutch, once you are accustomed to it, but come through and let me examine you.'

Despite my earlier reluctance, I found I did not mind removing my breeches and my rolled up left stocking, while Bolton washed his hands thoroughly in a basin of warm water and scrubbed his nails with a small brush. Then with remarkably gentle fingers he probed what was left of my leg.

'It is unfortunate that you have lost the knee, for the replacement of the lower leg is far less complicated, but as you could see from the diagram I showed you, we now have the knowledge to construct jointed knees.'

I opened my mouth to protest that I could not pay for one of the mechanical legs, but he held up his hand.

'Later. I have a proposition to make to you. Now, I need to take some measurements.'

He drew from his pocket a tailor's measuring tape and told me to remove the stocking from my right leg.

'Now, if you will lie down here on the bench, Master Bennington?'

I did as I was bid. He measured my good leg – the length of its various sections, the width of the widest and narrowest parts of thigh and calf, the length and width of my foot – writing down everything in a small notebook. Then he measured the stump.

'You have lost some muscle here,' he said, lightly tapping my left thigh. 'That is because the leg has been idle. Once you begin to use an artificial leg, the muscle will grow stronger again.' He rolled up the tape and tucked it into a pocket. 'You may put on your right stocking again.'

I did so, and sat up on the edge of the bench. Bolton pulled forward a joint stool and sat down opposite me.

'I can provide you with a simple wooden leg today,' he said, gesturing toward a rack, where I had already noticed rows of wooden legs in different sizes. 'This will strap on to your stump and you can use it to give you some support, but there is no knee joint, so you will find it awkward. When you sit, you will need to thrust it out like this.' He thrust out his own left leg as if it were rigid. 'And you will find it difficult to get up and down.' He demonstrated, hopping and grabbing hold of the door frame to steady himself.

'It will be sufficient for the moment, but I have another suggestion to make.'

I could not imagine what he meant, but I waited patiently as he walked back to the stool.

'I have been experimenting with a new design. Most artificial limbs are made of metal, for strength and durability, but they are very, very heavy, and can be exhausting to wear. Like this.'

He jumped up and rummaged about on his work bench, which was behind me.

'Here. See for yourself.'

He laid a metal leg on my lap. It was indeed remarkably heavy.

'Now a natural leg of flesh and bone is also heavy, but it is controlled by an intricate web of muscles and tendons and nerves, which we learn to use as tiny children when we first walk. Then as we grow, our natural control of our limbs grows with us.'

He restored the metal leg to his work bench and sat down again.

'Ambroise Paré made his original legs of iron. I have seen examples myself, and they are very like this one I showed you. This is the type I learned to make. However, in his book he states that he worked with a Paris locksmith, whom he calls "Le Petit Lorraine". No Christian name. I suppose he must have been a small man. A locksmith would, of course, have excellent mechanical skills for the designing of movable joints. This Lorraine came up with the idea of making part of the artificial limb out of leather, to reduce the weight. The moving parts, naturally, must be metal, and probably the foot, with sufficient weight in it to draw the leg down to the ground, but it should be possible to make the outer "skin", as it were, from leather. This would both lessen the weight and make the leg less unpleasant to wear – warmer and less hard to the touch. Unfortunately, no examples of Lorraine's work seem to have survived.'

It was certainly fascinating. I had no idea all these discoveries had been made some hundred years ago.

'But your proposition?' I said.

'I need someone young and healthy, not too heavily built, and living in London, to try wearing one of my experimental legs, so that I can modify it and develop it. You are young and slender. You are far healthier than most of the injured soldiers I see, who often have multiple injuries and are undernourished, as well as severely troubled in their minds. Often they do not live in London, while you will be here some time for your studies. What do you say?'

I was taken aback. I had come to Bolton to purchase a simple wooden prop, but the man's enthusiasm was infectious. I could never afford one of these marvellous inventions, but I could perhaps help him develop one.

'Well then, I accept,' I said, 'if I can be of help to you.'

'Excellent, excellent!' He leapt up. 'I have all the measurements I need. For now I will fit you with a plain wooden support, then I will set to work to design a mechanical leg covered in leather of the right dimensions to match your undamaged leg.

Allow me a little over a week, let us say until a sennight this coming Monday, and I will have a prototype for you to try. I will need to give you instruction in how to use it.'

After that he found a wooden leg of the right height and showed me how to buckle it on to my stump. A kind of cloth sleeve at the top fitted quite comfortably over the stump, and my breeches could be pulled down to hide the join, but I confess that it felt very strange and somewhat uncomfortable, although Bolton had padded the top of the wood, inside the sleeve, with lamb's wool and a felt pad. I put my rolled up stocking into my pocket and we went through into the front room of the shop.

'Now,' Bolton said, 'I hope you will join me in some refreshment.'

From somewhere upstairs he carried down cold meats and a fresh loaf, as well as some cold pickled turnips and soft cheese. From the side table he brought wine and glasses, and we drank to the success of our collaboration. When the carter arrived to convey me back to Gray's Inn, I was still feeling somewhat stunned. Bolton had put me through my paces with the wooden leg, which was not at all easy to control, although I did manage to walk across the room once using only a single crutch.

'Now you must practise every day,' he instructed, as he saw me into the cart. 'You will need to strengthen the muscles of the left leg in order to use the mechanical device.' He gave me suddenly a smile of great sweetness, and struck his chest and head again. 'Remember. Our legs are merely machines for carrying us about. The real man is within.'

When Anthony arrived back in chambers that evening, I was sitting at my desk in the office working at an imaginary case Bencher Whittaker had set me. I was to write out the arguments on both sides, as if the case were being debated in a court of law. It was difficult to be even handed about it and not favour one side or the other. It reminded me of trying to play chess against oneself, as I had spent long hours doing when I was recovering from the amputation. I had taught Kitty to play, but she rarely had time to sit down with me. It was the time last summer when Mercy was under trial with the witchfinders in Lincoln, and later lying ill with a fever upstairs. Playing chess against myself, I often found I was favouring one side or the other, so that the outcome was easy to predict.

'Good even to you,' Anthony said, coming into the office and dropping his satchel together with an armload of books on his desk. 'And how did it go with the sawbones?'

'That is not a name I particularly enjoy hearing,' I said.

'I apologise.' Anthony looked contrite. 'That was thoughtless of me. How did you find the maker of artificial limbs?'

'Quite extraordinary,' I said. 'A man of great enthusiasm and equally great talent. He also makes clocks and automata. Very clever ones.'

Then I rose carefully from my desk, propped one crutch under my left arm, and proceeded to hop my way across to the parlour, the wooden prop making a loud tapping on the floor. I was beginning to understand the way of it, but I found it tiring.

'God's bones!' Anthony said. 'Only one crutch!'

'Aye. Though I am not sure how far I could walk at present. I used two crutches to get myself from the gatehouse to here. Bolton said the muscles in the upper part of my left leg are somewhat wasted from lack of use and I must build up their strength again. Indeed, I find my leg is beginning to shake with the effort.'

I lowered myself thankfully into a chair.

'Well, we must drink to your new device. You may not be dancing a jig yet, but you will surely be able to move about more easily.'

He fetched us both a beer and sat down opposite me.

'So did you see any of these remarkable moveable limbs?'

'I did. And a great volume in French with detailed drawings of the mechanical parts. And got a lecture, too, not only on mechanical limbs but on the wickedness of cauterising amputations and the thick headedness of most surgeons.'

'He sounds an interesting character, your Master Bolton.'

'Indeed he is.'

'And I suppose the mechanical legs cost a king's ransom and are only to be purchased by noblemen and their like.'

'We did not discuss their cost, and he has loaned me this wooden leg for nothing. I am now to take part in the advancement of medical experiments.'

He raised his eyebrows, looking at me over the top of his cup, so I explained how Bolton and I were to collaborate in the development of a leg made partly of metal and partly of leather.

'Extraordinary,' he said. 'Has he explained how it will work? I do not understand how you can make it move, bend the knee or ankle, for example.'

'Nay, he has not told me yet. I expect it will be easier to demonstrate once the leg is constructed. I am to go back Monday sennight for a first fitting. I shall ask then. From the drawings I saw, the joints look very complex, like the mechanics of a clock, but there must be some way to move them, or they would have abandoned these mechanical limbs by this. It was a Frenchman who invented them, about a hundred years ago. One Ambroise Paré.'

'I have never heard of him.'

'Neither had I, but it seems that is merely our ignorance. Master Bolton considers him to have been the greatest master of surgery who ever lived.'

'Well, I hope your experiments prove successful. These studies of mechanics and natural philosophy are the very height of fashion, it seems.'

'I would not say Master Bolton cares a fig for fashion. He is one of those true inventors, always wanting to devise something new and strange.' I smiled. 'He is also a kind man, which is perhaps even better.'

'And when this experimental leg is perfected, will you be allowed to keep it?'

'I did not like to ask,' I said.

I spent the next few days growing accustomed to the wooden leg, and it was something of a trial. The remaining upper part of my left leg grew very tired, the muscles aching with the strain of lifting the thing each step, although my right shoulder benefited from no longer pressing down on a crutch. The wooden leg could also prove embarrassing. When I entered the Inn chapel for service on Sunday morning, the loud tap of the wood on the stone flags of the floor caused everyone to turn round and look at me, to my chagrin. They had grown used to my maimed state, now I drew attention to myself all over again.

The fragile skin which had healed over my stump began to grow sore with the chafing of the prop. Bolton had warned me of this, and given me a pot of salve to rub into it, not so much to sooth it as to toughen the skin. By the fourth or fifth day I was ready to abandon the wretched leg and one morning even threw it across my chamber in fury. Then I retrieved it, ashamed of my weakness and lack of determination. I remembered Bolton's words. I must rely on brains and courage to carry me through this painful period.

Toward the end of the week I received a note from Bolton, saying that he would need a little longer before the first model of the leg would be ready. I had told him that I was not free on Wednesdays or Thursdays. Instead of the Monday I was to go to Bucklersbury on the Friday following. And at the end of that first week learning to manage the wooden leg, I received an answer to the letter I had sent Mercy, asking her to discover, if she could, the name of the Dillingworths' lawyer at Lincoln's Inn.

> *My dear Brother,*
>
> *As you must understand, it would have been difficult for me to visit the manor myself to make enquiries as to the name of the lawyer. However, as you know, Jack sells some of his sheep to a farmer in Crowthorne who, thank God, is not such a purse mouthed Puritan as many in that village. This man (his name is Joshua) has had some dealings with Sir John over a disputed piece of woodland and has received letters from a lawyer in London. Jack believes it may be the same man, as he is a Member of Lincoln's Inn. His name is James Blakiston.*

Here she went on to tell me of all that was being done on the farm, the number of lambs and calves born, the crops planted.

> *Gideon and I are to be wed on the first day of May. I wish you might be here, but know that you cannot. I beg that you will think of us then, and pray for our future together.*
>
> *Your loving sister,*
> *Mercy Bennington.*

So my young sister was to be married. When I left home, Gideon and Mercy had found no clergyman to perform the service, so something must have been contrived. Mercy was wise to give no hint as to who the man would be, for if her letter had fallen into

131

the wrong hands, it would have been dangerous for him. Any clergyman performing the traditional wedding ceremony using the Prayer Book was liable for prosecution or even imprisonment. I wished I could be there to see them wed, but circumstances divided us now.

And although she wrote quite cheerfully about the farm, the number of new lambs seemed smaller than usual, yet we had not lost any of our ewes. They had been settled safe in the glebe lands as usual during the winter, well before the flood came. It also seemed that the spring sowing was somewhat late, but that might have been due to the waterlogged state of the fields after the flood. I must not worry and question her decisions. The farm was hers now, to manage as she thought best. She would make her judgements knowing the state of the land. How could I try to outguess her, from faraway London? My mind should be on my studies, not on Turbary Holm.

'James Blakiston, it seems, is the name of the Dillingworths' lawyer,' I said to Anthony. 'At any rate, my sister writes that they have employed such a man at Lincoln's Inn on one occasion, and they are unlikely to have used the services of more than one, surely?'

'Unlikely. Very well, let us seek out this James Blakiston tomorrow, if you think you can walk as far as Lincoln's Inn.'

'Aye, I am growing accustomed to this prop,' I said. 'I shall manage well enough.'

Privately, I knew it would be difficult and exhausting to walk so far, to the end of Gray's Inn Lane and then down Chancery Lane, but I was restless and impatient, having to leave all the work of the search to Anthony. If we could speak to James Blakiston, the whole matter could progress at once. If he had made a thorough search and failed to find the charter, it might mean that the copy kept in the Rolls House had somehow been lost or gone missing. There might be other places we could search. Indeed, the other copy, the one once held by the Dillingworths, might still exist. Like all old manors, their house would have chests of ancient documents, probably in disorder and chewed by mice, but had Sir John ever taken the trouble to search for it himself?

On the other hand, if James Blakiston had found the charter, I should demand to know why it had not been handed over to the commoners. At least we should have been informed, so that we could brief him to prepare for a case at law. I was glad Anthony would be with me. Already qualified as an utter barrister and a strong man in the prime of life, he would carry more weight, both professionally and physically, with a Lincoln's Inn barrister than I would, a crippled unqualified law student from the country.

The following morning we set off early, immediately after breaking our fast. It was Goodwife Gorley's day to clean, but the clerk Edwin Latimer was not due to be working for Anthony as Henry Grantham had a difficult case in hand. Anthony had agreed he should have Edwin's services that day, in exchange for an extra day when he too was over burdened with work.

Once again it was a beautiful spring morning. Had I still my old health and strength, I would have enjoyed the walk, but I hobbled along as best I could. I found the wooden leg a little easier to manage each day, and the muscles of my left thigh were certainly growing stronger, but I knew I made a sorry sight. Anthony considerately slowed his own pace to match mine.

'We are fortunate with such weather,' he said. 'I was speaking to one of the Benchers yesterday, who has just returned from visiting a client in Northamptonshire, and he said the weather was terrible there – very cold, like November, with both thunder and hail storms.'

'Mercy has been late with the spring planting,' I said. 'Perhaps they have suffered as well, in the Fens. Indeed,' I squinted at the sky, 'it is almost a little too bright here today. There is a brassy tint to the sunshine. And although the sky is clear here, is that not a faint trace of cloud building up in the east?'

'You are right,' he said. 'Ah well, this is England. We cannot expect the sunshine to last. I hope we may be back at Gray's before those clouds reach us here.'

We arrived at Lincoln's Inn at last, and I confess my stump was throbbing with pain. I had not attempted to walk so far before.

'Is that the Rolls House?' I asked, gesturing at a cluster of buildings on the other side of the road. It appeared to be an ancient hall house on to which various wings and excrescences had been tacked over the centuries.

'It is. A very labyrinth of a place. You could be lost and crying for help, and no one would find you.'

133

We turned instead to the gatehouse of Lincoln's Inn. Anthony had worn his lawyer's gown and I my student gown, for we wanted to impress on Blakiston that we were professional colleagues and not mere idle outsiders. It had been agreed that Anthony would take the lead, as the more senior man. I would take the role of his assistant. As both of us were familiar with the Fens and with the nature of the case of the common lands, I was content for Anthony to wield his greater authority.

The gatekeeper made no difficulty about admitting us, and pointed out the chambers belonging to James Blakiston in the first courtyard. My heart sank when I realised that I should need to climb a flight of stairs. I had been practising going up and down a few of the steps leading to the floor above Anthony's chambers, but never more than four at a time. I could barely manage, in a dot and carry fashion. I looked at Anthony in dismay as we made our way across the court.

'Do not let it worry you,' he said softly. 'We will go very slowly. I can steady you with a hand on your back.'

'And can you pick me up, when I tumble all the way down again?' I gave a nervous laugh, which did not deceive him.

'You are not going to fall,' he said firmly.

I did not fall, although I came close, about halfway up, when I misjudged the height of the step and lurched precariously sideways, but Anthony braced his hand against the small of my back and I was able to regain my balance.

Anthony's rap on the stout oak door was answered by 'Come in' and we stepped through into a very fine set of chambers. James Blakiston employed three men. Their positions were not clear, but I took one to be his junior, for he wore a lawyer's gown. The other two were probably clerks, though well dressed and experienced looking.

Anthony introduced us both, explaining that we had come from Gray's Inn and would like to consult him on a legal matter with which he might be familiar.

Blakiston was a man of middle age, just beginning to go slightly to seed, with the pasty look of a man who spends little time in the open air. His head was long and narrow, the eyes set too close together and his mouth narrow lipped. Perhaps I was prejudiced, for he noticed my wooden leg at once and gave me the sort of contemptuous look one might give a spavined horse or an old blind hunting dog overdue for having its throat cut.

However, he ushered Anthony into his inner office courteously enough and offered him a chair. I was left to stand behind it. After the long walk and the treacherous climb up the stairs, both of my legs were trembling and I ached to sit down, but I was thankful that my gown would conceal my weakness from Blakiston.

Once they were seated, the older man behind an impressive desk, Anthony explained that we were searching for the charter granting the common lands in perpetuity to the people of the five parishes, which Sir John Dillingworth had requested him to search for the previous year.

'As nothing has yet been heard as to the success or otherwise of your search,' Anthony concluded, 'and as I am acting for the remaining commoners in this case, I felt it right to consult you and consider whether we might work together on this matter.'

He was very impressive, I thought, giving every impression of being a senior barrister properly briefed in the case. James Blakiston should respect that. Surely he would be prepared to tell us what he knew.

Blakiston leaned back in his chair and steepled his hands under his chin.

'Ah, indeed. I recall Sir John's interest in the matter. It seems that the local copy, formerly held by the Dillingworths, is no longer to be found. Naturally, in such a case, one would expect that a copy of the charter would be lodged at the Rolls House. You have searched there?'

'I have,' Anthony said. 'Myself.'

I realised that Blakiston would not have dirtied his own hands amongst the dust of the old scrolls. He would have sent his junior, or one of the clerks, to search. His glance flicked over me and said, as clearly as words, that I was incapable of carrying out such a search.'

'It yielded no success, I assume?'

'Indeed,' Anthony said.

'The charter was believed to date from Henry II's time.'

'As I understand it.'

'Very unfortunate. There is such an abundance of documents from that reign.' Blakiston gave an odd little smirk.

I could not understand his attitude. Why should he admit that Sir John had approached him about the charter, and yet appear to be privately amused that Anthony's searches in the Rolls House had proved unprofitable? I felt myself flushing with annoyance, but I contrived to keep my expression bland, while gazing over Blakiston's left shoulder. Clearly Anthony was also somewhat taken aback by the other lawyer's odd manner.

'As you say, there is a great abundance of documents from Henry II's reign. There was a possibility that it might date from the time of his grandson, but it seems unlikely.'

'Unlikely, I am sure. What is it that you wish to consult me about?'

I noticed that Anthony's back had stiffened. He too was becoming annoyed, but he kept his voice level.

'As Sir John Dillingworth requested you, a year ago, to locate the charter, so that the commoners could take a case to court against the drainers, I assumed that you must have located the charter, or else had other advice to offer. I had hoped that we might work together.'

Blakiston leaned forward and rested the palms of his hands flat on the desk. He was smiling openly now.

'There is, however, a difficulty, Master . . . Thirkettle, did you say? I am currently retained as lawyer for a company of adventurers who are investing in land improvement in that wilderness of fenland. Young and inexperienced as you clearly are, you will understand that any collaboration on my part with you or your . . . clients, would represent a conflict of interests.' He stood up. 'I must therefore wish you good day.'

Anthony surged to his feet, his gown swirling about him. The back of his neck had grown very red.

'I wish you good day, sir. I am sorry to have troubled you.'

The words came out as though through clenched teeth. Anthony stood back to allow me to go out through the door first, for which I was grateful. It blocked Blakiston's view of my stumbling progress. As we crossed the other office, the three men gave us curious looks, but the junior lawyer was courteous enough to open the outer door for us. Blakiston had remained in his inner room.

Negotiating the stairs, half blind with fury, I would have fallen had Anthony not grabbed me by the elbow and held me steady. When we reached the ground, we stopped and stared at each other. We were both breathing heavily.

'He has the charter,' I said.

'Aye.' Anthony nodded. 'I believe you are right. He has it, or he knows where it is. A very pretty case of treachery and betrayal.'

Chapter Seven
Mercy

Gideon's return to Turbary Holm turned into a celebration. When he hugged Kitty and said he was so glad to find her recovering, she began to cry, for she was still weak from the fever, at which point he teased her until she laughed through her tears. Nehemiah shook Gideon's hand until I thought he would never stop, then took off his woollen cap and scratched his head, a sure sign that he was deeply moved. Gideon spoke gently to my mother, who seemed at first to recognise him, calling him 'Reverend', but then that confused look came over her face again and she became very quiet.

After he had washed the dust of the journey from his face and hands, he demanded to know what work he should do.

'For I know it has been hard for you all, while I have been away, with the lambing and Kitty so ill. Had it been less important, I would not have stayed away so long.'

'If you are able for it,' I said, 'you might help Nehemiah fetch the cows in for milking. The milking can be done in half the time with two. That will mean I can salt and turn the cheeses, before I prepare our supper.'

'I am willing to try,' Gideon said, with laughter in his eyes, 'though I fear my skill at milking will hardly halve the time.'

'May I fetch the eggs, Mistress Mercy?' Kitty said eagerly. 'I can easily do that. I am much stronger now.'

'Very well,' I said. 'But do nothing else. Come straight back. I do not want to look out in a few minutes and see you sweeping the yard.'

138

I went into the dairy with my heart singing. It had been a dull, overcast day, with a chilly wind blowing down from the north, but now that Gideon was back, the air seemed somehow brighter, despite the gathering clouds that foretold rain.

After we had eaten our supper, my mother taking hers as usual in her chamber, I sent Kitty to her bed, for she was looking tired after the excitement of Gideon's return.

'I am off to the village,' Nehemiah said, pulling on his cloak of thick grey frieze. 'I said earlier that I'd meet with Joseph and his nephews in the yel-hus this evening.'

With that he was off. Gideon smiled at me. 'Has he not been on the farm all day? When did he make this arrangement?'

'When his kind heart told him that we might wish to be alone together,' I said, reaching out to take his hand.

He lifted my hand to his lips and kissed it.

'It is somewhat cold for a spring evening, but will you go along the lane a little way with me? Wear your thick cloak.'

For a while we walked in silence, my arm tucked in his, till we reached the point where we could look across to the field where the settlers had built their houses.

'Not a trace left,' Gideon said.

'Nay. We found a few of their household goods, washed up against the hedges, sometimes several fields away. A few cooking pots, a wash tub. There was even some bed linen, but it was of little use.'

I was remembering how Tom and I, together with our friends, had crept to the edge of the settlement in the dark, carrying our scythes and axes and pitchforks. How we had torn down part of the incomers' houses as children screamed and the men chased us away. And how Tom had tripped over my scythe and injured his leg again. The memories were painful and shaming. Yet they had built on our land, destroying part of our badly needed crops. And their countrymen, van Slyke and his workers, had beaten Hannah and Nehemiah, burnt down their homes, and shot Tom. The blame for all this violence lay neither with us nor with the Dutchmen, but with the arrogant and greedy company of adventurers whose sole aim was to steal our land and turn it to their own profit. It would all start again, once van Slyke returned. Tom must find the ancient charter, so that we could take our battle to the courts. Until he did, we might need to take to violent actions again.

'I thought there would be something left,' Gideon said. 'Timbers, ditches where they laid the foundations.'

'All the timbers that remained were salvaged to be used in the new cottages, then before the field was ploughed, the men filled in the ditches.'

'What is planted here now?'

'Wheat. But it has barely sprouted. It was been so cold and wet.' I shivered, partly from the cold, partly from fear for the crops. Gideon put an arm around me and drew me close. We began to walk slowly back to the farm.

'As I explained,' Gideon said, 'Amyas plans to come on the last day of the month, so that he can hold the ceremony on the first day of May, but I thought we might hold a hand-fasting before that. What do you say, dear heart?'

I felt my colour rising. A hand-fasting is as good as a marriage and some never have a church ceremony at all. A hand-fasting held before witnesses would make us man and wife in the eyes of our neighbours and the law.

'There is little time to prepare, but, aye, let us have a simple hand-fasting. We can hold a feast after the church wedding, for I know that everyone will want to celebrate. Times have been so hard, we need a chance to make merry.'

'And it will compensate for no May Day revels,' he said, 'for I think we should not risk them this year.'

'Nay, we should not. When shall we hold the hand-fasting, and where?'

'Tomorrow?'

'Gideon!' I said, 'We must give some warning.'

'The following day, then. And at the church door, as the most fitting place. If we save the celebrations for the wedding, there is nothing to arrange. Our waiting has been long enough. Do you not long to put an end to it?'

'Aye,' I whispered. My heart was beating fast. Many couples are bedded after a hand-fasting, not waiting for a church ceremony, but Gideon, as a clergyman, would surely wait. After his long absence, it seemed everything was now happening very suddenly.

The next morning Gideon helped again with the milking, and Nehemiah declared that, with perhaps another ten years' practice, he might make a cowman. At that, Gideon laughed and said it would take more like twenty, but he managed to herd the cows back to the medland by himself, with only Jasper to help. He took my advice to lead Blackthorn, and the others would follow. When he returned, he came to me where I was kneaded loaves in the bread trough.

'I am going to the village, to let our friends know that we will hold our hand-fasting tomorrow. May I take Blaze?'

'You do not need to ask my permission, Gideon.'

'I was not sure whether he might be needed.'

'Nay, he is not needed. And be warned, it will not be our closest friends only. The whole village will come.'

'Are you having a hand-fasting?' Kitty looked up from the spinning wheel, her face glowing. 'Oh, I have never seen one!'

'You have seen Alice's wedding,' I said. 'A hand-fasting is like a simple wedding.'

'Then you will be married?'

'Not exactly.' I found myself blushing again, to my embarrassment. 'It is a pledge of marriage, but we will still have a church ceremony.'

Gideon smiled at Kitty. 'And that is when we shall have feasting and bride cake.'

When he returned from the village, he came in, shaking his head and laughing. 'You were right, my love. Already the women were for rushing off to start preparing a feast. I said we would wait for that until the first of May, but the only answer I got was that the first of May was only a week away, so they must make a start at once.'

'I warned you.'

It could not be the same as Alice's wedding last year, when food was abundant, when I had plaited a crown of flowers for her, and when for the first time I had danced with Gideon. Nevertheless, I remembered something from that wedding. Before I went to bed that night, I opened my clothes coffer and gently lifted out the silk shawl that my great-grandmother, Mary Dillingworth, had brought with her when she married the yeoman farmer, Thomas Bennington, against the wishes of her family. Both my mother and my father were descended from them. I would wear it at my hand-fasting to the man I loved, and again in a week's time, when Amyas Cooper would make us man and wife in the eyes of God, as well as in the eyes of the law.

For once in this cold spring, the sky was clear and there was a little warmth in the sun. After the morning work about the farm was done, I dressed in my best bodice and kirtle, which I had not worn since that day last year when I was the May queen, for times had been hard in the months since, with little to celebrate. I wrapped Mary Dillingworth's shawl about my shoulders and marvelled, as I did whenever I saw it, at the shimmer of the silk, and the wondrous colour, the very shade that you may see on a peacock. Jack once told me that the sea sometimes took on that colour. He had seen it in the fjords of Norway during the years he went for a sailor. I had never seen the sea. Sometimes, when the light is falling in a particular way, the colour of one of the meres in the Fen make take on, just for a moment, something of the same colour, but it never has this richness and depth. And the silk is so light, you can hardly believe you are wearing it, yet it is warm too.

Clad in my finery, I made my way slowly down the stairs. Gideon held out his hand to me. He had no need to speak, for I could read his thoughts in his eyes. With Kitty and Nehemiah following, we turned to go.

Mistress Norton had come to stay with my mother, for we feared that she would find the ceremony confusing or distressing, yet my heart ached that my mother could not be with me when I pledged my faith to Gideon. It was the one cloud on my beautiful day.

When we reached the village, Alice came running up and set a small garland of flowers on my head.

'I managed to find a few wildflowers,' she said, 'but I am afraid it does not match the one you made for me.'

'It is lovely,' I said, kissing her on the cheek. For some foolish reason I wanted to weep, yet I was so happy I felt like a child, swept away by my joy.

All the villagers were gathered about the church door, and all the Dutch settlers too. Griet was holding her children by the hand and gave me a broad smile. Every one who had endured our time crowded together in the church during the flood was here. Everyone, except the soldiers, who had still not returned from their military training.

Gideon led me to the threshold of the church, then we turned and faced the villagers. He took my right hand in his. Without any further ceremony, he spoke the words of the hand-fasting, which would make us one flesh for life.

'I Gideon take thee Mercy to my wedded wife, to have and to hold from this day forth, for better for worse, for richer for poorer, in sickness and in health, to love and to cherish, till death us depart, according to God's Holy ordinance, and thereto I plight thee my troth.'

Both our hands were trembling. He gently released mine. Then in my turn I reached out and took his right hand in mine.

'I Mercy take thee Gideon to my wedded husband, to have and to hold from this day forth, for richer for poorer, in sickness and in health, to love and to cherish and to obey, till death us depart, according to God's Holy ordinance, and thereto I plight thee my troth.'

He leaned forward and kissed me on the lips. I found that my legs were shaking and I kept hold of his hand, to steady myself.

There was a cheer from somewhere in the crowd of villagers. It sounded like Tom's friend Toby Ashford, then it was echoed by several others of the young men. Will Keane was pushing forward through the crowd. With a grin, he handed something to Gideon.

'I have no gold, Mercy,' Gideon said, 'but I did have a pair of silver shoe buckles. Will has melted them down and fashioned us a pair of rings. He set aside everything to make them, since I gave him the buckles yesterday.' He opened his hand to show a pair of silver rings. Each was fashioned of three strands, plaited together, simple but beautiful. I did not know that Will could do such fine work.

'We should not wear them until we are truly wed, by the church,' I said.

'Aye, but you may wear this on a ribbon about your neck for this next week, and I shall do the same.' He placed the smaller ring on my palm and folded my fingers over it.

'I have ribbons at home,' I said.

'I think Alice has already thought of that.'

143

'Was everyone in the village in on the secret except me?'

'Not everyone.'

Alice came forward with her ribbons and soon the ring was hanging inside my bodice. I touched the lace on my stomacher, where the ring lay, and felt a great surge of happiness, so great I was almost dizzy with it.

'Come,' Alice said, 'I know you wish to save the celebrations for the church ceremony, but Mistress Sawyer and I have prepared a dinner for your betrothal. It could not pass quite unmarked.'

Soon we were sitting around the table at Jack's house, with Kitty and Nehemiah too, eating roast mutton and drinking Mistress Sawyer's own brew of ale. It was an act of great generosity, for meat was still in short supply.

It seemed strange to return to the farm, to don my ordinary clothes, and to work for the rest of the day as though nothing had happened that morning to change my life for ever, although from time to time I touched the ring which lay between my breasts. When all the rest of the household had retired that night, Gideon took me in his arms, crushing me so hard I could barely breathe. With my cheek pressed against his chest, I could feel the rapid beating of his heart, matching my own.

'I shall not take you to my bed tonight, my love, though the law permits it. We must wait, even if it seems almost unbearable.'

'Aye, we must wait. I would be your wife in God's eyes first.' I tried to speak calmly, though I burned with desire to lie with him. I reached up and took his face between my hands. 'Only a week to wait.' And then I kissed him, feeling our bodies and souls burning with one flame.

Amyas Cooper arrived a day earlier than he had expected, on the evening of Saturday, the twenty-ninth day of April, riding out at once from the village to Turbary Holm. He was a serious-faced man, like Gideon about thirty years old, but already balding, so that he looked older. He greeted me warmly and the smile that lit up his face erased some of the stress left there by the trials caused him by expulsion from his parish and his present lowly occupation.

144

'I am glad Gideon has found you, Mistress Bennington,' he said. 'I knew as soon as he began to talk of you that he had discovered his true love. Few are so fortunate.'

I found it difficult to answer him, for Gideon had told me that Amyas had been in love with the daughter of the local lord in his Kentish village. The marriage had been refused and the girl married off to some friend of the father's. Within a year she was dead in childbirth. Amyas had never married. It seemed, however, that he would not allow his own sad history to mar our happiness, and I stumbled out some response, asking him to call me Mercy, and not Mistress Bennington.

Gideon had arranged for Amyas to stay with Will at the smithy, so that there should be no obvious connection between this traveller and ourselves. As Will saw to the shoeing of carters' horses, it was not unusual for him to provide a bed for a traveller, especially if the yel-hus had no room.

They went off together, and when Gideon returned he seemed a little anxious.

'Jack has heard that the Reverend Edgemont is conducting one of his hellfire services here tomorrow. I hope he is not bringing his friend, our new rector, early, else all our plans will fall apart.'

'But he was not to come until some time in May!'

'Aye, but plans change.'

All our household, except Gideon, walked to the village on Sunday morning for the service. Gideon must remain concealed, for the Reverend Edgemont knew him and might seek to have him driven away or even arrested. Since the flood, which had kept him away for weeks, the Puritan preacher had only visited us occasionally, no doubt feeling that his fine three hour sermons were as wasted on us as if he preached to a field of goats or to the empty wind. I entered the church in trepidation, fearing that this visit might mean that he was bringing the new rector.

As usual he rode up to the church door only just in time for the service. I let out my held breath in a sigh of relief, for he was alone, and I sat back to endure his sermon while thinking of other more pleasant things. When he spoke – as he always did – of the agonies of Hell, Kitty reached out for my hand. I laced my fingers through hers and gave her a reassuring smile. The seemingly interminable sermon came to an end at last, but before he dismissed us with a curt blessing, he had a message.

'You will all be relieved to hear that you will not much longer stumble in darkness, without a sound hand to guide you. Your new rector, the Reverend Webberly, will arrive sometime during this following week. I want the rectory made clean and ready for him, so see that it is done. And if any animals are still grazing on the glebe lands, they must be removed. I observe that the arable fields of the glebe land have not yet been ploughed. That too must be done at once. Reverend Webberly will instruct you on what crops he wants planted, as soon as he arrives.'

With that he muttered a brief blessing as though he did not mean it, and rode away.

As soon as he was gone, there was a burst of indignant talk.

'Clean the rectory! Plough his fields! We have no tied service to the rector!'

The village was angry. When Gideon was rector, he paid one of the village women to clean the house from time to time and do his washing. He prepared his own food, though I think he fared poorly in those days. As for ploughing, the men of the village ploughed and planted his land in return for grazing the stock on the higher ground of the glebe when the winter floods were out, an arrangement beneficial to all, which had existed for many years, through the incumbency of many rectors. And at harvest time Gideon wielded scythe and pitchfork along with everyone else.

Jack was all for refusing to comply with Edgemont's high-handed orders, but wiser counsel prevailed. We must not make a bad start with the new rector, for he had the power to make our lives miserable, if he so chose.

When I repeated Edgemont's speech to Gideon, he looked worried.

'This new man is coming so soon, this very week?'

'So he says. Though how he expects the fields to be ploughed by then, I do not know. At least nothing needs to be done at the rectory. After the last of the soldiers moved out, every nook and cranny was cleaned.'

'Perhaps the new rector will be a less difficult man than Reverend Edgemont,' Gideon said. 'We must not hasten to blame him for another man's highhandedness.'

146

'Perhaps.' I was not convinced. This man Webberly was, after all, a Puritan friend of Edgemont. 'Jack has said that Ephraim told him the people of Crowthorne are growing weary of their Puritan vicar. They are beginning to drift away from his extreme views.'

'It is not to be wondered at,' Gideon said. 'He and his like suck all the love and kindness out of Christianity and replace it with guilt and shame and sorrow. Man cannot live with so much misery. And as for teaching that every man is either saved or damned at birth, the doctrine itself is damnable, and contrary to the teaching of Our Lord.'

I thought it was good news about the villagers of Crowthorne. I had felt less hostile toward them ever since we had worked together last year to rescue our confiscated livestock, under the cover of a football game. At the time, the company of adventurers, together with the soldiers sent to enforce their drainage works, had counted on support from Crowthorne. Things were changing, especially since work had begun on the fenland surrounding the neighbouring village. The parish of Crowthorne was also covered by the charter granting our common lands. If Tom could secure it, they too would have a weapon against the drainers.

'It will be safe, do you think, for us to go ahead with the marriage tomorrow?' I asked.

'Aye,' he said with a smile. 'We shall not allow the fear of this man's arrival to put a stop to it.'

'Besides,' I said, 'the women of the village would never forgive us if all their preparations for the wedding feast were to go to waste.'

The next morning, as I dressed again in my best clothes, I saw Nehemiah through the window, driving the cows back to pasture. He must have risen very early to ensure all the farm work was done before we needed to leave for the village. There were already two calves at foot, and more due soon. I had baked the day's bread the evening before and Kitty would let the hens into the run when she collected the eggs. For today I should live like a gentlewoman, with no farm tasks to occupy me.

It had rained in the night, heavily, so that the lane was deep in mud.

'You cannot walk through that mud in your finery,' Gideon said. 'We will take Blaze.'

I was not sure that, sitting astride Blaze, I would fare much better, but Gideon and Nehemiah between them had thought of that. Gideon mounted first, and laid a folded blanket in front of the saddle, then Nehemiah lifted me up to sit sideways, with Gideon's arms around me, holding the reins. It felt very strange to be so cosseted, but I was glad that I would not arrive at my wedding mud bespattered. Gideon's arms tightened around me and he whispered into my hair.

'Are you ready?'

'Aye, my love,' I said, 'I am ready.'

As we rode down the lane I thought of last May Day. The very May blossom itself was barely open this year, and the eglantine no more than tight buds. But the birds were singing as if they cared little that the spring was late. For the first part of the way, a male blackbird followed us, winging from branch to branch in the hedgerow and singing joyfully each time he perched, until he flew off at last to his own mate.

At the church door, Jack and Abel both reached to lift me down, so I felt as light as a child – for to tell truth, Nehemiah had struggled a little in lifting me on to Blaze. I shook out my skirts, and there were Alice and Griet with a fresh crown of spring flowers, much more elaborate this time, with ribbons of blue and white fluttering from the edge. Once again the whole village was gathered, though they were a little quieter this time, for this was a service in God's name. Amyas stood at the door in his surplice, his prayerbook in his hand.

The marriage ceremony itself is quite short. It is a wonder that something which changes the lives of two people for ever is so simple and clear. We repeated our vows and this time slid the silver rings on our fingers. Amyas joined our hands together and blessed us.

I was trembling. It seemed much more solemn than the betrothal, here in the sight of God. Gideon kissed me when Amyas finished speaking, but it was a chaste kiss, then we followed him into the church, the rest of the village crowding in behind.

Amyas did not prolong the service. I think we were all a little nervous after Reverend Edgemont's visit the previous day, but he did preach a brief sermon on the blessings of matrimony in promising love and companionship for life. I gripped Gideon's hand throughout, thinking of Amyas's own lost love. The sermon ended with a few light-hearted memories of their student days in Oxford, then we sang a psalm, and it was over.

'And now the festivities begin,' Alice said, when she was able to draw me away from all the men of the village who wanted to exercise the privilege of kissing the bride. 'Let us lead them away from here to the tithe barn. Rafe, bring Gideon before he is swamped by all the matrons.'

Gideon was indeed somewhat red in the face. Never before had the women of the village had the opportunity of kissing their handsome rector, and they were seizing the chance now. *My husband*, I thought.

I was astonished when we reached the barn, for I did not believe there was so much food left in the village.

'It is too much, far too much,' I protested, but Alice and the other women merely laughed. Soon everyone was feasting happily, for none of us had eaten so well for months, though we all knew it would mean short rations for the coming weeks. Spring can bring starvation, as winter supplies run out before the new season's food is ready.

They had even made a bride cake. It was not very large, but there was just enough for everyone to have a mouthful. The rain having begun again, it was too wet outside for dancing, so we cleared away the trestle tables and danced in the barn. Robin Morton, Alice's brother, brought out his fiddle and then one of the Dutchmen shyly offered to play his as well. Johnny Samson had his pipe, so the three of them struck up a lively tune as Gideon led me out to the centre of the floor to begin the dance.

I was already dizzy with the strangeness of the day and the thought that now I was indeed married to Gideon. A generous helping of ale had contributed to my sense of floating somewhere a few feet above the ground. I had not meant to drink much, but someone kept filling my cup when I was not looking. Soon everyone was joining in the dancing, except the old and frail. Even little Rob Higson had dragged Kitty into the dance, though he was two years younger and six inches shorter. Her eyes were bright as they whirled past me.

The music grew faster, the laughter and shouting louder, so that at first we did not hear the noise from the door. Robin stopped playing, then the others. The chattering of the company died away. My back was to the door, but I felt Gideon stiffen. I twisted round to see what was amiss.

The young soldier Ben stood there, gasping and holding his side. He was red in the face and so short of breath that after the first shout he could not speak. He waved his hand desperately to the east. Gideon took his arms from around me and strode over to the door.

'What's to-do, Ben lad? Take a deep breath now, and tell us what is the matter.'

'Edgemont,' he gasped. 'And the new fellow. On the way here.'

There was a shocked silence.

'Where have you come from?' Gideon was holding Ben by the shoulder, steadying him. 'We thought you were in an army camp.'

'We was, but it's nobbut a mile t'other side of Crowthorne. We're sent back here today. Them drainers are coming back, and we've to keep you in order.'

He gave a sickly smile around at all these people who had become his friends during the winter.

'But what has that to do with the Reverend Edgemont?'

'Nothing. But we was stopped in Crowthorne for our dinner, and there was a whisper going round that a wedding was to be held here today. Mebbe someone told their preacher, mebbe it's just chance, but he and the new man, they've set out to come here.'

He looked round wildly. 'If they catch you–'

'Have you run all the way?'

'Aye. I had to warn you.'

Already the women were gathering up the remains of the feast, shovelling food and dishes together hugger-mugger into their baskets. Toby pushed past Ben to roll a cask of ale out into the street and along it to the smithy, which was nearest. After a moment of panic, everyone was clearing away all signs of our wedding celebration.

150

Gideon turned to Amyas. 'Was everything left as before in the church?'

'Aye,' he said. 'I even removed the stubs of the candles.'

'Then you'd best go back to Will's and keep out of sight.'

'Aye.' Amyas laid his hand on my arm. 'I am sorry it must end like this, Mercy. I may not see you again, for I shall be away at dawn tomorrow.'

I took his hand and pressed it between both of mine. 'I shall be grateful to you all the days of my life. Without you, we could not have been wed.'

He hurried off to the smithy. All around us people were rushing about, piling the trestle tables back against the sides of the barn, sweeping any fallen crumbs into dark corners. All the children had been hustled away home, many of them crying.

'Gideon! Mercy! What are you doing still here? You must go! Anyone may see that you are the bride and bridesman.' It was Jack, urging us forward out of the barn. 'Here's Nehemiah with your horse.'

Gideon leapt into the saddle and reached a hand down to me. 'Put your foot on mine,' he said.

I hitched up my skirts and did as I was bid. Jack seized my other foot and heaved me up. I thought I would pitch head first over Blaze's back and land in the mud on the other side, but after a scramble I managed to regain my position sitting in front of the saddle, though the blanket had fallen to the ground. By now it was raining hard, so when Jack thrust the blanket up to me I wrapped it around my shoulders to protect Mary Dillingworth's shawl.

'Where is Kitty?' I cried. 'We cannot leave her behind.'

'Alice has sent her home,' Jack said. 'Nehemiah will follow when we have all straight.'

'Ben,' I said. 'Take care of Ben. God be praised, he came in time to warn us.'

'We must go, Mercy,' Gideon said. 'Now.' He turned Blaze's head to the lane and suddenly we were flying along, through the rain, great gouts of mud flung up behind us from the horse's hooves.

I was suddenly frightened. Everything had happened so quickly. It was like slipping from a joyful dream into a nightmare. We were going so fast I thought I might slip off. One hand clutched the blanket, with the other I grabbed hold of Blaze's mane, but it was slippery with the wet and offered little support. I began to feel myself sliding.

'Gideon, I'm falling!' My shriek seemed to fly away and be left behind us, but he must have heard me, for he took one hand off the reins and gripped me firmly about the waist.

Ahead I could just make out through the sheeting rain a faint glimmer of light from the farm. Mistress Morton must have lit candles against the early dark brought on by the storm. As we drew nearer, I saw Kitty just running from the gate to the door. At least she was safe, although she would be soaked from head to toe.

Gideon took his arm from my waist to lean over and unlatch the gate. Blaze pushed his way through, as anxious as we were to escape the storm. He slithered to a stop beside the door, breathing heavily, a line of foam on his lips. It had been a hard ride, carrying two of us at that speed through the clogged earth of the lane. Gideon leapt down and held out his arms to take me by the waist. I let myself slide down the horse's wet side and my husband held me close.

'You are safe now,' he said.

I laughed a little shakily. 'I hope every one in the village is so. This is a wedding no one will ever forget.'

'I will not, for one,' he said, and I saw that he did not look fearful. He seemed almost to be excited. Then he drew me close into his arms, with the rain half drowning us, and I forgot everything else.

Somewhere, a blackbird was singing. The square of window showed dark grey, barely discernible from the surrounding wall, yet already a blackbird was singing. I have always loved blackbirds, for they seem to delight in the music they make, the first of the birds to burst into song before ever there is a sign that the sun is returning to grace the earth. And in the evening, long after the sun has sunk below the horizon, I will hear a blackbird somewhere about the farm, still singing as though life itself is too short to express the joy which their frail bodies can barely contain. I wondered whether it was the same blackbird who had followed us on the way to our wedding, and who now sang a triumphant epithalamion over our marriage bed.

152

Gideon was still asleep. He lay on his side, turned towards me, his hand resting on my waist, his breathing quiet and steady, after a night of such passion that I still felt breathless. Yet now he looked young and vulnerable, as he had when I had cared for him after he was beaten nearly to death. My heart twisted at the remembrance. His hair had grown long while he was away and a lock fell across his face, stirring slightly as he breathed. As gently as I could, I brushed it back.

Not gently enough. His arm slid round my waist and he drew me to him, though his eyes remained closed.

'I did not mean to wake you,' I whispered.

He smiled, but did not open his eyes. 'I was awake. I wondered how long you would listen to the blackbird.'

'He is still singing.'

'Aye. Let him rejoice, for my love is mine and I am hers, and none shall part us.'

He opened his eyes. Our faces were but inches apart. 'Is all well with you, my beloved, on this, the first morning of our wedded life?'

I ran my fingers down his back, feeling the muscles beneath the skin and the curve of his spine.

'All is well.'

I kissed him softly on the lips, and felt my whole body tremble.

'Ah, Mercy, you set me on fire!'

He raised himself on his elbow and looked down at me. The lock of hair fell forward again, and I reached up to brush it back, but never had the chance.

We had decided to remain quietly at Turbary Holm while the Reverend Webberly made himself known to the village. Sooner or later he was certain to come to the farm, if he was conscientious about his parish duties. Somehow we must prevent news of Gideon's presence reaching the Reverend Edgemont in Crowthorne.

'I think I must change my name,' Gideon said. 'If word spreads outside the village that one Gideon Clarke is living at Turbary Holm, we may expect retribution. What do you say to my taking my mother's unmarried name?'

'Perhaps it would be wise.' I was just growing accustomed to thinking of myself as Mistress Clarke. Who would I now become?

'What was her name?'

'Margaret Chandler.'

Gideon rarely spoke of his parents, who had died of the plague within days of each other, just a few weeks after he had gone up to Oxford. I reached out and touched his arm, leaving a powdering of flour on his sleeve, for I was making pastry.

'Very well,' I said, 'we shall be Master and Mistress Chandler as far as the outer world is concerned, but Master and Mistress Clarke in our hearts. We must alert all the village.'

'If we have not already been mentioned by name to the new rector,' he said. 'I fear we lay an unfair burden on our neighbours, forcing them to keep our secret. Even the children.'

'They will be glad to keep our secret. They have not forgotten little Huw's christening and what you suffered for holding the service. You could have died. Nor have they forgotten all you did during the flood. As for the children, they have learned to watch their tongues. Even little Rob Higson did not give us away to the drainers last year, despite their striking him.'

'I know they will do their best,' Gideon said, 'but we churchmen have a way of wheedling things out of people.' He gave a self-mocking smile. 'I am worried I may put you in danger.'

'We are one flesh now, dear heart. You cannot shake me off, try how you may.'

So we became known as Master and Mistress Chandler, as far as outsiders were concerned. The Reverend Webberly, it soon became clear, was an outsider. Gideon now attended church with the rest of the family on Sundays, for it would soon have been noticed, had he stayed away. He allowed his hair to remain rather long, where before he had worn it quite short, and I altered some of my father's clothes to fit him, so that he dressed like a yeoman farmer instead of a gentleman. They were, in any case, more practical for his new life. He soon came to like the cows, but had little time for the sheep. I saw that when it was the season for shearing, I should need to ask for help once again from Jack and Toby, for Nehemiah and I between us would not be able to manage.

I was very frightened the first time we attended church with the Reverend Webberly conducting the service. Gideon turned up his collar and wore a woollen cap pulled well down until we entered the church. As the leading family in the parish, we occupied the front pew, directly under the gaze of the rector when he preached, but I soon realised he was a man too self absorbed to pay us any attention. A Puritan out of the same mould as Edgemont, he was perhaps less violent in his sermons, although they lasted quite as long. The entire village had been told of our assumed name and soon made perhaps a little too much of using it as often as possible within Webberly's hearing, but I do not think he noticed.

The days passed peacefully enough. After the near disaster at our wedding celebrations, life settled down to its regular pattern of the farming year. We were all worried that the yield of the crops this year would be meagre, for the weather continued very cold and wet, more like November than early summer, so the crops grew thin and poor. The Dutchmen worked hard at their vegetable growing in their specially raised beds, rich in manure and covered with straw against the cold. Many in the village laughed at this, saying that carrots and leeks and cabbages did not need to be tucked up in bed like sick maidens, but in truth the vegetables did grow well. Hans invited me to examine his own plot.

'See now, Mercy,' he said. (I had at last persuaded him to call me Mercy.) 'Put your hand in here.'

He lifted part of the blanket of straw and urged me to push my hand into the soil between the rows of tightly packed cabbages. My hands were cold and chapped, and I had no wish to be thrusting them into cold wet earth, but I did as I was bid.

'But it is warm!' I said. Indeed the soil was far warmer than the surrounding air.

'It is the manure in the soil,' he explained. 'As it . . . dies?' He looked at me, questioning.

'Rots down,' I said.

'Rots down, it gives off heat. In our big farms at home we can grow fruits in heated buildings, like–' He searched for the words. 'Like the south. Italy. Southern France. Even in our cold Nederlands. Peaches. Grapes.'

'Could you do that here?'

He shrugged and smiled. 'Too much money. Only the big landowners. You keep stoves burning all the time for heat.'

I could not imagine us having such a heated building on Turbary Holm, just for early and rare fruits, when we could hardly afford to heat the house unless we could cut turf freely again. Nevertheless I was impressed by the Dutchmen's vegetable beds. When a very late frost blasted much of the crops in the fields, those vegetables remained safe and warm in their heated beds.

Tom wrote from London to say that he and his friend Anthony had paid a visit to Lincoln's Inn and tackled the lawyer James Blakiston, who had refused to help them find the charter, even revealing that he was retained by a company of adventurers, though Tom did not know whether it was those who were trying to steal our land. These companies operated in much secrecy, so that it was difficult to know who they were. They instructed men like van Slyke and other surveyors through 'an intermediary, so I suppose even he did not know who they were. If the case ever came to court, this could prove a difficulty for us.

Nothing had yet been seen in the village of either Piet van Slyke or any of the men who worked for him, but it could only be a matter of time. News trickled in from Crowthorne. Van Slyke had been surveying the fenland over to the north of Crowthorne. He had discovered how their pumping mill had been stopped at the time of the flood and it seemed they had not been too gentle about it. Not understanding how the mechanism worked, they had smashed it with heavy hammers and broken the framework of the sails. Van Slyke, it appeared, was bent on retribution. Will, who had some knowledge of simple machinery, had stopped the pump on our land without damaging it, although he told us that he had removed one small but essential piece, which meant that the pump could not be started again until it was replaced. We had done no damage to the sails. The flood and the winter weather had accomplished that for us. I did not know how van Slyke could have expected them to survive without regular visits, but perhaps he had been occupied in other drainage schemes, in the Low Countries or elsewhere in England. In any case, the flood would have kept him at bay for weeks.

Ben had been followed back by the rest of the soldiers who had been billeted in the village and who had shared the time of the flood with us in the church. The day after our wedding, our own five soldiers returned to Turbary Holm, and I was glad that Kitty was well again, for the feeding of such a large household took up many hours and put a strain on our supplies of provisions. Nehemiah taught the soldiers the art of trapping eels, although they did not greatly care for eating them, and all the men about the farm, including Gideon, went wild fowling. The birds were fewer than usual, however, due to the cold weather and the lack of food. Those they did bring home were thin and wasted.

I had planted my own small vegetable plot as usual near the house, but everything was very slow to grow. Perhaps next year I would ask Hans to show me how to grow them the Dutch way. In the meantime, to augment our food supplies, I traded one of last year's fleeces with Hans in return for a supply of whatever vegetables he had ready for the next six weeks. Griet began at once to spin the wool, which she would use to knit warm clothes for the family in readiness for the winter.

'I shall ask Hans to build me a loom,' she said, one day when she had come to collect the three pullets I had promised her, in return for her help when Kitty was ill. 'He has never made one, but Ned Broadley has said he will show him. He has some ends of wood Hans can use. Then I shall be able to weave blankets. Now, we make do with old sacking.'

I would have liked to offer her blankets, but with my full house, I had none to spare.

'Little by little, you will make a home,' I said, passing her a piece of the spice cake I had made that morning. We were sitting in the kitchen, close to the cooking fire, for although it was early June it was too cold to sit outside.

'Jack says that the drainers are coming to the village tomorrow.' She blushed as she spoke, for it was awkward for her, speaking of the scheme which had brought her here and at the same time wrought so much damage for us.

I stiffened. Van Slyke would undoubtedly be angry when he discovered just how much damage had been done to his drainage works. Most of it was due to the flood, but we had assisted a little in the weeks since the flood had gone down, shovelling earth back into the ditches to block them, ensuring that the Fen returned to its ancient ways, absorbing the water from the higher ground and providing us with food and fuel. That very day Gideon and Nehemiah had gone out to the moss, where Gideon was to have his first lesson in the correct way to lift peat for fuel.

When they returned late in the afternoon with a barrow load of peat, I went out to the yard to meet them and told them what Griet had said about van Slyke. As Jasper wound about our legs, Nehemiah spat contemptuously on the ground. He had good reason to hate the men who had cracked his skull, stolen his eels, and burned down his home.

'Let them try their tricks again,' he said, 'and we shall be waiting for them.'

'Still no word from Tom about the charter.' Gideon frowned. 'We do not want to put ourselves too much in the wrong. It could jeopardise our case in court.'

I knew he would not be in favour of violence, but with men like van Slyke, sometimes violence is the only language they understand. Last year I had been an unmarried girl and could join the men in attacking the drainage works. Now, as a married woman, I might need to be more circumspect.

'I wonder whether we should approach Sir John again,' I said slowly. 'Perhaps if I went to see him–'

'Surely you do not want to set foot in that house again!' Gideon stared at me. 'After your treatment by the Dillingworths.'

'I am not sure. I think someone should speak to him. Tell him that we are now looking for the charter ourselves and urge him to help us to take the case to court. It would be too risky for you to go. He might recognise you. As Tom's sister, I think perhaps I should go.'

'I do not like the idea of you going there, to be insulted.' He took my hand and gripped it hard.

'I am not afraid,' I said, though I was not as brave as I sounded. It would be unpleasant to return to the manor house, which I had left so thankfully before. 'Let us see first what van Slyke intends. Then we may decide.'

There was not long to wait. The following day the Dutch surveyor returned with a large group of his men – Dutchmen like himself, a few of the Scots prisoners, and some disreputable Englishmen who were jeered through the village. I had gone to the village myself to see just how strong was the party of the enemy.

In a body we followed the men in silence as they made their way to the medland where they had dug their first ditch, running from the Fen to join Baker's Lode. At the junction they had installed a sluice, now shattered, partly by some of our own actions, partly by the flood.

At the far end of the ditch, by the marsh, the pumping mill had been built on the spot where Hannah's cottage had once stood. It was powered by wind, like a grain mill, but instead of producing flour for nourishing daily bread, it drove a pump whose function was to suck the water out of the Fen, robbing fish and eels and waterfowl of their homes and turning the precious peat into useless dust.

Still in silence we stood at the edge of our medland while van Slyke strode about, growing angrier and angrier, swearing in English and Dutch. Our beasts grazing there took fright and retreated to the hedge at the far side of the medland, till they could go no further. Finally he turned on us.

'You will pay for this, you filthy peasants!' He was so angry that spittle flew from his mouth. 'All this damage, this work destroyed, I will see that you pay for it! My masters will take you to court and strip you of everything you own, down to the shirts off your backs.'

Jack took a step forward, but I grabbed his arm and shook my head.

'Not here,' I whispered. 'Let him rant. What can he do? It is clear most of the damage was done by the flood and the winter storms. Be patient. We will defeat him yet.'

Jack was breathing heavily, but he nodded.

'At least he will find we have not smashed his pumping machine, unlike the people of Crowthorne.' He gave a small smile. 'Though Will promises it will not work, without the piece he has removed, and it will take them some time to discover why.'

As van Slyke made his way to the mill, we melted away, each to our own homes. The settlers had stayed well away from the confrontation, for they were in an unenviable position. I wondered what would happen when the adventurers' bailiff came to collect their rents for the plots of land they no longer occupied. That might mean more trouble.

Back at the farm I hurried to catch up with my neglected tasks, but an hour or so later the door to the kitchen was thrown open and van Slyke walked in, without so much as a by your leave. My mother was spinning, Kitty was chopping onions and I had just hung the pot for the midday soup over the fire. Gideon was sitting on my father's chair, prising off his boots.

'You!' Van Slyke pointed at Gideon. 'You, Bennington, you are behind all this trouble!'

He started toward Gideon, but I moved from the fire and blocked his way.

'Meneer van Slyke,' I said coldly, 'you enter our home with little courtesy. In your country, do you not knock and wait to be invited to enter?'

He stopped and glared at me.

'You! You hoyden, you are no better than your brother.'

He pointed again at Gideon.

'That is my husband, Master Chandler. If you seek my brother, Master Bennington, he is gone to London.'

Gideon stood up. Even without his boots he was a good handspan taller than van Slyke. He laid his hands on my shoulders and moved me gently to one side before stepping so close to van Slyke that the man backed away a step.

'You have invaded our home without leave, fellow,' Gideon said, taking another step forward, 'and you have insulted my wife. Your behaviour is unpardonable. Get out.'

In his anger, Gideon sounded more aristocratic than I had ever heard him. I was not sure whether van Slyke's ear was attuned to English voices, but he could not mistake the tone. He muttered something in Dutch, which it was as well we could not understand, and turned to the door.

As he went out, he flung over his shoulder, 'You will hear more of this. I will have the law on you.'

Just before he moved away, Seth and Col, on their way to the kitchen for their midday meal, came near to colliding with him in the yard.

'Is this man troubling you, Mistress Mercy?' Col said.

'Do your duty, damn you!' van Slyke said. 'You are here to ensure that these rogues do not interfere with our work.' With that he stormed off.

The two soldiers came in, looking somewhat embarrassed. Gideon laughed and clapped Col on the shoulder. 'Well spoken, Col. Come and take your dinner.'

Later, when Gideon and I were alone, I said, 'I do not think I should delay any longer. Tomorrow I will visit Sir John and urge him to support us. That man means trouble.'

Chapter Eight
Tom

After our visit to James Blakiston at Lincoln's Inn, I needed to rest, for the long walk had exhausted me. I had also rubbed the skin of my stump raw, so that I was obliged to remove my wooden prop and resort to two crutches again. I sat in one of our cushioned chairs with my eyes closed, too tired and in too much pain to think clearly. Anthony had papers to prepare for his senior, so he spent the rest of the day in the office working on them, while I alternately dozed and fretted. I had work to do for Bencher Whittaker, but I had not the heart for it.

The meeting with Blakiston had left me confused, and I wished we could have questioned him more closely, but it would have contravened the accepted courtesies between barristers. Who were the adventurers for whom he was acting? Were they the company bent on stealing our land, or some other company altogether? The Fens cover a large area, from Essex northwards, even touching the southern parts of Yorkshire. The company he represented might be carrying out their unscrupulous schemes as far away as Cambridgeshire, where my grandfather had led the resistance to their activities nearly twenty years before. In any case, why had Sir John Dillingworth engaged Blakiston on the other side of the quarrel? Was it simply because the Dillingworths had employed him before?

That seemed to make little sense. Had Blakiston already been employed by Sir John when he undertook work for the drainers? Or was it the other way about? In either case, it would mean a conflict of interests, not merely if he were to deal with Anthony, as Blakiston himself had pointed out, but in dealing with two such opposed clients of his own. Was Sir John aware of these other clients? Perhaps Blakiston had kept him in the dark. Or was Blakiston playing a double game, as Anthony had suggested, hoping to use information or evidence from one side to benefit the other? It resembled one of my two-handed tasks for Bencher Whittaker, arguing first for one side and then for the other, except that this was no student exercise. The fortunes of real people were in danger here. If Blakiston was engaged in some kind of treachery, we would be the ones to suffer. *Had he already found and hidden the charter?*

Anthony delivered the papers he had prepared to his senior and returned to our chambers in the late afternoon.

'I have sent for a meal from the Peacock,' he said as he flung himself down in a chair. 'I think neither of us is in the mood for dinner in Hall tonight.'

'Hardly,' I agreed. 'What did you make of James Blakiston?'

Anthony clasped his hands behind his head. 'Arrogant. Supercilious. Deceitful. Sly.'

'But does he have the charter?'

'Like you, I suspect he has. Or else he knows where it is. But he has not chosen to use it yet.'

'The only way he can use it,' I said slowly, 'is either to hand it over to the company of adventurers who covet our land, so they can withhold it if we take them to court. Or else he can destroy it.'

'I wonder.' Anthony got up and poured us each a cup of beer. 'I think for any lawyer, even a corrupt one, as I suspect Blakiston to be, the destruction of a royal charter would take a great deal of courage. What if he should be found out? I think he would be debarred from ever practising at law again. Nay, I think he is more likely to conceal it.'

'But where?' I sipped my beer. I realised that I needed it, as I needed the dinner Anthony had ordered.

'In his chambers? But then one of his clerks or his junior might come across it. Or else . . . I wonder.'

'What?'

'Do they not say that the best place to hide something is where it is least suspected, in plain view? If you wish to hide a book, place it between many other books on a shelf. If you wish to hide a paper, slip it into a pile of similar papers.'

'But a charter?'

'Amongst other old parchment scrolls. It would need to be somewhere he could lay his hand on it when he wanted it.'

He thought for a moment.

'Perhaps amongst the old parchments in Lincoln's Inn library? Their library is better organised than ours. While we still kept our books in one of the Bencher's rooms, they had a separate building for their books and manuscripts. Someone told me they have had a library building for more than a century and a half. I wonder–'

He began to pace about, but before he could say what was on his mind, the servant arrived with our dinner. When we had satisfied the first pangs of hunger – for I realised that I had eaten nothing since early morning – Anthony wiped his mouth on his napkin and took a long drink of his beer.

'Supposing he has hidden the charter amongst the old scrolls kept in their library,' he said. 'I expect few people need to consult them, and he could lay his hand on it whenever he wished.'

'That is little help to us,' I said.

'Bear with me. My senior has another case involving ancient land laws, some of which date from before the Normans came. Some were still cited several centuries later. He is something of a scholar, my senior, and loves finding these old cases, whether they are of any practical use or not. I think I might persuade him that I could make a search in the Lincoln's Inn library, to see whether there might be anything of interest to him there. He could gain us permission to use their library. Now that you have become an assistant to our librarian, that would be reason enough for me to say I needed your help.'

'It might be worth a try.'

'Of course it is.'

'What if Blakiston should catch us there?'

'We would be there quite legitimately. The Inns do cooperate, when it is in their interests to do so. Besides, we could choose a time when he is in court. That should not be too difficult to discover.'

It was agreed, therefore, that Anthony would try to arrange for us to visit Lincoln's Inn library some time the following week, after I had seen Gilbert Bolton on Monday afternoon, to try the mechanical leg. In the meantime I must complete my task for Bencher Whittaker and serve my two days in the library. We were progressing slowly with our catalogue of the books, but there was work enough to keep me occupied for many weeks yet.

On Monday I attended my usual session with Bencher Whittaker, having completed my assigned task with more enthusiasm now that Anthony and I had something definite planned. We were to go to Lincoln's Inn the following day. Anthony had been able to discover that Blakiston would be in the Court of Chancery, in a case that would last most of the day.

As I was leaving Bencher Whittaker's chambers, I asked, 'Master Thirkettle and I were discussing a theoretical case. If someone were to conceal or destroy a royal charter, what crime would that constitute?'

He tapped his fingers on his desk and gazed out of the window.

'It is not something I have ever come across.'

'Might it be lèse-majesté? A form of treason?'

'Indeed, it might count as such. An interesting point. I shall need to think about it.'

So, I thought, as I made my way back to our chambers, it is probably not something Blakiston would risk.

I could not travel to Bucklersbury with the wine carter this time, for he would have gone early in the morning, but he had agreed to collect me for the homeward trip. In order to reach Gilbert Bolton's shop, I was obliged to hire a man to take me. I had not the coin for one of the hackney carriages the gentry used in their journeys between the City and their homes along the Strand, but I found a jobbing carter who was prepared to convey me for a tenth of the cost. When I stepped inside the shop at the sign of the Golden Ram, the surgeon was already there, eating bread and cheese with one hand and turning over the pages of Paré's book with the other.

'Ah, Master Bennington!' he cried, leaping up. A shower of breadcrumbs spilled on to the floor from his lap. 'Come through, come through. The leg is ready for you to try.'

He watched me keenly as I hobbled into the back room, using just one crutch. In the days since our walk to Lincoln's Inn my skin had healed again, but I had also added some extra padding at the top of the prop, a soft folded cloth Goodwife Gorley had given me. I had discovered that her fierce manner was no more than a pretence. Underneath it all she reminded me – although she was much younger – of Hannah Greene, who had comforted us after our scrapes and tumbles in childhood.

'Good,' Bolton said. 'Your balance is much improved, I see. Now let us examine the muscles of that left leg.'

I noticed that he always spoke of it as a 'leg', although less than half of it remained. I must learn to do the same, and stop thinking of it as a pitiful stump of the leg I had once possessed.

Again I sat on the bench, after removing the wooden leg and my breeches. I had not worn a left stocking, but Bolton had told me to bring one. He leaned over and began probing my left thigh with firm but gentle fingers.

'Excellent,' he said. 'It has been – what? – two weeks? And already the muscles are stronger. Can you feel it?'

'Aye,' I said. 'At first I found it very difficult to lift or move the wooden leg, but it is much easier now.'

'This is what I hoped. You will need to use those muscles even more with the mechanical leg. Let me see you clench and relax the muscles of your thigh.'

At first I was not sure I could do as he asked, but after a few minutes he said, 'Imagine that your whole leg is still there. Stretch out your leg. Point your toe. Then draw your leg back, with your knee bent.'

I looked at him as if he were mad. Then I remembered than when my leg was first amputated, I kept imagining it was still there. My foot would itch, so that I longed to scratch it. Yet the foot was not there. I would feel a pain in my calf, but my calf was gone. Even now, usually when I was in that dim land between waking and sleep, I would think I could feel my leg. So I did what he asked. I closed my eyes and moved the leg which no longer existed, while he laid his hand on my thigh. When I opened my eyes, I saw that he was beaming.

'You see! You still have the memory of your leg.'

166

'It's true,' I said, 'I sometimes feel that it is there, but why? Is it some kind of devil's deception?'

He gave a scornful snort. 'What nonsense! The human body is God's most beautiful and complex design. This memory which remains when a part of the body is lost bears witness to that beauty. We do not yet known why it is so, or how it happens, but we can make use of it. I have seen a man who lost a hand use a mechanical one to pick up and wield a sword, guide his horse by the reins, lift a cup to his lips. What you will learn to do is much simpler, just as a leg is much simpler than a hand.'

He removed a cloth from something which was lying on his workbench. It startled me, for it looked much more like a severed human leg than the metal ones displayed in his shop windows. I realised, of course, that this was because the outer layer was made of some soft leather, probably calf skin. He lifted the leg carefully and brought it over to where I sat.

'I have made this to the exact measurements of your right leg. It is braced within by a metal tube in sections, replacing the bones which give rigidity to the human leg. The foot is weighted, as I think that will give you more stability.'

He placed the foot in my hand, so I could feel the weight.

'The knee and ankle are jointed, as you have seen in my metal legs and in Paré's illustrations. You will manipulate them partly by flexing your thigh muscles and drawing on your memory, and partly by the way you lean forward and back.'

He moved the joints of the leg so I could see. The leather, being soft and pliable, moved quite easily.

'The foot is not yet perfected,' he said. 'When we walk, we use our toes more than we realise. Watch my foot.'

He discarded his shoes and walked slowly up and down the room so that I could see the movement of the toes. He pulled on his shoes again, but left the laces untied. I was still holding the leg and saw that the toes were made in one simple piece, hinged to the rest of the foot. He sat down on the bench.

'I am sure I can improve on the toes, but I want you to try this for now. We will practise until your carter arrives, then I want you to practise further – shall we say for another week? – before I see you again. I would like you to send me a message every day or two to tell me how you are faring, how well the leg is performing. Can you do that?'

'Of course,' I said, although I was feeling a little overcome by all of this.

'And if you have any problems, any at all, you must return and I will try to solve them.'

With his help, I strapped on the leg, which fitted much like the wooden one, though the leather meant that it was more pleasant to handle. I took up my crutch and stood up, somewhat unsteadily.

'Good,' Bolton said. 'Now try a step or two.'

I took a single step with my good leg, managed to swing the new leg forward to take a second step. Toppled forward and fell flat on my face.

'Oh, my dear sir!' Bolton was kneeling on the floor, peering at me anxiously. 'Are you hurt!'

The crutch had struck me an unpleasant blow on the chin, and I had twisted my right leg slightly, but I shook my head as best I could, with my face on the floor, a few inches from his dangling shoe laces.

'Is the leg broken?' I gasped, for the unexpected fall had winded me.

'Nay, I do not think so. Let me help you up.'

When he had me sitting on the bench again, he suddenly struck his forehead with the heel of his hand.

'I am a fool! I forgot to tell you to bring a left shoe!'

I looked at him blankly. 'I have no left shoes in London. What I had, I did not bring with me. Why do I need a shoe?'

'I have tried to be too clever,' he said with a groan. 'Usually we make a mechanical leg so that it is complete in itself, but I have made this so that it is an exact pair to your own right leg. I hoped to make it possible to conceal the mechanical leg from view, because so many – like you – feel ashamed of an amputation. Though, I may say, there is nothing to be ashamed of.'

'But, a shoe?' I prompted.

'Without a shoe, you are unbalanced, so naturally you fell. Let us remove your right shoe and try again.'

I was not sure if he was proposing that I should walk about London with my right foot bare, but I did as he asked and removed my shoe. This time when I stood, I felt much steadier. With great care I took one step with my right foot, then swung the artificial leg forward as I had swung the wooden one. I did not fall. I took several more steps until I reached the opposite wall, when I hopped around until I was facing back the way I had come and managed to reach the bench again.

'Excellent,' Bolton said. 'Now your balance is right, but you must not swing this leg like the wooden one. It has a jointed knee. Try to imagine it bending. Lean down on it slightly, and forward, as you step. It should bend.'

I tried hard, but the leg would not bend.

'I think I have the mechanism too tight.' Bolton inserted a thin probe into the knee joint through a small aperture in the leather and turned something. 'Try again now.'

This time the leg flapped loosely, like the limb of a cloth doll.

'Too much,' he said, adjusting the joint once more.

Now I felt the knee flex slightly as I walked. It was a strange sensation which almost caused me to lose my balance, but I managed to reach the other side of the room without falling.

'I think the ankle is still a little tight.'

Bolton made some adjustments to the ankle joint until he was satisfied, and I practised walking up and down the room. I still leaned heavily on the crutch, but the leg felt a little less strange.

'Now try sitting down and getting up.'

When I sat down, the leg remained sticking out straight, so that I took hold of the knee and bent it with my hands. Getting up was more difficult and I nearly tipped forward on to my face again, but by pushing myself upright with my crutch I was able to regain my balance and took a few steps.

'That is good. You are growing accustomed to it, but you must practise, practise, practise.'

'I cannot walk about London with my right foot bare,' I said.

'Nay, you cannot. You must have a left shoe made to match your right shoe. Until then . . .' he took off his own left shoe. 'Our feet are much the same size. I think this will fit the mechanical leg, and the heel is the same height as yours, so you will maintain your balance.'

'You cannot give me your shoe.'

'I am merely lending it, until you have a shoe made. I have another pair of shoes. Did you bring your left stocking?'

'Aye.' I pulled it out of my pocket. 'The foot is cut away, so that I could roll it up.'

'It will suffice for now.'

He helped me pull the stocking over the mechanical leg and then put on my breeches, before I put my right shoe on again and we fitted his shoe on to the mechanical leg. The two unmatched shoes looked strange, but for the rest, if you did not peer too closely, it nearly seemed as though I had two sound legs again. Despite the ache in my back and a throbbing in my left thigh, I began to feel a stirring of excitement. I would always walk awkwardly. I would never run again. Yet I might almost begin to look like a normal man.

'Shall I ever be able to discard the crutch?' I asked.

He smiled. 'Much will depend on how well you learn to manage the leg. Some have walked with an iron leg, but found it tiring. My hope is that this design will come nearer to replacing what you have lost, but you must practise, practise. In the meantime, I shall work on a better design for the foot.'

When the carter arrived to take me back to Gray's Inn, his eyes widened as I walked out of Bolton's shop, apparently on two sound legs. I saw his hand twitch as he came near to crossing himself, a gesture that would have had him seized as a Catholic.

'God's bones, sir!' He said, looking furtively from me to Bolton, who stood in the doorway, watching to see how well I managed the climb into the cart.

'Nay,' I said, as I heaved myself awkwardly up. 'Merely a better artificial limb.'

When I reached Gray's Inn, I was glad to see that the gatekeeper Potter was deep in conversation with one of the clerks and did not glance my way. I had no wish to discuss my new appearance with him. I was disappointed that Anthony was not in our chambers, but at least it meant that I could practise walking back and forth, in and out of the rooms, sitting down on my bed, on chairs, and getting up again. I was still awkward and I thought I should always need a crutch, but I found I did not lurch quite so much when I walked. Sitting and standing smoothly were very difficult.

170

Anthony was amazed when he arrived, and wanted to examine the mechanism of the leg.

'Not possible, I am afraid,' I said. 'It is all concealed inside the leather sheath. If I can remember, I might be able to draw you a rough sketch.'

I did my best, but I am no artist, nor could I remember the Paré illustration in detail.

'Something like this,' I said, handing Anthony the paper. 'It is very ingenious, and supports me much better than the wooden leg, but I am not sure how well I shall be able to manage it.'

'Astonishing,' Anthony said, as I did my best to demonstrate the leg. 'And shall you be able to keep it?'

'I do not know. But as it was made to my precise measurements, I cannot suppose it would be of use to anyone else.'

The next morning we made our way once again to Lincoln's Inn. As Anthony wanted to spare me the fatigue of walking both ways, he persuaded my friend the carter to go a little out of his way and carry us as far as Chancery Lane before he set off for the City. I was grateful for his forethought. I had spent longer than I should the previous evening following Gilbert Bolton's instructions to 'Practise! Practise!'

The library at Lincoln's Inn was impressive. The librarian assured us that the building had been erected in the fifteenth century and the Inn had been accumulating books and manuscripts ever since. It would be some while yet before we could match this comprehensive collection at Gray's, though the recent legacies by former Members (perhaps prompted by comparison with Lincoln's Inn) would go some way to improving our literary collection.

Aware of this difference, the librarian did not seem at all surprised that we might wish to consult his superior resources. He showed us the great ledgers in which all the books were recorded, and which were arranged very like the ones Master Hansen and I were creating. The books were shelved according to the subjects they dealt with, and it seemed relatively easy to locate them.

'My senior has sent me to search through your oldest records,' Anthony said. 'The earliest centuries of the Normans, and anything you may have from before their invasion. These will

171

almost certainly be scrolls rather than folios. How do you catalogue and arrange those?'

'As you know,' the librarian gave me a brief nod, as one engaged on a similar task, 'scrolls are particularly difficult to accommodate. They cannot be shelved like books, and they have no spines to make them easy to locate. Like the Rolls House, we keep them stored horizontally, stacked up in divided shelves like open boxes. Insofar as we can, we group related material together, but it is a nightmare, a true nightmare. I have suggested to the Benchers that we should donate them to the Rolls House and rid ourselves of the problem, but they wish to retain them in our own library.'

'We shall just have to do the best we can,' Anthony said. 'If you would be good enough to direct us?'

'They are stored in this room at the back,' the librarian said. 'Follow me.'

Anthony winked at me, and we followed.

My first reaction was dismay. Lincoln's Inn's collection of parchment scrolls filled shelf after shelf, with nothing to distinguish one from another but an occasional seal which had been left to dangle over the edge of a shelf. They were piled up about six deep in each box-like compartment, with nothing showing but the tattered edges of the rolled up parchments, some with fragments hanging loose. No one ever dusted or swept here, so some of the parchment fragments lay scattered about the floor. I wondered whether mice presented a problem.

Anthony seemed undaunted, but I supposed his searches in the Rolls House had prepared him for this. The librarian had carried in the ledger recording the scrolls and set it on a table for us, before returning to his work in the other room.

'This will take us days!' I murmured in dismay to Anthony. 'Although . . . look, this whole section in covered in cobwebs. Thick cobwebs. No one had disturbed them for some time. I think we may ignore those.'

'You are right,' he said. 'At least a third of the shelves are in a like state. This section here, someone has been consulting these. And that section over to the right. You start looking at those and I'll search these. All you need to do is unroll the top section of each scroll and check the first few lines.'

He had brought a small notebook with him, to keep up the pretence that he was looking for information for his senior. He laid this down beside the ledger and as he worked his way through the scrolls he made occasional notes. I started on the section he had pointed out and began lifting out the scrolls and checking them, one by one. It seemed to me, although they were not covered with cobwebs, that they looked as though they had not been disturbed for a long time.

I had made little use of my Latin in recent years, but it had been well drilled into us at school, while at Cambridge many of our books were in Latin. The Latin formula at the beginning of each scroll was easy enough to read. Almost all were legal documents of some kind, as was only to be expected in the library of one of the Inns of Court, so their opening words followed a standard form, the type of case, the parties involved and the year of the current reigning monarch.

Time passed slowly as we worked our way through the only sections which appeared to have been searched at some recent date. A drowsy bluebottle buzzed in a corner and occasionally made a sluggish flight from one side of the room to the other. Once it made a heavy landing on my face, startling me. I batted it away in disgust. Although there were few or no cobwebs amongst the scrolls I was examining, there was dust everywhere and as we disturbed it, it began to float about in the air, so that we both suffered bouts of coughing.

I found a few documents from the time of the first two Henrys, and a few dealing with land transactions, but no charter granting rights in common land. I did turn up one scroll from the twelfth century which I thought might be of interest to Anthony's senior, and he made a note of it.

'I'm am replacing it here,' I said, 'on the top row of this top shelf, at the far right, should he want to consult it.'

'Good,' he said. 'I have found – let me see – eleven other documents for him. But no sign of your charter.'

We looked about us. There was nowhere else. We had checked every shelf which was not cloaked in a thick accumulation of cobwebs. It was dispiriting.

'We guessed wrongly, then,' I said.

Anthony shrugged. 'It was worth a try. At least we now know one place where it is *not*.'

I was tired from standing, but not as tired as I would have been either leaning on two crutches alone or on the wooden leg. I realised that because my balance was much better with the mechanical leg, my back was not twisted. Before, I had suffered a good deal of back pain.

Anthony carried the large ledger back to the librarian, who looked up, surprised, as though he had forgotten we were there.

'Did you discover anything of use?' He sounded as if he thought it unlikely.

Anthony held up his notebook, open at the page where he had been taking notes. 'About a dozen documents. We thank you for your assistance.'

We bowed and took our leave.

I had to use caution in walking down the few steps to the court, not being quite certain of the new leg on steps, and I kept my eyes on my feet, so I did not notice the man approaching us until he was nearly upon us.

'Tom Bennington! What do you here? Who is your friend?'

I looked up to see someone I could hardly have expected to meet here in one of the Inns of Court.

For a moment I was too startled to speak.

'Anthony,' I said, clearing my throat of the dust, 'this is Edmund Dillingworth, son of our neighbour at home, Sir John Dillingworth. He is a sort of distant cousin. Edmund, this is Anthony Thirkettle, barrister of Gray's Inn.'

The two men bowed. Anthony looked alert, for he knew of Edmund Dillingworth's attempted rape of Mercy and how he had brought a band of rogue soldiers to smash our church and beat Gideon Clarke nearly to death. And also how we suspected that he had been behind the accusation made to Matthew Hopkins, that Mercy and Hannah had practised witchcraft, for he claimed they had raised Gideon from the dead. Anthony's face held a look of reserved politeness.

I also realised that Edmund resented my addressing him with such familiarity, and my reminder that we were cousins, though I cared little for that. I despised the man. He had fought for the king, but now tried to ingratiate himself with the followers of Cromwell.

I despise any man who turns his coat instead of keeping faith with his beliefs and his friends.

'But what are you doing in Lincoln's Inn, Tom?'

'I might say the same of you,' I said. 'I have returned to the study of the law. I spent a year at Gray's Inn after Cambridge, but then the war came. I am now accepted back as a student and we have been working in the library here. But you – are you now studying at Lincoln's Inn?'

I doubted it. I knew that Edmund had been one year at Cambridge, which he spent drinking and whoring, after which he was sent down. He was never a university man. And indeed men from his background sometimes spent a year or two at one of the Inns to gain a smattering of the law, but I could not imagine Edmund Dillingworth accomplishing even that much.

He laughed, eying our lawyers' gowns with a supercilious air. He was himself richly dressed in a velvet doublet more suited to the king's court than Presbyterian London. If he wished to join the Cromwellians, he would need to learn to dress differently.

'Nay, I am merely here on some business for my father.'

'Perhaps with your father's man of law, Master Blakiston?' I asked, and saw him give a start.

'What do you know of Master Blakiston?' His tone was aggressive.

'Why, we all have an interest in the matter of the common lands,' I said smoothly. 'Your family has a small share in them, though your living does not depend on them, as ours does. It is more than a year now, since my father and his friends came to see your father. He promised to help in the matter of the drainage works and – so he said – briefed his lawyer, Master Blakiston.'

We had not known the lawyer's name last year, but Edmund would not be aware of that. I felt Anthony touch my arm and realised that he was warning me not to go too far. I bit back my words. He was right. I could feel my anger growing, but I must take care what I said to Edmund Dillingworth, who was probably on his way to see Blakiston.

'Are you still pursuing that hopeless cause?' he said, with a smirk. 'The land improvers will have their way, you know. Why not accept it?'

I clenched my fists, but did my best to keep my voice level.

175

'A charter was granted by the king to our parish and four others, giving us the rights to the common land in perpetuity. At one time, your family held one copy of the charter, although you seem to have lost it. The other would have been lodged with other royal charters. With the charter in our hands, we can fight these invaders in the courts. Even the Dillingworths have some interest in that.'

He gave an odd smile. 'Indeed we have. Well, perhaps I can assist you. I shall see what I can discover from Blakiston. He's a tight mouthed old woman, but I will find out what he knows.'

I saw that he was eyeing the mechanical leg with its odd shoe. He must have been wondering at it, but he said nothing.

'Let me think.' He tapped his chin in a parody of deep thought, though I suspected he already knew what he was going to say.

'I will speak to Blakiston, find out what I can. Do you know the Black Eagle? Down a side turn, just off the top of Chancery Lane.'

'I can find it,' I said.

'Meet me there – on Friday, let us say, at nine of the evening. I shall be occupied all day. If Blakiston has managed to lay hands on the charter, I will bring it with me and we can put our heads together, consider what is to be done next.'

My heart gave a leap of hope. If Blakiston did have the charter, Edmund Dillingworth was likely to have some influence over him, for Sir John was a rich man, with powerful friends. Perhaps we were nearing the end of the hunt.

'Very well,' I said. 'The Black Eagle, nine, Friday evening.'

'Best come alone,' he said, flicking a glance at Anthony. 'I may need to bring Blakiston, and he will not like another lawyer present.'

We all bowed. Edmund turned toward Blakiston's chambers, while Anthony and I made our way out of the gatehouse.

'You never spoke a word,' I said, as we headed up Chancery Lane.

'Do you trust him?' Anthony said. 'I thought he was a very blackguard.'

'So he is, but it is in the Dillingworths' interests to send these adventurers packing.'

'Hmm.' He shook his head. 'Why does he wish to see you alone, and after dark? I know the Black Eagle. It's a lowlife tavern, not at all the sort of place I should imagine your fine cousin choosing.'

I felt uncomfortable at his mentioning that cousinage. I had only referred to it because I wanted to prick Edmund's look of superiority.

'I shall fare well enough,' I said.

'Are you sure you do not want me to come?'

I was grateful, more than grateful, for all Anthony had done for me, but it was time I learned to manage things for myself. I could not depend on him for ever.

'Truly,' I said, 'you are very kind, but I shall fare well enough.'

He did not press the matter, and we returned to Gray's Inn. He merely pointed out the narrow alley leading to the Black Eagle as we passed it.

The following day all the talk at Gray's was about the war. With the king a prisoner of the army in Carisbrooke Castle on the Isle of Wight and the New Model Army seemingly in control of the whole country, everyone had felt that we had obtained peace for a time, if an uneasy one, although no one knew – not even Parliament, I suspect – what the future would hold. Everyone walked warily. Parliament, once united in opposition to the tyranny of King Charles, was now divided against itself, the Army and the military men, the so-called Independents, falling out with the Moderates, who were anxious to bring in legislation to rein in the king's power but not to dethrone him. Added to the mix, word began to spread that the army had not been paid for months, and was existing on short rations. In some places they took matters into their own hands and raided towns and farmland for food. And they were not above pillage and rape amongst the civilian population. I had heard nothing from Mercy for some time, save for a brief note to say that she and Gideon were now married and were keeping his identity hidden by taking the false name of Chandler. The soldiers who were billeted at Turbary Holm were no danger to them, I was sure, but I could not forget the attack last year on the church during Huw's christening.

Although the king remained a prisoner, it seemed he still had support in the country and was even dealing with those supporters through secret letters. A few weeks earlier we had heard of an uprising in Wales, although it was put down by the Army. There were rumours of the Scots invading England from the north. At first they had been as opposed to King Charles as strongly as anyone, both for his tyranny and for his intolerance towards their religion. It was difficult to believe that they could now be supporting him, but perhaps they simply wanted to make trouble in the north. It would not be the first time.

Now news had come that there had been a Royalist uprising in Kent. This was a little too close for comfort. Fighting in Kent was on the very doorstep of London. The New Model Army was spread thinly, in Wales, in the north, and in the southeast. There was talked of calling out London's Trained Bands, the citizen militia, but they were scorned by the Army and any weapons they might once have had were now confiscated. At Gray's Inn, Pension held a meeting to discuss what ought to be done in the face of the possible threat to London, but it seemed little had been decided, other than to place the Inn's silverware in concealment.

Amidst all this fear and excitement, I could not forget my own search for the charter. I asked myself whether it would serve any purpose to meet Edmund Dillingworth on Friday evening. Reflecting on his proposal in the sober light of the following day, as I sat at my desk in the library, entering the details of the next parcel of books into the appropriate ledgers, I thought it unlikely that Blakiston would hand over the charter to him, even supposing he possessed it. And should Edmund obtain it, would he give it to me? I had been a fool even to suppose he might. Nay, he would take it home to his father.

Still, there seemed no harm in meeting him at the Black Eagle and sharing a mug or two of beer. I detested him and did not much like his father, but if we were to take the company of adventurers to court, we would need to work with them.

On Friday evening I set out in good time. Although I managed the mechanical leg a little better each day, I still moved slowly. I did not want Edmund to arrive and –not finding me there – to leave again. I had not taken the precaution of discovering where he was lodging, although he might be staying at Lincoln's

178

Inn, so I had no means of contacting him unless I went to the meeting.

Anthony looked up from the book he was reading as I prepared to go.

'I hope all goes well. Perhaps he will have secured the charter.'

'Perhaps,' I said. 'I have no great hopes of it.'

He did not offer again to come with me, having detected, perhaps, that I needed to strike out on my own, but as I stepped through the gatehouse into Gray's Inn Lane I was aware how dark it was growing and admitted to myself that I would have been glad of his company. The weather had continued dreadful, as cold and wet as many a winter, and heavy cloud had closed down over London, shutting out the last rays of the setting sun. I realised before I was halfway down the lane that I should have brought a candle lantern with me, for it would be even darker on the way back. In the City, householders are obliged to set lamps before their doors during the dark hours, but out here in the country there was only the occasional lit window to be glimpsed from a cottage. The few taverns along the lane burned torches to welcome customers, but they were spaced far apart, with long stretches of dark in between.

Chancery Lane was little better, although there were more buildings here, stretching down the hill ahead of me. I found the opening to the narrow alleyway which Anthony had pointed out to me. The Black Eagle was about a hundred yards down it, and I could make out a flickering light which I supposed must be the torch at its doorway, but no one else was showing a light in this unsavoury backwater.

I paused at the entrance to the alley, the hairs on the back of my neck stirring slightly. I did not like the look of the place. Why had Edmund chosen it? For someone with his pretensions to gentility it did not ring true. The Peacock Inn was not far away. That was a meeting place more suited to a Dillingworth. I should have suggested it, but I had been taken aback, first by encountering Edmund here in London and then by his unexpected suggestion that we should meet this evening.

It had grown steadily darker as I made my way here, so that I was anxious I might miss my footing in the rough alley. My confidence was ebbing away. Should I turn around and make my way back to Gray's? I had no real belief that this meeting would profit me, but to retreat now would be the act of a coward. The man I had once been would have despised me for my present fears. I drew in a deep breath and stepped carefully under the jettied storeys which nearly met overhead, turning the alley into little more than a dark tunnel.

I suppose I was about halfway between the entrance in Chancery Lane and the faint light of the tavern's torch when I sensed that I was not alone. I did not so much see anything or even hear anything, but there must have been some stirring in the air that alerted me.

'Edmund!' I called out. 'Is that you?'

There was no reply, but this time I did hear something, the faint crunch of a boot against pebbles, instantly hushed. I stopped. There are cutpurses everywhere in London, but they tend to haunt the places where the pickings are good – marketplaces, the New Exchange, London Bridge, the public hangings at Tyburn. Once the theatres were excellent hunting grounds, but they were all closed down now. Cutpurses do not normally waste their time in deserted alleyways. I was carrying little that would have interested a thief, for my purse contained only enough coin for a couple of beers, and it was stuffed down the front of my doublet, a precaution familiar to any Londoner.

My breath was coming fast and I tried to hold it, only to hear the beat of my own heart, so it seemed, in my ears. I waited a moment too long. As I turned awkwardly to make my way back to Chancery Lane there was the thud of footsteps in the mud of the alley, and they were upon me. Someone aimed a blow at my head, but misjudged it in the dark and instead struck the base of my neck painfully at the collar bone. Another punched me in the stomach and I doubled over, barely able to keep my balance. I swung out with my crutch and felt a satisfying jolt to my arm as I struck one of my assailants, who let out a muffled yelp.

It was impossible to tell how many there were, but it was probably three. Although I managed a few more blows with my crutch, they soon had me down on the ground. One was kicking my head, another the base of my spine. I found myself wondering, quite clearly, how I should get back to Gray's if they broke the mechanical leg. Would I need to crawl?

Then something harder than a boot hit the back of my head, and everything went black.

There was a guttering candle a few feet from my face. I remembered that I was lying in the mud of the alleyway. Why would a candle be standing on the ground? I could hear voices murmuring, but I could not make out what they were saying. My head felt as though a wall had fallen on it.

'His eyes are open,' someone said. I was able to hear the words clearly, so perhaps my hearing had not been damaged after all.

A man squatted down beside me, a complete stranger, and I became aware that I was not lying on the ground, but on a wooden bench.

'Where am I?' My voice came out in a croak and I realised that my throat was throbbing.

'Bar of the Black Eagle,' the man said. 'We carried you here.'

'Drink.' I whispered.

'Aye. Give him some small ale. Not strong beer. Not after that blow on the head.'

I knew that voice. 'Anthony?' I said.

'Aye. Lie still and drink this.'

He raised my head and held a cup to my lips. It was poor stuff, but I was glad of it. My whole head and throat seemed to be on fire. And there was a sharp pain at the base of my spine.

'What happened? I know someone attacked.'

'Aye. Three great rogues.' It was the stranger speaking. 'I saw them hanging about in the lane when I came in for a beer, then when I heard you shout . . . I fell over you in the dark.'

I was still confused. I did not remember shouting. Who was this stranger, and where had Anthony appeared from? As if he could read my thoughts, Anthony pulled up a stool next to the bench. There was someone else standing behind him, but I could see no higher than his waist and I did not care to lift my head just then.

181

'I was uneasy about this meeting with Dillingworth,' Anthony said, 'the more I thought about it. Why choose a place like this, down a dark alleyway, unless he had some unsavoury business in hand? So after you left, I fetched Henry Grantham and we came after you, just in time to be nearly knocked down by those rogues running off. We found John here, trying to lift you, to bring you inside. So the three of us carried you in.'

Henry. So it was Henry standing behind Anthony. But who was John? The stranger grinned at me. He was young, perhaps no more than eighteen, and very slight. He could never have carried me on his own.

'John Farindon at your service, sir,' he said. 'Post office runner.'

'I'm obliged to you, John,' I said. My voice came out again in a croak. I touched my neck with my finger tips. It was very sore.

'They tried to throttle you,' the lad said. 'Probably thought they had, for you was lying still as death. But when they see me, they run off.'

'Good fortune to me that you came.' I struggled to sit up, but found I was dizzy and weak. 'Anthony, the leg. Is it broken?'

'Your stocking and some of the leather is torn. I don't know about the mechanism. It does not seem to be smashed. They were more intent at aiming for your head and your kidneys, I'd say.'

'Dillingworth?'

'Who else? Why would they lie in wait for a stranger? Not Dillingworth himself, though. He'd not want to dirty his hands. Men working for him.'

I shivered. But for the swift actions of the boy and my friends, I would be lying dead now in that filthy alley.

Someone else came into view, a big man, his bulk cutting off the light from the other side of the room. A fire, probably. It was cold enough for a fire, even in summer.

'When are you going to get him out of here? This a'nt doing my business no good. This is a respectable house, and there's blood everywhere.'

Blood? That must be from my head. I remembered that they had hit the back of my head. With a stone, perhaps, or a cudgel. I felt the back of my head and my fingers came away sticky.

'Anthony,' I said, 'can you help me sit up?'

Once I was upright, the room swam a little until I managed to focus my eyes. It was a filthy place, one of those London drinking shops which serves cheap ale made of unmentionable substances, where the poorest dregs of London come to drink themselves into a forgetfulness of their miserable lives. The post office runner, who was respectably if humbly dressed, did not look as though he belonged here.

Henry was gazing at me curiously. 'That is an extraordinary device the surgeon has made for you, Tom. Can you really walk with it?'

'After a fashion. Though I fear it may be damaged.' I looked in dismay at the rip in the leather of the calf just below the knee. I could see the strengthening bar within. Perhaps if the mechanical joints had taken no harm, the leg would still function.

The tavern keeper was eager to be rid of us, and I was just as eager to be away from the place. I wanted to ensure that I could walk. And I wanted to wash the wound in the back of my head. I could remember now the foul stink of the mud in the lane as I lay there.

Anthony and Henry helped me stand, and John fetched my crutch from where it was propped up against a table.

'They threw this out of your reach,' he said. 'I only found it when I went back with your friends' lamp and searched.'

I propped myself on the crutch and took a few tentative steps. I could manage, I thought, with the help of my friends, though I felt the leg was somehow twisted. Anthony put some coins in the tavern keeper's hand, though he hardly seemed grateful. It was only now that I realised that there were other customers in the room, sitting well away from us and watching with wary curiosity. They were threadbare workmen of the poorest sort, and again I wondered at the post office runner coming to such a tavern. Had I known the sort of place it was, I would never have agreed to meet Edmund here.

The four of us left the tavern, John leading the way with the lantern, Anthony and Henry on each side of me, steadying me whenever I stumbled. When we reached the wide stretch of Chancery Lane, John held out the lantern to Anthony.

'I'll be off then.'

'Can you not come as far as Gray's Inn with us?' Anthony said. 'We would like to stand you that drink you never had back there. We have an excellent beer.'

The boy hesitated, then he smiled. 'Very well, gentlemen. I'll come gladly.'

It took us a long time to make our way back up Gray's Inn Lane, and by the time we reached our chambers, I was shaking with exhaustion and pain. They half carried me inside and propped me up in a chair, while Anthony fetched beer and Henry lit a fire. It had grown so cold outside, I almost expected to see frost under the light of our lantern as we crossed the court.

'That's a bad blow to your head,' John said. 'You should wash it.'

'Aye.' I struggled to get up, then sank back again. 'Later.'

'Have you water?' John was asking Anthony. Before I knew what they were about, Henry had warmed some water on the fire and John was washing the back of my head, as if he had known me all my life. I felt like a small child.

'You need not–' I said.

'My grandmother was the wise woman in our village,' he said. 'I know what to do.'

We had no salves such as Mercy keeps for the small injuries which frequently occur on a farm, but at least the wound was clean, and John judged that it had not gone too deep. While I was being cared for, Anthony had laid out beer and the pasties he had bought from Goodwife Gorley, meant for tomorrow's dinner. Indeed it was tomorrow already, for I had heard the church clock strike midnight. John seemed too shy to sit down with us at first, but with the beer and the pasties, he soon relaxed.

'What I do not understand, John,' I said, 'is what you were doing in that place. You seem a decent lad, and that is a filthy tavern.'

He looked very embarrassed. 'I am not paid much, sir, and since my mother died and I lost our lodgings, I have to share a room that's no more than a cupboard. I have to eat where I can. The brother of that landlord married a cousin of mine, so I go there sometimes to eat cheaply. But you are right. It is a filthy place.'

'Well, it is my good fortune that you were there tonight.'

When we had finished eating and Henry had taken himself off to his own chambers, John said he must go too, and make his way home.

'And where is that?' Anthony asked.

'Southwark.'

'Southwark! You would need to take a wherry, the Bridge will be closed. And I doubt there will be a wherry to be had at this time of night. You may sleep here if you wish. There's a truckle bed in the kitchen.'

At first the boy would have none of it, but Anthony persuaded him in the end.

'He rolled himself up in the blankets and fell asleep at once,' Anthony said, coming back to where I was still sitting by the last of the fire, too weary to walk the few steps to my chamber. 'I think we can trust him. He seems an honest lad.'

'I probably owe him my life,' I said soberly. 'Those men might have had time to finish the task if he had not come when he did.'

'Aye, that's true. Come, now, I'll give you an arm to your bed.'

I was glad of his arm. The mechanical leg seemed to have suffered some harm as well as the tear in the leather. When I was sitting on my bed and Anthony was halfway through the door, he stopped and turned back,

'What do you want to do next? Dillingworth must have been behind the attack, but was it because of the old enmity between you, or because of the charter, do you suppose?'

I shook my head. 'I cannot tell. Both, perhaps. One thing I can say for sure. It has made me more determined than ever to find the charter.'

Chapter Nine
Mercy

The morning after Piet van Slyke had burst into Turbary Holm uninvited, I set out for the manor house, to confront Sir John Dillingworth. I should lie, were I to say that I was not a little afraid, but I strove to conceal it. I must go, so there was no reason to delay. Better to have done with it.

'I hate to hide behind your skirts!' Gideon burst out as I took up my cloak. 'What kind of man am I, what kind of husband am I, to let you go to that place where you were humiliated and attacked? Stay, and I will go in your stead.'

I sat down on the bench beside the table, while he strode up and down the kitchen in frustration. Kitty gave me a sympathetic look, then slipped out to feed the hens.

'We have already discussed this, Gideon,' I said mildly. We had indeed discussed it for the whole of the previous evening. 'We both know that you must keep out of the sight of your enemies. 'Tis pure common sense. I shall come to no harm. Edmund Dillingworth is away from home. We know that. And Sir John, though arrogant, is not uncivil. His lady is barely civil, but I shall have no need to see her.'

'Let me come with you, at least part of the way,' he said.

I shook my head. 'To Crowthorne, and risk Reverend Edgemont recognising you? In broad daylight, what harm can come to me? I have walked these lanes all my life.'

'You know that we have had word that fighting has broken out again, between the Royalists and the Army. What if there should be renegade soldiers roaming about?'

I smiled. 'You know as well as I that the fighting is miles away – the other side of London, down in Kent, or else up in the far north, near Scotland. The soldiers here are our friends.'

'Those who attacked Huw's christening were no friends of ours,' he said grimly. 'What if they are still about?'

'There has been no sight of them for months. Nay, Gideon, I shall come to no harm and you must get on with the farm work. All this wet weather has brought the weeds on apace out in the arable. Everyone is going out to hoe the fields today. Nehemiah will go, and so must you. As soon as I am home, I will join you. It must not be said that we left others to care for our crops.'

He continued to protest, but he took up his hoe and set off with Nehemiah for the fields. Kitty came in with her basket of eggs just as I was about to leave.

'What shall I do while you are gone, Mistress Mercy?'

'Best start a new batch of cheese,' I said. 'And if there is time, we are running short of bread. With so many men to feed, we should open a bakery!'

For once in this miserable year it was not raining, but it was hardly sunny. The sky was a uniform pale grey, as though a painter had loaded his brush with a single colour and washed over the entire dome of the skies with it. We have wide open skies, here in the Fens, and you can see for miles, but nowhere was there a break in this dull, listless grey, neither a rip in the veil to show a fragment of blue sky, nor even a respectable solid cloud.

I had debated long over what I should wear to the manor house. They had seen me last in the poor clothes of a lowly kitchen maid, the rank in which they had condescended to employ me. I could wear one of my everyday gowns, such as I wore about the farm. Or I could wear my Sunday gown, which was made of finer cloth, but was not too ostentatious under the eye of a Puritan preacher. Or, finally, I could wear my best, the clothes in which I had been wed.

Nay, the memories attached to those were too precious to be sullied by contact with the manor. I would wear my Sunday clothes, and my silk Dillingworth shawl. It was unlikely the people at the manor would recognise it for what it was, but I would know, and it would give me the courage to conduct myself as a relative of the family, however little they might wish to remember it.

With the silk shawl about my shoulders, I decided I would not need a cloak after all. Although the weather continued so cold that it was difficult to believe it was June, yet I knew I should grow warm with walking. There were three different ways I could go. The shortest was across the fields, the way I had come home when I left my service at the manor, but that meant jumping ditches and was likely to be boggy in places, after so much rain. The longest way was to head for Crowthorne, then skirt round the village to the north, along a network of paths between small scattered patches of the moss. It was somewhere here that the military had pitched their camp. Although our soldiers had returned, the camp might still be there. Despite my brave words to Gideon, I did not care to encounter a group of soldiers, alone on a deserted lane.

In the end, the best way to go seemed to be through Crowthorne, then out along the lane to the manor. At one time I had always avoided Crowthorne, but I was no longer so intimidated by the people there. I had met Jack's friend Joshua a few times since the flood and he seemed harmless enough.

The first part of my route took me past the place at the far end of the village where the three cottages had stood, the ones which had been washed away in the flood, then over the new bridge to the Crowthorne road. When I reached the bridge, I saw that three of the village boys were fishing from the bank beside it.

'Any fish?' I asked.

Rob Higson shrugged. 'Enough to feed a cat. But us'll keep trying.'

'Aye,' I said. 'Patience is the answer.'

The next part of my way led between high banks topped with straggling hedges. The rain seemed to have brought on their growth, like the rampant weeds in the fields. The men needed to come along here when they had time, to cut back the new growth of the hedge trees and the whippy tendrils of brambles which reached out to snatch at the unwary passer-by. As I neared Crowthorne, I saw that someone had been out here to trim the hedges. No doubt the Reverend Edgemont had issued his orders.

The village was quiet. As at home, the able bodied, men and women alike, would be out in the fields, seizing this rare opportunity to tackle the weeds while it was not raining. The soil would still be claggy with the wet, which would make the hoeing difficult, but it must be done. Neglect it and you have a crop of burdock and sow thistles instead of wheat or barley. It is remarkable, sometimes, that the corn survives at all.

There were a few of the elderly people about in Crowthorne, minding the small children. The older children would be out in the fields with their parents. I nodded to one or two of the elders, sitting before their doors, to take advantage not of the sun, for there was none, but of the cessation of the rain. I followed the main street of the village to the end. Like our own village it consisted of houses built along this one street, with outbuildings and plots of ground behind, where there was room to grow vegetables and keep a pig. Narrow paths led between the houses to these back premises, just barely wide enough for a horse and cart. At the far end of the village, the street narrowed a little between more hedges and became the lane that led to the manor house.

The overhanging grey of the sky seemed to lean down ever more oppressively as I drew near the manor house, and my steps began to slow and drag. I had taken care to keep up a steady but unhurried pace as walked, for I had no wish to arrive hot and flustered. As usual, the house looked deserted, standing aloof amidst its formal gardens. The family rarely seemed to venture outside, except when Sir John or his son went hunting. I had never heard of Lady Dillingworth leaving the sanctuary of the house in recent years. It occurred to me for the first time what a very dull and even unhappy life she must lead. No one in the neighbourhood was of her rank in society, and she was not a woman to mingle with the lower orders. Before the war, I believe the family used to spend part of each year in London, for Sir John owned a house there, but like many of the country gentry they had retreated to their estates and kept their heads down during the struggle. Although many of his rank were royalists, Sir John had made much of his distant relationship to Cromwell since that man had come to power. My own father had believed that Cromwell would prove the champion of the common man, and it had been the subject of many arguments between him and Tom, for Tom did not trust Cromwell. When it was rumoured that Cromwell was involved in the draining and enclosure of our common lands, the arguments had grown fiercer. I do not know what my father believed at the time of his death.

189

I walked boldly up to the front door of the manor. I would not allow myself to be intimidated by my previous experiences here. As I raised my hand to the knocker, I heard the first sounds of human activity from the stableyard. A dog barked and a man spoke to it. There was the clatter of a bucket which I judged came from the well-hus, out at the back, near the kitchen premises.

The door was opened by Master Rogers, Sir John's steward. A momentary astonishment flickered over his face before he composed it to a look of bland indifference. I wondered whether he would admit to knowing who I was.

'Yes?' he said, looking down his nose at me, and effectively blocking the doorway.

'Good morning to you, Master Rogers,' I said, without expression. 'I am here to see Sir John on parish business.'

Rogers raised his eyebrows, clearly indicating that he doubted whether a woman could have any business, parish or otherwise, with Sir John.

'It is . . .' he made a show of ignorance, '. . . Good . . . Mistress Bennington, is it?'

I clenched my teeth. The pretence of nearly demeaning me to 'Goodwife' was deliberate. Of course, when I had worked here, I had been merely 'Mercy', or more often simply 'You'.

'I am married now, Rogers. I am Mistress Chandler.'

His face hardened at my form of address, but I could not resist playing him at his own game. His brief hesitation gave me the opportunity to step forward into the house.

'I know my way to Sir John's study,' I said, 'if he is at home. Or will you announce me?'

This was by way of calling his bluff. He would be forced to announce me, or be clearly failing in politeness to his master. Without a word he walked ahead of me, turning into the left hand wing of the house and following the hallway to the end, where Sir John's study stood.

Rogers knocked on the door, then opened it. 'Mistress . . . Chandler, Sir John.'

He stood slightly to one side to let me enter, but not quite far enough, so that I was crowded. I let my skirts brush his legs and ignored this petty discourtesy. Sir John rose and I realised that he did not at first know me. Then I saw recognition in his eyes.

190

'Mistress Bennington!' Clearly I was the last person he expected. He bowed. 'Thank you, Rogers.'

The steward withdrew and I dropped a polite but not obsequious curtsey.

'Good day to you, Sir John,' I said. 'However, I am no longer Mistress Bennington. I am married now. I am Mistress Chandler.'

I hated using this false name. As a name, there was nothing amiss with it, but I wanted to shout to the world, 'I am married to Gideon Clarke!' I wondered whether the day would ever come when he could emerge from the shadows and resume his rightful name and vocation.

'My felicitations, Mistress Chandler.' He bowed again. 'Please, be seated.'

As I sat, I remembered when I had last been in this room. My father was imprisoned and the whole family had struggled to raise the money to pay the fine for his release. I had been received with little courtesy then. I drew Mary Dillingworth's shawl closer around my shoulders. I do not suppose Sir John recognised it, but I could see that he appreciated its quality. Clearly I had not returned to my position as his lowest kitchen maid.

'I wished to see you, cousin,' I said, 'on this matter which touches everyone in these five parishes. The matter of the drainage works undertaken by the company of adventurers.'

If his eyebrows had been raised a fraction when he assessed the quality of the silk shawl, they rose higher when I mentioned our kinship. Yet it was much closer than his supposed connection to Cromwell. My great-grandmother had been his great-aunt. Or to put it another way, he was my mother's second cousin. When I mentioned the drainage works, his eyes narrowed and I saw that he looked wary. For the moment he said nothing, either to encourage me to explain, or to discourage me.

'It is more than a year now since my late father and many men of our village came to you for help in resisting the attempts to steal our land. At that time you promised us help. You said you would set your lawyer to work on the matter. Yet in all this time, nothing has been done.'

'Matters at law are slowly dealt with, Mistress Chandler,' he said. I saw that he was not going to acknowledge the kinship. His tone was patronising. What could I, a mere countrywoman, understand of the law?

'Ah, but some matters have moved on,' I said smoothly. 'My brother Tom has returned to his legal studies in London, at Gray's Inn. Moreover, he has called upon your man of law at Lincoln's Inn, James Blakiston.'

His eyes widened when he realised I knew the lawyer's name.

'Now here is a strange thing,' I said, 'for Bencher Blakiston has told my brother that he is retained by a company of adventurers, and therefore it would be a conflict of interests for him to work with my brother in taking them – or any such company – to court in order to stop their activities. He did not tell Tom *which* company of adventurers he serves, but surely it cannot be in your interests to retain such a man in your service.'

'Indeed,' he said, but his tone was reserved. I thought I saw calculation in his eye. It was clear he was taken aback by the fact that Tom was in London and had found the lawyer.

'So it seems all this time has been wasted,' I said, 'while the drainers have gone about their destruction of our lands. They have extended their works to Crowthorne now. You are aware, of course, that the devastation wreaked by the recent flood was due to their ill-judged activities. Even here on the manor you must have suffered, although much of your land stands higher than our villages.'

'We did indeed suffer some damage,' he conceded. 'So Blakiston is retained by a company of drainers? I wonder who they might be.' There was something insincere in his tone.

'They seem very skilled at hiding their identities,' I agreed. 'I wished to be sure that you knew the truth about Blakiston, but that was not my principal reason for seeing you.'

'And that is?'

'My brother is determined to find the royal charter granting the common lands to us in perpetuity. There must be a copy in London. And I believe that the Dillingworths held the other copy.'

He spread his hands apologetically. 'I am afraid that it appears to be lost. There was a fire here in this very room, some century and a half ago, and an entire chest of documents was destroyed. Alas, that copy of the charter appears no longer to exist.

You say your brother hopes to find the other. Is he not somewhat disabled?'

'He has lost a leg, certainly,' I said coldly. 'That will be no impediment to my brother, once he has made up his mind. Besides, he has friends amongst the lawyers who are also assisting in the search.'

It was clear that Sir John was listening very carefully to me now.

'I have come to ask that you support your neighbours and fellow commoners in putting a stop to the work of the drainers until the matter can come to court, and to lend us your assistance when we do take the adventurers to court.'

'That may be difficult, if you do not know who they are,' he murmured.

'Oh, I am sure we will find them out in time. Meanwhile, will you help us put a stop to their present activities? You are a Justice of the Peace. Surely you can do something, within the law. It would be a pity if it came to violence again.'

'It would, indeed it would.' He rose to his feet. 'I will see what I can do, Mistress Chandler, but it may be difficult. I understand that damage was done to the drainers' two pumping mills.'

'The pumps had to be stopped, or the flood would have been even worse,' I said. 'The damage to the mill on our land was mostly done by the flood and the winter storms. The machinery was merely stopped. I believe the Crowthorne mill suffered worse, but people were desperate and in danger of drowning. Are you aware of all the homes swept away or severely damaged?'

'Some sad losses,' he said, but without a great deal of sympathy.

I wished he could have suffered what we had suffered. I stood up. Clearly he wanted me to be gone.

'I will see what I can do about the drainers' present activities,' he said, as he opened the door. 'It may not be possible to do anything at once.'

'I understand,' I said, 'but perhaps you will keep us informed?'

'Certainly.'

He began to walk with me toward the front door.

'And I hope you will keep me informed about your brother's attempts to find the charter.'

'I will indeed. Once the charter is found, we shall be able to take the adventurers to court.'

He held the door open for me.

'You seem very certain that it will be found.'

'My brother does not easily abandon a task, once he has undertaken it. If the charter still exists, he will find it.' On the threshold I dropped him a small curtsey. 'I wish you good day, cousin.'

He smiled. I believe he even admired my boldness. 'Good day to you.'

I walked briskly back to Crowthorne. Now that the interview was over, I was anxious to reach home and return to all the tasks that awaited me there. I could not decide whether my meeting with Sir John had been successful or not. He had promised to look into putting a stop to the resumption of the drainage works, but he had made promises before. And when he told me that a chest of documents had been destroyed in a fire, he had not actually said that the charter was amongst them. And there was something else that worried me. When I had told him that Blakiston was working for the adventurers, I could have sworn that he knew it already.

The farm was deserted when I reached home. Apart from my mother, resting in her chamber, everyone – including the soldiers – was out in the fields, hoeing. I changed quickly into my workaday clothes and laid the silk shawl safely away in my coffer. It had, I was sure, fulfilled its function today. Then I checked that Kitty had done what I had asked her to do. There was a batch of bread dough rising in the bread trough under a cloth. Out in the dairy the curds had been set to drain. She was a good girl. Hardly past her thirteenth birthday, she could do almost a grown woman's work. One day we must find a good husband for her, but I should be sorry to lose her companionship.

I found an old hoe with a worm-eaten handle, but decided it would have to serve, and made my way along the lane to the wheat field. All my neighbours were strung out across the field, valiantly hoeing up the pernicious weeds, but the stunted stalks of wheat seemed hardly worth all their hard labour. A moment of real fear seized me. Our stores of flour were growing perilously low with having to feed the soldiers as well as ourselves. Many in the village had lost far more of their stores than we had. What should we do if we ran out of flour over the winter? At least we would have fleeces and woollen goods to sell at market. Because of the wretchedly cold weather during the spring and early summer, we had delayed this year's shearing later than I had ever remembered. We must shear within the next few days or the sheep would not grow their new coats in time for the following winter.

As I stepped across the adland into the field, Gideon and Jack walked over to me, wiping the sweat from their brows. Despite the chilly weather, hoeing is hot, dispiriting work, especially when you can see a large field stretching away in front of you. The soil, sticky from all the rain, had slowed them, but the field was about halfway done.

'How was your meeting with Sir John?' Jack had barely reached me before he asked.

I gave them a quick account of the meeting, and Sir John's offer – somewhat reluctant – to see whether he could put a halt to the drainers' work, for a time at least. I did not repeat my misgivings about his knowledge of the lawyer Blakiston's doings.

'If they begin again to dig ditches across our land as they did last year,' Jack said fiercely, 'then we must show them once again that we are not to be trifled with. As fast as they dig their ditches, we can fill them in, and as fast as they construct sluices and pumping mills, we can burn them down.'

'We must not put ourselves on the wrong side of the law,' Gideon cautioned. 'It will only do us harm if the matter comes to court.'

'Gideon is right,' I said. 'But so are you, Jack. However, we can thwart them in more subtle ways. Remember, in the autumn of last year, we did not confront them directly. We loosened hinges and bolts in the sluices at night. Blocked their drains seemingly through natural landslips. Besides,' I added, 'they will have a hard time of it, digging ditches in such sodden soil. They will probably collapse at once.'

'That is true enough,' Jack conceded. 'Well, we shall see what mischief our friendly fenland boggarts may work by night.'

'There has been other news while you were away to the manor,' Gideon said, as we walked across the field to join the line of those hoeing between the poor stalks of wheat. 'A summons has come for the soldiers. They are to be redeployed down in Kent against the Royalist forces. That is reckoned more important than keeping a few fenland farmers in order. In any case, I think their officers have come to realise that these men have more sympathy with us than with van Slyke and his men.'

'Aye,' Jack said. 'They have come out to the hoeing, to give us one day of their labour, in return for feeding them for months.'

'That is not their fault,' I said, in defence of the men. I had grown fond of the soldiers lodged with us. 'The Army was supposed to pay us for their food, and has not done so.'

'They have not paid the men either,' Gideon said. 'Not for months. I think it may not be long before the men grow weary of their masters.'

We worked hard all the rest of that day, the soldiers and the Dutch settlers along with us. Like the soldiers, the Dutch had no share in these arable lands, but laboured with us out of gratitude that we had not turned them away. Little by little they were learning to speak English, which, it seems, is often close to Dutch, at least in simple words. The children learned the fastest, as children will, for their minds are not yet locked into one language only. Dutch and English children played together and had soon shared their language along with their games. The village children had even picked up a few words of Dutch.

It was difficult to believe that we were near the summer equinox, so dull and cold was it, except that the day seemed to drag on, for hour after hour. The hay should have been in by now, but it was already near ruined by the rain, and there was little hope of drying it. The stock, as well as ourselves, must look forward to a hungry winter.

The wheat field was finished and a start had been made on the barley when we women left the men while we went home to prepare an evening meal. Everyone would be ravenous after the heavy labour of the day. Kitty and I stowed our hoes in the barn. While she shut the hens away and turn the curds into the cheese press, I set about making the supper. Nehemiah had been out early to his eel traps, so with onions from Hans and some handfuls of

196

dried peas from last year, I was able to make an eel pottage. I knew the soldiers had not much liking for eels, but I had little else to give them.

'Kitty,' I said when she came in, 'take this jug and fetch me cream for the eels. We will make them as tasty as possible for the men.'

The pottage was simmering when they returned. Nehemiah went at once to the milking and Ben begged eagerly to go with him.

'For it will be my last time,' he said sadly. Then he brightened. 'When the war is over and I'm out of the Army, I'm going to be a farmer.'

Col cuffed him lightly on the shoulder. 'And how will you find the coin to buy or rent a farm, lad? With all your back pay?'

The others laughed grimly.

'I think the generals hope we will all be killed off,' Seth said. 'It will save them a deal of money.'

I saw the look of panic on Ben's face. 'Off you go with Nehemiah, Ben, or the pottage will be spoiled before you are back.'

Once the door had closed behind him, I turned to the other soldiers. 'Watch your tongues. You are frightening the boy.'

Aaron, who was cleaning the dirt from under his nails with the point of his knife, gave a shrug. 'I was no older than Ben when I was in my first battle. He's seen no real action yet. He'll learn.'

'I suppose he will,' I said. I thrust the bread paddle into the oven beside the fireplace and drew out the loaves I had baked from Kitty's dough. I slipped them on to the table, where they steamed gently.

'And keep your hands off them, Col,' I said, as he reached out. 'We need them for supper.'

Although everyone tried to remain cheerful that evening, I suppose we were all thinking that this was the last time we would sit down together. I had resented the billeting of the soldiers at first, and it had meant a worrying depredation of our stores, but they had come to seem like members of the family. I knew I should miss them when they were gone. There was no ignoring the fact that they were going to war and might not survive.

197

At the end of the meal, I made hot spiced ale for us all, while Kitty and Ben washed the dishes. I even took a mug of it up to my mother, but she was asleep, with her tray of supper barely touched. It was not the first time she had left her food uneaten and she was growing very thin.

We sat late that night. For the first time the soldiers talked more about their families, and their lives before the war, than they had ever done before. It was a good evening, despite our fatigue after a day of hard labour, and I think we were all sorry to end it. I was the last to retire, setting bread dough to prove overnight.

In the morning, I crept out of bed early, taking care not to wake Gideon, and shaped my dough into individual rolls for the men to carry with them. I hard boiled eggs, cut slabs of cheese, and fried some of our precious bacon for them to eat cold. Kitty came out of her room yawning as I was tying up each bundle in a piece of cloth.

'I'm sorry they're going, Mistress Mercy,' she said.

'So am I. But they must go where they are ordered.'

'You know, they didn't all choose to join the Army. Some of them were forced.'

'Aye,' I said. 'They were. The same happens with sailors.'

'I'm glad I'm not a man.'

I smiled at her. 'There are some advantages to being a woman.'

Breakfast was eaten hastily and almost in silence. The men were all pathetically grateful for their bundles of food.

'They scarce feed us, you know, Mistress Mercy,' Seth said. 'As well as not paying us. They reckon we can survive by stealing from people as we march through their lands.'

'It a'nt right,' Ben said. 'It a'nt as if we was in enemy country. They're our own people.'

The others nodded glumly, but there was no time to debate this, they must hurry or find themselves in trouble with the officers. To my astonishment, every one of them kissed me in farewell, as well as Kitty, and I found I was weeping as we waved them off down the lane.

Gideon put his arms around me. 'I am sure they will be safe. I expect the fighting will be over by the time they reach Kent.'

I was not so sure, but I pretended to be comforted. The rain was still holding off and there was work to be done. The barley field was waiting.

We managed most of the hoeing and salvaged what we could of the hay, but it was poor stuff and much would probably rot before winter. Jack and Toby came to help Nehemiah and me with the long delayed shearing and Gideon did his best to help, while Kitty rolled the fleeces and carried them to be stored at one end of the hay loft. She was strong for her age, but I am not sure how she managed to get them up the ladder. I was too busy myself to see. I was glad to discover that I was better at the shearing than last year, when I had been learning for the first time, while Tom was suffering from his first injury, caused by van Slyke's bullet. This year I could even manage the older, bigger sheep.

Seeing Gideon struggling to turn one of the smaller ewes and grip her between his knees, I smiled encouragingly.

'It was the same for me last year. It gets easier.'

Not that it seemed to grow any easier for Gideon. I think he was more tender towards them than I had been and they sensed it. They took advantage of his soft heart and wriggled away time after time, but he continued to struggle valiantly.

When we stopped for a midday meal, I sat down next to Jack.

'We have not seen much of van Slyke. Do you suppose Sir John has put a stop to his work?'

Jack shook his head. 'Nay, they're working over at Crowthorne. They have repaired the mill building and have started clearing their ditches of the winter debris. They've been helping themselves to food from the village as well. Cheeses and hams. They're even taking sheep. Whenever anyone objects, they say it is in payment for the damage to the mill.'

I felt the anger growing hot inside me. 'How dare they!'

'Indeed. And our lord of the manor seems to be powerless to stop them, or chooses not to.'

'Will they be coming here, do you suppose?'

'Oh, certainly. We have been carrying out a little quiet sabotage to be ready for them. None of their sluice gates will quite work now. Nothing too easy to detect. And while we are sure they are not about, we have undermined some of the banks of their ditches. As soon as they start walking along them, they will collapse.'

He grinned. 'If we are lucky, some of them may fall in.'

I laughed. 'As long as they believe that it is the work of nature.'

'We're being careful. The next task is to see whether we can undermine the mill. After all, it is right on the edge of the Fen. Who is to say that the flood did not eat away at the foundations?'

'Who indeed?'

In return for their help, Nehemiah and I lent a hand to Toby and Jack with their shearing. Toby had only a small flock, but Jack's main interest was sheep. Although he kept a few of his fleeces for his mother to spin and weave, he sold most of them to dealers in Lincoln or Peterborough. Nehemiah had resumed his practice of making baskets to sell, and Kitty and I had built up quite a store of knitted caps. When Jack was ready to take his fleeces to market, he offered to take our goods as well. Nehemiah would set up a stall, as he had done before, and take eels as well, although we were pickling most of them for the winter.

'Perhaps Hans and some of the other settlers would like to sell their vegetables,' I said. 'When they first set up their gardens, they talked about selling at market, but instead they have been trading for other goods in the village.'

'I will ask,' Jack said.

The result of this was that quite a procession set out for Lincoln, with goods packed into two carts – fleeces, woollen goods, baskets, straw hats, eels, and mounds of fresh vegetables. As well as Jack and Nehemiah, Hans and two other Dutchmen joined the expedition. They planned to spend two or three days there, selling their goods and buying some essential supplies. I had asked for sugar and vinegar. I was afraid there would be few autumn fruits this year, but I intended to preserve everything I could lay my hands on. I needed the vinegar for pickling eels and eggs. At least my hens continued to lay and I had increased my flock. When meat is scarce, eggs are a great comfort. I also needed more salt for my cheese making.

While they were away, Turbary Holm seemed very quiet, even deserted, after our full household of recent months, with only

Gideon, Kitty, my mother and me at home. Gideon's skill with the cows had improved beyond his expectations, so that he was able to do the morning and evening milking on his own. It took him longer than Nehemiah, but not so very much longer.

'I want to learn to make cheese, Mercy,' he said to me, the day after the Lincoln party left.

'Cheese making is woman's work.'

'I have seen you doing men's work. You can shear a sheep as well as Toby. So why should I not learn to make cheese? It is like a miracle – is it not? – that a white liquid can be turned into solid yellow cheese!'

I laughed. Having lived all my life on a farm, I had never thought of it like that, but I supposed he was right. It was a kind of miracle.

'I suppose the greatest miracle,' I said, 'is that while milk will go bad in a few days, cheese will keep, and feed us, for months and months.'

'That is indeed a miracle,' he said soberly, 'and one we should thank God for. With the poor harvest we shall have this year, it will be cheese that will keep us alive. I wonder who first discovered the miracle of cheese. It was known in very ancient times.'

'We have no time for a history lesson now.' I often teased him when he became pensive like this. 'Come. If you want to learn how to make cheese, we will start now. Kitty and I will show you how.'

We had shown Gideon how to set one lot of curds to drain and had packed the drained curds from the day before into the cheese press, when I heard the gate slam and running footsteps across the yard. Rob Higson was banging at the kitchen door.

'We are here, Rob,' I called, going to the door of the dairy.

He ran across to me, gasping a little, for he had clearly run hard.

'Mistress Leiden says, can you come? There's trouble in the village.'

'What kind of trouble?' Gideon was rolling down his shirt sleeves.

201

'There's a man come. He says he's the . . . the bailiff, I think he said. Come to collect rent from the Dutchmen, but they a'nt got no coin, and they don't know what to do.'

'They aren't living in the settlement any more,' I said. 'They are in our village. In any case, the settlement was on our land. This man can claim no rent from them.'

'Will you come?' Rob said. 'He's a mean 'un.'

'We will both come,' Gideon said.

I looked at him and nodded. There was no danger of this man recognising him. But I wished this had not happened while Jack was away. Still, Rafe and Will and Abel must be somewhere about. Surely between us we could make a stand against one rent collector.

'We'll take Blaze,' I said. 'It will be quicker. We have ridden him both together before. Kitty, you must take charge. My mother has not come down yet this morning. If she wishes to stay in her chamber, can you take her something to eat?'

Kitty nodded and ran back to the house. Gideon was already putting Blaze's bridle on. There was no time to saddle him.

'I'll run on,' Rob said, and was off.

Gideon led Blaze out to the mounting block in the yard. I hitched up my skirts and mounted, he mounted behind me and we turned Blaze down the lane toward the village. As we caught up with Rob, I leaned down to him.

'Do you know where Rafe is?'

'He went up to the medland to physic one of his ewes with the scour.'

'Then don't go to the village. Go to the medland and fetch Rafe. Tell him it is urgent.'

'Aye, mistress.' He scrambled up the bank at the side of the lane and set off across the fields to the medland.

A crowd had gathered in the lane leading to the new cottages. Gideon and I both slid to the ground and Gideon handed Blaze's reins to one of the village lads to hold. We pushed our way to the front of the crowd. The settlers were huddled together in a frightened group, the children and most of the women crying. The men were stony faced, but they looked desperate. A large man, not fat but heavily muscled, was shouting at them, that they must pay

202

up at once, or he would fetch soldiers to arrest them and send them all to prison.

'That is all bluster,' Gideon murmured. 'He has no power to do such a thing.'

'They do not know that,' I said. 'They are terrified.'

Will and Abel had come out of the smithy. They were both big men. Not as big as the bailiff, but in their leather aprons they looked quite intimidating. Abel still had his hammer in his hand. The bailiff, however, did not seem in the least intimidated. I suppose such men are chosen for the work because they are better able to threaten than to be threatened.

Matters might become dangerous. If the men of the village should decide to take up the settlers' cause and attack the bailiff, it could prove disastrous. Neither Will nor Abel had much gift for words of conciliation or negotiation. Perhaps it was as well Jack was not here. He might have rushed in without thinking. As Tom would have done, I realised.

Gideon was a man of a different stamp. He stepped forward and held out his hand to the bailiff.

'Gideon Chandler at your service, goodman. And you are?'

There was no mistaking his tone of authority. It was clear that the bailiff recognised it, as he recognised a gentleman, even though he might be dressed like a farmer. He hesitated only a moment, then shook Gideon's hand.

'Jasper Needler, master.'

That put matters on the right footing.

'And what is the problem here?' Gideon's voice continued to be calm, reasonable. And aristocratic.

'These people–' the man waved scornfully at the huddled settlers, 'they owe rent for the smallholdings as they rent from my principals.'

'But they are living here in our village,' Gideon pointed out gently, 'on land belonging to us. They are not farming any smallholdings belonging to anyone else. Do you perhaps mean our common land over there?' He waved his hand in the direction where the settlement had briefly stood. 'Everything there was destroyed in the flood.'

The bailiff shifted from foot to foot.

'I was told to collect their rents,' he said stubbornly.

'Do you have any written authorisation?' Gideon said it so charmingly, you would have thought he was the man's dearest friend.

Needler began to look very uneasy. 'I don't need no writing,' he blustered.

'Oh, I think you will find that in law you do,' Gideon said firmly. 'Otherwise, you see, it would count as obtaining money by menaces. That is a form of theft. It would carry a prison sentence for you.'

The bailiff now looked really alarmed. 'They said I was to collect the rents.' But he said it with a good deal less conviction now.

'Then they were wrong on two counts. These people are now part of our village, so they cannot possibly owe any rents. And as for your principals' attempt to steal our land, you will very shortly see them in court themselves, when we bring our case against them. Now, have you come far? From London? From Lincoln? Will you take a glass of ale in the yel-hus with me? Or would you rather be on your way?'

The man shook his head, as if a fly were buzzing round it, and began to push his way toward a horse he had left tethered beside the first of the settlers' houses. The crowd of villagers opened courteously before him. Without another word, he mounted his horse and rode off toward the Crowthorne road. Until he was out of sight, no one said a word, then a great noise of yelling and laughter broke out, to greet Rafe who came running along the lane from the medland with Rob.

'Too late,' Alice said with a laugh, slipping her arm through his. 'You have missed all the excitement. Gideon has trounced the enemy with sweet words.'

The Dutchmen were crowding round Gideon and shaking his hand. The children, come out from behind their mothers' skirts, rushed off squealing to play with their friends amongst the village children. Griet ran over and threw her arms around me. She had held back her tears in the face of the bullying bailiff, but she was crying now. She kissed me.

'Oh, Mercy, I give thanks to God that you came to help us.'

'It is Gideon you should thank,' I said with a laugh.

'I shall. I shall kiss him too.'

204

And she did.

When our intrepid merchants returned from Lincoln, we had a tale to tell them. Gideon's reputation in the village had grown ever higher. He had always been known for his kindness and sympathy, and for his courage at the time of Huw's christening. Now his crafty diplomacy in the face of a naked threat gained him great admiration. There is nothing a villager likes better than seeing an arrogant outsider put in his place.

The expedition to market had been successful. The settlers had now earned some much needed coin to purchase goods for their homes. I even had a little left over after my purchases were paid for. Yet there remained two clouds on the horizon. The summer continued colder than many a winter anyone could remember. And Sir John had done nothing to stop van Slyke. Any time now, the drainers would turn their attention to us once more.

Chapter Ten
Tom

I was grateful that the day following the attack I suffered from Edmund Dillingworth's thugs was a Saturday. I stayed in bed and slept for most of the day. Some time in the afternoon, to my astonishment, Anthony brought Goodwife Gorley to see me. He had sought her out in her lodgings and asked her help in treating the injury to my head.

She came in scolding.

'And what did you think you were a-doing, Master Bennington, that is what I would like to know? Master Thirkettle tells me you were set upon by rogues down a dark alley, going to meet an enemy in some dirty tavern!'

She rolled up her sleeves and fetched a pot out of her basket, carefully removing the square of cloth that was tied over the top.

'You young men, you think you can stand up to anything. My man was the same, fool that he was. Thought it would be exciting to go for a soldier. Turn on to your side, so I can see the back of your head, *if* you please.'

Too astonished to protest, I did as I was told.

'Hmph.' She made a sceptical, snorting noise. 'At least someone has had the sense to wash it. I am going to clip away the hair near the injury. You don't want that getting caught up in it.'

I tried to protest, for I confess to being somewhat vain of my thick locks, but she ignored me and I could hear her snipping away. Anthony gave me a comical grin.

'Never fear, Tom. She has not removed much.'

Goodwife Gorley sniffed the wound and pronounced it apparently clean. She smeared it with whatever salve she had brought with her, which smelled fresh and pleasant enough.

'Where do you find the herbs for your salves?' I asked, addressing the hem of her skirt and trying to maintain some dignity. 'Or do you purchase your salves from an apothecary?'

'There's plenty of healing herbs to be found in the Walks,' she said. 'Any that lack, I can find in the fields beyond. I'd no more trust an apothecary, rogues every one of them, than I'd ask a blacksmith to make me a pair of shoes, or a lawyer to charge an honest fee.'

Anthony suppressed a snort.

'You may laugh, Master Thirkettle, but there's a-plenty rogues in the Inns of Court.'

'Indeed there are, Goodwife Gorley,' he said solemnly, 'but not all of us are rogues.'

'Ah, but the two of you are but apprentices still to the trade. Let us judge you when you have been twenty years at the bar.'

'If I am ever called to the bar,' I said, sitting up with a groan, 'then you may pass judgement on me.'

'You will not live to be called,' she said sharply, 'if you do not have a care. That is a nasty blow you took to the head. What else did they do to you?'

I described the kicking I had received.

'And do you feel yourself dizzy at all?'

'A little.' I wondered that I was allowing myself to be questioned by this woman, as though she were a licensed physician. Many years of surrendering my injuries to the care of my mother and Hannah and Mercy, I suppose, had accustomed me to the tyranny of women.

'You must stay abed,' she said, 'or at most sit quiet in a chair here. For a week at least. A blow like that to the head is serious.'

'But I must see Bencher Whittaker on Monday, and I must go to the City. And my work in the library–'

She shrugged. 'Be your own assassin, then. What care I?'

She picked up her basket.

'I am sorry, goodwife,' I said with appropriate meekness, 'I will do as you say. And I thank you for your care. What do I owe you for the salve?'

207

'Nothing!' She gave me a haughty look and strode out of the door.

Anthony raised his eyebrows and grinned at me.

'A formidable woman.' I said, 'she should be in charge of the New Model Army.'

He nodded. 'She terrifies me. Will you follow her instructions?'

'I do find myself somewhat dizzy,' I admitted. 'And my sight is a mite blurred. Perhaps she is right. I can leave the search for the charter a week or so. As for my duties here at Gray's, that is no problem. I will send notes to Bencher Whittaker and Master Hansen, but what of the surgeon? He is expecting me on Monday afternoon. And I believe the mechanical leg has suffered some damage as well as the tear in the leather.'

'If you write a letter explaining everything,' Anthony said, 'I will see that it is sent to him.'

'I will write the notes now.' I got awkwardly to my feet and began to make my way to the office. 'By the way, what became of that lad, John?'

'He went off while you were still asleep. Said he would lose his post if he failed to report to his master. He will come back in a few days to see how you fare.'

In fact the first person I saw from outside Gray's was not John but Master Bolton. I was half dozing by the fire in one of the cushioned chairs on Monday afternoon when I heard a brisk knock on our front door followed by Anthony's voice speaking to someone. It had remained so cold, even though it was supposed to be summer, that we kept the fire alight during the day. However, since the blow to my head the warmth of the fire was apt to make me sleepy. It seemed to be disgraceful to be sitting here idle, but I found that I had little energy to bestir myself. Perhaps Goodwife Gorley was right and my head injury was worse than I had thought at first.

'And what is this I hear?'

Gilbert Bolton came bouncing into the room in his usual irrepressible way, carrying a large bag that clanked as he set it down on the table. I was surprised that he had left his business to come all the way out of the City to Gray's Inn. He shook his finger at me.

'Riotous behaviour and damage to my precious leg?'

I gave him a weak grin. 'Nothing riotous on my part, I assure you! As I explained in my letter, I was set upon by three thugs.'

'Aye, in a dark alley where you had no business to be.'

'Enticed there by someone who meant me harm,' I conceded. 'It was foolish of me. But thanks to the timely rescue by a kind stranger and the arrival of two friends, I have survived to trouble you all.'

'But the leg has not.'

'I am not sure how serious the damage is. I can walk with it, but it does not seem to move as well as it did before. The leather is ripped just below the knee, so perhaps the knee joint has been knocked sideways.'

He crouched down and studied the leg.

'I see you are going barefoot.'

'Anthony,' I nodded toward him, 'has taken my right shoe to have a pair to it made by a shoemaker in Holborn. So I am going about our rooms shoeless. I should have the pair by this evening, so I can restore your shoe to you.' I pointed to his shoe, which was sitting on the windowsill.

'Well, we had best remove the leg, and I will examine it.'

'Do you wish me to leave?' Anthony said.

'Stay if you wish.' I turned to Bolton. 'My friend is most interested in your inventions.'

Bolton removed the mechanical leg and laid it on the table, then began unpacking his tools while he explained the gears in the joints to Anthony. I felt one of those periodic waves of sleepiness washing over me, which had been affecting me since the attack. I leaned my head on my hand and closed my eyes.

I woke when Bolton shook me gently by the shoulder.

'Let us try this now, Master Bennington.' He gave me a sharp look. 'You are not well?'

'Just tired.' I smiled. 'Have you been able to repair the leg?'

'Aye. No serious harm done. The gears in the knee had been knocked a little out of alignment, so they were not engaging as smoothly as they should. Nothing was bent, fortunately. And I have replaced the section of leather that was torn. Luckily I still had some of the same skin left over from when I made the original casing. Now, let us see you walk.'

He helped me strap on the repaired leg and as soon as I stood I could feel the difference. The leg no longer felt slightly twisted. I picked up my crutch and walked back and forth across the room until he was satisfied, sinking at last, thankfully, into the chair again.

'Good,' he said. 'You are making excellent progress.'

He began to pack up his tools into the bag. I could hear him speaking quietly to Anthony.

'I think that blow on the head was quite severe. You say he then walked all the way back here from Chancery Lane? That was quite an undertaking after such an injury.'

'We needed to get him home. And away from that place. For all we knew, those fellows might have come back with reinforcements.'

'Quite, quite. But I think now he should take plenty of rest. I have seen it with war injuries. Immediately afterwards the victim may make great efforts to reach a place of safety, only to collapse once the immediate danger is past. I think he should have several weeks' rest. No straining of the intellectual muscles. No rambling about dark alleys at night.'

'I think he is well cured of dark alleys at night,' Anthony said. 'I am not so sure about his intellectual muscles.'

'I can hear you,' I said. 'I can assure you that my intellectual muscles are quite as fit as yours, Anthony.'

He laughed, and they both came over to me.

'I am serious, Master Bennington,' the surgeon said. 'You must rest. These head injuries can be dangerous things. When you are quite recovered, come to see me again. I have not been able to create the perfect foot with flexible toes yet, but perhaps I will have succeeded by the time you are well. I will bid you good day now.'

'I thank you for coming,' I said. 'I did not expect it. Now I can walk comfortably again.'

'But not too much!' He shook his finger at me again.

'Not too much, I promise. Do not forget your shoe.'

It was not long after he left that the shoemaker's boy delivered my shoes, the old one and the new one he had made to match it. I put them on, one on my good right foot and one on the mechanical leg. I took a turn about the room, the boy gaping in wonderment. The balance was right, so I paid him his master's fee and sent him off.

When he was gone, I sank back in my chair and Anthony sat down opposite me.

'That is two people now, who have said you must rest. I hope you will take their advice.'

At one time I might have argued, but I was feeling dizzy again and the room seemed to waver, as though I were looking at it through water.

'Very well,' I said. 'I will rest.'

In the event, it was nearly three weeks before I resumed my studies with Bencher Whittaker and my work in the library. John Farindon had visited us twice, and taken a meal with us each time. He was curious about the study and practice of the law. We were now well into summer, past the end of term, but as Whittaker was in residence and I had missed so much, he was kind enough to supervise my studies for a few more weeks, although he said he would then give me a long reading list of books to be digested over the summer. That was his word, 'digested'. When I eventually received the formidable list, I feared it might be a somewhat indigestible diet. In an act of surprising generosity, Pension continued to pay the wages for my library work while I was ill. For part of the summer, Master Hansen would be away visiting family in Shropshire, but he would leave me a list of tasks to be done. Secretly I suspected I would work more quickly without him fussing about me.

At the end of my second session with Whittaker after my illness, I decided to ask him for help. I explained that I was attempting to trace the royal charter which had granted our common lands in perpetuity.

'I have learned that Bencher Blakiston of Lincoln's Inn is the lawyer acting for our local lord of the manor, Sir John Dillingworth,' I said. 'About a year and a half ago, Sir John promised my father and other men of the village that he would set his lawyer to find the charter so that we could fight these adventurers in court and establish our rights to the land. As there had been no word from Bencher Blakiston, I went to see him, to discover whether he had traced the charter or whether he could help us find it. He told us that he was acting for one of the companies of adventurers and so it would be a conflict of interests for him to help us.'

I had decided I would say nothing about Edmund Dillingworth and his almost certain connection with the attack on me.

'Indeed,' Whittaker said, 'it would be a conflict of interests.'

'But you see, he was retained by Sir John for the express purpose of finding the charter.' I swallowed. Having come this far, I must make my point. 'I wondered whether you might speak to Bencher Blakiston? Ask whether he has been able to trace the charter? If he can give any advice? Coming from you, as a disinterested party, it would not be so much a conflict of interests.' My voice trailed away in uncertainty.

Whittaker looked at me in astonishment.

'But that would be most improper! I could not make such an approach to a distinguished colleague, a senior Bencher of another Inn. Besides, it would be for me, also, a conflict of interests.'

'I am sorry,' I said. 'I do not understand.'

'I am myself retained,' he said, 'by a company with property in Cambridgeshire. It is a well-established, reputable concern, which is working to convert a marshy wilderness into useful farmland.'

My heart gave a painful jerk as I felt the blood rising in my face. Cambridgeshire! This was the very drainage scheme that had cost my grandfather his life, though by now there might be other men, faceless men hiding behind their agents like Blakiston and Whittaker, who were in charge.

I scrambled awkwardly to my feet.

'I am sorry to have troubled you, sir.'

'You were not to know.' He gave me a small smile, which seemed genuine enough. 'Continue your search. If you can find the charter, you should have a good case at law. However, I cannot help you.'

When I told Anthony what Whittaker had said, he gave a low whistle.

'Whittaker as well! At least he was honest with you, and encouraged you to continue the search.'

212

'I suppose these adventurers pay their lawyers fat fees,' I said miserably. 'No wonder men like Blakiston and even Whittaker are willing to act for them. It is nothing to them but lawyer's business, but to my people it could mean survival or death.'

'We shall merely need to continue the search on our own,' Anthony said calmly. 'Did you hint to Whittaker that you thought Blakiston might have the charter in his possession and might be concealing it?'

'I am not such a fool. As soon as he began talking about Blakiston being a distinguished colleague, I reined in.'

'Aye, that was best. Did you tell me you are to visit the surgeon this afternoon?'

'I am.' I grinned at him. 'Do you want to come with me?' I knew Anthony was keen to see Bolton's other devices, especially the automata.

'If you do not mind?'

'Of course I do not mind. I can see whether he has managed to complete his perfected foot and you can play with his mechanical toys.'

After our midday meal, we hired the same carter who had taken me to Bucklersbury before. He was obliged to let us down a few houses away from the Golden Ram, for the street was blocked by two ox carts which had become entangled.

'Mostly apothecaries in this street, I see,' said Anthony, as we inched past the carts and their arguing drivers.

'Aye, surgeons as well. All of them in a medical way of business, though I think there are no physicians.'

'Too grand to mix with these lowly practitioners, I daresay.'

When we reached Bolton's shop, I stared at it in dismay. The windows were shuttered and a large padlock was affixed to the door. With little hope, I banged loudly on it. I had sent a message to Bolton to say that I would call on Monday afternoon. I could not imagine that he would not have warned me if he did not expect to be here.

'No use your knocking.' A wizened little man had come out of the apothecary's shop next door. 'He's not there and he won't be back. Not for a long while, at any rate.' He wiped his hands on a dirty apron and took a tobacco pipe out of his pocket.

I stared at him. 'What do you mean?'

'Fetched away to the Army, wasn't he?' The man made a great business of lighting his pipe. He drew in a deep breath through the stem, so that the tobacco glowed, then expelled a vast cloud of smoke in our faces with a sigh of pleasure. Anthony and I both coughed.

'You see?' he said smugly. 'Wonderful for clearing the lungs. I have a new shipment of the finest New World tobacco, none of this rank weed fellows are trying to grow in England. I can make you a very good price.'

I shook my head, fanning the unpleasant smoke away from my face. 'We are not interested in your tobacco. What do you mean, that Master Bolton has been fetched away to the Army?'

'Just what I say. Two captains came yesterday and fetched him away. He's worked for the Army before and he's known for clean amputations. If the Army grandees say you are wanted, you go. No questions asked. He won't be back until the latest fighting is over. Seen it before.'

Then, judging we were a poor prospect for a sale, he returned to his shop and shut the door in our faces.

'Gone!' I said, looking at Anthony in dismay. 'What shall I do?'

'Continue to use the leg, I suppose. He wanted it tested, did he not?'

'Aye, but it wasn't finished. He was going to fit a new foot.'

'Well, you are managing well with it as it is. All you can do is carry on until the Army releases him. Still, I am sorry not to have seen his automata.'

We turned away from Bolton's shop, squeezing past the ox carts, which were still entangled, and heading up toward the Stocks Market.

'We can probably hire a cart there to take us back to Gray's,' Anthony said. 'There are certain to be some driving west.'

Ahead of us there seemed to be some kind of a scuffle going on, and a voice shouted, 'Let me go! I am a government servant!'

'That sounds like John Farindon,' I said.

'It does.' Anthony broke into a run and I hobbled after him, cursing my maimed leg.

A couple of officers of the Army, with half a dozen common soldiers, were rounding up young men and tying their hands together. Most were City apprentices in their blue tunics, but amongst them was John Farindon, protesting loudly. Anthony strode up to the nearest officer, looking impressive in his lawyer's gown and cap.

'What is the problem here, captain?' he asked. His voice was reasonable but stern.

'Recruiting for the Army, sir,' the captain said politely. 'Have to make up for the losses in the recent campaigns.'

Several of the apprentices looked sick. They were well aware that they might form the next batch of losses.

'Are you not required to get their masters' permission, before you recruit them?'

'Not any longer. The Army needs men and we mean to get them.'

I had reached them now and took my stand next to John Farindon.

'You must settle the matter of the apprentices how you will,' I said, 'but this man is telling you the truth. He is known to us. His name is John Farindon. He is a post office runner, employed by Parliament. You may not recruit him.'

'So you say.' The other captain sneered at me. He was a great brute of a man, with whom it might be unwise to pick a quarrel.

'Very well, pursue the matter if you will,' Anthony said, 'but I am his legal representative, Anthony Thirkettle of Gray's Inn, and this is my junior, Thomas Bennington. We will take charge of Farindon now. If you wish to take the matter further, you will know where to find us.'

The big officer opened his mouth, but before he could speak the other captain, who appeared to be more senior, shrugged and said, 'If you can vouch for him, we'll not take him, Master Thirkettle. We should have enough without him.' He turned to the frightened apprentices. 'Come along, lads. You're off to glory now. You'll soon be wielding a musket instead of a broom, and we all know how the wenches like a man in uniform.'

A few of the apprentices laughed nervously as they were led away.

'Poor lads,' Anthony said. 'I wonder how many of them will even have learned how to load a musket before they are sacrificed to this senseless war.'

'How are you, John?' I said. The runner was mopping his face with his sleeve. His hands were shaking.

'That were a b'yer lady close thing!' he said. 'If you gentlemen had not come along, they would have taken me. I've just been visiting my married sister in Old Jewry, and I walked right into them, not keeping my eyes open, as I should have done. The streets a'nt safe any more.'

'Let's take a glass of beer before we find a cart to carry us back to Gray's,' I said to Anthony. 'That tavern looks clean.' I pointed across the road. 'Come along, John. You must need it more than we do.'

We ordered a beef pie to have with our beer, for the encounter with the recruiting captains had left us all hungry. The landlord pointed out his small garden behind the tavern, where we sat gladly, for it was one of the few days of the summer which did not feel like winter. The tavern, which had five storeys, cut off the noise of the street, while the wooden fence around the garden made it a pleasant sheltered spot, shaded by a couple of apple trees. John began to relax, chattering about his sister and his small niece, who was nearly three years old and as clever as an African monkey.

'If ever I can do anything for you gentlemen,' he said, wiping the traces of the pie from his mouth, 'you've not but to ask.'

'You've already saved my life,' I said. 'I think we are quits.'

'I never understood why you was down that alley,' he said.

So I explained briefly our search for the charter, and Edmund Dillingworth's promise to meet me there and hand it over, if he had got it from Bencher Blakiston.

'But it was just a trap? This Dillingworth hadn't got the charter, nor yet this Blakiston?'

'It was a trap, right enough,' I said grimly, 'and I was a fool to fall straight into it.'

'We aren't sure about Dillingworth,' Anthony said. 'The Dillingworths are Tom's neighbours at home in the Fens. There's been trouble before. That old trouble might lie behind the trap. Or it might be that Dillingworth wanted to frighten Tom off trying to find the charter.'

'He didn't succeed,' I said.

'But you've searched everywhere for it?' John's eyes gleamed. Clearly he was intrigued by our story.

'Not quite everywhere,' I said. 'The Rolls House, which is where the state copy of the charter should have been deposited. The library of Lincoln's Inn, where we thought Blakiston might have concealed it, if he stole it from the Rolls House. The only other place we can think of it Blakiston's chambers.'

'He could have destroyed it.'

'We don't think so,' Anthony said. 'It would be a serious crime. If he were to be found out, it would mean the end of his career as a lawyer. Whatever the adventurers are paying him, it would not be worth sacrificing his future for.'

'So all you need to do is search his chambers.'

Anthony and I both laughed.

'Aye, that's all,' I said. 'Get into Lincoln's Inn – preferably when Blakiston is not there. Break into his chambers, which are sure to be locked if he is concealing anything of value. Search his chambers. If we find the charter, steal it. Then escape from Lincoln's Inn without being caught. Quite simple, really!'

John grinned at me, but said nothing while the landlord brought us a fresh jug of beer and went back inside.

'I told you that the brother of that scoundrel at the Black Eagle is married to my cousin. He's not such a bad fellow, but he goes in for some petty crime. When I was little lad, he showed me how to pick a lock with a bit of wire. I think I remember how to do it. Take me with you. I can probably open any locks.'

It was a crazy offer, but perhaps it might just work.

'Anthony?' I said. 'What do you think?'

'I think John should practise, to see if he really can pick a lock. Blakiston may not keep his chambers locked, but if he has the charter, you may be sure he keeps it in a locked strongbox.' Anthony poured himself more beer. 'As for getting into Lincoln's Inn, I suppose we could pay another visit to the library, though I am not sure how we would explain John.'

'The most difficult part would be finding a time when Blakiston is not there,' I said. 'With term ended, he will not be in court. And it would be best if we could do this at night. We would be less likely to be noticed entering Blakiston's chambers.'

We talked it round and about until the beer was finished. John promised to practise his criminal skill, while we said that we would try to discover a time, for choice an evening, when Blakiston would be away from Lincoln's Inn.

'Then send word to me and I will come at once,' John said. 'I do not work in the evenings.'

He told us where he was lodging now, not far from Gray's, along a lane off Holborn.

'It took me too long, walking back and forth to Southwark,' he said. 'Now I must be getting back to work. I was delivering to the office in Three Needle Street and took the opportunity to see my sister, but I've been too long absent. The brush with the recruiting officers will be my excuse. And I shall say I was rescued by two friends who are distinguished lawyers. That will impress my master. He is ever trying to curry favour with the gentry.'

We laughed to hear ourselves so described. John drained the last of his beer, caught up his postal satchel and ran lightly off.

'Do you think he can indeed pick locks?' I said.

'What have we to lose? We will test him with a few before we set off on this madcap adventure.'

'It is my last hope.'

'Aye, it is. Come, let's look for a carter. We both have legal work to do. You to struggle through Whittaker's reading list and I to find some precedents for my principal on standard weights and measures. What it is to be a distinguished lawyer!'

John came to see us the following Saturday, bringing an assortment of wires, some ending in hooks of different sizes, some in loops. He laid out on the table several locks of different designs.

'I have been practising, as I promised,' he said, 'and I have found that some locks are very much easier than others, although it is difficult to tell from the outside. The larger locks are not always the more difficult ones.'

He demonstrated his skills on each of the locks in turn and we could see which were easy and which hard. The smallest lock, surprisingly, was the most difficult.

'It is Italian,' he said. 'I believe they are very clever at making locks.'

Anthony and I tried to open the locks with John's bits of wire. We both managed a large, crude looking one, which John said was the easiest, but we could not move any of the others.

'Now let us try you on some you haven't practised,' Anthony said. 'We have but three: the front door of these chambers for one. In my office I have a locked coffer and a strong box.'

John managed the front door lock with ease. We looked at each other.

'So the chambers are not that secure,' I said.

'Let us hope Blakiston's aren't either. Now for the office.'

It took John some time to unlock the coffer, but he succeeded and turned to the strong box. This proved a much greater challenge. He tried one tool after another and began to look anxious. I glanced at Anthony. If Blakiston had the charter, it was likely to be held in a similar strong box.

At last there was a familiar click from the lock and John lifted the lid. He sat back on his heels.

'That was the hardest I've ever had to do.'

'But you did it at last.' Anthony clapped him on the shoulder. 'Well done. I think that deserves a glass of wine.'

When we were sitting with the wine in front of us, John grinned and raised his glass. 'Well, at least if ever I lose my position, I can find employment as a petty thief.'

'Here's to lock pickers and petty thieves!' I said, raising my own glass.

'You are a pair of scoundrels,' Anthony said. 'I am a respectable barrister. What if we are caught?'

I sobered at once. 'You are right,' I said. 'You must not risk it. You have too much at stake. If we are caught, well, John can outrun any captor. I can always go home to my sister's farm.'

Even as I spoke, I hoped fervently that Anthony would not give up on the idea. As I had said before, it was my last hope and I was not sure I could carry it out with only John to help.

'Of course I shall risk it! What is life if we do not take a few risks? It will make a pleasant change from weights and measures.'

Anthony had found an old lawyer's gown left behind by Jonathon Dawes, who had shared his chambers before I arrived. It was a little short for John, but it would serve for our visit to the library. The librarian had not seemed someone who would pay us much attention. All parts of the plan were now in place. Except the most crucial part. How could we know when Blakiston would be absent from his chambers? We even toyed with the idea of breaking in one evening when he was dining in Hall, but it seemed too dangerous. We had no idea how long our search would take and he might return from dinner to find us there.

John went home to his lodgings to await our summons, if ever it came. I pored over the heavy tomes Whittaker had set me and worked at the library catalogues. I found I missed the odd fellow, Hansen, when I was there alone. Anthony yawned his way through his notes on historic weights and measures.

And then we had an unexpected stroke of luck.

A fellow townsman of Anthony's from Ely was a Bencher at Inner Temple, one of the Inns of Court down nearer the river. He invited Anthony to dine there at High Table one night. Anthony went off cheerfully, reckoning that dinner at High Table at an Inn with a reputation for good cuisine was worth an evening in the company of his erstwhile neighbour, whom he described as something of a pompous bore.

I contented myself with a couple of apples and our usual bland cheese, nibbling at them alternately as I struggled with *infangtheof* and *outfangtheof*. At least, I thought, the Anglo-Saxons had vivid names for their categories of crime and the privileges of landowners to exact punishment. The text had lulled me to sleep when Anthony came bounding in with all the verve of Gilbert Bolton.

'Wake up, you sluggard!' he said. 'I have news!'

'What?' I blinked at him in the semi dark, for my candle was down to the very end.

He grabbed another candle and lit it from the stub.

'Blakiston is dining at Inner Temple tomorrow night. It came out quite by chance. Their Treasurer made some polite remark about a guest from Gray's tonight and a guest from Lincoln's tomorrow. I managed to insinuate an innocence question and learned that it is to be Blakiston. The gods have favoured us!'

I grinned at him. 'Careful the Puritans do not hear you. That's a very pagan sentiment.'

'Never mind the Puritans. We must send a message to John first thing in the morning. Do you know when he starts work?'

I shook my head. 'Early, I expect. Possibly before dawn.'

'Well, we must manage it somehow, even if I have to go myself.'

And he did. He had to rouse the gatekeeper, grumbling, to let him out of Gray's long before the gate would normally be unlocked. I was just getting up when he returned.

'Caught John just in time,' he said cheerfully. 'You were right, he does start before dawn. He will come here when he finishes this afternoon and we will make our scholarly visit to Lincoln's library. And then we shall see.'

Neither of us did much work that day. As usual when I was distracted, I found that I read the same page of Anglo-Saxon law over and over, and in the end I could not have told you a word of what had been on that page. Anthony sat at his desk with his papers spread out, but I noticed that most of the time he was staring out of the window, chewing the end of his quill until he ruined it. It was a relief when John arrived and we could stop pretending.

'Before we set off,' Anthony said, 'I think I will tell Henry what we are about, if you do not object, Tom. It would be as well if someone knew where we are going. In case something should go wrong.'

I nodded. 'A good plan.' I sounded casual, but I had a sinking feeling in the pit of my stomach. Many things could indeed go wrong. And if they did, Anthony could be debarred, I could be dismissed as a student, and John could lose his job. We were embarking on a criminal act.

When Anthony returned from seeing Henry, John and I stood waiting. Wearing a gown, John looked quite different and could easily pass for a young law student, one of straitened means, who could only afford an old and shabby gown. If we were questioned by the librarian, Anthony could pass him off as one of his students, but I doubted that the librarian would bother.

'Henry will come down to Chancery Lane at dusk,' Anthony said as we set off. 'Just in case. He might bring some of the other fellows as well.'

I was alarmed. 'We do not want to start a major disturbance.'

'Henry is a sensible man. He will not make trouble if no trouble is needed.'

The librarian at Lincoln's Inn greeted us pleasantly and did not seem surprised either at our return or at the addition to our numbers. I supposed that, since Lincoln's had such an excellent library, he was accustomed to visitors. We made our way to the scroll room and took the time to check whether there had been any changes since our previous visit. We would look very foolish if we broke into Blakiston's chambers while all the while the charter was concealed here instead.

We had skirted well round the door to his chambers on our way to the library, but out of the corner of my eye I had seen the lawyer I took to be his junior going up the steps. So business was still afoot there. I hoped fervently that the junior or the clerks had not been set tasks to carry out while their master was dining away.

Time dragged as we pretended to be busy, but at last the light began to fade. Blakiston must have set out for Inner Temple by now, but we needed greater dark before we attempted our break-in, or we would certainly be seen. That is the problem with communal life. Your every move is observed by someone. Our plan suddenly seemed hopeless and I was on the point of telling Anthony that we should abandon it, when I noticed it had grown considerably darker. Great masses of grey clouds were building up overhead.

'Storm coming,' Anthony murmured. 'That should favour us. People will stay indoors. There's a clump of trees near Blakiston's building. I suggest we withdraw there.'

We bade the librarian a pleasant good evening and sauntered out into the court. It was empty, everyone having hurried to take shelter before the storm broke. We slipped into the shadow of the trees and waited. My stomach churned with the suspense, and I found the palms of my hands were sweating.

'I think it is dark enough now,' I said. The other two nodded agreement.

As we had planned, John ran lightly over to the steps leading to the chambers. If the door was secured, he would try to open the lock before we joined him. Either it was already unlocked or else he had freed it very quickly, for we soon saw him beckon us before slipping inside. Anthony ran across and I limped after him.

We had been worried about how we should be able to see in order to search, without showing a light that would bring someone to investigate. The shutters were closed, but no shutters fit perfectly, there is always a crack through which a sliver of light may be seen. John had found a candle lantern with moveable panels at the side, so a small beam of light could be directed where one was searching. We did not ask whether he had borrowed it from the same thief who had taught him to pick locks.

The outer office looked just as it had done when we had visited it before. There were neat piles of papers on shelves, though no sign of a scroll. I remembered Anthony's theory of hiding something in plain view, but there was nowhere here that a scroll could lie innocently. We moved through to the inner room, Blakiston's private office. Between the two rooms, a staircase led up to the floor above, where he must have his living quarters. My heart sank at the thought that we might have to search there as well. How long would it take?

The inner room, like Anthony's office, held both a locked coffer and a strong box. While John prodded at the lock of the coffer, I quickly checked the desk, but there was nothing here but writing materials and a note about bills owing to the Inn for dinners. Behind me I heard a satisfying click as the lock of the coffer sprang open. Anthony and I turned our attention to it at once, while John moved on to the strong box. To my dismay I saw that this had not one, but three locks.

'We'd best try to leave these papers looking as undisturbed as possible,' Anthony said, gesturing at the coffer.

I leaned over as far as I could, propped on my crutch, and took the lamp from John to shine down into the coffer.

'I can't see any sign of a scroll there. It's all neat stacks of flat paper.'

Anthony took the lamp from me. Leaning over, he ran his hand carefully down the sides of the coffer, between the papers and the wood, then between the stacks of paper.

'You are right,' he said, passing the lamp back to John. 'Everything is too smooth. No scroll there.'

As he lowered the lid of the coffer back into place, I heard one of the strong box locks spring open. John freed the second one quickly, but the third was either jammed or it was a more complicated lock. I was sweating freely now, although the darkening storm had brought a wave of cold air and I could hear rain beginning to drum against the window shutters. At least it should keep the Members indoors. They must have finished dinner by now.

At last the third lock snapped open and John gulped and grinned. He was sweating as much as I was. He sat back on his heels and wiped his face.

'Can you lock the coffer again?' I asked. 'We want to leave everything as intact as possible.

He nodded and crawled across to the coffer, not bothering to get up. Anthony lifted the lid of the strong box and we both peered in.

At the bottom, there was a layer of papers. There were three large bags, presumably holding coin. There was a heavy gold chain, such as aldermen wear.

And there, at the top, was a scroll.

I lifted it out. My hands were shaking so much I could hardly unroll it. What if we had run all this risk and it should prove to be nothing but some old will?

Old it certainly was. It crackled as I unrolled the first few inches and a sliver of parchment drifted off the outer edge. I read the opening words. I looked across at Anthony and nodded.

'It is the charter.'

'God be praised,' he said. 'Let us get out of here as soon as John has fastened the locks.'

He was about to shut the lid, when I laid my hand on his arm.

'Wait! I know that seal.'

Beneath where the scroll had lain there were two letters, both with the same seal. I lifted them out.

'This is the Dillingworth seal,' I said. 'No time to read them now, but I am taking them as well. They may cast some light on what part the Dillingworths play in all this.'

I stuffed the letters down the front of my shirt for safety, but the scroll was too bulky for that. John had locked the coffer. Now, with what seemed like agonising slowness, he secured the three locks of the strong box and slid his wires into his pocket. He got to his feet and brushed the knees of his hose.

'Now, out!' Anthony said. 'But as quietly and carefully as possible.'

We crossed into the outer office and once we were standing beside the door, John dowsed the lantern. Anthony eased the door open a crack and we all strained our ears to listen, but there was nothing to hear but the rain. John gave a faint grunt. He thrust the lantern at Anthony and groped in his pocket. Of course, the outer door would need to be locked! I think we had all forgotten that.

Anthony and I eased our way down the steps and sheltered under the trees. A few moments later, John joined us. It occurred to me then – and it was foolish of us not to have considered it before – that it would look very suspicious if we were to walk out of the gatehouse now, hours after we were known to have left the library. The same thought must have struck Anthony.

'Wait a moment,' he murmured, and slipped away.

'John,' I whispered, 'if we cannot get out, would you be able to climb the wall?'

Lincoln's Inn is surrounded by a brick wall, a wall I would once have been able to climb myself.

'Easily.'

I handed him the scroll. 'Take this. If anything happens, or we can't get out of here, go over the wall and run to the Peacock Inn in Holborn.' I felt in my purse for a few coins. 'That should be enough for a meal and a beer. If we haven't come by the time the inn closes, take the scroll back to your lodgings. I'll come to you later.'

'Right,' he said.

Anthony slipped up to us. 'The gates are locked. I'm a fool. I should have thought of that. We have taken much longer than I expected.'

'John has the scroll,' I murmured. 'He's going to climb the wall.'

I turned to John. 'Go now. If you see Henry, tell him what has happened.'

He nodded and slid away into the shadows.

'He should be safe,' I whispered to Anthony. 'I am not so sure about us.'

'We can't leave by the gatehouse. I wonder if there is some way out through to Lincoln's Inn Fields.'

'If there is a back gate, it will be locked,' I said. 'I have been stupid. I was only thinking of getting the scroll to safety. John could have unlocked the back gate for us.'

We were already wet, but the rain was sheeting down even more heavily now, so I tightened the strings of my shirt. I did not want those letters to be soaked. They might be quite innocent, or they might not. I did not want them to disintegrate in the wet before I had a chance to read them. Even with the protection of the trees, our outer clothes were soaking.

'We cannot stand here all night,' Anthony whispered. 'John must be over the wall by now. Let us go through the grounds to the wall next to Lincoln's Inn Fields. There may be a low place we can climb over.'

He was giving me more credit than my due. I doubted I could climb over even a broken piece of wall. And it was likely the Inn took its safety seriously, if the imposing gatehouse was anything to judge by. The wall would be in good repair.

Anthony took my elbow and urged me forward. The storm meant that everything was darker than it would usually be at this time of night, and the ground was unfamiliar. We stumbled toward the path across the court which led in the direction of the Fields. I was glad of Anthony's steadying hand, but the mechanical leg was serving me well. I could never have managed with the wooden prop. It seemed we might make our way successfully to the far end of the Inn. Perhaps we could conceal ourselves somewhere there and scramble over the wall after dawn. I was sure I could not manage it in the dark. The rain and wind had plastered my hair across my eyes and I raised my hand to push it irritably away.

Just as I did so, a light shone suddenly in my eyes. I covered them with my hand, confused. Where could a sudden light come from? Then I thought of John's shuttered lamp. This must be another, and someone had opened the shutter to shine a beam of light directly in our faces.

'Well now,' a familiar voice said. 'It is the crippled peasant and his lawyer friend. Just what are you doing, creeping about Lincoln's Inn in the dark?'

Edmund Dillingworth. I felt his father's letters crackle inside my shirt.

'We have been working in your library,' Anthony said boldly. 'Ask your librarian. And I have my notes here. We have been accidentally locked in and are looking for a way out.'

'Indeed?' He laughed. 'And how do you account for the fact that the library closed hours ago, before dinner, and you were seen not many minutes since, coming out of Bencher Blakiston's chambers? We have been watching you, you see. Very curious, that you should spend so long there, when he is out this evening. And were there not three of you?'

As my eyes grew accustomed to the light, I became aware of more men standing behind Edmund. The rogues who had struck me down before, no doubt. Now another man ran up.

'No sign of the third, Master Dillingworth.'

'Then we shall just have to amuse ourselves with these two,' he said. He gestured to the men behind him.

Suddenly they were upon us. Anthony went down first, for I suppose they thought I could give them little trouble. Then someone punched me in the stomach, so that I doubled up. Another kicked my feet from under me, and swore as his foot hit the mechanical leg. I was on the ground and someone was kicking my head. Apart from grunts, they went about their work in silence. Yet, just before blackness overcame me, I thought I could hear yelling from the direction of the gatehouse. Then I heard nothing more.

Chapter Eleven
Mercy

It was not long after Gideon had seen off the bailiff that Piet van Slyke began to take an interest in our land again. He had spent some weeks working over at Crowthorne, and Joshua reported to us regularly about the progress of the drainage works there. The man Ephraim, who had also taken part in our rescue of the confiscated stock the previous year, came over to the village with him from time to time. He spoke to me quite civilly, so I supposed he had overcome his antipathy to working with a woman.

One cold July afternoon Gideon and I were sitting with Alice and Rafe near the fire in Jack's kitchen. They had moved back to Rafe's parents' house, but their time living with Jack had awoken the idea again that they might have a home of their own, especially with another child on the way. Having helped to build the new cottages, Rafe was now planning a simpler house himself, which he could enlarge and extend later. There was a suitable spot, just beyond the village green, on the nearer side of the new cottages, and it had been agreed he could build there. He had come to ask for help.

'I would like to move in before winter, and before the new babe,' he said. 'Do you think we might have it built by then?'

'Harvest will be late this year,' Jack said. 'What there is of it.'

'Nehemiah and I will help,' Gideon said. 'Apart from the milking, things are quiet for now.'

I nodded. 'Now is a good time. And if you ask the Dutchmen to help, you can have most of the work done before harvest, then move in before the winter. What do you plan?'

'Something very simple at first,' Alice said, getting up to steer Huw away from the dresser that held Jack's mother's best dishes. Huw was walking now, and he was also climbing. He would be up that dresser like a squirrel. Alice brought him back to the table and gave him his piece of slate and a bit of chalkstone, so he could scribble away.

'We will have a big kitchen on the ground floor, large enough to live and eat in, like yours, Mercy.'

'Aye,' I said. 'We hardly ever use the parlour. I believe Thomas Bennington added it for Mary Dillingworth, but I doubt whether she ever had time to sit there and be a lady.'

'Well, a kitchen is always the heart of a house. We will have some small storerooms behind, and perhaps a bedchamber for a servant girl, if we should ever have one. Then upstairs, two big bedchambers or three smaller ones. The size will depend on what we can afford to pay for timbers to build the frame. All the spare timber salvaged after the flood has been used to build the other new cottages.'

I felt a stab of guilt. Last year when the court officials had come to seize some of our stock as security for my father's fine, Tom had sold our draught oxen to Rafe for coin, coin which he had used towards paying the fine, only to discover that Father was already dead. It was money Rafe had been saving to build a home for Alice and himself. The agreement was that we would buy the oxen back when we had the money, but in all our troubles since, that had not been possible. The only coin I had now was the small amount left over after the trading in Lincoln.

'Rafe,' I said hesitantly, 'we have never bought the oxen back from you, for we have never had the money.'

'I know that, Mercy,' he said. 'Do not fret about it.'

'But I do fret about it. You could build a better house if you could afford the timber. I do not have the coin, but I have this year's fleeces. Suppose I give you enough fleeces to cover the cost of the oxen. Then you can sell them to buy the timber. Or Alice could spin the wool and sell that, it would bring in more profit.'

I saw that Gideon was smiling at me encouragingly, but I was aware, as perhaps he was not, that feeding the oxen over the winter would mean that more of the rest of the stock would need to be slaughtered at Martinmas.

'You cannot do that,' Alice said. She understood perfectly all the implications of my offer.

'I can,' I said. 'All that is needed is for Rafe and me to agree on a fair exchange.'

It took some time, Rafe claiming I should give him perhaps three fleeces and I insisting that ten would be nearer the mark. He had none of his own to sell, for Master Cox still owned the stock, although it was Rafe who did all the work on their farm. In the end we settled for six fleeces, and I promised myself I would choose six of the best, for I wanted Alice to have a solid and roomy house – as roomy as possible – before the new baby was born.

We had just reached this point in our discussions when Joshua and Ephraim arrived, as they often did, to share a pot of ale with Jack at our yel-hus, for they said that the Crowthorne yel-hus was ever under the reproving eye of the Reverend Edgemont.

'And what news of the drainers at Crowthorne?' Jack asked. It was what we all wanted to know.

'They have the mill almost repaired,' Joshua said.

'That must have cost them a few headaches,' Gideon said, 'from all that I have heard about the state of it.'

Ephraim grinned. 'Aye, we did not leave them much of the machine. It was useless. They had to send for a new one, away to the Low Countries.'

'And three of the sails were past mending,' Joshua said, 'though they cannot hold us at fault for that, it was the winter storms. There was a corn mill, about five miles north of here, that was left unattended, and the sails there were destroyed, or so I've heard. A man must care for his property.'

'The sails of the mill the drainers built here were badly damaged as well,' Rafe said, 'but we did not smash the pump. They will try to make you pay for that.'

'Let them try,' Joshua said. 'They shall need take us to court first, for we have no coin. The flood has cost us dear.'

'And the damage the flood did we owe to the drainers,' Jack said. 'It is the drainers who should be paying us. Well, let them come. We have a few surprises prepared for them.'

Soon after this, the men went off to the yel-hus, Gideon and Rafe with them. I said that I would stay with Alice for a time. We walked slowly back toward the Coxes' house, Alice taking her time and Huw hopping about us, in and out of the puddles on the village street.

'Huw, come away! Grandmother Cox does not want all that mud on her clean floors!' Alice gave me a despairing look and I smiled sympathetically.

'Things are difficult?' I said.

She shrugged. 'She is fond of Huw when he is quiet and biddable, which is not very often, I fear. They are both pleased to have an heir, Master Cox is particularly glad I gave them a boy, but it is difficult stop Huw breaking things and causing havoc, now he can go everywhere.'

'They had a son themselves. Do they not remember when Rafe was a child?'

'To hear Mistress Cox speak, he was no ordinary child. He was a little angel, come down to earth.'

'And what does Rafe say?'

'He does not recognise himself.' She grinned. 'He does not contradict his mother to her face, but he has recounted one or two little stories to me . . .Though I think myself that he was kept on a tight rein, poor little lad. Do you not remember how he must always keep his clothes clean, when the rest of us were roaming through the fields? It is hard for him to be obliged to go on living in the same house, and to submit to his parents' orders as if he were still a boy. Our freedom while we lived at Jack's house has opened his eyes.'

'Well, you shall soon have your own house. I will send over the fleeces tomorrow, so set up your spinning wheel and get to work. If Rafe sells one or two fleeces in the raw, he can buy the timbers for the foundations, then when you have spun the rest, he will get a good price. Kitty and I are hard at work already, spinning, weaving and knitting. In another month or two I shall hope to sell at market again.'

We had reached the Coxes' door, and although Alice invited me in I realised it would be difficult for us to gossip freely, with Mistress Cox in attendance. Normally at this time of year we would have sat out in the orchard, but it was far too cold for that.

'How fares your mother?' Alice asked, as she tried to scrape some of the mud from Huw's shoes with a stick. Most of the

231

village children went barefoot, but Rafe had stitched a pair of small shoes for Huw, once he could walk.

'Not well, I fear.' I looked at her bleakly. Alice might need to endure living with Rafe's parents, but both of her own parents were strong and healthy and she had a brother too. With my father dead, my brother gone, and my mother lost somewhere in the darkness of her mind, I had some cause to feel bereft. I gave thanks daily for Gideon, but he too had lost his parents.

'Do you think she will ever come to her wits again?' Alice asked gently.

I shook my head. 'Do you remember Jack's grandmother? She was the same. She just slipped away, until she could barely speak. My mother is losing her words too, and she grows so *angry*. Sometimes I think she hates me. And now she is refusing to eat. She told Kitty that we were trying to poison her.'

I turned away, so that Alice should not see my tears. She put her arm around my shoulders.

'You have so much to burden you, Mercy. Gideon is a truly good man, but he is no farmer. Nehemiah is growing old and Kitty is scarcely more than a child.'

I shook my head. 'Gideon is learning every day. He even demanded that I should teach him to make cheese!'

We both laughed.

'As for Nehemiah, he works as hard as a man twenty years younger. And without his eels and fish and an occasional duck, I think we should have starved by now. Kitty does the work of a grown woman. I have asked Gideon to teach her to read, but the days are so full of work, there has been little time for it.'

'Why should she learn to read? What use will it be to her?'

'You and I will always disagree about this!'

'Never mind,' Alice said. 'I will ask my mother to come and see Abigail. I think she is some comfort to her.'

'Indeed she is. My mother is much calmer when your mother is with her. Perhaps she may even persuade her to eat.'

Alice kept her word, and the next day Mistress Morton arrived, bearing a basket of her own baking. My mother never left her room now. When I tried to lead her downstairs, she backed away, frightened, and retreated to her room. It was better, I suppose, than when she had gone wandering in the night.

'Now, Mercy,' Mistress Morton said, when I offered her a chair and one of Kitty's gingerbreads, 'I am here to look after Abigail, I am not a guest. Away with you to your work and forget about me. Abigail is not come down this morning?'

I shook my head. 'She seems afraid to leave her chamber. And she is refusing to eat.'

'Poor soul. She is so confused, I do not suppose she even knows where she is any more. And not eating? Well, we shall see. I have brought her some of my raspberry cakes, made with some of our few raspberries. They were always her favourites when she was a girl.'

With that she bustled away upstairs, and soon I could hear the murmur of her voice, although I did not hear my mother answering. However, my attention was soon drawn by voices out in the yard.

'Mercy!' It was Jack calling.

I went out to him.

'What's to do?' I said.

'Van Slyke has come, with a dozen of his men. I wanted to warn you to be prepared, in case he storms over here again.'

Gideon came out of the barn, carrying two full buckets of milk.

'There is little we can do,' he said.

'Well.' Jack grinned. 'We shall see whether they enjoy the little surprises we have prepared for them. I thought I would call and tell you before Gideon comes to the village to help with the digging of the foundations for Rafe's house.'

'He has laid it out, then?'

'He has been busy with pegs and string and scribbles on paper since dawn.'

'I will just put these in the dairy,' Gideon said, 'then I will come with you. Nehemiah went off fishing at dawn, but he will be back soon.'

'I have loaded the fleeces on to the handcart,' I said. 'You can take them with you. Then Alice can make a start on her spinning.'

When Gideon and Nehemiah came home that evening, Jack came with them, and they trundled the hand cart into the barn. They were all tired, and grubby from digging in the damp soil, but seemed pleased with the day's work.

'There is no time to rest yet,' Jack said. 'The drainers have just gone back to their camp at Crowthorne, so we must not waste this opportunity. They will be making camp here, as they did last year. This may be our last chance to work unhindered. The others are already away to the ditches, but we wanted to bring the cart back first.'

'What are you planning to do?' I asked.

'Undermine the mill,' Jack said. 'We need any spades and mattocks you have.'

'I'll fetch 'un,' Nehemiah said, and headed for the barn.

'I am going to make sure there is no violence, if the drainers return.' Gideon looked at me seriously. Did he think I would condemn him for joining in the sabotage?

'I am sure you have as good a pair of arms as any of them,' I said cheerfully. 'And I am coming with you.'

Gideon opened his mouth – to protest at this, I was certain – but then he had the good sense to close it again.

'I will just see whether Mistress Morton needs anything. She is still sitting with my mother.'

I ran up the stairs and looked into my mother's room. Mistress Morton put her finger to her lips.

'She is sleeping, but I'll bide with her. If you do not mind, Mercy, I will stay the night. She has been very weak but restless all day.'

'Of course I do not mind. Did she eat your raspberry cakes?'

She shook her head sadly. 'She did but take a single bite of one. She said she could not eat, her stomach was full.'

'Yet she has hardly eaten for days,' I said, pressing my hands to my chest, for I could feel a dull ache there. The bedclothes scarcely showed the gaunt shape of my mother lying beneath them.

'Aye. I can see that. You must be prepared, Mercy. I do not think she has long. But I may be wrong. It may be no more than a passing fancy, that she will not eat.'

I left them there, my mother sleeping, Mistress Morton quietly knitting as she sat in a chair by the bed, and I flew into the room I now shared with Gideon, which had once been Tom's. I dropped my skirt and petticoat on the floor and found a pair of Tom's old breeches in his coffer. I had worn them before and knew that with a tight belt, and folded over at the waist, they would serve well enough. I ran down the stairs again.

'Shall I come, Mistress Mercy?'

Kitty stood at the door, her face alive with excitement. I ought to tell her to stay, in case Mistress Morton needed anything, but I could not disappoint her.

'Bring a candle lantern and a strike-a-light,' I said. 'It is so dull these days it will be dark coming back. You can keep watch for us.'

I did not expect the drainers would return tonight, they were probably gorging on stolen Crowthorne mutton, but it would do no harm to be sure.

The men had already started along the lane, perhaps thinking I was not coming, but I picked up a spade, and Kitty and I hurried after them.

All through that evening's work, I kept thinking of Tom and how we had defied the drainers together last year. He had been a leader of the young men then, one of the fastest runners, a fine horseman. Where was he now? Would he ever come back to us? The loss of his leg had hurt him very deeply, I knew. It was more than a mere physical injury. It had destroyed his whole life and his place here amongst us. I brushed away angry tears, which no one was likely to see in the gathering dark, as I thought how these unknown speculators had been the cause of everything that had happened to Tom, and to all of us later in the flood.

On inspecting the previous work Jack and the others had done in cutting away under the banks of the ditch across the medland, we found that the banks had indeed collapsed when the men walked on them, just as Jack had planned. Tonight one group set to work to damage more of the banks – Will and Abel, along with Joseph Waters and his two nephews, and a few more. The rest of us crossed to the far end of the medland, where Hannah's cottage had once stood. It was here that van Slyke had built his mill to pump water out of the Fen, and feed it along their ditch to

Baker's Lode. The pumping mill stood on the very edge of the field, where it dropped a few feet into the beginning of the Fen.

All the wet weather we had endured over the past weeks had done little good to the crops, since there had been no intervals of sun, but the reeds were flourishing. The whispering of the reeds is the song of the Fens, and it sings to us fenlanders from birth to death. It is so much a part of our lives that I suppose we almost forget that we are hearing it, and only notice it when it stops, which is hardly ever. Only when a truly hard frost turns even the reeds into upright pillars of ice, and one of those bitter still nights of a frozen winter kills any breath of the wind, does the music of the reeds cease.

I missed it too when I was carried off for trial in Lincoln. The town was full of noises: harsh noises of people shouting and dogs barking and iron-clad wheels clattering over cobbles. But no song of the reeds.

'Now,' Jack said, when we had gathered beside the mill. 'What we want to do is leave the mill looking exactly as it did earlier today when van Slyke inspected it, so we will do no obvious damage to the mill itself. We need to go out on to the moss and dig away into the bank, underneath the mill. We will fill the holes with loose rushes, just to keep the earth in place for the moment. What I hope will happen is that, as soon as men begin climbing about in there, the extra weight will cause the earth to collapse. It may not work, but it is worth a try.'

'How do we know it is safe to walk on the moss just there? With all the rain, it may be treacherous.' It was the carpenter, Ned Broadley.

'We'll test it carefully first, not all rush on to it together. The causeway into the marsh starts here, and it will give us access to the left side of the mill. If we can't go further, we must just undermine the one side.'

'The earth we dig out,' Gideon said. 'Won't they see that? It will be quite clear in daylight.'

'Aye,' someone said.

'Well thought of,' Jack said. 'We must just make sure we heave it well away into the marsh. No being idle and dropping it at our feet.'

'I will test how firm the ground is, under the bank,' I said. 'I am the lightest.'

'I am the lightest.' It was unusual for Kitty to speak out in such a large company, but she was wild with the excitement of it all.

'You are supposed to be keeping watch,' I said severely. 'Besides, I know this part of the Fen better than most of you. I used to go out along the causeway with Hannah.'

Before anyone could stop me, I had pulled off my shoes and stockings and stepped down on to the beginning of the causeway. Mud oozed up between my toes, but the causeway held. The last time I had stood here it was with George Lowe, when I fetched him out of the Fen. But I must not think of George, drowned in the flood. I began to take my first precarious steps off the edge of the causeway onto the surface of the moss.

'It is quaking,' I called up to those leaning over the bank above me, 'but it is holding. I think those of us who are lightest should work at this end, the heavier ones keep to the causeway.'

Soon we were at work, a row of us like a colony of badgers, digging tunnels under the mill and throwing the waste soil as far as we could heave it into the wetter parts of the Fen, in the hope that it would be drawn down and out of sight before the drainers returned.

Gradually I became aware of whispered voices above us, and turned to Ned, who was next to me.

'Who is that, up there?'

He was taller than I and could just see over the top of the bank. He clicked his tongue in annoyance. 'It is Rob and some of the other children. They must have followed us. I'll send them off.'

He was about to climb the bank, but I laid a hand on his arm.

'They could be useful. We still need reeds to stuff into our tunnels. Tell them to go and gather armfuls of reeds. We should not cut them here, it will just draw the drainers' attention. Tell them to go over to the mere, where Nehemiah's cottage used to stand, and gather them there. And to take care not to fall in!'

I knew it was unlikely they would, and most of them could swim like fish, but it was getting very dark.

Soon, from the rustling and the giggling, we knew that the children were back. Jack declared that he thought we had done enough.

'We do not want it to collapse too soon,' he said. 'We want them to think it is their fault. Now, you young 'uns, pass us down those reeds and let us finish the work. Not a single reed to be left lying about, do you hear?'

We shoved bundles of reeds into the damp burrows we had dug into the bank, until each one was stoppered like a bottle and we were all of us covered from top to toe in mud. As we clambered up on to the bank, I realised I could hardly feel my feet, they were so numb with the cold. I began to grope about on the ground where I thought I had left my shoes, and stubbed my toe painfully on something in the dark.

I let out an involuntary yelp, which brought Kitty over to me, carrying the candle lantern.

'What's amiss?' she said. 'Have you hurt yourself?'

'Stubbed my toe.' It was quite painful. 'Here are my shoes.'

I picked them up. What had I stumbled over?

'Give me the lantern a moment, Kitty.'

I swung it around, trying to find the cause of the pain. A large stone? A tool left behind by the drainers? I crouched down, the better to see.

'It is a tree,' I said. 'At least, there is a hummock here, which must cover an old stump. That is what I banged into. And there is a new young tree growing up from it.'

I sat back on my heels. Hannah's cottage had stood just there. And here?

'It is Hannah's cider apple tree.' My voice was shaking. 'Her tree. It is growing again.'

I think every one of us would have liked to see what happened when the drainers came back, but we could not all stand about staring at them. It was agreed that Jack, as instigator of the plan, along with one of the Waters boys, would make a pretence of tending some of the sheep in the medland, where they could observe what happened when the drainers entered the mill. In the meantime, every man in the village was helping with the building of Rafe's house, digging the ditches for the foundations and filling them with stones, packed down hard, on which the base timbers could be laid. These must be stout beams of well weathered oak, for they would need to support all the weight of the house. Ned would then drill and chisel out the sockets for the mortise and tenon joints, where the upright timbers would be fitted.

Rafe himself had set off before dawn to sell two of the fleeces and buy these first vital beams. There was a woodsman halfway to Lincoln who might be willing to take the fleeces in exchange instead of coin, which would save Rafe the journey all the way to Lincoln and back. Since the war had brought so much uncertainty, including suspicion about the quality of the coins circulating through the country, many people preferred goods in their hands instead of metal coinage of sometimes dubious value.

With Gideon and Nehemiah working in the village, all the farm tasks fell to Kitty and me, so we laboured hard all day. Mistress Morton, having spent the night at my mother's bedside, was kindness itself, cooking meals for us, and even taking time to shut up the hens in the evening. The men returned after dark, hungry, although they admitted that Mistress Cox and Mistress Sawyer had fed them well while they worked.

'Rafe managed to make an exchange with the woodsman,' Gideon said, stretching his legs out before the fire. I noticed there was a hole in the toe of his hose. 'He brought back as much as his cart would carry. All the beams for the base, and some of the uprights. He will fetch more tomorrow.'

'All that for two fleeces?' I was astonished.

'The woodsman has trusted him with the timbers, in advance of the remainder of the payment. His wife died of the marsh fever two years ago and he has three young boys. He has ordered blankets from Alice, and warm winter clothes for the lads. He has no woman to weave and knit for the family. Alice will go with Rafe tomorrow, to measure the children.'

'A good exchange for all, then,' I said.

'Aye, Rafe has been lucky. We should finish the foundations tomorrow, then we will start to put the frame together. Ned will be in charge of that, and the rest of us will be his apprentices and labourers.'

He grinned suddenly. 'I only hope that Rafe has worked out his calculations correctly. He has planned it all in such a rush.'

'Ned will set him right,' I said with certainty. 'He knows how to frame a house, though he cannot read and can only draw plans based on rule of thumb.'

'Aye. Sometimes I am almost ashamed of my book learning, now that I am coming to know the skills of our unlettered neighbours all the better.'

'Like cheese making?' I gave him a wicked grin, and dodged when he threw a cushion at me.

The house building continued at a fast pace, for we had been spared rain for a few days, and everyone was eager to do as much as possible while there was the opportunity. The crops recovered a little under the thin sunshine, and we all hoped that it would mean there would be some food to be gathered when it was time for harvest. Kitty and I continued to run the farm by ourselves and were so busy making cheese and pickling eggs for the winter that we had no opportunity to deal with the rest of the fleeces. Mistress Morton stayed on with us, and turned her hand to some spinning. She also dyed some of the spun yarn with onion skins, woad and madder, so we should have a supply of different coloured wools when we had time once more for weaving and knitting. I saw nothing of Alice. Gideon brought word that she was working like a woman possessed, to make the goods for the woodsman.

'She is determined Rafe shall pay for all the wood before the house is complete,' he said. 'He must not be foresworn!'

'That is like Alice,' I said. 'She will always put those she loves before herself, but she should have a care. There is the unborn child to think of as well.'

'She will do nothing foolish,' Mistress Morton said, as she dished out our evening meal. 'My girl has a sensible head on her shoulders.'

To our disappointment, the drainers had not returned to the mill since we had undermined it, and we began to worry that the tunnels might begin to collapse before they came. It was a relief that there was no more rain at present, for that would certainly have caused the weakened bank to crumble.

The whole framework of Rafe's house was assembled and erected before van Slyke and his men returned to the medland. Shortly after they were seen, Jack, accompanied by Dick Waters, sauntered out to the flock grazing on the medland, well away from the ditch. Jack came that evening to tell us the tale, rubbing his hands in glee.

'At first I thought all our labour would go for nothing,' he said. 'They were working on their ditch first, shoring up the banks which had collapsed. I began to think we could hardly pretend to go on tending the ewes for much longer, when at last van Slyke and about half a dozen of his men went over to the mill.'

He took a swig of the beer I had poured for him. 'They seemed for ever to be poking about outside, then one of the men climbed up a ladder to inspect one of the sails, and came down shaking his head. I thought they would leave then, but at last they all went into the mill and closed the door. Dick and I stood there, holding our breath.'

'And?' I said. I knew Jack was teasing us by prolonging his story.

'Then we began to hear a creaking noise. It reminded me of my time as sea. The ship used to creak like that in a storm. It's the sound of tightly fastened timbers under strain. There was only that creaking at first, then a crackling, the noise you hear just as a felled tree begins to fall.'

'Did the mill fall?' Kitty was as impatient as I was.

'Aye, Kitty lass, the whole mill keeled over like a felled tree and collapsed into the moss.'

'We did it!' she said with shining eyes, clapping her hands together.

I began to feel I was not setting her a good example, were I to gloat as well. There had been men inside the mill.

'Were they injured?' Much as I loathed them, I hoped we had not killed any of the drainers.

'They all climbed out, eventually. The door had ended above their heads, so they must have had to scramble up through it somehow. Then they made their way crawling along to the base, which was the only part still on the bank, and slid down from there. A few of them were limping, and one man was holding a bloody clout to the side of his head, but none seemed seriously hurt.'

'God be thanked,' Gideon said. 'We should none of us want to be a party to murder.'

241

'Such considerations do not hinder them,' Jack said seriously. 'Remember how van Slyke shot at Tom. He could have killed him.'

'That does not make it any better for us,' Gideon said. 'What state is the mill in?'

'Badly smashed. It will need to be completely rebuilt.'

'Do you think they will suspect what we did?' I asked.

Jack shook his head. 'There was such a mess of timber and earth and rushes, no one would think the collapse anything other than an accident. The ground is still very soft since the flood – their flood – and then all this rain. I think we may take it that they will believe it a natural disaster.'

'Well, that will hamper them for a good while,' I said, 'since it is clear that Sir John has certainly used none of his powers as a Justice of the Peace to curb their activities. If only we can hold them back until Tom finds the charter.' I sighed. 'If ever he does.'

All of us would need to help with the harvest before the weather broke again, poor as the crops were likely to be, but we wanted to see the outside of Rafe and Alice's house secure against the rain before then. The spaces between the timber framework would first be filled with panels of woven withies and rushes, like the hurdles we use for penning sheep. Then these would be plastered over with a daub made of clayey soil, sand, animal hair, and cow dung. Laid on thickly, inside and out, it would eventually harden, whenever we had any warmth in the sun. Afterwards it could be lime washed.

Even the women could help with the daub, so the next day, after Kitty and I had finished the milking, we donned our oldest clothes and walked to the village. Some of the men had already prepared several large heaps of daub, turning it with spades until it was well mixed, and everyone from the village crowded about to help. A few of the elderly sat on upturned barrels and told us we were doing it all wrong. The children ran about, gloriously dirty, but they were useful, pushing their small hands in where others could not reach. The younger men perched on ladders, coating the upper panels and sometimes dropping gobs of daub on unsuspecting heads below, not altogether by accident. Kitty and I found places out of their range, and began to slap and smear daub on to lower panels. If you do not think about where it has come from, cow dung does not smell too unpleasant, not like human waste. I think it is because cows feed on simple clean things like fresh grass or hay. And applying the daub to the woven panels is like being a child again, playing in a sodden lane, making mud villages for imaginary games.

It is quite hard labour as well, for you must work the daub well in amongst the woven withies, not simply smooth it over the surface. We were all glad when it was time to stop for a midday break of beer, bread, cheese, and pickled eel. Some of the men ate theirs with their daub-covered hands, but I took Kitty firmly off to the Coxes' house, where Alice gave us a bucket of water to wash in.

'It is really beginning to look like a house now!' she said excitedly.

'If only there were more sun,' I said, 'to dry the daub. Then you could have it lime washed before harvest.'

'Never mind,' she said. 'It will dry in time. I expect it is better for it to dry slowly. There are still the inner dividing walls for the rooms to build, and the floors, and the stairs. Once the house is water tight, that can be done even when it is raining.'

Involuntarily, I glanced at the sky. Clouds were gathering out to the east, over the sea. They would not reach us today, but perhaps tomorrow.

'Toby and Ned and Robin plan to start thatching the roof this afternoon,' I said, 'on the far side, where the daub is finished.'

'Let us hope they can finish this side as well,' she said, 'before the rain comes again.'

'Nehemiah wanted to help, and he is an excellent thatcher, but the others said he was too old to go climbing about the roof.'

'He would not be pleased about that.'

'He was not.'

We all continued to work hard for the rest of the day, and by dusk all the daub had been applied. The roof was about three-quarters thatched, but the rain clouds were rolling nearer. The men working on the roof decided to continue by the light of lanterns, which they hung from the branches of nearby trees, not wanting to risk candles too close to the reed thatch. It seemed an impossible task, to complete it before the rain came, in the dark, but Nehemiah, ignoring the protests of the younger men, climbed up with a bundle of reeds on his back and the handle of his legget tucked into his belt, to begin work on the unfinished area. It was a delight to watch him, for I think no one understood the reeds as he did. Or perhaps the reeds understood him, waterman that he was. In any case, the layers of reeds fell into place smoothly and were tapped level with the legget, with none of the cursing and fumbling of the other men. Finally admitting his greater skill, the younger thatchers passed up further bundles of reeds and twisted hazel staples as he gave his orders.

Leaving them to finish the work, Gideon, Kitty and I began to walk up the lane to Turbary Holm.

'I hope Mistress Morton has made us a supper,' Kitty said. 'I could eat an ox!'

'And there is still the milking to do.' I groaned. I had forgotten the milking.

'I'll fetch the cows in,' Gideon said, turning aside to take the shortcut to the medland.

'Can you manage without Jasper?' I asked, for I had left the dog at home, fearing that he might find the heaps of daub irresistible to roll in.

'Aye. If I lead Blackthorn, the others will follow.'

Kitty and I continued on our way, stumbling occasionally in the dark. A sudden rumble of thunder startled us.

'A good way off still,' I said. 'I hope they finish the thatching in time.'

'Nehemiah is very good, isn't he?' Kitty said. 'For such an old man.'

'He does not think he is so old. And he isn't as old as he looks. He has had a hard life. I think he must be about five and fifty.'

Kitty's eyes widened. To her Nehemiah at such an age must have seemed a true Methuselah.

The house was very quiet when we entered. Jasper was asleep by the fire, and there was something simmering in the iron cookpot hanging at the side of the fire. Mistress Morton would be up in my mother's bedchamber. However, she must have heard us come in, for we had scarcely removed our muddy shoes before she was there, coming through from the stairs. Her face was pale, and streaked with tears.

244

She put her arms around me. 'I'm sorry, Mercy. I was going to fetch you, but it happened so quickly in the end. I am afraid Abigail is gone.'

I looked at her in disbelief. My mother had been sitting up in bed when I left in the morning, recalling with Mistress Morton some adventure of their youth. She had even laughed a little and, looking up at me standing in the doorway, she had smiled. Not as if she knew I was her daughter, but merely sharing a happy memory.

Nothing seemed real. I took up a candle and began to climb the stairs, only aware that every joint ached. Below me, I heard Mistress Morton telling Kitty to wait. There were candles burning in my mother's chamber, giving light where there was no one to see. In the big bed where once my parents had slept, the bed where I myself came into the world, there was only a tiny figure, who seemed no bigger than a child.

I set down my candle and knelt by the side of the bed. One of my mother's hands lay, palm up, on the cover, and I took it in both of mine. It was not quite cold. I pressed it to my lips.

'Oh, Mama,' I said, 'surely you must remember me now, wherever you are. I hope you find Father, and your sister Elizabeth.' Her hand, which I had always known so busy, spinning, weaving, sewing, cooking, kneading bread, lay forever still. 'I wish I could have comforted you these last terrible months.' A sob rose in my throat, choking me.

I saw that her face looked peaceful, as though all the fear and confusion had been swept away. But I had never in all my life felt so forlorn.

The storm broke in its full strength that night, and raged for a day and a half. When the clouds finally blew away and a fragile sun peered out, Gideon rode to the village to see the Reverend Webberly and arrange the funeral. I went about my usual tasks automatically. Although my mother had been lost to us for months, yet I suppose I had always clung to the hope that she might find her way back to us, although I knew in my heart of hearts that it was a vain hope.

When it came to the time for the funeral, all the village gathered to support us, for my mother had lived here all her life.

245

The elders of the village could remember her being born. And until the blight of a wandering mind fell upon her, she had been busy about the village and well loved. It was she who had taken in the foundling Kitty, and she who had provided many a meal for Joseph Waters and other paupers. I went through the service without truly hearing the words, only coming to my senses when clods of wet earth began to be shovelled down upon the coffin. Then I turned aside, feeling sick. Even Gideon's arm, gripping me firmly around the shoulders, was little comfort. We held a modest wake afterwards, but the new rector disapproved of such things, so it was brief and quiet. Afterwards I went to bed and slept for a day.

The rain storm had flattened the crops. Although we had a week of mild sun, there was little hope of gathering much at harvest time. Before we attempted to reap what we could, I wrote to Tom, telling him of our mother's death, and begging him for news, for I had not heard from him for a long while. I told him too that I was growing very doubtful of Sir John's honesty. As more time passed and he did nothing to stop the adventurers or to send us any word about the search for the charter, I began to grow more and more fearful. Had Sir John somehow betrayed us? I wanted Tom's opinion and I wanted to know what he was doing in London.

At long last we trailed out to begin harvesting what we could from our meagre crops. It was heartbreaking. The pitiful yields of wheat and barley were perhaps a quarter of what we could expect in a normal year, or even less. Much of the crop lay flattened and rotting on the ground. The beans had fared a little better. Some had rotted, while some, in the parts of the field that were better drained, had gone almost too far, so that the beans were large and tough. Still, if we dried them they could be added to pottage flavoured with an end of bacon or a beef bone, to make a dull but sustaining meal. The stalks that were not rotted we cut for forage for the sheep and pigs. I was worried lest our share of the hay we had cut earlier in the summer should prove insufficient for our cows. We had two male calves we would slaughter before winter for beef, but I was anxious to over winter all the cows, for our cheeses were one sure food which could sustain us, summer and winter.

The final day of cutting the wheat was coming to an end. Everywhere there were worried faces, and voices subdued by anxiety. The last cart set off to the village with its pitiful load as we shouldered our scythes and began to trudge homewards. As we reached our lane, I saw a figure approaching from the direction of the village and shaded my eyes from the mocking light of a sun which had come too late to do us any good. It was a young man, by the look of him, but limping and weary almost beyond endurance. When he drew nearer, I recognised him.

'Ben!' I cried. 'It is Ben! Whatever can he be doing here? And where are the others?'

As he reached us, he seemed to stagger, as though he would fall, and I saw that that his left sleeve was blood soaked. There were the dark stains of dried blood and the fresh crimson of wet blood from an open wound. He took a few tremulous steps towards me and held out his hand pleadingly to me.

'Mistress Mercy,' he said. His voice was dry and cracked. 'Help me. Please help me.'

Then he slid to the ground at my feet.

Gideon thrust his scythe at Nehemiah and stooped to lift the boy up.

'He's nothing but a skeleton,' he said grimly. 'He weighs no more than a child.'

'We must get him home quickly,' I said. 'Run ahead, Kitty, and put water on to heat. Don't trip over your sickle! We will need to put him in your room by the kitchen.'

She nodded and sprang away without a word.

We followed as fast as we could. Toby was still with us, and Alice's brother Robin, who both offered to help.

'Nay,' I said, 'we will manage. He is hurt, but it cannot be serious if he has walked all this way. You go back to the village and help with unloading.'

I was not sure I knew where Ben had walked from, but I could see that his injury needed attention without any delay.

Kitty had a pot of water heating when we reached the farm. She had moved her belongings out of the small chamber and piled them in a heap on Father's chair.

'Lay him down on the bench, Gideon,' I said, 'and we must take his shirt off.'

The shirt was so tattered it fell almost to pieces in our hands. I recognised a patch I had put on it many months before. Ben cried

247

out as we peeled away the bloodied sleeve, and I nearly cried out myself when I saw the state of his arm.

'Sword slash,' Gideon said.

I nodded. Kitty brought me the warm water and rags, and I knelt beside the bench and began to sponge away the dried blood that was crusted with dirt and pus. The wound, which was deep and more than a handspan long, continued to bleed. Ben moaned, but bit his lip and tried not to cry out.

Gideon and Nehemiah stood watching helplessly, which made me nervous.

'Gideon,' I said, 'bring me one of your leather belts. Then can you both go to the milking? Kitty and I are enough to care for Ben.'

They did as they were bid, recognising that they were of no help to us.

'Kitty, can you carry on cleaning Ben's arm?' I got up and went to fetch what I needed – poppy syrup and a salve of woundwort, a needle and stout thread. I added some of the poppy syrup to a mug of small ale and lifted Ben's head and shoulders so he could drink.

'This will ease the pain a little,' I said.

He drank thirstily. I hoped it would ease the pain. I did not dare give him much, he was so emaciated.

Kitty moved over so I could reach Ben's arm.

'Now, Ben,' I said, 'this wound must be stitched. I won't lie to you, it will hurt, but I will do it as quickly as I can. It will only heal properly if it is stitched, do you understand?'

He looked at me with frightened eyes, but he nodded.

I put the leather belt in his right hand.

'It will help if you grip this between your teeth.'

He looked even more frightened. 'You a'nt going to cut my arm off, Mistress Mercy? That's what they done in the army.'

'Of course not,' I said briskly. 'It isn't that serious, but it's deep, and we must give the two sides of the wound the chance to grow together again. Now, bite on the belt.'

I turned to Kitty. Her face was very white, and she too looked frightened.

'Do you want to go away?'

She swallowed uncomfortably. 'I'll stay, if you need me to help.'

'It will help if you can hold his arm steady, because he will probably flinch. He can't help it. But you do not need to watch.'

She nodded and gripped Ben's lower arm hard with both hands, but she turned her face away.

It needed eight stitches to pull the wound together. It is a hateful business, even though I had done it before and on larger wounds. Ben yelped despite the belt, and Kitty gave little sympathetic cries. It was done at last. I smeared the whole of his upper arm with the healing salve Hannah had taught me to make, then wound a clean bandage around it.

Kitty went outside into the fresh air to recover, while I cleared everything away and brought Ben more ale.

'We'll have supper soon,' I said, 'and then you will feel better. Do you want to tell me what has happened? Where are the others?'

I drew up a stool next to the bench where he lay, so that I did not at first see the look on his face.

'What is it, Ben?'

I took his right hand, which was dirty and callused, the nails bitten down to the quick.

'It was terrible, Mistress Mercy,' he whispered. 'I never thought it would be like that. I dunno. I suppose I'm just stupid. They tell you fighting is noble, you're a hero. It a'nt. It's a bloody Hell. Never mind what old Edgemont talks about Hell. You don't need to wait for Hell, it's right here.'

He seemed to be staring at something he could see, beyond the kitchen wall, and he had begun to shake.

'It was all yelling and blood and pain. Cannon balls and shot was flying around, but that a'nt the worst of it. You're there, right face to face with another man like yourself and you don't know him but he's just another man like yourself and you have to kill him because if you don't he'll kill you first and he's just another Englishman like you not some b'yer lady foreigner. And then somebody's head flies through the air like a football and lands at your feet. And it's Aaron's head. Do you remember that football game you had in Crowthorne last year, when you stole the stock back? Me and Aaron watched it together and then there he was

249

staring up at me from the mud and I wanted to say, "What are you doing down there, Aaron?" Only this other man, this man that was a man just like me, he slashes at my arm with his sword. Why didn't he shoot me? I thought, then I saw he hadn't got a gun so maybe he lost it. And I didn't know where any of them were, my pals. So I started to run and I got out of the fight and I saw Seth sitting on the ground leaning against a tree and clutching his belly and I said, "What are we going to do?" and he said, "Get out of it lad, I'm not going to make it." And it was getting dark and I scarpered. I don't want no more of their damned army, so I came back here.'

He had struggled to sit up and I slipped my arm round his shoulders, for I feared he would fall on to the floor, he was so distressed.

'I've deserted, Mercy.' His voice as hysterical. 'They'll shoot me if they find me. What am I going to do?'

I put both arms around him. He was scarcely older than Kitty. Just a boy.

'Hush, Ben,' I said, trying to hold back my own tears and keep calm. 'You are going to stay right here on Turbary Holm.'

Then he fell against my shoulder and began to sob.

Chapter Twelve
Tom

Someone was manhandling me. I could hear grunts and curses. What did Edmund Dillingworth intend? Would he dare go so far as to kill us? If we were dumped in one of those dark alleys off Chancery Lane, knifed in the back, no one would be surprised – just another two young men foolish enough to be out at night in these troubled times. There flashed through my mind what the carter Joseph Thompson had said, about the masterless men and renegade soldiers roaming the heath north of London since the war had begun. We were not so very far from the heath here, outside the City itself. Found murdered, we would be regarded as just two more of the incidental casualties of wartime.

My shoulder was wrenched painfully and I let out a yelp, smothered as a large hand was clamped over my mouth. I bit it.

There was an answering yelp.

'Have a care of your friends, Tom, or we might just leave you here.'

It sounded like Henry, but how could that be?

I felt myself being lifted up, then dragged. My hand scraped painfully on stone. My head was throbbing and I could not clear it enough to make out what was happening.

Then I heard Anthony whisper, 'Don't leave his crutch behind!'

Anthony was recovered, then, though he sounded breathless.

'What's afoot?' I just managed a faint croak.

I felt someone's breath in my ear. A voice I did not recognise said, 'We're over the wall into Lincoln's Inn Fields. We'll need to make a run for it, before they realise where we've gone.'

251

I gave a choked laugh. 'Can't run.'

'Well, hobble, then. No time to waste.'

They propped me up, sitting on soaking grass with my back to the wall. Brick. That was what had scraped my hand, not stone. It was still raining and I could feel the wet from the grass soaking through my breeches. Anthony was sitting next to me, swigging something out of a leather flask. He passed it to me and I took a deep draught. Choked. Coughed. Aqua vitae!

'Quiet!' someone hissed.

'Can you walk?' That was Henry. 'We need to get away from here.'

I nodded. Passed the flask back to Anthony, who took another swig and handed it up to Henry. I could just make him out now, silhouetted against the sky. The clouds must have cleared a little.

Anthony and I staggered to our feet, helped by unseen hands. Someone handed me my crutch.

I lurched forward, not sure which way to go, but Henry had me by the elbow, guiding me. The grass in the Fields was long and lush, from all the rain of this miserable summer, so that we had to wade through it, like water. The ground was uneven, with hummocks and hollows to trip us up in the dark and thickets of thorn bushes and brambles to claw us. At one moment a briar or blackberry branch slashed my hand, and at another I would have fallen full length when I slipped on a cowpat, if Henry had not tightened his grip. I am not sure how large Lincoln's Inn Fields are, but they seemed to stretch for miles. In the night and the rain, we probably followed a roundabout course, but at last we reached the beaten earth track that was the continuation of Holborn out into the country.

There we stopped. The heavy clouds had begun to clear away, though a mizzling rain continued. All of us were soaked and shivering. For the first time I could make out our rescuers. Besides Henry there were five other students and young lawyers from Gray's, most of whom I scarcely knew. What were they doing here?

As if he had heard my unspoken question, Henry grinned at me as he wiped the rain from his face with his sleeve.

'When Anthony told me about your escapade, I decided to recruit a few friends in case we were needed. I reckoned you could well run into trouble. We have had a few quarrels with Lincoln's in the past, a right battle back in '45. At Gray's, we've no love of them, so I thought if they caught you, they wouldn't spare you a beating.'

'Did John find you?'

'That young lad, masquerading as a student? Aye. Said you were locked in and might have trouble. Said he was to wait for you at the Peacock. Come on, lads. Let's make our way there.'

'But I don't understand how you got in,' I said. 'The gates were locked.'

'Two of them climbed over the wall,' Anthony said.

'And the rest of us created a hullabaloo at the gate, banging and shouting, till the gatekeeper came to see what was afoot.' It was one of the lawyers speaking, one I did not know.

We began to walk down Holborn, in the direction of the Peacock.

'We gave the gatekeeper a light tap on the head,' Henry said. 'Nothing serious. Just to keep him quiet. Then we stormed through the gates and found those rogues beating you both, with their gentleman master looking on and smiling at the sight.'

'Henry knocked him out,' someone said, 'and the rest of us gave him a kicking.'

'He had asked for it, the way his men were laying into the two of you. Anthony was still conscious, but you were away with Queen Mab.'

'Tom has just recovered from one blow to the head, inflicted by those same brutes,' Anthony said. 'No wonder that he was unconscious.'

'Anthony said you were making for the Fields,' Henry said. 'It seemed like a good plan. The Inn was beginning to wake up and the gate might have been barred again. So we picked you up and made for the wall.'

'And dragged me over,' I said, thinking of my grazed hand.

'There was no time for finesse.'

'I realise that. I'm grateful. We're both grateful. Jesu knows what they would have done to us if you hadn't come.'

'There's the Peacock,' someone called. 'And the torch is still lit. I'm ready for a meal and a gallon of beer.'

We all shouted our agreement.

We found John sitting alone at a table near the back, nursing a cup of beer and looking frightened. As he glanced over and saw us, he face cleared and he stood up.

'You got away!'

'Thanks to our friends,' Anthony said. 'And to you alerting them. You got here with no trouble?'

'No trouble at all.'

We pulled up stools to the table. The landlord came bustling over, surprised at so much business this late in the evening, but pleased nonetheless.

'I can offered you gentlemen beef and onions or a dish of pike or roast goose. What shall I fetch you?'

'All three!' Henry roared. Now we were away from Lincoln's he clearly regarded the whole episode as no more than a student prank.

'Aye,' Anthony said. 'Bring all three.'

I took off my sodden lawyer's gown and laid it over a stool near the fire. It might dry out a little before I needed to put it on for the walk back to Gray's. I was glad of the rest at the Peacock. The beating and the long walk had exhausted me. Perhaps the lavish food, washed down with the beer in the jug the landlord brought, would restore me. As I sat down again next to John, I felt Sir John Dillingworth's letters rustle under my shirt. I was anxious to read them, but this was not the place.

I turned to John. 'You have the scroll safe?'

He nodded. 'I wrapped it in the lawyer's gown, to keep it from the rain.'

He lifted the bundled gown from a bench behind him and unwrapped it. The scroll lay there in the folds of the gown, undamaged by the wet. I lifted it up and laid it on the table in front of me, where the others eyed it curiously.

'So all this adventure, and the beatings you endured, were just for an old dusty scroll?' Henry grinned at me.

I reached out and touched it with the tip of my finger.

'An old dusty scroll,' I agreed, 'but it holds the future of five parishes within it.'

Mercy

The sword slash in Ben's arm was healing cleanly, but I feared it would be some while before his spirits were healed as well. During the day, he helped with any tasks about the farm that did not require the full strength of two arms. He had always loved the cows. Every morning and evening he went with Gideon to bring them in for milking, and as his arm grew better, he took over half the milking, freeing Nehemiah to go in pursuit of fish and wildfowl to augment our present diet and our winter stores. Kitty and I were experimenting with smoked and salted fish, while the rendered meat of the wildfowl, sealed in jars under a layer of purified duck fat, seemed to be keeping well enough.

I think Ben found Gideon's company a comfort. His quiet, undemanding presence was what the boy needed after his experiences of the battlefield. By day, he seemed almost to have returned to the cheerful lad he had been before the soldiers were sent away. But at night it was another matter. Night after night he woke screaming in terror. After his first few nights in the room off the kitchen, he moved in to share with Nehemiah, for we all thought he would be the better for the companionship, but the terrible dreams that afflicted him meant that Nehemiah suffered broken nights. He worked long hours by day and needed his sleep, so I moved Ben once again into the downstairs chamber. Kitty was back in her attic room and Nehemiah was far enough away that he was not often disturbed, but night after night Gideon and I were woken. We spent many hours comforting Ben and quietening him, or sitting with him beside the kitchen fire, all of us drinking spiced ale, Ben wrapped in blankets which could not stop his shivering. Gideon and I both began to feel the lack of sleep.

When we were not occupied in our usual farm tasks, or preserving food for the winter, Kitty and I were busy making more knitted and woven goods for the next trip to market. As well, Kitty was weaving a striped blanket as a house gift for Alice and Rafe, while I was sewing a winter tunic for Huw and knitting a lace cap for the new baby. Alice was certain it would be a girl and I hoped she would prove right, as it would look a mite dainty for a lad.

Despite all that we had to keep us busy, I could not stop worrying about Tom. I had heard nothing from him for weeks, and my last two letters had gone unanswered. That might mean nothing more than my letters – or his – having miscarried. Unless you had the use of the government mails, sending a letter was always unchancy, but I thought there should have been some word by now. London was a sickly place, far more endangered by the plague than we were. We had the marsh fever, but it was not so certain a death sentence as the plague.

The drainers had returned to camp in the medland where they had set up their quarters the previous year. A group of men from the village had gone to Piet van Slyke, to try to make him understand the danger of draining the Fens, instead of allowing them to absorb the excess water during the winter rains. They explained that by forcing the marsh water out of the Fen and pouring it into Baker's Lode and the river, the pumping mill had caused both to burst their banks and created the flood which had caused so much damage. Van Slyke's response had been to swear at them, yelling that they knew nothing of the management of water. If they did not leave the drainers' camp, he said, he knew how to deal with them, waving his short-barrelled musket in their faces. In despair they retreated and van Slyke's men began the rebuilding of the shattered mill.

They also began to steal our sheep once more.

Sheep-stealing is a hanging offence, conviction should lie within the jurisdiction of the local Justice of the Peace. But we knew that the stealing of sheep by the drainers when they were working over at Crowthorne had called down no punishment from Sir John. If he ignored a crime committed on his very doorstep, what hope was there that he would act on our behalf? It had begun to seem as though we had no existence. As if we had become invisible to great men.

Alice and Rafe were nearly ready to move into their new house, although they had very little to furnish it. An excellent kitchen hearth and bread oven had been one of Alice's first requirements, for she loved baking, like her mother, something I have little time for. I enjoy making bread, for kneading is a fine way to work off the petty annoyances of life, but I have not the patience for fine baking. Rafe had built a sink and dug a well, so their cooking needs were well provided for. Otherwise they had not much. Ned Broadley had made them a bed as his house gift, while Nehemiah had constructed a sturdy table out of timber left over from the house building. Others had contributed stools and cooking pots, and for dishes Alice had salvaged and mended her mother-in-law's dishes which had been broken or chipped in the flood. Her parents had provided bed linen, while Rafe's mother had given them one very small rug.

'I shall keep it for our bedroom,' Alice said. 'If I put it in the kitchen, Huw is certain to tread on it with muddy feet and I shall never hear the last of it from Mistress Cox. A bare floor can be swept and scrubbed easily. I quite enjoy it.'

I laughed. 'You may come and scrub my kitchen floor any time you like,' I said, 'for I do *not* enjoy it.'

The day before the great ceremony of moving in, Jack was taking his cart to Peterborough market to sell a mixed lot of our goods. He would not have such high prices as at Lincoln market, but it was nearer and he could be there and back in a day.

'Now,' I said, as I gave him a basket of knitted caps and two baby shawls to sell, 'I want you to take my earnings and buy a set of the best dishes you can find. Nothing crude, mind. Two large plates, two small plates, two bowls, and two ale cups. The very best you can find. If there is not enough coin, I will pay you the rest from my next earnings.'

'Have you not enough dishes already, Mercy?'

'They are for Alice and Rafe. And mind you keep it secret.'

I hoped there would be something pretty to buy in Peterborough. There would have been more choice in Lincoln, but no one would be going there for another month.

There was to be a feast in the new house that evening, to which the whole village had been invited, so late in the afternoon we all walked down the lane, carrying our contributions – two roast wild geese, one large whole drum of cheese, a pot of pickled

257

eels, some of our smoked fish and potted duck, as well as Kitty's blanket and my clothes for the children. For once it wasn't raining.

It had taken some persuading to convince Ben that he should come. He was still nervous of crowds of people, but we kept reminding him that he had known everyone here for months, and indeed had spent much of the previous winter sharing the church with them. Eventually he agreed to come, but he trailed along behind us, his face tense and unhappy.

Alice was delighted with all the food and with the gifts we had made. As when she was carrying Huw, she bloomed during this pregnancy, her skin glowing and her eyes bright. She had still nearly two months to go, but she patted the neat round of her apron.

'I think this will be a large baby, like Huw.'

I was surprised, though pleased, that she looked so content. Huw's birth had been dangerous. She had nearly died, and would have done, left to the mercies of Meg Waters, the village midwife. It was only the intervention of Hannah that had saved both mother and child.

'This is a wonderful feast,' I said, as I helped Alice lay the food out on the new table, which shone with wax, undamaged as yet with the hard use inflicted on a farm table.

'I feel a little guilty,' Alice said. 'We are all low in provisions for the winter, and everyone has been so generous.'

'We had no harvest feast this year, for there was nothing to celebrate. Let us enjoy celebrating your new home before the winter depresses us all.'

'It has already seemed like winter for months,' she said. 'If they repair the pumping mill, do you suppose that will cause another flood?'

I sighed. 'It could, especially if we have a heavy winter rain storm. At any rate, Will knows how to stop the pump. Another time we will stop it at the first sign of a flood. He has also explained to Joshua and Ephraim how to stop theirs, so they will not need to smash it.'

'Van Slyke may leave men here to keep a watch on the mills in future,' she said.

'He may. If only we could take them the court! Not van Slyke and his men, but the people they work for.'

'We need to discover who they are, first.'

I nodded.

'Jack says Joshua told him that Edmund Dillingworth is come back to the manor,' she said.

I shuddered. 'In that case, I shall not be calling there in a hurry.'

Alice walked to the open kitchen door and looked out down the street.

'I hope they will be back from Peterborough soon,' she said. 'I asked Jack to buy some fancy cakes from the baker there.'

'There was no need for that! Your own cakes are better than any bought in Peterborough.'

I went to join her at the doorway.

'Look,' I said. 'There they are. Just coming up the slope from the bridge.'

We both ran out into the street. Jack's cart came rumbling up toward us, lurching a little in the ruts. Toby had gone with him to Peterborough, but there were not just two men in the cart. There were four.

'It is Tom!' I cried. 'That is Tom sitting next to Jack! And another man I have never seen before.'

I flew down the street, my cap falling off and streaming behind me on its ribbons. He had not been taken by the plague, or any other London mishap. Others followed after me, alerted by my shout. Jack drew up with a flourish in front of his house and Tom climbed down. He was a little awkward, but he moved as though he had two legs, and he was using only one crutch. I could scarce believe my eyes.

'You are safe!' I hugged him hard, only too aware how worried I had been. 'Why have you not written?'

Before he could answer, Gideon was there, clapping him on the shoulder, and Nehemiah shaking him by the hand, and Alice standing on tiptoe to kiss his cheek. All the village was firing questions at him.

'Where have you come from?'

'We thought you were in London.'

'How do you come to be with Jack?'

Toby answered this last question. 'We were just taking down our stall in Peterborough market when Joseph Thompson, the London carrier, drove up, with Tom sitting up beside him.'

'We thought we must stay in Peterborough overnight, and come on by carter tomorrow,' Tom said. 'Then I caught sight of these two rogues.'

'Then you are just in time for our celebration,' Rafe said.

'Aye, Jack and Toby have told us that you now have a house of your own.'

While all this was happening, I kept a firm hold of Tom's arm, but I noticed that the stranger had climbed down from the cart and was standing a little apart.

'Tom,' I whispered, 'who is this other gentleman?'

'Anthony!' Tom called, 'Don't hide away there! I said you should meet my sister, and here she is.'

The man stepped forward, smiling.

'Mercy, this is Anthony Thirkettle, barrister-at-law. I do not know how I should have fared in London without him. I should probably be lying dead in a ditch now. Anthony, this is my sister, Mercy Bennington.'

'Mercy Chandler,' I corrected him. 'I am married now.'

The man bowed and smiled more broadly. 'I am honoured to meet you. I have heard some remarkable tales of your adventures.'

I blushed, wondering which of my unmaidenly exploits he had heard about.

'And where is my new brother-in-law?' Tom was clearly in high spirits. 'Gideon, where are you now? He was here a moment ago.'

'By your elbow, Tom,' Gideon said. 'Master Thirkettle, I am equally honoured to meet you. I am not sure how you preserved Tom from dying in a ditch, but having known him since he was a boy, I am not altogether surprised.'

He laughed. 'Please call me Anthony. I feel I know all of you already, for Tom never stops speaking of his family and friends.'

'But I do not understand,' I said. 'I thought you would both have duties at Gray's Inn.'

'Term has finished for the summer,' Anthony said. 'The courts are closed and all lawyers with a grain of sense escape the heat and smells of a London summer to enjoy the peace of the country.'

'It is well past most of the summer by now,' I said bluntly. 'Past harvest too. And I know nothing of the weather in London, but there has been little heat here.'

Tom laughed. 'I warned you, Anthony. My sister possesses a relentless logic. She would make a good lawyer.'

I found myself blushing again. 'I did not mean to sound ungracious. We are so pleased to see you, both of you. After the celebration for Alice and Rafe, we will all go back to Turbary Holm.'

Some of the villagers were beginning to drift toward the new house. I spoke to Tom in a lowered voice.

'So, you did not succeed in finding the charter.'

He turned away from me and rummaged in his knapsack, which was still lying on the seat of the cart. He drew something out and waved it in the air.

'The charter granting our rights to the common lands!' he shouted.

There was a moment of absolute stillness, then everyone came rushing back, shouting, crowding around Tom, reaching out to touch the scroll he held in his hand with the tips of their fingers, as if they could not believe it was real.

I turned to Anthony. 'It is truly the charter?'

'It is.'

'And it grants us the rights to our lands?'

'Unequivocally.'

'I cannot believe it.'

'It is true. We have quite a story to tell you. Of course, this is only the first step. We must next identify all the partners in the company of adventurers and take them to court.'

My face fell. 'It will take a long time and cost us a great deal of money.'

'It is like to take a long time, but we can probably secure a court order to stop the works until the case is settled. As for cost, I have told Tom I will act for you, for no fee.'

'You cannot do that.'

'I can. I have been involved in the search from the first. I want to see this through to the end.'

261

'Come.' Rafe was urging everyone toward his new house. 'Now we shall have a double celebration. A new home for Alice and Huw and me, a new hope for future for all of us.

The celebration that evening was one of the most joyous I have ever known. Alice and Rafe were popular in the village, and everyone was glad to see them in a home of their own. If the over-excited children did run in and out spreading mud on the spotless kitchen floor, even Mistress Cox seemed not to mind. It was not her kitchen floor, after all. Perhaps she was as glad to have her immaculate house back to herself as Alice and Rafe were glad to move into their own home.

Yet I think the most powerful sense of joy came from the knowledge that we now possessed the charter. Anthony was right, of course. It was only the first step. The long battle in the courts lay ahead and I do not suppose many of us had illusions about that. Our enemies were powerful men, and rich. They would be formidable opponents.

When little remained of the feast but crumbs and dirty dishes, people began to drift homewards, some carrying sleepy children, until only a few of us were left in Alice's kitchen. Huw was asleep on Rafe's lap as Kitty and I cleared the table.

'Leave that,' Alice said, stifling a yawn. 'I shall deal with it all tomorrow. My mother is coming to help us move in.'

'At least let me make a space for this.' I fetched my basket from the shelf where I had placed it when Jack had passed it to me quietly. He winked at me now.

'This is a small present so that you and Rafe do not need to eat always from cracked dishes.'

Alice removed the cloth and lifted out the dishes Jack had bought for me in Peterborough. They were not the sort of fine wares one might buy in London, but they were neatly made, glazed in white and painted with a pattern of blue flowers and orange berries. Alice's face lit up with a joyful smile.

'They are beautiful, Mercy!' She hugged me, as best she could over the hump of the baby.

'I had to trust to Jack's judgement,' I said, 'but he seems to have fared none too badly.'

Jack threw up his hands in mock despair. 'Gratitude!'

'I am grateful, Jack. You did very well.'

Kitty had cleared the rest of the table and wiped it over, despite Alice's words. Now she sat down on a bench, very close to Tom, I noticed.

'Good,' Tom said. 'I am glad we have some space now. I have something else to show you, besides the charter.'

He glanced at Anthony, who nodded, then he reached inside his shirt and pulled out two folded papers which bore wax seals.

'We have not had time to tell you the full story, but when we were searching Bencher Blakiston's chambers, I found something else. Something locked away with the charter. Could we have another candle?'

Gideon fetched a candle from the mantel shelf and lit it from the one already standing on the table. We all leaned closer, even Ben, who had forgotten his reluctance of earlier.

'They look like letters,' I said.

'They are letters. Do you recognise the seal, Mercy?' Tom held one so that I could make out the seal in the candlelight.

'It is the Dillingworth seal.'

'It is. These are letters of instruction from Sir John to Blakiston. I am sure there must be others. These were both sent this year.'

He paused and looked around at the intent faces. Alice and Rafe, Toby, Will and Liz, Jack, Ben, Anthony, Kitty, Gideon and me.

'These letters instruct Blakiston to keep the charter carefully concealed and to make sure that I should have no chance to lay hands on it. They also contain orders to be conveyed to van Slyke with regard to the drainage works. He writes with the authority of the company of adventurers, of which he is the leading member.'

For a moment there was a stunned silence, then I gulped for air, for I felt all the air had been struck from my lungs.

'Betrayal!' I cried.

'Betrayal,' Tom echoed. 'All this while, when our father and the others when to him for help, when he has made us promises, specious promises . . . he was behind the whole scheme from the start. And sent his son to prevent me from finding the charter.'

'How–' I could hardly find the words.

263

'It was Edmund Dillingworth who was behind the attacks on Tom,' Anthony said quietly. 'He might have been killed.'

I looked at my brother, shocked, and reached out to take his hand.

'Later,' he said. 'I will tell you everything later.'

'But I don't understand,' Kitty said in a small voice, as if she hardly dared venture her opinion. 'Why would Sir John want to destroy the commons? He is a commoner himself.'

Tom smiled at her. 'That was why we were misled, Kitty. You are quite right. He is a commoner. But his share of the common land is tiny. Nothing to compare with the rest of his estate. That was why we supposed he would not stir himself much in our defence. But if he holds the largest share in this company, and if they seize the common lands in five parishes, he will become a very, very rich man indeed.'

'I see.' Kitty suddenly looked furious. 'I hate him! He should be hanged!'

Anthony leaned across the table and took her hand. 'No one will hang him, Kitty, but I will fight with every weapon and argument I can command to destroy him in court.'

For a while we sat discussing all the news Tom and Anthony had brought, but I think the rest of us were still so stunned that we could barely take it in. Alice took the sleepy Huw from Rafe and said she must put him to bed. Kitty and Ben set off for the farm. Tom said he would take Anthony along to the yel-hus to introduce him to the sort of decent brew of beer a fenland country landlord could provide, and most of the others said they would go with them.

As we stepped out into the cool night air, Anthony said, 'Tom is forgetting I am a fenlander myself, though not a countryman.'

'You are a fenlander?' I said.

'From Ely.'

'Then you are one of us.' That seemed to make it right that he would fight our battle for us in the courts.

Gideon and I bade the others good-night and began to stroll slowly up the lane toward Turbary Holm. I slipped my arm through his.

'Tom is looking well,' he said, 'despite these beatings he has suffered.'

'He does. And this new mechanical leg is remarkable. He was so bitter after the amputation. Perhaps now he can begin to live his life again.'

Gideon laughed and squeezed my arm. 'I think he has already begun to live quite a lively life already!'

We walked on in silence for a little way. We were rarely alone together, and there was something I wanted to tell him.

'Look at that sky,' he said.

In the west, where far away the inland wolds rose up, the sun had sunk behind the land, leaving the sky glowing as orange as new-minted pure gold. And by some trick of the light, thin banks of clouds out to the east had caught the reflection, turning bright gold themselves. Over toward the Fen, here and there amongst the whispering rushes, a wink of gold showed where a mere lay.

'It is beautiful,' I said. 'I know we have not won the battle yet, but I feel such a lift of my heart, despite the betrayal of the Dillingworths. Tom finding the charter – it gives us hope after so much despair. Our lands will be ours again. And our children's after us.'

I stopped, standing there in the lane under that golden sky.

'I have something to tell you, Gideon.'

Suddenly I felt both elated and shy.

He cupped my face in his hands. 'What is it, dear heart?'

'I am with child.'

He drew a deep breath. 'Then our joy is complete.'

The very gold of the sky enfolded us, and he kissed me.

We resumed our walk along the lane as a blackbird – surely the same blackbird – sang in the hedgerow, and a hoolet, hunting early, swooped silently over our heads.

The Author

Ann Swinfen's first three novels, *The Anniversary*, *The Travellers*, and *A Running Tide*, all with a contemporary setting but also an historical resonance, were published by Random House, with translations into Dutch and German. *The Testament of Mariam* marked something of a departure. Set in the first century, it recounts, from an unusual perspective, one of the most famous and yet ambiguous stories in human history. At the same time it explores life under a foreign occupying force, in lands still torn by conflict to this day. Her second historical novel, *Flood*, first in the Fenland Series, based on true events, takes place in East Anglia during the seventeenth century, where the local people fight desperately to save their land from greedy and unscrupulous speculators. The second novel in the Fenland series, *Betrayal*, is set partly in East Anglia and partly in London. *This Rough Ocean* is a novel based on the real-life experiences of the Swinfen family during the 1640s, at the time of the English Civil War.

Currently she is also working on a late sixteenth century series, featuring a young Marrano physician who is recruited as a code-breaker and spy in Walsingham's secret service. The first book in the series is *The Secret World of Christoval Alvarez*, the second is *The Enterprise of England*, the third is *The Portuguese Affair*, the fourth is *Bartholomew Fair* and the fifth is *Suffer the Little Children*. A sixth novel in the series is due in 2015.

http://www.annswinfen.com

Printed in Great Britain
by Amazon